"NO GENTLEMAN WOULD EVER THREATEN A LADY"

"That didn't stop you before!" Rianne snapped.

"That night I threatened a female highwayman, not a lady," he corrected her mildly. "Tonight, all I've done is make up my mind about something. That can't possibly be considered a threat."

"Then tell me what it is that you've made up your mind about," she said through clenched teeth, fighting the urge to shout.

"You *will* find out all about it. Discussion is so unnecessary."

Rianne was startled to feel his hand slide down her arm to her side. The heat of his flesh set hers afire, and it was all she could do not to move under its caress.

He turned her toward him and then his lips came to hers . . .

Other **AVON ROMANCES**

BELOVED PRETENDER *by Joan Van Nuys*
DARK CHAMPION *by Jo Beverley*
LORD OF THE NIGHT *by Cara Miles*
MASTER OF MY DREAMS *by Danelle Harmon*
OUTLAW HEART *by Samantha James*
PASSIONATE SURRENDER *by Sheryl Sage*
WIND ACROSS TEXAS *by Donna Stephens*

Coming Soon

FOREVER HIS *by Shelly Thacker*
TOUCH ME WITH FIRE *by Nicole Jordan*

And Don't Miss These
ROMANTIC TREASURES
from Avon Books

FASCINATION *by Stella Cameron*
FORTUNE'S FLAME *by Judith E. French*
SHADOW DANCE *by Anne Stuart*

FLAME OF FURY

SHARON GREEN

AVON BOOKS ◆ NEW YORK

FLAME OF FURY is an original publication of Avon Books. This work has never before appeared in book form. This work is a novel. Any similarity to actual persons or events is purely coincidental.

AVON BOOKS
A division of
The Hearst Corporation
1350 Avenue of the Americas
New York, New York 10019

Copyright © 1993 by Sharon Green
Published by arrangement with the author
Library of Congress Catalog Card Number: 93-90346
ISBN: 0-380-76827-5

First Avon Books Printing: November 1993

AVON TRADEMARK REG. U.S. PAT. OFF. AND IN OTHER COUNTRIES, MARCA REGISTRADA, HECHO EN U.S.A.

Printed in the U.S.A.

RA 10 9 8 7 6 5 4 3 2 1

For Marian Stensgard,
the best researcher ever.

And thanks to Ron and Sheila
for Bryan's wedding gift to Rianne.

Chapter 1

England, 1751

Rianne Lockwood heard the conversational noise in the salon when she was still ten feet from the room, and shook her head. Her stepfather's guests were wide awake and gossiping even at this early hour, as though afraid they'd miss some choice bit of news. They'd been at it since they'd arrived the day before, and didn't seem to subscribe to the belief that Saturday mornings were best greeted with peace and quiet.

"But what else would you expect from friends of *his?*" she asked herself in a mutter, the only proper answer clear in the question. Not all of them were really close friends of her stepfather's, but they were all the sort of people he most approved of. Even those who came to see *her,* and maybe especially them. Wealthy young men with marriage in mind, not to mention visions of the inheritance that came with her, as well as an acceptance in her stepfather's social circles. Some few already had that acceptance, but the rest, despite their wealth, would be admitted only through *her* . . .

"And they really think they have a chance of that," she murmured with a hidden smile, pausing in the hall to brush at the day gown she wore. "They're fools to keep coming back every time, but their eyesight must be sharper than their reason."

Rianne's smile widened just a little at the thought, her amusement deep and real. She'd once been laughed at by the daughter of one of her stepfather's friends, a small,

1

dark-haired girl who knew just how appealing her own petite loveliness was. She'd ridiculed Rianne, saying that she was much too tall to attract *any* man, and had declared that Rianne would end up a spinster if her father didn't *force* some man to marry her. Rianne had ''accidentally'' stepped on the small girl's petite foot to get even for the remarks, but the idea had still bothered her.

At least until her first formal ball, that is. It was certainly true that Rianne was much taller than the other young ladies at the ball, but it was also true that the young gentlemen found the difference to be largesse rather than excess. Few of the young men topped her by more than a finger joint and most were her height or smaller, but fascination with her golden-red hair, her beautiful face and changeable green eyes, her large breasts and comparatively small waist drew them to her side and kept them there. She was delightfully more than a simple handful, she'd once heard one of them comment to another . . .

''Ah, there you are, dear lady,'' a voice said, and Rianne looked up to see Jonathan Coleridge grinning at her from the doorway. ''We were becoming certain you meant to sleep away all of this glorious morning.''

''With so many fascinating people in the house, Mr. Coleridge?'' Rianne asked with a smile as she resumed walking. ''Certainly not.''

The man's dark gaze moved over her as she approached, and he offered his arm with a small bow. He was new to the circles constantly hovering around Rianne, and seemed convinced that his dark-haired handsomeness would impress her more than the less-classical looks of his fellow suitors. He also clearly enjoyed the fact that he was at least a full finger taller than she, something none of the others were. Rianne, unimpressed with anything about him, treated him with the same friendly distance she did the others.

''Do allow me to help you choose your breakfast, dear lady,'' he urged, the smooth attempt to take command adding to Rianne's earlier amusement. ''Since I've already sampled the dishes, my advice should prove invaluable.''

"Mr. Coleridge, I *live* in this house," she pointed out as he led her toward the buffet. "This is hardly the first breakfast I've had here, so what good would your advice—"

"Now, now, a lady such as yourself should never be burdened with the need to make decisions," he interrupted, ignoring the other young men who had begun walking toward them through the large salon. "It's a man's place to see to such tiresome activities, and the pleasure of doing so will be mine."

"I suggest, Mr. Coleridge, that you look for your pleasures elsewhere," Rianne told him, her friendly, confident smile making him pause. "Despite the dangers and unreasonable rigors, I'll choose my own breakfast."

She patted his arm before leaving him in the middle of the floor and continued to the buffet alone, hearing the soft chuckling of those men who had been close enough to be aware of what she'd said. At one time or another they'd all tried proving how masterful they were, but it hadn't worked any better for them than it had for Jonathan Coleridge. Rianne was young, but she'd never had trouble handling men. She had a mind of her own, and never hesitated to let them know it.

The servant filled her plate with what she pointed to, then followed her with it to the chair she chose to sit on. After she'd relieved him of her plate, Rianne asked him to also bring her a cup of tea and sat back with a sigh. She hated large buffet breakfasts, hated the way the men closing in on her would try to get her attention, but there was no helping it. She still needed to be where she was, for at least a short while longer. After that she would be free, but until then she had to put up with being bothered.

And bothered she was. Jonathan Coleridge led the pack, but the others weren't about to give up without a fight. They took turns talking at her, coming up with what they considered charming conversation, but she did have the excuse of food on her plate to explain her lack of response. She pretended to be listening closely as she chewed, but in fact she was remembering the conversation her stepfather had initiated a few weeks earlier.

"Every one of them is considered a catch, Rianne,"
he'd said, referring to the bevy of gentlemen who so often
followed her around. "Which of them do you intend settling on?"

"Why, I hadn't thought about it, Father," she'd answered, giving him an open, innocent stare. He'd always
insisted that she call him father, despite the bad taste using
the name for *him* put in her mouth. At one time she'd
thought about refusing to do it any longer, but then she'd
changed her mind. She continued to call him by a name
he didn't deserve, but hopefully would not have to do so
for much longer.

"It's more than time you did think about it," he'd replied, stepping closer to the chair she sat in. "I'm not
getting any younger, and I'd like to see you with a family
of your own before my hair turns completely white. Which
of them do you like the best?"

"I think it would be most accurate to say that I like
them all just about equally," she allowed, betraying her
real meaning only by the glint of laughter in her eyes.
Although knowing her stepfather's plans for her tended to
overshadow all humor . . .

Robert Harding was a fairly tall man with black hair
and eyes and a still-handsome face, but he was a terrible
actor. He'd been trying to show fatherly concern for his
young daughter's welfare, but Rianne had been able to see
the heavy impatience he forcefully held down. Until she
married, the estates and very large income left to her by
her grandmother and father were out of the reach of both
of them, and her stepfather didn't care for that state of
affairs.

"You like them all equally," he'd echoed flatly, staring
down at her with frank disapproval. "What about young
Rochard?"

"Jean is very sweet, but possibly a little *too* sweet,"
she'd answered, making sure her expression didn't change.
Robert Harding had introduced her to Jean Rochard, obviously hoping she would accept the man's almost immediate proposal. Jean was a nice young man and really very

handsome, but was so obviously under Robert's thumb that her inheritance would become her stepfather's to manage the very day that any marriage ceremony took place—which, Rianne knew, was exactly what Robert Harding planned. What her stepfather had done to Rianne's mother apparently hadn't been enough for him. Now he was after his dead wife's daughter's possessions, but Rianne wasn't anything like her poor mother.

"So Jean is too sweet, and you like the others all equally well," he'd summed up, annoyance clear even in his stance. "What you like most, I think, is all the attention being paid you, but the time for that is over. Choose one, else I'll do it for you."

"Now, Father, you know that would never do," Rianne had replied with a smile, making no attempt to avoid his commanding gaze. "Every one of those young men knows I would never allow myself to be forced into marriage, so what would be the use in *your* choosing one? They would look foolish when I refused the vows in front of everyone, and *that* would be all they got out of the effort. If you feel I'm threatening rather than promising, do feel free to make the attempt."

"You, young lady, should be ashamed of yourself!" he'd stormed, obviously stung by her smile and the truth she'd spoken. "You took the love you were shown while growing up, and turned it into license to do just as you please! You are wild and spoiled, but that will change when a strong husband takes you firmly in hand. I look forward to the day."

He'd bowed stiffly and then had stalked out of her sitting room, obviously furious over the way he was being balked. He, like other men, much preferred sweet, obedient women to order about; Rianne knew how he felt at a loss when he had to deal with one who knew her own mind. She also knew just how far she was able to go. Rianne *had* had love while she was growing up, her mother's love, and it had made her stronger than the gentle woman had ever dreamed was possible.

". . . what a truly beautiful day this is," Jonathan

Coleridge was saying as Rianne returned from her thoughts. "I do believe a ride around the estate is just what the two of us could use."

"I think not, Mr. Coleridge," Rianne answered, smiling again as she put her empty plate aside. "I much prefer the thought of a stroll, and afterward a game of some sort. I've always been rather fond of games."

"That, dear lady, is easily seen," he countered, his dark eyes showing only a hint of disapproval. "Most ladies of your position would refrain from gaming in the knowledge that it was far too unladylike, but you surely indulge in that as often as you attempt domination. A pity your suitors until now have allowed you to believe such domination of men would be possible. It's the man who dominates, dear girl, a fact I would like to teach you."

"Would you really," Rianne said in the softest of voices, a reaction that caused some of the men around her to draw back. At one time she'd tried showing fits of temper in the hopes of driving away the boring hordes, but as long as her tantrum wasn't aimed at them, most of them came right back. Under normal circumstances Rianne preferred laughing to screaming and throwing things, but circumstances hadn't been normal in quite some time.

"Your words seem to indicate an interest in challenging my intention," Coleridge said, mockery in the smile he showed as he leaned back unconcernedly in his chair. "Challenge me as you like, dear girl, I shan't mind in the least. I do mean to tame you, quenching the raging flame of your willfulness. After that, I will make you mine."

"The raging flame of my willfulness," Rianne repeated flatly, beginning to believe that this man was as much a creature of her stepfather's as Jean was. Harding must have decided it was arrogance she was looking for, and had provided it in the form of Jonathan Coleridge. "You turn a neat phrase, Mr. Coleridge, but I find more interest in another word you used. *Quenching.* Yes, I do like that word."

With that Rianne raised the cup of hot tea the servant had brought, and threw it straight into Coleridge's face. It had been too hot even to sip, but it served its secondary purpose beautifully. Coleridge howled and jumped to his feet, both hands going to his face, and stumbled back after knocking his chair to one side. Rianne rose to her own feet.

"And now that you have the tea, you should also have the cup," she growled, then threw it at him with all her strength. Rianne had always made a habit of hitting what she aimed at, and the fragile china cup shattered against the man's head. He howled a second time and retreated even farther, then cleared his sight in time to see her now reaching for the plate she'd emptied. That the plate would follow the cup was in no doubt at all; seeing that, Jonathan Coleridge chose the better part of valor and made a hasty, uneven escape from the room.

"Bravo, my dear Rianne, bravo," Jean applauded with a laugh from the midst of the laughter of the others. "The boor deserved all you did to him and more besides. A gentleman would never speak to a lady as he did—proving, of course, that he's no gentleman. You are truly magnificent in your justifiable anger, and I mean to tell you so as we stroll about the garden."

"Perhaps later, Jean," Rianne denied immediately, holding up one hand to keep the entire pack at bay. "The fool has put me in such a monstrous mood, I'm not fit company for anyone. I'll take a short stroll alone, and rejoin you gentlemen later."

Having been given no choice at all the young men bowed, allowing Rianne her own escape from the room. The guests who hadn't been in the immediate vicinity of the disagreement stared at her with raised brows as she swept past them, and the women immediately began chattering among themselves. Rianne Lockwood's temper was quickly becoming legendary, which meant it was a choice topic for gossip—just as she was.

The object of discussion took herself directly outside, delighted that things had worked out so well. Not only was she rid of that Coleridge boor, she would even have some time to herself. It was a really lovely summer day, warm and sweet with the quiet of the country. Some of their guests complained that it was *too* quiet, that compared to London it was dull and uninteresting, but the rest disagreed. Out here they could breathe freely, they said, and enjoy the sight of open grounds and thick woods just by looking out their windows.

Rianne herself was undecided. She did love the country and its beauty, but she also yearned to visit and learn the streets of London. So far, she'd never had the chance, and now she probably never would. She'd gotten the impression from overheard comments that it was a place where marvelous things were done everywhere and at all hours, as though the city were magical and all those living in it were enchanted. Peace and quiet were all well and good, but after a lifetime of it she longed for a taste of enchantment.

Like the sort mentioned in all those wonderful books she read. Handsome men suddenly appearing in times of trouble to rescue beautiful ladies, with whom they of course fell in love. *He* would immediately profess his love, speaking the lady's name softly and caressingly. She, being much too shy to say anything so forward, would show her love and devotion in other ways. And he would know how she felt, without the words, and would cherish her for all time.

Cherish her. Rianne paused on the walk for a moment to sigh, wondering what it would feel like to be cherished. It had been so long since *she* had experienced the feeling, all the way back to the time before her father had died. If only she could believe something like that was ahead of her. It was a silly dream, she knew, but still . . .

With another sigh she continued along the stone walk which led around to the gardens. In the process the walk passed in front of the guest stables; as luck would have it Cameron Campbell was just coming out, and that gave Rianne another idea.

"You, boy," she called, gesturing imperiously and showing the frown she'd been wearing indoors. "You'll walk with me until I decide I want refreshment, and then you'll run and fetch it for me. Come along.''

"Yes, m'lady,'' Cameron answered, showing a nervous expression as he hurried over to her. "As ye say, m'lady.''

Rianne sailed along with the stable boy hurrying in her wake, and in another moment moved between the start of the hedges. No one was in sight up the long path between the hedges, and the majestic green wall kept them from being seen by anyone in the house.

"Come on, Ree, slow down!'' Cameron hissed from behind her, his stable-boy accent now discarded. "I've been up and running since before dawn, so please take it a little easier.''

"Sorry, Cam,'' she apologized with a smile, glancing at the young man as she immediately slowed. "I'm supposed to be in a temper, and galloping along is part of it. Will you and Angus be ready to ride out with me this afternoon?''

"Just try to keep us away,'' he returned with a snort, then grinned. "So you're supposed to be in a temper again. Who did you bash over the head this time?''

"Jonathan Coleridge,'' Rianne told him with a soft laugh. "He decided to be 'masterful' with me, but it didn't work out too well. And I didn't 'bash' him. I threw hot tea in his face, then broke the cup over his head.''

"He's lucky your sword is hidden with Angus's and mine,'' Cameron said, with a matching laugh. "Any man who tried being masterful with you when you were armed would probably find himself run through. Are there many more guests arriving this afternoon?''

"Hopefully enough to add a lot of gold to what we already have,'' Rianne replied, her amusement fading. "I don't know how much longer I can stand it, Cam, not without going crazy. We have to get out of here and start building our new lives, we simply *have* to.''

"We will, Ree, and it won't be that much longer,'' the young man reassured her, looking as though he wanted to pat her shoulder comfortingly. "Angus is ready and so am I, and as soon as we have enough we'll go.''

Rianne looked at the young man who was her friend, and smiled faintly in thanks for his support. He and his older brother Angus were both fairly tall, with sandy hair and bright-blue eyes. Angus was Rianne's age with Cam a year behind them, and the three had been friends since they were very young. It might not have happened if Robert Harding hadn't told his little stepdaughter to stay away from the low-class gutter rats. The order made her that much more determined to befriend them, and for that Rianne was grateful to him. It wouldn't have been possible to find more loyal friends, even if she'd looked forever.

If Cameron Campbell had been asked, he would have said the same thing. He could still remember the day the gangly little brat had first come to insist she be allowed to play with him and his older brother, and that in spite of the fact that she'd had to sneak out to join them. Angus hadn't trusted her and had tried to chase her away, but the skinny little girl had put her hands up like a boy and had dared him to do his worst. Angus had accepted her challenge and the two of them had fought, but he hadn't been able to make his opponent cry defeat. Or cry at all, for that matter. The girl had given as good as she got, and when the two of them had stepped back the seeds of friendship had already been sown.

The three had grown up together almost like brothers and sister, but Rianne had been a sister like few others. Cam smiled as he watched her move to a stone bench and sit with all the grace of a great lady, remembering when she hadn't been graceful at all. She'd been resisting her lessons in ladylike comportment with all of her usual stubbornness, but Angus knew that her gawkiness upset her deeply. So he'd casually mentioned the new gardener who had once been a fencing instructor. The man was down on his luck and had taken the job as a gardener to keep his family fed, and could certainly be trusted to keep silent if Rianne paid him to teach her to fence.

Angus had wanted Rianne to learn a womanly grace the easy way, and so she had. What he hadn't counted on was her paying for lessons for himself and Cam as well, lessons the brothers would have done anything for. All three of them learned to use a sword, and after the instructor left to open a school again, they also practiced together. But only with wooden swords. Angus and Rianne were both too good, and it took a while before Cam began to catch up.

"He's talking again about cutting my allowance," Rianne said suddenly, drawing Cam's attention back. "He claims that having too much money to spend ruins a young girl, so he's threatening to cut the allowance down to a mere pittance. If the trustees let him do it—and they just might—I won't be able to keep adding to our fund."

"Why would he do that?" Cam demanded with a frown. "And *how* can he do it? Isn't the money yours from your father's estate?"

"With Mother dead it *is* mine, but as my stepfather his word carries a lot of weight with the trustees of the estate," Rianne explained. "They don't know him the way I do, and they also don't know that he's trying to force me into marrying. Not that they would think that was all so terrible. They'd do the same thing themselves to see their daughters married."

Cam watched her make a face at the idea, just the way she always did. Rianne had grown into the most beautiful woman he had ever seen, with golden-red hair and green-blue eyes that were enough to stop a man's heart, matched to a face and body guaranteed to start it up again. She was breathtaking, maddening—but wanted nothing to do with being married. What she wanted was to be free and on her own, and was even willing to turn her back on all the money and property waiting for her in order to do it.

"I wouldn't worry too much about his threats," Cam told her, trying to bring her smile back. "Since Angus and I already have what clothes and accessories we'll need, we won't need to spend on *that*. We also have the passage money, so all that's left is the amount of our stake. If we have to go with a smaller stake, well, we'll still make out."

"Oh, Cam, I can always count on you to make me feel

better,'' she said with the smile he'd been looking for. "And you're right, of course. If it gets to the point where I can't stand it any longer, we'll simply pick up and go. If our stake is small, it won't matter in the least. We're going to make our fortunes in America, and *no one* will be able to stop us.''

With the way her beautiful face glowed as she said that, Cam didn't doubt it for a minute. She'd lived with the dream for years, and had made it the dream of Angus and himself as well. All the time she'd taken to teach them to speak the way men of property would, the gold she'd given them to buy the clothes of gentlemen. Rather than face their new lives with hat in hand, they would stand with heads held high and demand a place rather than beg for it. He and Angus would have gone with her even as servants; it had been her choice that they pose as her brothers instead.

"And we may have to go sooner than we thought," Cam put in, wondering how she would take the news. "Angus says the victims of those three desperate high-waymen who have been robbing coaches in this area are wild over having lost their gold. They're screaming to the authorities that something be done to catch the miscreants, and everyone is starting to run in all directions. As soon as they start setting traps, the game is over."

"I'm surprised they haven't yet noticed that only certain people are being stopped and robbed," Rianne said with such a devilish grin that Cam blinked. "All of them being cronies of my stepfather. Did I mention that some of them demanded *he* reimburse them? They claim they wouldn't have been robbed if they hadn't accepted his invitation to visit, and they have no idea how right they are."

"Ree, I was trying to tell you that we can't keep pushing this," Cam said, attempting to put the sound of authority in his voice. "We've only been at it for a short while, and already everyone is shouting for our blood. No matter how much you're enjoying yourself, you have to remember that hanged people don't do well with starting new lives."

"Then we'll have to be sure we stay *un*hanged," she

answered with a laugh, the glow in her eyes teasing him for his caution. "Although if I had to choose between hanging and going back to the attentions of those . . . gentlemen, the sight of the rope would begin to be a lot more appealing. But I suppose I *do* have to go back, at least for a little while. And if we do well enough this afternoon, we may even be able to leave after tomorrow, when all the guests head home."

The idea excited Rianne so much that she got immediately to her feet, kissed Cam's cheek, then headed back toward the house. She would meet the brothers later in the usual place, and after she changed her clothes they would play highwaymen again. Cam shook his head with a sigh as he watched her go, then took himself off to find Angus. Leaving in a day or two might be the best idea after all, and he wanted to talk to his brother about it. Rianne was enjoying herself too much with the very dangerous game they were playing, and if they didn't get her away soon they might find that time had run out faster than they were expecting . . .

Rianne headed back toward the house, but rather than go all the way around the yards, she took a narrow side path through the hedge. She felt wonderfully better after talking to Cam, and didn't care to spoil the mood by returning to the vicinity of her suitors. There wasn't one among them who would have understood what she planned to do and why, let alone join her even half as enthusiastically as Angus and Cam had.

The side path led to a pretty little bower, a single stone bench surrounded by vines and flowers and, a bit farther back, yew trees. As she sat on the bench she remembered all the marvelous afternoons she'd spent there, reading books and dreaming. The idea of becoming highwaymen had come from one of those books, the notion of running away to the colonies from another. Of course in the books it was men who had done those things, but by including Cam and Angus she was simply stretching the point.

And it's not as if I'll find the life I want by doing nothing more than sitting here, she thought. All those heroes *did* go to where the ladies were, but she'd been waiting for what felt like forever and no one even remotely resembling a hero had appeared. Which wasn't surprising, when every suitor coming after her had to be approved of by Robert Harding. He didn't want her to have a hero, just a pawn who would obey him the way Rianne never had.

Well, traveling to the colonies would change that. Rianne closed her eyes and raised her smiling face to the warmth of the sun, letting herself slide down into her favorite daydream. She would reach the colonies with her adopted brothers, make her mark as an individual in her own right, and then her hero would appear. He would be so impressed with what she'd done that he would fall immediately in love with her, telling her so almost as soon as they met. And *she,* knowing his love was real, would *not* be too shy to say the same, and they would be happy for the rest of their days.

A gentle breeze tickled through Rianne's hair, but she was much too busy enjoying her dream to notice.

Chapter 2

Bryan Machlin grimaced inwardly at the coach waiting in his drive, but outwardly he nodded pleasantly to the bearded driver standing with cap in hand who was holding open the door for him. The man was trying very hard not to look impressed, but his efforts fell a good deal short of success. He gaped up at Bryan, plainly shocked at how big the other man was, and Bryan nearly grinned. To him everyone else was small, and he himself the normal one. He passed the driver without speaking and climbed into the coach, then settled back for what would be a very short trip. He wore a sword in a scabbard attached with lockets as a gentleman was entitled to do, but had left his pistols at home. The sight of them tended to upset people, and that wasn't what he wanted to do during the coming visit.

But that coach was coming close to upsetting *him*. A white body trimmed with gold, red wheels, a large and ostentatious coat of arms on the door, red-dyed leather inside covering the seats, matching lap robes neatly folded on the seats in case the summer weather suddenly turned freezing cold—all of it enough to embarrass anyone but a king on parade, which Bryan didn't happen to be. As a matter of fact he didn't even *want* to be a king, not when the position required even worse ostentations than that. And that coat of arms was all but meaningless, which meant it just *had* to be Harding's.

As soon as his case was put aboard the coach they pulled away from his house, heading for the road that would lead to the very next estate. Bryan had intended riding over

15

across the fields on his favorite hunter, but Robert Harding wouldn't hear of it. Bryan was not only his new neighbor but a very special guest, and nothing would do but that he send his best coach.

"Obviously he's afraid I'll get lost on my own," Bryan muttered softly, but a small, private grin creased his rugged, masculine features. Getting lost was the last thing he intended doing, at least until he had the answers he wanted. Harding had those answers now, but if Bryan's plan worked, in a very little while *he* would learn all he needed to know.

Bryan ran a hand through his very dark red hair, then forced himself to relax. The end of the chase was nearly in sight, and another few days would see the quarry bagged. It had been five years since his brother had taken his own life, and after all that time Bryan was finally closing in on the man who was responsible for causing that tragedy. It had cost him a fortune in gold to find out the little he had, but he'd finally discovered that a man named Robert Harding knew all about the way his brother had been trapped and threatened. Bryan had decided that Harding would talk no matter what he had to do to make it happen, but luck had suddenly touched him with a gift.

Bryan had bought the estate adjacent to Harding's, but hadn't had to force a meeting with the man. He'd been invited to join the private club the area notables attended, and his first night there Harding had come over to *him*. The man had welcomed his new neighbor in the sort of condescendingly hearty way Bryan detested, and then had offered to have a drink with him. The one drink became four, with Bryan answering a large number of not-very-discreetly put questions, and then Harding had gotten around to the real reason he'd approached Bryan.

"It's my stepdaughter, you see," Harding had explained, the expression on his face trying to be concerned. "She's an exquisitely beautiful girl, and once she marries she'll also be extremely wealthy. Even she doesn't know just how wealthy, but there's no need at all *for* her to know. Her husband will have control of her property, of course, him and any friendly advisors he might have. He will also share her social position, something all the gold in the country can't buy. She's directly related to the royal family through her mother, you see, and blood will always tell.''

Bryan had wondered briefly just what it was blood was supposed to tell, but kept the question to himself.

"And you control the estate now?'' he'd asked instead, expecting the answer to be yes. That was usually the way it worked, but Harding had surprised him by shaking his head.

"No, the estate is overseen by a board of trustees,'' Harding had told him with something like an unconscious grimace. "Lockwood was a baronet, but his private holdings far exceeded his official ones. It came from another branch of his family, and at his death became subject to administration by a previously selected board. My stepdaughter, being Lockwood's only living child, is his sole heir. Her late mother was provided for with lifelong funds supporting her in proper style, but being a Lockwood only by marriage meant she wasn't able to inherit.''

For the briefest instant Harding's expression had turned furious with apparent frustration, giving Bryan the impression the older man hadn't expected *that* when he'd married the woman. He must have thought *he* would have control of all that gold, and then had come the crushing truth. The man really was a fool if he hadn't first gotten the facts straight before plunging into marriage, Bryan had thought.

And then Harding's expression had changed, telling Bryan that the man was about to make him an offer. Bryan suspected he was going to be extremely interested in that offer, but first there had been more pretending to do.

"So your exquisitely beautiful stepdaughter isn't yet married,'' he'd commented, deliberately sounding *un*interested. "I'm sure the lack of suitors is only a matter of your being this far from London. Have you considered taking a house there?''

"God forbid!'' Harding had exclaimed, actually looking shocked. "If the flock she has around her now is a lack, in London I'd find myself feeding half the city. No, a lack of suitors isn't the problem. They're at her endlessly and propose on what seems to be a prearranged schedule, but she won't have any of them."

"Won't have?" Bryan had echoed, brows high over light-gray eyes. "Why haven't you simply picked one and told her to accept?"

"She . . . isn't that easily told things," Harding had admitted, now looking embarrassed. "I must say I had no idea she would grow to such willfulness due to what seemed like harmless indulgence on my part, but all of that is water under the bridge. She needs the hand of a stronger man than I, and one who won't be a father to her."

"So she's a screaming hellion who has you under her thumb," Bryan had said with a grin. He was curious to know just how far he could go with Harding, just how desperate the man really was. "Why are you telling *me* about it? Women have a habit of behaving themselves around me, so I'm hardly the one to ask advice from."

"That, sir, is exactly the point," Harding had pounced, not in the least insulted. "A man of your size and determination would soon have the girl put properly in her place, and would then be able to sit back and enjoy the fruits of his efforts. I have recently conceived a plan to circumvent her refusal, and I would be delighted to share it with you—as soon as we come to a firm understanding. I couldn't possibly give my daughter's hand to just anyone, you understand."

Harding had smiled then, and Bryan *had* understood. He was a very wealthy man with no wife, and Harding was offering him a priceless opportunity. If he married the girl he would not only have her wealth to add to his own, he would find an acceptance in the highest social circles that his children would share. That acceptance would otherwise never be his, but the offer wasn't without strings. Harding had a price, and didn't mind saying so.

"This firm understanding," Bryan had probed, keeping his eyes on the other man. "Just what would it entail?"

"You would need to give me a third of your new wife's estates, and control over enough more to make a full half," Harding had answered without hesitation as he leaned forward. "A man of your resources will never miss so piddling an amount, and it will also buy my friendship and support. Do you agree?"

Bryan had grinned and gotten down to bargaining, and the final agreement came at one quarter of the inheritance given outright, and control over enough more to make a third. Harding had insisted that the agreement be put in writing, and Bryan had insisted that he first get a look at his prospective bride. If she pleased him he would sign the agreement, and then they could get to Harding's new and brilliant plan to get around her refusal . . .

"And now things are finally working out," Bryan murmured as he glanced out of the coach window and saw the road ahead. He would take a look at the girl, but it really didn't matter whether or not she was attractive. His plans called for marrying her anyway, and then he would have Harding right in his hand. The man was obviously desperate for money, and his one and only chance at some was to share in his stepdaughter's estate. If he hadn't been desperate he wouldn't have concocted some wild scheme to overcome the girl's refusal, which until then he'd obviously been willing to live with.

And that desperation was what Bryan was counting on. If *he* married the girl, Harding would lose his very last chance at a very large sum of money—unless he cooperated with Bryan. If he answered Bryan's questions truthfully and fully, he would get what he needed. If he didn't, his only other option would be to go begging on the streets of London. Just meeting the supercilious and fastidious Harding had told Bryan how impossible *that* choice would be, which meant he would get his answers.

And the girl would be no worse for the episode, either. Bryan shifted on the leather seat, knowing that part of it was very important. No matter what she was like, Hard-

ing's stepdaughter was still an innocent in the affair that
had caused his brother's death. The only honorable course
open to him would be to keep her in his house after the
wedding, and once he had his answers he would arrange
for an immediate annulment. Sufficient gold and an untouched bride would end the marriage quickly, and then
they'd all be able to get on with their lives.

As Bryan stared out at the trees lining the road, his
thoughts left his bride-to-be and returned to her stepfather.
He'd been tempted to take the man and torture the information out of him, but that had to be left as a last-resort
effort. Men like Harding either turned out to be stronger
than they looked, or they collapsed at once and became
useless. No, his plan was what he was counting on, and
there was very little chance it wouldn't work.

Even if that daughter of Harding's tried being difficult.
It would hardly interfere with his plans, and after all, how
much trouble could a girl be anyway? Bryan chuckled,
knowing the answer was nothing he had to be worried
about . . .

"Luck doesn't seem to be with us this afternoon," Angus commented as Rianne watched the third coach pass
their hiding place. "Since we're not going to rob just anyone, we might as well go home."

"Just one more," Rianne decided in annoyance. Two
of the three coaches had held neighbors rather than Robert
Harding's guests, and the third had belonged to a man who
was forced to do business with her stepfather despite his
obvious dislike of Harding. "The next one *has* to be
someone we can stop, and if it isn't *then* we'll leave."

"Cam and I have been talking," Angus said after a
moment, and Rianne realized he was no longer watching
the road. "We've decided that what we've already gotten
will do us nicely, so there's no reason to delay. When all
the guests have gone, we'll leave too."

Rianne turned her head to look at him, wishing they
weren't all wearing masks. She'd waited so *long* for it to
be time . . . !

"Angus, are you sure?" she whispered, patting her horse as it shifted under her. "What if the gold *isn't* enough? What if—"

"Ree, we'll make it be enough," he interrupted, reaching over to touch her gloved hand with his own. "I don't like this robbing people, even if they're people who deserve to be robbed. Let's go now while we still can, and put all this effort into something worthwhile. Are you with us?"

"Just try to keep me away," she answered with a grin he could only hear in her words. They were all dressed in old breeches and coats, frayed shirts, cracking boots, dirty caps, and long masks and gloves. The bulky clothing along with Rianne's height made it very difficult to tell she was a girl, which meant she always let the other two do the talking. The only well-tended things any of them wore were their swords and swordbelts, but that was only to be expected.

"If you two aren't too busy to be interrupted, you might like to know there's another coach coming," Cam said, taking a firmer grip on his longbow. "Since we get to go home after this, why don't we decide whether or not we want it?"

Rianne joined Angus in immediately looking toward the road, and even though the coach was still a distance off, she quickly made a sound of pleasure.

"Tell me that isn't one of *our* coaches," she declared, knowing she couldn't be mistaken. "If he bothered sending *that* coach for someone, they must be close enough to him to be his twin. This is exactly what we were looking for, so let's not let it go by."

The two men couldn't deny what Rianne had said, and since this was the very last time they'd be robbing a coach, they didn't hesitate. Angus drew his sword as Rianne drew hers, but Cam urged his horse out onto the road and put an arrow in his string. Chasing a coach did nothing more than waste time they didn't have. Stopping it was more to the point, and that they knew how to do.

By the time the coach drew close enough to hail, Cam

had drawn his bow and was clearly aiming at the driver. When they were sure the man understood that, Angus gestured with his sword.

"Stand and deliver!" he shouted, one hand on the reins of his dancing horse. "Halt there or die there!"

Rianne noticed he'd deepened and roughened his voice even more than usual, and knew he'd done it to keep the driver, Ritchie, from recognizing him. She also knew *she* would have to be even more careful, because Ritchie was nervously pulling the coach to a halt.

"You in the coach!" Angus rasped. "Toss out your purse, and then you can be on your way again. But don't try to hold back any of the gold, or the only place you'll be on your way to is heaven—or hell."

Rianne expected to see the purse come flying out as it always had in the past, but there was nothing but silence. Then the coach door opened and a man who was a complete stranger stepped out, the sight of him bringing her the definite urge to gasp.

He had to be the largest man she had ever seen, with shoulders so wide his carefully tailored coat seemed to strain against them. His hair was that very dark red called black-red, and it rested in unruly thickness around a square, handsome face. In that face were eyes of very light gray, surely the color of gray ice. *Isn't that strange,* Rianne mused. *I know I've never seen him before, but it's almost as though—it feels as if we've—I can't possibly know him, so why does it feel as if I do?*

"I think I'll hold back *all* of the gold," the man answered Angus's orders in a deep, deliberately offensive voice as he drew his own sword. "If you want to continue thinking of yourselves as men, you'll step down off those horses and face me squarely. Unless you're afraid."

Rianne could see Angus stiffen with insult where he sat his horse to her left, and then the damned fool was actually dismounting! He knew as well as she did that staying mounted gave them the advantage, but his sense of honor refused to let him keep it. He meant to answer the big man's challenge the way a gentleman should, and Rianne was furious but had to do the same. She had the sudden conviction they were making a terrible mistake, but it was far too late to undo it.

As she stepped to the front of the horses she saw that Angus had already moved ahead to face the stranger, and a sudden thought made her glance around. Yes, Cam *was* on the other side of the coach, still keeping the driver in his sight. The coach itself was between him and the big man, which meant that if Angus needed help the only one who could give it to him was—

"Not a bad pass," the stranger said as the clang of swords came. "Certainly not good enough for your intended purpose, but not a complete waste. Try again."

Rianne could hear Angus's low growl as he engaged the big man again, his pride no doubt stung over how easily his first pass had been parried. She could tell Angus was only trying to wound the man, which made things even harder. *She* could see that her adopted brother's opponent wasn't one to be toyed with where weapons were concerned, but Angus seemed to be missing the point. Didn't he know the man in the same strange way she did?

The stranger couldn't be toyed with, but he was clearly one who *did* the toying. His blade rang as he stopped every one of Angus's attacks, his movements fast and deceptively smooth. The faint smile on his face pointed up the fact that he wasn't attacking in turn, and that plainly made Angus even angrier.

"You'd better give it up, boy," the stranger said after a very few moments, the easy drawl of his voice showing how little effort he'd made. "Put that blade up and surrender, and you'll continue to live for a while. Keep coming at me with it, and the hangman will be out his price."

Rianne saw Angus stiffen, and could almost hear his thoughts. If he surrendered they would all be hanged, his younger brother and adopted sister with him. Rather than be the cause of that he would give up his own life, at the same time giving the other two a chance to escape.

"You two get out of here *now!*" he shouted, then attacked his opponent in earnest without waiting for an an-

swer. Clearly he had now steeled himself to killing the
man if he could, but the desperation in his cautious lunges
showed he didn't believe he could.

Rianne threw an equally desperate glance at Cam, but
he was still on the other side of the coach. The way he
had straightened said he wasn't about to leave Angus any
more than she would, but he didn't know what to do. They
were both aware of the crossbow Ritchie kept in the boot
beneath his feet, and if Cam tried to help Angus by shaft-
ing the stranger, Ritchie would use the opportunity to bring
his own weapon into play.

And then the whole problem was almost ended in the
worst way possible. The stranger had now begun replying
to Angus with his own attacks, and Angus wasn't moving
fast enough. He parried awkwardly *en sixte* to keep the
big man's thirsting blade from the middle of his chest, but
didn't succeed in keeping it away from him entirely. He
cried out as a sharp edge of the sword sliced along his
side, and his free hand came up to be greeted with swiftly
running blood.

"I think that does it," the big man said, his point hovering very close to Angus's throat. "Let the sword fall to
the ground, and then we'll—"

His words broke off as Rianne leaped forward and
knocked his point away from Angus, silently taking up the
gauntlet of defense. She couldn't blame the big man for
defending himself, but that didn't mean she would let him
hurt her beloved brother even more. He would have to kill
her before he would get at Angus again, and she wasn't
all that easy to kill.

"I know," the big man said lightly as his sword moved
very slowly in front of him. "You're jealous of the attention the other boy got, and now want some of your own.
Well, I don't mind showing little boys the error of their
ways. Come ahead, lad, and take your licking like a man."

Rianne made a very soft sound of ridicule, and did exactly as she'd been invited to. Being called a boy rather
than a man meant nothing to *her,* and she proved it with
her first attack. She forced the big man into defending

himself rather more briskly than he had with Angus, and after her point nearly reached his flesh a third time, he disengaged and took a short step back.

"Well, we seem to have a *real* swordsman here," he drawled, but despite the insulting tone Rianne noticed he was careful not to drop his guard. "A pity you're putting such skill to so low a use. Why don't you surrender, and we'll see if we can't get you paroled into *my* custody? There's always room for a likely lad in my employ, and we might even do the same for your friends. What do you say?"

Rianne's answer was to step forward and go *en garde* again, the only answer she *could* give. A "likely lad" might be welcome in the big man's employ, but what would he do with a likely girl? And that was assuming she believed his offer, which something inside her was tempted to do; but it was a belief she knew she could in no way afford. If her odd feelings turned out to be mistaken, it wasn't only her own life that would be forfeit.

"Now *that* was a mistake," the big man said, referring to her silent but obvious choice to continue with the fight. "But if you want it all that badly, there's nothing I can do but oblige you."

As he came back *en garde* himself, Rianne couldn't help but notice how self-assured he sounded. Anyone facing him would begin to doubt their own ability in the presence of such colossal confidence, and that must surely have won most of his duels even before steel was raised. If her need hadn't been so great she might have thought twice herself, but she couldn't afford to be bluffed. The only way that this man would best her would be with cold steel thrust into her heart, not with distracting words.

And, very suddenly, steel was what he was trying to use. His attack came so abruptly that Rianne had no time to think, only to react. Frantically she beat away his glinting blade, but his impossibly long reach made it very difficult to counterattack. And the strength behind his blows! The impact of his sword on hers made it seem that he was trying to drive her into the ground, and she had to grip the hilt tightly despite her numbing arm. She tried desperately to disengage, to put some space between them, but he continued to loom close with his sword arm battering at hers. She had to disengage before he killed her, but she couldn't!

And then she discovered that killing her wasn't what he had in mind. His wrist twisted around in the sort of circle she was very familiar with, and the next thing she knew, her blade went flying out of her hand and away. Rianne was the one who was used to disarming her opponents like that, and she nearly cried out as she stumbled back. Her only weapon was gone, and now the big man would be free to hurt Angus again. As she took a second stumbling step backward, her boot heel caught against a protruding stone and she went down, sprawling on her back in the dust and dirt of the road.

"Well, children, I hope this is finally the end of it," the brute said with a chuckle, looking twenty feet tall where he stood beyond her feet. "If the third of your number doesn't immediately take that arrow from his string, I'll make this one's throat match his side. And I'll do it even if that arrow ends up in *me*, take my word on that."

He had returned his point to Angus's throat, and Rianne's glance at Cam showed he *did* believe the brute. Even if Cam could kill the big man, he was sure to kill Angus before he went down, and the idea, Rianne knew, was more than Cam could bear. He put off the need to make a decision by not doing anything, but Rianne was aware that inaction would be the end of them. She rolled to her side and put her hands to the ground to help her sit, and just that easily found what she hadn't known she was looking for. A palm-sized rock, just the right size for throwing.

Rianne's hands wanted to tremble in cadence with the thudding of her heart, but she simply couldn't allow that. All she could do was grip the rock tightly in her gloved hand as she sat straighter, ignore the way her cap had slipped to one side, and throw with all her strength. She also prayed very hard, but her prayers were more for Angus and Cam's sake than her own.

The brute was too busy dividing his attention between Angus and Cam to see her throw, and the rock struck him hard in the right temple. And all the practice she'd gotten as a child, and in throwing dishes and cups and things had paid off! Without a sound he collapsed to the road like a felled tree, and Rianne quickly scrambled to her feet and over to Angus.

"Resheathe that sword and lean on me!" she whispered fiercely, putting an arm around his waist. "We're getting out of here *now.*"

"More than time, *I'd* say," Angus muttered as he did as she'd ordered. "Thought we were goners for sure."

Rianne didn't mention that she'd thought the same; apologizing could wait until later. She helped Angus to his horse and pushed until he was in the saddle, then she went at a run to retrieve her sword. It was sheathed by the time she got back to her horse, so she mounted instantly and reached for Angus's rein. He was slumped in the saddle, and Rianne gave thanks that he hadn't fallen off.

"You two get started," Cam said in a gruff rasp. He was taking his turn at issuing orders, but at the same time was still watching Ritchie. "I'll catch up as soon as you've got a decent head start."

If Angus hadn't been bleeding so hard Rianne would have argued, but as it was the idea made sense. They wouldn't be able to ride very far or fast, but once into the woods it shouldn't be possible to follow them. Without a word, then, she began leading Angus's horse off into the woods, and simply kept going even when the road was completely out of sight. She wanted to stop to tend Angus's wound, but with possible pursuit behind them she didn't dare.

She didn't realize she'd been afraid to breathe until Cam caught up with them, but once he had the constrictive fear eased from around her heart. Acting like highwaymen had been *her* idea, and if her brothers had been killed or captured she would never have forgiven herself. As it was, the guilt over Angus's wound was making her feel like the lowest of the low, and the groan Angus gave made it even worse.

"We've got to put something against that wound," Cam said as he pulled his mask off, his voice uneven with worry. "Here, let's use this until we get to a place where we can do better."

He was already tearing out the lining of his coat even as he spoke, the sweat clear on his forehead as he hurried. Rianne pulled off her own mask and stuffed it in her pocket, wishing she could get out of those heavy, bulky clothes. Angus had to be taken care of first, but as soon as he was . . .

"Did I kill him?" she asked Cam tonelessly without looking at him, dreading even to speak the question but needing to know. The man *had* been a brute to threaten Angus like that, but there was still that strange something about him . . . The thought of having killed him was unexpectedly painful . . .

"No such luck," Cam answered at once with disgust, too busy tending Angus to notice how upset she was. "He was starting to groan even as I slipped into the woods, but I didn't hang around to see more. At least he can't come after us on foot or in that coach. If he had a saddle mount, I seriously believe he'd have followed even with his head split open."

Privately Rianne agreed, but she didn't have time to do more than shiver at the idea. Cam put the cloth to Angus's side as gently as he could, then shifted fast from his horse to sit behind his brother.

"The only way we can move faster is if I hold Angus up," Cam told her. "You follow with *my* horse, and pay attention to tracks."

When Rianne nodded he kicked Angus's horse, and the two of them moved ahead quickly. Rianne grabbed the reins of Cam's horse and followed, and when Cam turned off onto the rock that would show no hoofprints, she carefully followed. No blood to drip down and make a trail, no hoofprints to do the same, and soon they would be at the cave they'd prepared for just such an emergency. If only they hadn't needed that cave, if only she'd had the sense to call a halt *before* someone was hurt, if only they'd already left. But now they *would* leave, and soon. Just as soon as Angus could travel . . .

Bryan's head clanged with the sound of every church bell ever cast, and he groaned as hands helped him to sit up. He was outdoors somewhere, and couldn't remember what had been going on.

"What happened?" he croaked, putting his fingers to the place on his head that hurt the most. When he pulled them back covered with blood, he wasn't surprised.

"Th' one on th' ground threw a rock, sor," the driver of the coach answered, his bearded face worried. "Are ye all right? Can ye reach th' coach, 'r should I run fer help?"

Bryan looked around to see no one but them, memory rushing back of the three highwaymen. He'd wounded the first—accidentally, as it happened; he hadn't wanted to hurt the boy—disarmed the second, and had almost gotten the third to put up his bow . . .

"The one on the ground threw a rock," Bryan repeated, again not in the least surprised. The boy had proven he had courage to spare, even if he *was* too thin to have strength. And even if he did move in a strangely liquid way which Bryan had never seen with prior opponents. And was there something he remembered about the boy's hair, a strand of golden-red that had come loose from under his tumbled cap . . . ?

"I can make it to the coach," he told the man looking at him so anxiously, knowing the much smaller man had immediately dismissed the idea of carrying him. "Give me a moment until this dizziness passes."

The driver bobbed his head in relieved agreement, and kept silent while his passenger worked at pulling himself together. He had no idea how disgusted Bryan was with himself, disgusted and exasperated. He should have watched the thin one more closely, should have planted his boot in the middle of that skinny chest. That the boys understood the concept of honor and had behaved with

courage bothered him even more; finding men to handle
weapons was easy, finding those to handle them with honor
wasn't. He could have had these three in his employ, but
instead had lost them all. If the law got them first they'd
be wasted, and it was his negligence that had let them ride
off . . .

His negligence and the arm of a skinny boy. Bryan
growled deep in his throat as he touched his head again,
beginning to look forward to running into that boy again.
He'd take him into his service, all right, but first he would
take him to the stables for a good switching. He had the
feeling it would take at least that to get the boy to respect
him, that and some very careful handling.

"We won't be mentioning this attack to Mr. Harding or
anyone else," Bryan informed the driver as he got slowly
to his feet. "We'll say there was a tree down which was
half on the road on my property, and when we went to
move it out of the way of the coach I was caught by one
of the branches. Is that clear?"

"Yes, sor," the driver answered at once, his expression
showing he understood none of what he'd been told, but
would still do as he'd been ordered. "A branch on a tree
on yer own property."

"Exactly right," Bryan commended him, then bent
carefully for his sword. The first boy's blood was still on
one of its edges, so he pulled out his handkerchief to wipe
the sword clean, quickly resheathed it, then put the handkerchief to his head. Blood mingled with blood to disguise
the fact that someone else had been hurt, and then Bryan
was able to climb back into the coach. As soon as he had
the preliminaries with Harding taken care of, he would
start his own people on a search of the neighborhood. A
boy with golden-red hair shouldn't be *too* hard to find,
and once he had the first he would have the other two as
well.

But before that he had business with Harding and his
innocent bystander of a daughter . . .

Chapter 3

R ianne looked at herself in the mirror with very little enthusiasm, and that despite the oohing and aahing of her maid. Her gown *was* beautiful, a pale-green silk trimmed with golden lace and daringly low-cut, but no gown would have pleased her right then. She was still too worried about Angus despite the fact that Cam swore he would be fine, and too annoyed over the way her stepfather had behaved. She'd taken supper in her rooms with the intention of also skipping the ball, but he'd had the nerve to insist she attend. Her mother would have expected it of her, he'd blandly pointed out . . .

"Damn him for using that against me," she whispered to herself, hating the fact that they both knew he was right. Her mother would have been there for her guests even if she'd been ill, and technically those people in the house were *Rianne*'s guests. Worried or not she couldn't betray her mother's memory, but she swore to herself that this was the first and last time. Letting Robert Harding take over her life the way he'd taken over her mother's was *not* going to happen, not even if he threatened her. As soon as Angus was able to ride they would be gone from there, and her stepfather would never be a problem for her again.

The thought of leaving made her feel a good deal better, so much so that she was able to summon a smile as she left her rooms. She'd been exhausted enough to sleep for a while when she'd finally gotten back after helping with Angus's wound, and she'd eaten enough to satisfy the feeble appetite she'd had. Now she would play hostess for a little while, mingle with her guests, then retire with a

31

headache. Cam was spending the night in the cave with
Angus, but she wanted to be there as well.

Strains of music floated up to her as she descended the
wide stairs, but rather than put Rianne in a festive mood
it depressed her. She could still remember the parties
they'd had when she was a little girl, happy parties with
kind, happy people. But then her father was killed in that
hunting accident, and after a proper period of mourning
her mother was introduced to Robert Harding. Her mother
had married the man because of the pressure brought to
bear by some of the people who supposedly cared about
her, but she had never stopped mourning her first husband.
When she'd finally had enough and stopped caring about
life, she went to join her beloved husband. Rianne sometimes wondered whether her mother realized she was leaving a young daughter behind all alone . . .

"Ah, there you are, my dear," Jean Rochard's voice
came, and then he was putting her arm through his own.
"Do allow me to escort you. You are without doubt the
most beautiful woman here, and every man in the house
will envy me. Why, just think how blissfully happy I would
be if you were to agree to making the arrangement permanent . . ."

Rianne smiled faintly and let Jean's words float past her as
they entered the ballroom, and then the rest of her suitors
were there, clustering around. It was fascinating how not one
of them was interested in her for herself, not one who would
think about her before themselves. All the men she was allowed to know were like that except for her adopted brothers,
but once she escaped to the colonies . . .

"As I've already said, I'm delighted we needn't delay
business because of your unfortunate accident," Harding
told Bryan with one of his insincere smiles when they
paused for a moment between groups of people. Harding
had been introducing him to the other guests, and had all
but preened in front of the women. He obviously considered himself a ladies' man, and some of the women had

apparently agreed. "Are you certain you're feeling recovered?" he added.

"Completely recovered," Bryan assured him as he glanced around. The works of art they'd passed on the way to the ballroom had been magnificent, as was the ballroom itself. *Someone* had excellent taste, but he doubted the someone was Harding. "Resting before dinner made me good as new, and I admit to feeling disappointed that your daughter didn't join us for the meal."

"She was feeling faint and so took a tray in her rooms," Harding answered quickly with another of those smiles. "She will, however, attend the ball, so no more than a small amount of time was lost. Introductions can be made and then on to business."

Bryan nodded absently as they moved around the ballroom, privately wondering why Harding was in such a hurry. Time was clearly on his mind, rush and hurry, hurry and rush. His daughter's feeling "faint" had nearly enraged him, giving Bryan the impression that "stubborn" would have been a better word. She hadn't felt like coming down to dinner, and so she hadn't. If she failed to put in an appearance at the ball as well, Bryan intended suggesting they go and visit her in her rooms. He needed that girl to make his plan work, so he wasn't about to let her get away with a fit of temper.

"Ah, there she is," Harding exclaimed, looking across the very large room. "There in the green and gold gown."

Bryan looked in the direction Harding was facing, trying to see through the crowd. Everyone in the neighborhood was attending the ball, along with a surprisingly large contingent from London society. The crystal chandeliers gleamed with the candlelight, the orchestra played with smooth perfection, fortunes in jewels and gowns were displayed by the ladies—

And then Bryan felt as though he'd been hit again with a rock. The girl his searching gaze had found was stunning, completely captivating even from that distance. Tall and graceful with an incredible figure, her manner of ignoring the men around her apparently only inflaming their

interest. She toyed with them even as she let them follow
her, and they crowded close like lap dogs, eager for the
least pat on the head.

But there was also something else about her, something
beyond mere looks. Bryan had met many beautiful women
in his life, but none of them had impressed him in quite
the same way. Was it her manner of tossing her head, as
if rejecting something stupid being told to her? The steadiness of her gaze, which clearly made the men around her
uncomfortable? Possibly it was the way she held herself,
as though silently announcing to the world that she was
more than just another beautiful woman. Whichever, it
was definitely something Bryan hadn't been expecting.

"Let's make our way over there and I'll introduce
you." Harding interrupted his thoughts with a touch to his
arm. "And you can see now that I wasn't exaggerating
about her beauty."

"You certainly weren't," Bryan admitted, letting Harding believe it was only her looks that had impressed him.
And in point of fact, it made very little difference. No
matter how attractive the girl was, he wasn't really there
looking for a wife. Possibly if things had been other than
what they were—but they weren't, so what was the sense
in thinking about it?

Despite that very sound decision, as the two of them
made their way across the ballroom Bryan couldn't keep
from staring at the girl who would soon be his temporary
wife. The closer he got the more beautiful she became,
with her flawless, pink-tinged complexion, eyes of flashing
green, and full, beautifully formed lips. And that hair! A
glorious crown of golden-red, done up with jewels and
pearls and all the rest of that nonsense. Bryan would much
rather have seen it flowing free below her perfect shoulders and neck—

No, stop that! he scolded himself. *Can't you remember
you're here on business? She's nothing more than your
means to reach Harding, nothing more than just another
woman . . . just another innocent, helpless, beautiful
woman . . .*

By the time they reached the girl, she stood talking to two older ladies who had chased away the gaggle of men who had surrounded her. Most of the men seemed to have used the opportunity to go searching for refreshments, and the ladies themselves moved off just as Bryan and Harding arrived. Bryan was strangely pleased that the girl's lapdogs were momentarily elsewhere, and then Harding stopped beside her and spoke.

"Rianne, my child, there's someone here I'd like you to meet," he said, and Bryan heard tension in the man's voice. "My dear, this is our newest neighbor, Mr. Bryan Machlin, who will be our guest for a short while. Bryan, may I present my daughter, Rianne Lockwood."

"My lady, I'm honored," Bryan found himself saying with a bow, not at all what he'd intended. He suddenly felt like a schoolboy attending his first important social function, which was completely ridiculous.

"Mr. Machlin," the girl acknowledged with a regal nod of her head. "So you're new to our neighborhood. How do you like it so far?"

"I find the beauty of the area extremely compelling," Bryan answered with a smile as he drowned in incredible green eyes. "If I'd known about it sooner, I wouldn't have waited this long to move here."

"Yes, our forests and hillsides *are* rather lovely," she agreed dryly. "You're not the only one to think so."

"I would be very surprised if I were," he returned, charmed with the way she held him to a discussion of landscape. She knew his comments referred to *her*, but he was the one who had first mentioned scenery, so she would continue with it. "And your forests and hillsides aren't the only lovely things in the neighborhood," he added, conceding her the victory. "I'd heard the country produced breathtaking ladies as well, but never believed it until just a moment ago."

"When you saw the ladies I was just speaking to," she said with a nod, again interpreting his comment in her own way. "How very gallant you are, Mr. Machlin. Would

you like me to introduce you to them? I'm sure they would
be delighted to meet you.''

Bryan opened his mouth, but couldn't seem to find any
words to speak. The two women she'd been talking to were
blurs in his memory, except for the fact that they were
older ladies. He hadn't the least desire to meet them, but
how was he supposed to say that without sounding like a
boor? It looked like the beautiful minx had him trapped,
but then he was visited with inspiration.

"I can see there's no use in denying the truth you've
already noticed,'' he said with a sigh meant to suggest
defeat. "I do, however, ask the favor of your discretion.
I'm certainly not good enough for either of those ladies,
and meeting them would only add to my painful embarrassment. May we keep the truth between ourselves alone?
I somehow feel you'll keep my dark and terrible secret.''

She glanced around then, seeing, as Bryan already had,
that Harding was engaged in conversation with some people a few feet away. She *was* the only one who knew his
supposed secret, and now she was the one who had to
keep from looking boorish.

"People with dark and terrible secrets shouldn't rely on
others to keep those secrets,'' she said at last, apparently
amused in spite of herself. "What would happen if I forgot
myself and blurted it out? I'd feel awful, but the damage
would be done.''

"Why, then I'd be left with no choice,'' he answered,
producing another of those weary sighs. "I'd have to forget about being a gentleman, and lie like a rogue. I'd tell
the ladies it was really *you* who had me enchanted, and
although they would probably find that hard to believe, I'd
have to continue to insist on it. Coward that I am, I'd find
it impossible to acknowledge my real interest.''

By then she was obviously trying very hard not to grin
or laugh aloud, and Bryan was delighted. The silly little
game they were playing was unlike anything he'd ever engaged in with a woman, which certainly had to be what
was wrong with other women. He'd just told this gorgeous
girl that no one would believe she was attractive enough

for him to be interested in her, and she considered the suggestion funny! How many other beautiful women would react the same? Not many, if any at all.

"It's strange that a man of your appearance would be so unsure of himself," she said as soon as she had control of her amusement. "And I find it difficult to believe that you really are a coward. What you probably need is the support of a good woman, which you might very well find with at least one of those ladies. My advice would be to trust in yourself and them, and make the effort to approach them. You could very well be surprised with the result."

"It seems to be time to make another admission," Bryan said, now pretending to be embarrassed. "I'm very much afraid of surprises, and have even been known to hide under a bed to avoid one. You don't want to force me into hiding under a bed again, do you?"

"That would be something I'd have to see," she said with a sudden laugh, no longer able to keep to the silliness. "It certainly isn't something I can picture. You would—"

"Rianne, do excuse this interruption," a male voice said, and then the girl's collection of lapdog admirers was there again. "We saw that the ladies had finished having a private word with you, so we came back. Is this someone new visiting your father?"

"Yes, Jean, it *is* someone visiting my father," the girl answered in a strange voice, as though struck with a revelation that banished all amusement. She then went on to introduce the newcomer to the gaggle, but the newcomer was too busy fuming to pay much attention. If those idiots hadn't interrupted, Bryan would still be enjoying the girl's conversation. He felt robbed of something valuable, and had to fight to keep the feeling out of his expression.

"Whatever have you done to your head, Machlin?" the one introduced as Jean Rochard asked lazily. "A disagreement with an unseen door, perhaps? I certainly would hesitate to suggest an unseen husband."

Bryan's jaw tightened as the gaggle laughed in amusement, all of them knowing he couldn't make a fuss over

the allegation without making it seem true. The girl didn't
join in the general laughter, but suddenly there was a gleam
in her eye unlike anything he'd seen while they talked.

"Perhaps Mr. Machlin fell from his—horse," she
drawled, bringing laughter to the group again. Her slight
hesitation before the word "horse" suggested it might be
his own clumsy feet that he'd fallen from. Bryan found
himself speechless at that, not to mention incredibly hurt.
What could have happened in the space of a single minute
that would have changed her so completely? Now she was
laughing *at* him rather than with him, and the difference
was painful.

"I really do think we've taken up enough of your time,
Mr. Machlin," she said once the laughter stopped. "I'm
sure there are any number of people in this room who
haven't yet made your acquaintance, so you'd better return
to the round of introductions. I do hope you enjoy the rest
of your stay."

With that she all but turned her back on him, giving the
man Rochard her complete attention. Bryan just stood
there, finding it impossible to believe he'd been dismissed
like that, feeling horribly humiliated at the smirks being
sent to him by some members of the gaggle. The rest were
following the girl's lead and ignoring him, very pointedly
and very obviously. At last Bryan forced himself to turn
and stalk away, his mood black enough to shrivel plant
life at a dozen paces.

"What an incredible boor," Jean commented to Rianne,
looking over her shoulder. "Apparently he isn't even bright
enough to know what to do when he's dismissed. I thought
he'd never leave."

Rianne turned back to watch Bryan Machlin stomp
away, an odd feeling in the pit of her stomach. It was
unbelievable that she'd actually forgotten who and what he
was, even though it had been her stepfather who had introduced him to her. She'd expected the man to be at the
ball and had therefore decided to be cool and distant if
they met, but something had happened to ruin her inten-

tion. He was so very handsome in dark-gray brocade and
white silk shirt and cravat, his silver knee and shoe buckles gleaming in the candlelight. One distant word had led
to another, and before she realized it they were sharing a
silly pretense that not another man she'd ever met would
be capable of. Rather than mouthing a lot of meaningless
compliments, he'd even gone so far as to pretend she
wasn't attractive at all. It had been great fun, completely
unexpected—

And then Jean had come over to remind her exactly who
she was laughing with. The man wasn't only a friend of
her stepfather's, he was also the brute who had wounded
Angus. She'd felt immediately ashamed of herself then, to
behave like that with the man who'd hurt her brother, and
when the opportunity came to hurt the man in return, she'd
taken it without stopping to think. It was ridiculous to feel
that maybe she *shouldn't* have done it; feeling like that
would be disloyal to Angus, and she could never be disloyal. No, she wasn't bothered by what she'd done, she
wouldn't let herself be.

Besides, the man would probably get over it in no
time . . .

"Machlin, please, let me speak to you," Bryan heard
as he reached the hall. Harding was hurrying after him,
but hadn't had much luck in catching up. He sounded as
though he'd overheard the last of what his stepdaughter
had said, and once Bryan stopped to wait, the guess was
proven correct.

"Machlin, let me apologize for my daughter's behavior," Harding jittered as soon as he faced the bigger man.
"Her actions were reprehensible, but surely you won't allow *that* to keep you from finalizing our agreement. With
everything that's involved—"

"If you think what she did made me want to refuse your
offer, you're wrong," Bryan interrupted harshly, seeing
the other man flinch back from his anger. "What I want
is to conclude our agreement as quickly as possible, get it

signed and sealed and completed. After that I can forget
all about what she said.''

"Of course, my dear fellow, of course,'' Harding fluttered, so relieved he looked close to passing out. "Let's
go to my study immediately, and I'll tell you all about the
arrangements I've made. If I'm not mistaken, you'll be
absolutely delighted . . .''

He chattered on about unimportant things as he led the
way toward another part of the house, and Bryan didn't
bother to listen. What a damned fool he'd been, to get so
involved that he forgot why he was there. The girl must
have been playing with him, waiting for his guard to go
down before she attacked in earnest. Rather than refusing
to talk to him she'd encouraged his interest, and then had
jumped at the chance to show off for her toadies. That he
hadn't expected to be treated like that after the first part
of their conversation somehow made it worse, as though
she'd in some way betrayed the special qualities he'd imagined her to have.

Special qualities—what a joke! Bryan tugged at the lace
at his left wrist, struggling to get his temper back under
control. The only thing special about that girl was her
malicious sense of humor, which had made him believe
she was enjoying herself before abruptly dismissing him
like a beggar. Redheads were supposed to be notorious
for their tempers and mood changes, but she wasn't really
a redhead. Golden-red her hair was, a rather unusual
shade—

Bryan nearly stopped short, but caught himself just in
time. It was a ridiculous thought that had come to him,
one that couldn't possibly be true—but what if it was?
Those three on the road that afternoon, and the skinny one
he'd disarmed . . . that one had had the same golden-red
hair, a shade you didn't see every day. Had the eyes looking through the mask been green? The boy hadn't said
anything, not a word even when he was bested, and that
in itself was strange. Could it really have been *her* . . . ?

"Come right in and take a seat, Machlin,'' Harding
said as he opened the door to his large, tastefully deco-

rated study. "I'll get the papers out of my strongbox and be with you in a moment."

Bryan nodded and went to sit in one of the deep, leather-upholstered chairs in front of the wide desk, but his thoughts were still running riot. It was outrageous to think the girl was one of those three on the road, but if she were, there was suddenly an explanation for her behavior beyond malicious rudeness. The skinny one had come at him in attack while he was pretending to threaten the life of the wounded boy. If that had been her, she hadn't known he was only pretending; in her mind he was someone who would kill a wounded boy in cold blood, so why bother being in the least courteous? And hadn't she started out cool and regal, before the conversation turned silly? If she actually had been enjoying herself, it was the arrival of the gaggle that must have reminded her he was the terrible monster from the road this afternoon.

That interpretation bothered him quite a lot, since that wasn't the picture he would have wanted her to have of him. And the more he thought about it, the more likely it seemed it *had* been her on the road, and that part he really didn't understand. Was Harding so tight with money that she had to supplement her income as a highwayman? Just how much more *was* there to Miss Rianne Lockwood, beyond all the obvious points she allowed the world to see?

"And here we are," Harding said with thick heartiness as he took his place behind the desk. "Our—private agreement first, and then the marriage contracts."

He handed across the first of the papers, and Bryan read it carefully before he leaned forward and accepted the quill to sign it with. He sanded the ink before handing it back, and Harding beamed as he inspected it.

"Bryan Machlin," he read aloud with a chuckle. "I never realized how fine a name that really is. And now the marriage contracts."

Bryan took them and read them even more carefully than he had the first, then leaned forward and signed them.

His sprawling "B. G. Machlin" was boldly clear, but Harding didn't even glance at it.

"And now for the good news I've been waiting to tell you," Harding all but sang. "I've arranged things so that you and Rianne can be married tomorrow. How does *that* sound?"

"That's not possible," Bryan answered with an incredulous laugh. "I wouldn't mind if it were, but it simply isn't. And what about the girl's consent? How do you plan on getting it?"

"Getting an agreement will simply be a matter of explaining things clearly to her," Harding said in a lecturing tone as he sat back with his fingertips together in front of him. "Until now she has simply refused to take vows, and her stubbornness would have permitted her to make a fool of anyone who doubted the stance. Recently, however, it came to me that she reveres her parents' memory, and she would not find it possible to shame and tarnish that memory. I tested the theory this evening, when she attempted to beg off from the ball as well as from dinner."

"And it worked?" Bryan asked with surprise. "Without any trouble at all?"

"My dear fellow, you saw her in the ballroom yourself," Harding pointed out smugly. "She had no true wish to attend, and yet she did so. I'll explain that if she refuses to go through with the marriage, everyone attending will be certain to spread word of her shocking behavior far and wide. There won't be anyone who won't know how she brought shame to the Lockwood name, and her parents will turn over in their graves from the disgrace of it. The girl will never cause a public scandal of that sort, and so she will bow her head and obey me."

Bryan studied the other man's satisfied smirk, and decided that Harding really was a fool. That girl would never bow her head and obey anybody, least of all a man like Harding. She might be fond enough of her parents' memory to let herself be swayed on unimportant matters, but marriage would hardly be considered unimportant. No, if Bryan wanted to force this girl to marry him, he'd have to test a theory of his own—and he was quite sure he had guessed correctly about her "secret identity."

"And as far as marrying her tomorrow is concerned, it's not only possible, it's already arranged," Harding went on. "When we first came to agreement on the private part of the matter, I took the liberty of speaking to the vicar of a nearby village parish. I knew you would find Rianne acceptably attractive, you see, and therefore had the good sir make all the arrangements. He knows me well and appreciates the donations I've given his little church, and so will be here tomorrow afternoon to perform the marriage in our chapel. If the arrangements suit you, there's nothing left but to tell the bride."

"Tomorrow will suit me admirably," Bryan agreed, his smile enough to take the smirk from Harding. The smaller man must have thought Bryan was considering what he would do to his new wife, but in fact it was Harding himself who was foremost in his thoughts. That agreement Bryan had signed stipulated immediate payment of a very large amount of money to Harding, due the day after the marriage took place. Harding lived like a man with limitless wealth, but his rush to get everything settled quickly really showed that desperation Bryan had noticed previously. And Bryan would use the desperation to buy the name of the man he was after, and then it would only be a matter of reaching the treacherous scum . . .

"I'll put these papers away, and then we'll find your bride-to-be," Harding said, folding the agreement separately before taking everything to his strongbox. "She really should be told tonight, I think, so that tomorrow she'll be in the proper frame of mind."

"While you're telling her, I'll be taking a stroll in the gardens," Bryan said, not missing the vindictive satisfaction Harding doubtless thought he was hiding so well. "I really dislike the sight of a woman crying and begging—begging someone else, that is."

Harding laughed with true enjoyment at the remark, which had been calculated to make him believe Bryan was just as low as he himself. The words had left a bad taste in Bryan's mouth, but he made sure not to show it as the two of them left together. Rianne's stepfather was eager to get on to the next part of the plan, but so was Bryan. Not the same next part, of course, but definitely related.

Rianne closed the door to her bedchamber with a sigh, surprised that Jean and the others hadn't decided to camp in her sitting room. She'd had unbelievable difficulty getting away from them in the ballroom, and had half-expected to be followed upstairs.

"They're probably saving the camping idea for tomorrow," she muttered, glad she'd thought to dismiss her maid earlier. If she hadn't, she'd still be lacking the solitude she needed so badly. "Most of them will be leaving soon, so it's bound to be considered their last chance."

She shook her head as she began to cross the room, admitting she had no one but herself to blame that her final escape had had to be put off. If she hadn't insisted on stopping one more coach, Angus wouldn't have gotten—

A polite knock cut short the self-chastisement, and she turned to look at the door, wondering if the camping idea *had* occurred to someone.

"Who is it?" she called, making the words sound extremely annoyed. There was no sense in having a reputation like hers if she never used it to her advantage.

"It's your father, child," Robert Harding's voice came, surprising her. "I need a moment to speak with you."

"Whatever it is will have to wait until tomorrow," she answered, certain he would try to talk her into going back downstairs. "I have a beastly headache, so I'm going straight to bed."

"No, dear, it must be tonight," he returned, and immediately opened the door and walked in. Rianne was shocked that he would do that, and further shocked at the hint of a smile in her stepfather's voice. That was very unlike him. He was in fact smiling very broadly, and Rianne wondered what on earth could bring him to her bedchamber at this hour and in such a cheerful mood.

"All right then, it has to be tonight," she conceded, finding it was unnecessary to deliberately replace polite interest with impatience. She had no interest at all in what he had to say, and was burning to get back to Angus and Cam. "Just say it as quickly as you can, please, and then leave."

"Please," he echoed, that smile still firmly in place. "How polite a child you are, when no one is about to hear you but me. In the presence of others I receive nothing but haughty ridicule, as though I were too far beneath you to really notice. A pity you'll no longer be able to treat me so."

"Are you going away?" she asked, finding the idea pleased her. "If so, do have a wonderful journey and be sure to stay away as long as you like."

"I'm not the one who's leaving," he answered with a wide grin, obviously enjoying himself immensely. *"You* are, along with your new husband, after the ceremony tomorrow. It's all arranged, so don't bother your head over any of the details. I've taken care of them all."

"Except for the most important one," she pointed out, not terribly surprised that he was actually trying to do as he'd threatened. "I refuse to take wedding vows, so you and Jean will find nothing but disappointment tomorrow. Or was it Jonathan Coleridge you talked into making a fool of himself?"

"Neither," he responded happily. "Your husband will be Bryan Machlin, that very large man you were so sweet to earlier this evening. He's decided he wants you very badly as his wife, so that he might spend his time teaching you good manners with a free hand. A rather *heavy* free hand, I would venture to guess."

"A prospect that obviously delights you," Rianne told him, suddenly fighting to hide painful shock. "The disappointment will surely be crushing for the two of you, but my stance hasn't changed. I won't be married off at your whim no matter who the groom is."

"Ah, but you will, child," he disagreed, his continuing amusement setting Rianne's teeth on edge. "All of our guests tonight are at this moment being invited to the ceremony tomorrow, and any refusal you make will be in front of *them*. Think how notorious you will become, once they spread the word. There won't be a soul in the entire country who isn't aware of how thoroughly you besmirched the Lockwood family name. Even in their graves your mother and father will blush with the shame of it, the humiliation of . . ."

"How dare you bring my parents into this!" Rianne shouted, suddenly so furious that she took a step toward him with fists clenched tight. "You're not fit to have licked my father's boots, and my mother would never have looked at you twice if others hadn't insisted. Get out of here this minute, or by God I'll do to you what I should have done long ago! Get out!"

"Oh, how sad that I've made you so upset," Harding said in mournful pretense. "Your happiness and well-being are, of course, always my primary concern. I'll leave at once, and let you get your rest. Tomorrow will certainly be a big day for you."

His bow was on the hasty side, due to the second step she took toward him, and then he was gone after having pulled the door closed behind him. Rianne was so furiously angry that she had to stalk back and forth across the room an uncounted number of times before her hands stopped shaking. The filthy, slimy pig! That he would *dare* speak to her like that!

"And he's stupid, as well as slimy," she muttered savagely to herself as she tore open the doors of her wardrobe. "He was so eager to crow over his plans, it never occurred to him that he was also giving me warning. We'll see whose name becomes notorious when they find tomorrow that I've gone."

Well-hidden behind the clothing of a lady was a pair of supple leather breeches, a long-sleeved, white linen shirt, and a pair of calf-high brown boots. Rianne had always worn the outfit for special occasions like fencing lessons and practice, climbing trees, and learning to ride really well astride. Now she would wear it for running away, even though she would not be running very far. She would stay in the cave until the excitement over her disappearance died down, and by then Angus would be thoroughly healed and they could leave together.

It took something of an effort to get herself out of the green gown without help from her maid, but once it was lying in a heap on the floor she was able to get rid of the rest and climb into more practical clothes. With a party going on, the back stairs would be empty of servants. She would have no trouble sneaking down them for the last time, and then she would finally be *free*.

When the time came to marry it would be to a man of *her* choice, the sort of man she'd always pictured in her dreams. She'd somehow thought the man Machlin could be someone like that, but it was clear now how wrong she'd been. Anyone who associated with her stepfather had to be cut from the exact same cloth . . . She pulled the pins out of her hair and quickly brushed it down, then headed with a firm stride to the bedchamber door.

Rianne had to tug at the handle four or five times before she realized the door was locked. Fury came rushing back as she used the sort of language she'd heard in the stables to describe the man who had locked her in, but she wasn't even remotely beaten. She still had a balcony outside her bedroom windows, one she'd climbed down from a few times. Usually it was too much of a risk to leave that way, when one of the gardeners might come by at any time and see her. Right then it was no risk at all, but Rianne would have used it even if it were.

Again she strode across the room, the need to be out of there mounting ever higher, and this time she reached for the handle of a curtained door that *couldn't* be locked. She yanked it open—then took one step back with a gasp.

"Isn't it too late for little girls to be going out?" that giant brute Machlin asked very mildly. His body filled the single doorway, blocking it completely as he lounged with one arm leaning high on the door frame. "You should be in bed by now, getting your rest for tomorrow. It would be embarrassing if you fell asleep during the festivities."

"Embarrassing for whom?" Rianne retorted, fighting to keep her voice steady and hard. "I've already said there won't *be* any festivities, which you may have heard if you've been sneaking around out there for any length of time. Go away, Mr. Machlin, and take up any complaints you may have with my stepfather."

"That would be a waste of time," he answered with a shrug, apparently ignoring her comment about sneaking but hardly unaware of it. "I say there *will* be festivities, and I'm here to list the reasons why. Just to see if you agree, you understand."

He flashed her a brief, unamused smile, then stepped into the room and closed the balcony door behind him. Rianne found herself backing away from that advance, and forced herself to stop. She would *not* show this brute fear, not even if her heart pounded straight out of her chest.

"I have no interest in hearing anything you have to say," she stated, looking up into those cold gray eyes. "And I'm not the sort of tart you're obviously used to. Get out of my bedroom, and get out *now.*"

"Hasn't anyone ever told you that *too* much courage becomes foolishness?" he asked, for some reason suddenly and truly amused. "There isn't a man within fifty miles who would speak to me the way you've been doing, and it's not even because you're so good with a blade. You already know you can't best me, but you're not letting having lost to me stop you."

"What—what are you talking about?" Rianne asked, feeling a surge of fear and hearing it thin her voice. It sounded just as though he *knew*—

"What I'm talking about is this afternoon, and how I got the head wound you and your friends were so concerned about," he drawled, folding his arms where he stood. "Three highwaymen stopped my coach, and I got out to face them. I wounded the first, disarmed the second, and would have had the third put up his bow if I hadn't been knocked unconscious by a thrown rock. The one I disarmed did the throwing."

"Why are you telling *me* rather than the authorities?"

Rianne said, having fought her voice almost back to normal. "If you were robbed they should know about it, so they can—"

"Do the same sort of nothing they've *been* doing?" he finished for her. "Once I got here I heard all about those highwaymen, but I don't have a legitimate complaint. I *wasn't* robbed, and you know it."

"Mr. Machlin, you're beginning to annoy me," Rianne said, folding her arms in the same way he had. "I *don't* know what you're talking about, and don't want to know. If that's what you came here to say, you can leave now."

"Little one, it's no secret to me that *you're* the highwayman I disarmed, the one who threw the rock," the brute said bluntly, no longer playing the roundabout game. "You and your friends have made quite a reputation for yourselves, and I can understand why the authorities haven't been able to find you. Who would think to look *here*."

"If you really were hit with a rock, it obviously affected your balance," Rianne told him, feeling slightly more secure. "No one would ever believe a story like that, even if you happened to have proof. All you're doing is wasting my—"

"Ah, but I do have proof," he said, his gray eyes beginning to fill with that unexplained amusement. "When you fell this afternoon your cap became disarranged, and some of that hair came free. I saw it, and I'm sure the coach driver saw the same. Are you going to try to claim there are others in this area with exactly the same shade as yours? You may *try* claiming it, but it's not likely to do you much good."

"And what good do you expect it to do *you*?" she snapped, beginning to feel cornered. "Assuming anyone would believe you in the first place, I would then be taken out and hanged. If it's occurred to you that I'd *prefer* being hanged to being married to someone like you, you're absolutely right. I would."

"But would you prefer being hanged with company?" he asked, that light-gray gaze burning into her. "Once they had you they would *not* just toss you into a cell and call the hangman. They would ask you first about your two accomplices, in a way guaranteed to encourage answers. You *would* tell them, and then they would have all three of you to show off to the howling victims of your attentions. With the sort of people you've robbed, they can't afford to do anything else.''

Rianne felt the blood drain out of her face, and for the first time in her life she thought she might faint. He meant they would torture her to find out about Angus and Cam, and she was very much afraid she would tell them. Her brothers would die right beside her, and she would have to face eternity knowing their death was her fault.

''Steady,'' the big brute said, and suddenly she realized he'd closed the distance between them without her knowing it. His arms were around her and holding her up, keeping her close to him despite the way she'd begun trembling. She immediately jerked away and tried to stand alone, but those impossible arms pulled her to him again.

''I know what you're picturing, but it doesn't have to happen that way,'' he told her, for some ridiculous reason sounding faintly upset, as though her shock and horror were unexpected. ''I'm not likely to want to see my wife hanged or tortured, so you'd have nothing to worry about. Do you hear me? Do you understand what I'm saying?''

''I understand,'' she whispered as she stopped the useless struggling she'd been doing, staring at his ruffled shirtfront. ''Spilling my blood alone on a private altar of sacrifice will be enough to appease the gentleman inside you. And how insensitive of me not to have realized that you've seen in me your one true love, and you can't possibly rest until you've made me yours. What choice have I but to accede to your impassioned pleas?''

''I wasn't the one who put you into this position,'' he immediately protested, still sounding bothered as he set one big hand under her chin to make her look up at him. ''Taking to the highways was presumably your own idea— unless some *did* force you to it?''

The way he looked down at her was almost a hopeful plea, but that didn't mean she had to respond. Why she'd done as she had was *her* business, and nothing that he needed to know.

"For a woman, you have too much pride," he said after a moment, an odd expression in his eyes. "You'd rather take the blame for anything you were accused of, sooner than justify what you'd done—even if you *were* forced. Don't you know you're not big enough to keep yourself from being forced into things?"

She had no idea what he was talking about until he lowered his lips to hers. Still he held her to him with the strength of the brute that he was, but the touch of his kiss was as soft as silk on her trembling lips. It felt as she'd always imagined the kiss of a hero from her books would feel, full of desire and passion, but gentle despite that. Her heartbeat quickened as she felt an intense need to join in the kiss, but then memory brought her abruptly back to harsh reality. This man was a cad rather than a hero, and she'd be a fool to believe anything else. He let the kiss continue for another moment, then raised his head again to look down at her.

"You're not responding in any way at all, not even with hysterics," he said, and idiotically enough he sounded disappointed. "Hasn't any man kissed you before? I can't believe they haven't."

"I have no interest at all in what you believe," she said, totally taken over by a leaden numbness. Unless she escaped, he *would* force her to marry him, and then she would be his to do with as he pleased. And her chance at happiness would be gone forever, a worse fate than anything *he* could think of to inflict.

"You're just tired and upset," he said, and then, unbelievably, he was letting her go. "Get to bed and have a good night's sleep, and we'll continue this conversation tomorrow."

He looked down at her as though he wanted to add something; then he apparently changed his mind, for he simply turned and left. He used the balcony door just as he had to enter, and after a few moments when Rianne followed, she found he'd tied the doors closed from the outside. Through the glass, the lamplight showed that the rope was knotted tight. Even if she broke a pane to reach it, untying it would be just about impossible.

"Check and mate," she whispered, idly wondering if the man played chess. The phrase was so unbelievably appropriate . . .

Rianne felt dead inside as she went over to a lounge and sat, her head whirling with a sense of unreality. None of this could possibly be happening, she must be in the midst of a dream. Yes, that was it, she was dreaming, but it wasn't anything like the dreams she usually had. Yet that brute hadn't even tried to violate her—his kiss had left her shaken—it must have been a dream!

A whispering voice inside her refused to let her believe this comforting lie. *Of course he didn't try to violate you now. Why would he bother, when tomorrow it will be the duty you owe him?*

"I'll die first," she whispered back, feeling the resolve strengthen even in the presence of the numbness. She remembered the feeling when she first saw him, that somehow he was different from all the other men she'd known, and couldn't understand how it was possible to be that wrong. Why did she have those feelings, when he was just another brute?

Nothing in the way of an answer came, not even when she slowly lay back to stare at the ceiling. Angus and Cam would have helped her escape, but it would all be over by the time they found out. She would have to be strong and remember she was doing it for them, but giving up the dream hurt so badly. It hurt, it hurt . . .

Bryan stood in the shadows of the balcony until the girl discovered for herself that she couldn't get out, and then he used the trellis to climb back down to the darkness-covered ground. If he'd had someone there to bet with, he would have bet on her trying the balcony doors, even in the face of the possibility that he might still be there. His first look at those clothes she wore had banished all doubt: she was definitely the "skinny boy" from that afternoon.

"More nerve and guts than any man in her house," he murmured with a grin, then felt the amusement die. He remembered the way she'd gone pale at the thought of being tortured, the shock hitting her so hard she'd nearly passed out. What he'd told her was nonsense, of course, even if she so obviously didn't know it. No woman with her looks, wealth, and social position would ever have to worry about being locked up, let alone being put to the question. Her stepfather would be forced to make restitution while the scandal was hushed up, and that would be the end of it.

Bryan had sweated over the point he'd thought she *would* believe, that he would use his own people to find her accomplices no matter who or where they were. It had been clear from the first that she cared about those two, and so he'd decided to use them against her. He'd been waiting for her to laugh at the idea of personal danger, but had been shocked himself at the intensity of her reaction to the idea that her friends would hang with her.

He'd hit her really hard with his threat, and the life had gone out of her beautiful eyes. He hadn't wanted to see *that* happen, hadn't really expected it. If she'd screamed and cried and thrown a tantrum it would have meant nothing, but to see her just standing there, trying not to show how devastated she was—If he'd had any choice at all he would have told her to forget about his threat . . .

"But I have no choice," he growled low, all sense of pleasure gone. "I need her to be my wife, so she will be. If I leave her as I found her, Harding will believe he can sell her inheritance to someone else and will refuse to answer my questions. He can't be left with any way out but the one I provide, otherwise I'll be wasting my time. No, I can't turn my back on her . . ."

He ran his hand through his hair as he sighed, forced to admit there was another reason. The girl had shown how little she thought of him, and that bothered him even more now than it had earlier. He'd pictured himself being firm and distant with Harding's spoiled little stepdaughter, shrugging at her hysterics and then simply going on with his plans. But Harding's stepdaughter wasn't at all what he'd pictured, and keeping his distance wasn't going to be easy. There *was* so much more to her than just beauty . . . He hadn't intended to kiss her, but something had come over him . . . something that felt almost like an echo of a kindred spirit . . .

And now, like it or not, his plans had become more complicated. He *couldn't* change his mind and call the wedding off, but he also couldn't just dismiss the girl's feelings. And he couldn't tell her how brief their marriage would be. If she decided not to cooperate, his hold on her would be cancelled out by her knowledge of his plans. A word from her to Harding would end everything, and after all his planning, he wasn't about to let that happen.

Thoroughly dissatisfied, Bryan went back into the house. Maybe tomorrow, his wedding day, things would go better . . .

Chapter 4

R ianne awoke with a start when she heard someone at the door to her sitting room, and didn't need any time at all to remember what had happened the night before. It was all perfectly clear in her mind, but now without the numbness. She hadn't expected to fall asleep on the lounge, but she had slept deeply if not comfortably, and was now ready to fight. What good it would do—if any at all—she had no idea, but she still intended to fight.

She got to her feet to stretch the ache out of her body from having slept all cramped up, and watched as the door to her sitting room finally opened. If it had been her maid alone she would have walked right past the girl and out, trusting to luck and boldness to get her into the woods and out of sight before anyone caught up. But in addition to two housemaids there was a large new footman she didn't know, who stood himself in the sitting room beside her bedchamber door. And sailing in in front of the maids was a woman who advanced with a sweet, understanding smile that was so very familiar.

"Rianne, child, what a glorious day this is!" Lady Margaret Welford sang, waving one hand as the other held her full, fashionable skirts. Lady Margaret was about the age Rianne's mother would have been had she lived, and never had a harsh word to say about anyone. She was kind and charitable, open and compassionate, and visited often after Rianne's father was killed. When Rianne's mother died as well, Lady Margaret turned her attention to Rianne, sweetly determined to make her good friend's daughter a proper, well-fulfilled woman.

"Why do you think this day is so glorious?" Rianne asked as she eyed the footman just outside the door. If only she had her sword . . . or even a rock . . .

"What a silly question," Lady Margaret laughed in answer. "A woman's wedding day is always glorious, and that's what you'll soon be. A woman."

Lady Margaret gave her that special "Secrets" look she was so good at sending, letting Rianne know that soon the mysteries of the universe would be open to her. It was supposed to be a Woman's Thing, delicious secrets kept strictly from men, and it was all Rianne could do not to laugh. Angus and Cam knew a lot more about those "Secrets" than Lady Margaret ever would, and what they knew they'd shared with their sister.

"And now we must get you out of those dreadful clothes and into a bath," the older woman went on, her brows high as she studied Rianne. "And as soon as you're out of them, we'll throw them away. A lady is known by what she wears, dear child, a truism you must make more of an effort to remember."

"I have a new truism for you, Lady Margaret," Rianne retorted as she folded her arms, stung by the slighting reference to her very special outfit. "A lady shows her opinion of the world by what she wears. They may be able to force me into this marriage, but not into any other clothes. They'll take me as I am, or they don't have to take me at all."

"Dear child, you mustn't feel as though you've been betrayed," Lady Margaret said with a compassionate sigh, coming closer to put a hand on Rianne's folded arms. "It was your stepfather's duty to find an acceptable match for you, and now it's your duty to obey his wishes. Shedding an ocean of tears won't change things, dear, so why be difficult? Be happy on your wedding day, even if the happiness is only for yourself."

"I'd rather be difficult," Rianne stated flatly, looking down at the smaller woman's sincerity. Robert Harding had undoubtedly sent Lady Margaret to her, counting on the woman to talk Rianne into proper behavior. Well, if

Machlin's threat meant she wasn't going to be able to refuse the vows, she would show her pleasure with this situation in other ways.

"Oh, you'll change your mind after a good breakfast and a nice bath," Lady Margaret said heartily after clearing her throat. "And wait until you see the gown dear Robert had made for you. One look will tell you how lovely you'll be in it, and then we'll try it on you. I supervised the sewing of it quite carefully, so you needn't be afraid that only a man was involved."

She gave Rianne a beautiful smile and turned away to watch the maids setting out breakfast dishes on the table, having no idea what she'd just let slip. So Lady Margaret had supervised the sewing of the wedding gown, had she? That meant she'd known about Robert Harding's plans for weeks, but hadn't considered it necessary to mention them to Rianne. She was on "dear Robert's" side, which finally set her in proper perspective for Rianne.

"All right, dear, you can come to breakfast now," Lady Margaret announced as she turned from the table with a smile. "And I'll join you for a cup of tea."

"If you want a cup of tea, then help yourself," Rianne said with a small shrug. "As far as I'm concerned, I'm not hungry."

Which wasn't anything like a lie, Rianne thought as she turned away to sit in a chair. Normally her appetite was excellent, but right then there was nothing left of the normal—or an appetite. If she could only be sure that she *wouldn't* speak under torture, but that one time so many years earlier—She'd only been a child then, and had simply watched, but it had been the most horrible thing she'd ever seen. Rianne held to the chair arms with a death grip to keep from trembling at the memory, to force the picture back to the past and into the place it was usually buried.

"Well, then, you'll have your bath first," Lady Margaret decided to decide, just short of bustling. "A nice warm soak and a brisk scrub, and then you'll have a small bite or two. If the food has gotten too cold, we'll send for another tray. Girls, go down to the kitchen for your mistress's bathwater, and . . ."

"No," Rianne interrupted, beginning to be really annoyed. "No bath, no food, no fussing, and no gown. Just leave me alone until the time of the execution."

The housemaids had never been on the receiving end of Rianne's temper, but they knew enough to recognize and respect it. They curtsied at the order and made a hasty retreat, and Lady Margaret looked after them in mortification.

"Oh, Rianne, now see what you've done," she wailed, wringing her hands. "You've chased them off, and *now* who will I have to help me? I'm going after them to bring them back, and you must promise not to frighten them again."

She stood there waiting for Rianne to promise, but all she got was absolute silence. Was the woman too stupid to understand that she meant what she said, or was she just too used to the sort of girl who cried and carried on, then did exactly as she was told? Rianne suspected it was the latter, and the thought increased her anger almost to the point of fury. If you were challenged by an enemy to a meeting of swords, you were to expect no quarter and therefore give none. That was the way Rianne intended handling *this* little affair of honor, and all the wheedling in the universe would not change her mind.

But Lady Margaret was too used to the other kind of girl. She sat not far from Rianne and began giving all sorts of motherly, friendly advice, blissfully unaware of how dangerously thin her victim's patience was growing. Lady Margaret was the sort of person who *knew* what was right, and was therefore determined to see others do it. It was beyond her to understand that right for one person did *not* mean right for everyone, and Rianne didn't waste any breath trying to explain. The worst things in the world often came from others' good intentions, and you had to be very strong or you found yourself giving into well-meant, disastrous kindness.

Happily, Rianne had that sort of strength. She took her

attention away from Lady Margaret to keep from insulting
the woman, and spent some time thinking dark thoughts
about the man who had visited her bedroom the night before. For someone who had been so concerned earlier
about "likely lads," he had really enjoyed himself threatening her. He had taken off his coat and vest to climb up
her balcony, and somehow, clad only in the lace-trimmed
shirt, he had appeared even bigger and more threatening
than he had on the road, wielding his sword with such
expertise. And his kiss . . .

Rianne stirred in her chair at the memory, wondering
why he had stopped with just a kiss. It was true that he
would have her all to himself after the ceremony, but from
the stories Cam had told her, that didn't always hold a
man back. He hadn't liked the way she'd refused to respond to his kiss, and then he'd let her go entirely. It was
almost as though—

Almost as though he really didn't want her at all. Wasn't
there that one tragedy she'd read, where the young girl
was married off to a man who was in love with another
woman? He married the girl because he needed her dowry
to keep his ancestral home from being lost, but he was
never able to bring himself to consummate the marriage.
Whenever possible he left his untouched bride alone and
hurried to the arms of his real love, and one day he came
home to find that the girl had wasted away and died. She'd
known where he was and what he was doing, but had
never said a word, preferring death to intruding where she
could never possibly belong.

That book was one of the few things that had ever made
Rianne cry. She'd been able to feel the abandonment experienced by the girl, the sense of being completely unwanted and unloved. The man had been so cruel to do that
to her, using *her* life to repair his own and giving nothing
in return but an empty house and distant, uncaring servants. Rianne, too, would have preferred death to that sort
of life, but it had been such a terrible waste. The girl had
been willing to learn to love her husband, and had never
even been given the chance . . .

Rianne, unlike the girl in the book, had no interest in learning to love the man she was being made to marry. He, on the other hand, probably had more than one woman to occupy him, women who had experience in keeping him satisfied. What man with such abundance would want to leave it even temporarily for an inexperienced girl who loathed him? Very few, if any at all, and the brute didn't strike her as someone who denied himself.

No, her inheritance had to be all he was interested in, and experiencing as little fuss as possible. If she'd responded to his kiss he might have forced himself to make love to her, but without encouragement he would never take the bother. It was certain he was aware of her beauty, but beauty was obviously not his primary concern.

She stirred again as she remembered that when she'd first seen him it had been like something out of a beautiful book. The tall, handsome stranger showing up from nowhere, to help the beleaguered girl free herself . . . possibly to fall in love with her as she did the same with him. Now, unfortunately, it was clear this tall, handsome stranger didn't want her at all, not even for his bed. Her stepfather had outdone himself, finding her a husband who didn't even want her body. What a warm, wonderful marriage it would be.

"Rianne, dear girl, it hurts my heart to see you crying like that," Lady Margaret said as she leaned forward in concern, and for a moment Rianne didn't understand what she meant. Then she realized that tears were trickling down her cheeks, probably from thinking about that tragically sad novel. She used an impatient hand to wipe the tears away, then got up to stalk to the other side of the room. If she managed to be rude enough, Lady Margaret might get discouraged enough to leave.

But Lady Margaret seemed to thrive on discouragement. She left just long enough to bring back the housemaids, and while she was gone the footman refused to take his eyes off the prisoner. Rianne would have snuck up behind him with a brass candlestick or a water pitcher if she could have, but the man refused to turn his back. By the time it occurred to her that he might have done so if she'd started to get out of her clothes, it was already too late. And what if she'd started to undress and he *hadn't* turned away . . . ?

Rianne had spent a good part of her growing years swimming naked with her brothers in the woods, but Angus had eventually put a stop to the practice. She had already become a young lady with a nicely developed body, and he'd explained that he and Cam had also become men. It wouldn't have been fair to any of them to continue swimming like that, not when their bodies might react in a way their minds didn't agree with. They loved her dearly, but they wanted to keep loving her like a sister.

So Rianne had learned that men's bodies sometimes reacted to the sight of a woman's body and vice versa, no matter how the mind really felt. The knowledge had helped her judge just how near to let her suitors come, which hadn't been very near at all. She hadn't wanted to put herself into the position of desiring someone physically when she couldn't stand them ordinarily even to talk to, and things had worked out well. At least up until now . . .

Lady Margaret had bathwater brought up despite Rianne's refusal, so Rianne took the cold contents of her breakfast tray and gave *them* a nice warm bath. Another tray of food was brought just before they brought her wedding gown, and Rianne was so outraged she decorated the gown with every one of the fresh dishes. Her stepfather had had the nerve to copy Rianne's mother's first wedding gown for the daughter to be married in, as pure a travesty of decency as Rianne had ever seen. Her mother had *loved* the man she married in that gown, just as he had *loved* her. To soil the memory of something that wonderful—!

"I think I'm going to faint," Lady Margaret announced weakly with horror at sight of the ruined wedding gown. She'd screamed when it first became clear what Rianne intended and had tried to protect the gown with her body, but hadn't been able to stand fast and let her own gown be ruined. "Yes, I'm definitely going to faint."

"You'd better do it over near one of the chairs," Rianne responded heartlessly, so far beyond patience with the woman that it was a miracle that she hadn't committed murder. "There are no dear, sweet men around to pick you up off the floor."

"You are the most impossible girl I have ever met," Lady Margaret stated, and at long *long* last there was anger in her rather than unbearably sickening patience. "I'm going right this minute to that delightful Mr. Machlin, and tell him exactly what you've done this morning. In all fairness he must know what he's taking to wife, and even be given the opportunity to withdraw. If, as a man of honor, he does not, he will certainly give you what you deserve once you're his. I, personally, will insist on that."

Her parting nod was most emphatic, and then she was sailing out of the room with inflexible determination. Rianne watched her go with sour satisfaction, then went to collapse into a chair to brood. The big brute would never change his mind about marrying her, not even if she swung from one of the chandeliers in the ballroom. It was her inheritance he and her stepfather had to be after, and only marriage would get them that. If anything, he would decide to punish her, but just let him try. Even as big as he was, just let him *try* . . .

Bryan looked around at the beautifully decorated, well-filled chapel, and tried to bring his impatience down to a bearable level. He couldn't believe how intensely he wanted to get on with a ceremony he expected to have annulled in a matter of days, and in all honesty he had to admit that Harding had very little to do with the feeling. It was that girl he wanted to see again, the girl he wanted to talk to. He had also thought of other things to do with her, and had had to remind himself that he had no real intention of staying married to her.

But thought of those other things had kept him awake long hours the night before, and had refused to let themselves be chased away. What he didn't understand was why he felt like that, as though he were a boy taken with the sight of his first woman. So the girl was beautiful, and had a body that had fit surprisingly well pressed up against his, and was a pure joy to talk to when she forgot she hated him. Was that any reason for him to spend so much time thinking about holding her again, and this time succeeding in coaxing her into responding to his kiss? It was—

"The bride should be here any moment now, Mr. Machlin," the vicar said softly to Bryan, bringing his thoughts back to reality. "It will certainly be a lovely service, with all those flowers in this delightful chapel. Is there anything you would care to discuss before we begin? You needn't hold back just because I'm not familiar to you."

"I think not, Vicar," Bryan answered with something of a smile, wondering if the kindly old man had made a guess about the nature of his preoccupation. And as for how lovely the service would be, that remained to be seen. He'd had a visit from Lady Margaret Welford, and the woman had nearly been in tears. His sweet little bride had apparently gotten over her shock from the night before, and had been spending the morning terrorizing half the household. The other half had probably gone into hiding, Bryan thought with amusement, one small part of him admiring the girl. She'd been given no choice about marrying him, but still had found a way to show how much she disliked the idea. You *had* to admire a person who fought on against overwhelming odds when surrender wasn't an option. They usually didn't survive long, but they always ended on their own terms. That was the part of it Bryan *didn't* like, the thought of her ending in any way at all . . .

"Ah, here we are," the old man said, smiling as Harding appeared at the back of the chapel. "All ready to begin now—"

The poor man's words broke off as he stared, doubtless seeing the same thing Bryan did. His delicate little bride had been escorted in by two of the housemen, and both of them looked as though they'd been through the mill. Rumpled clothes and desperate expressions told him the girl had tried to get away from the men, but that was what *they* looked like. The girl herself was in a towering rage, and none of Harding's frantic efforts were calming her down. She hated being where she was, and intended for everyone to know it.

Bryan let his gaze touch her as she and Harding argued, startled to realize that he wanted to go over there and stand beside her against everyone else. It was getting harder for him to remember that *he* was the one forcing her into marriage, that he was the one whose plans demanded her involvement. He wanted to defend her against all attacks and then carry her off to his house, the way men did in some of those books women read. The only problem with that was the concept called real life, which had a way of ruining a man's best ideas . . .

"Uh, here she comes," the vicar whispered, sounding exceedingly nervous, the words more a warning than a statement. Through the buzz of scandalized conversation from horrified guests his bride stalked up the aisle, trailing a stepfather who looked as though he would welcome death by torture if only it would be performed right then and there. The girl reached the altar and stopped beside Bryan, but looked only at the vicar.

"All right, let's get on with it," she ordered in a growl, making the poor old man jump. "This wasn't my idea, but no one will be able to say it didn't have my touch."

"My dear child," the vicar began to protest, putting out one hand toward the girl, clearly disturbed. Even a blind man would have known there was something wrong, but Bryan was still stuck with reality.

"It's all right, Vicar," he said, reaching over and gently forcing the girl to give him her hand. "Both of us are ready, so let's get on with it. I'm sure the lady would rather have you speaking than someone else."

Bryan hated having to say that, but his bride-to-be did need the reminder. He looked down at her, half-expecting her to turn those blazing green eyes on him, but she didn't. She just stood there stiffly beside him with her eyes straight ahead, and didn't say another word.

The old man looked back and forth between them, then hesitantly began the ceremony. He seemed to be expecting interruption at any moment, but got all the way through to the end without incident. The bride's responses to his questions were flat with furious monotone, but they were also in the affirmative. When the ring was put on her finger, it had to be all but forced on. At the end of it all, he had no choice but to pronounce them husband and wife.

"And you may now kiss the bride," he said hopefully, but Bryan smiled without amusement and shook his head.

"I'll be best off saving that for later," he said, the words sounding ridiculously disappointed in his own ears as he looked down at his new wife. "Shall we go to the reception and thank our guests for coming, dearest?"

His wife looked around at everything but him and didn't bother answering, but he knew she couldn't ignore his hand wrapped firmly around her arm. He would walk her through the reception and then get her home, back to *his* house where they could exchange a few words in private. There had to be *something* he could say to make the situation easier for her, assuming he could get her to listen . . .

Rianne spent the short time they were at the reception refusing to speak to anyone or even to acknowledge their existence, which increased the exclamation-filled buzz to a level that nearly drowned out the music. It annoyed her that they all pretended not to know what had happened, that they tried to maintain the lie of being unaware that she'd been forced into marriage. They were so used to the victim going along with the sham quietly and gracefully, letting them pretend they were decent people there to help friends celebrate a happy time. Not one of them had objected to her being forced into something she didn't want, not a single one.

"Yes, I think it's time my wife and I left," she heard the brute beside her say pleasantly to her stepfather, loud enough for others to hear. His ridiculously large hand hadn't left her arm, and although he wasn't hurting her she couldn't wait until it was gone. "We'll expect you for dinner tomorrow night, around eight?"

"The pleasure will be mine," her stepfather answered,

almost sounding as though he were anticipating something other than dinner. He was still more than a little harried, and hadn't even glanced at her.

"Until tomorrow night, then," the brute said with a bow, then began dragging her through the shocked and staring crowd. He nodded affably to people as they went, as though it was a willing bride he led outside.

The coach waiting for them was the same one he'd arrived in the day before, and again Ritchie was there to drive it. The small bearded man stared with his jaw hanging down as the brute forced up her the steps and into the coach, then woke up to close the door when the two of them were inside. Another moment and they had begun moving, and only then was her arm finally released.

"You should have tried to enjoy the reception," the brute commented mildly, startling her. "Even if none of this *was* your idea, you still had the right to enjoy it."

"You're completely out of your mind," Rianne stated, looking up into cool gray eyes with all the disbelief she felt. "You force me into a marriage I want no part of, and then have the nerve to suggest I should have enjoyed the execution celebration? That's the most mindless thing I've ever heard."

"I've heard one or two worse," he replied, for some reason looking uncomfortable. "Sometimes someone does something that looks really bad to the people around him, but that's only because they don't know the whole story. Once they find out everything changes, but until then he has to live with their low opinion of him. It isn't easy, but sometimes it's necessary. Especially for a man of honor."

"A man of honor doesn't *ever* do anything low and vile," Rianne countered, certain about *that* point at least. "He's always kind and considerate and *honorable,* and the people around him never have any doubts. Some people, though, *pretend* to be honorable, but it isn't hard to see through them. Threatening someone to make her do as you demand, for instance, has never been high on the list of honorable endeavors."

"But people sometimes have reasons for doing things

that look dishonorable,'' he repeated, and now Rianne detected defensiveness in his manner. "When the truth finally comes out and he has what he's after, he's able to show he wasn't being dishonorable after all.''

"Ah, I see,'' she said with a judicious nod. "Marrying an unwilling woman for her inheritance is a fine and noble act, and as soon as you have my money and estates in your hands you'll prove it. I can hardly wait.''

"So you believe that the only thing I'm after is your inheritance,'' he mused, now studying her with a definite disturbance in those gray eyes. "Isn't it possible I also want *you?* When someone bathes and combs you you're not exactly unattractive, I've already mentioned your courage, and occasionally you even show signs of intelligence.''

"Please,'' she said with a grimace, finally turning away from him in disgust. "I could see from your ardent courtship just how interested in me you were. Whatever women you've been keeping in private are obviously satisfying you, so let's just leave it that way, shall we? It's the only bright spot I've found in this otherwise dismal affair.''

"Do you always use attack to defend yourself?'' he asked from behind her turned back, actually sounding curious. "I think I've already said that you're not big enough to make it work right.''

"With the normal part of the world, I'm big enough to do anything I please,'' she countered again, annoyed that he kept referring to her as small. "I'm not exactly helpless with those who are overgrown either, as they'll find out if they try bothering me. I'm not in the mood to laugh it off.''

"And I'm not used to being threatened,'' he said, and Rianne couldn't believe he now sounded amused. "I can see that the longer I keep you around, the more used to it I'll get. At least until you learn what a real catch I am.''

Outrageous comments like that couldn't possibly be dignified with an answer, so Rianne simply sat and watched the woods go by. They were almost to the road that would lead to the brute's estate, and after a short ride they would be driving on his property for a while. Rianne knew these woods, all of them, and wished with all her heart that she could be deep inside them rather than riding in that coach. It was too late to keep herself from being married to a man she detested, but it might still be possible to get on with her life if she managed to escape him.

And if he didn't have plans of his own that called for her "accidental" death. She'd read a novel about the marriage of an innocent young girl to a man who married women for their gold, and then did away with them when the dowry or inheritance was in his hands. He always made sure the deaths looked accidental, and the young heroine would have become his next victim if not for the man she was really in love with. *He* hadn't been able to marry her because of a feud between their families, but he continued to keep an eye on her even after she was married to another man.

Rianne almost sighed at the thought of devotion like that, the kind of support *she'd* only had from Angus and Cam. It wasn't the sort of thing one usually found in the world, the proof of that clear in the way her former suitors had behaved after the wedding ceremony. Even Jean had been hearty in congratulating the man who had married the girl he and the others had been pursuing so ardently, just as though they were all more relieved than disappointed. Just as she'd always known, every one of them was more concerned about himself than about her.

And her new husband was the worst of the lot. Rianne knew nothing at all about the brute, but he'd proven himself ruthless when it came to getting what he wanted. His freedom would no doubt be precious to him, much more so than the life of the girl whose fortune he coveted. He now had that fortune, or would have it soon. After that . . .

Well, she wasn't about to simply stand there and let him murder her! Rianne sat straighter on the coach seat as she promised herself that, and it was a promise she meant to keep. One way or another she would escape this man, and then she would find the freedom that had been all but snatched out of her hands.

It would have been nice if the ride took longer, but all too soon they were pulling up in front of the brute's house. It wasn't quite as large as her own, but it was a good distance from being a cheap little cottage. Rianne wondered how Machlin had been able to afford to buy it if he needed money so badly that he had to marry for it, then dismissed the question. He'd probably bought it with the last of the gold stolen from a previously married victim, and now, no longer a widower, was ready to begin to become one again.

"Welcome home, wife," the brute said as the coach came to a halt. "I think you'll like the house you're now the mistress of."

Rianne said nothing as he climbed out of the coach, trying instead to decide whether or not to refuse to follow him. Would he embarrass himself by fighting with her there, in front of the staff that had come out of the house to greet them? Maybe if she just sat there, he would get so annoyed he'd turn and walk away.

By then he stood on the ground with one hand held up to assist her, and a single look at those cold gray eyes told Rianne *she* would be the one who was embarrassed if she refused to leave the coach. He would sooner drag her out kicking and screaming than let her stay in the coach from where she could escape him, and there was no doubt to the conclusion. He was a big, overgrown brute, and wouldn't hesitate to act like one.

She put a bored, totally unimpressed look on her face, then began to leave the coach without paying any attention to the hand being held out to her. She had no skirts to trip over, after all, and a glance at the household staff showed they were shocked at the lack. Well, good, she was making a proper first impression, then. A small warning before the real storm struck—

"Oh!" Rianne cried out, so startled at suddenly being lifted into the brute's arms that she almost forgot to be outraged. He'd taken her off the coach steps without a word, and now stood holding her without the least effort.

"A bride is supposed to be carried across the threshold

of her new home," the brute informed her blandly, a touch
of amusement in those gray eyes. "If nothing else has
gone right, at least this will. And if you don't stop struggling, I could end up dropping you accidentally."

Oh, right, accidentally. Like the accident he must already have planned. Rianne might have said something
about that, but she felt too confused by her suddenly
strange feelings to respond, and in point of fact was most
uncomfortable. She'd never before been held by a man in
any way, and was upset to find herself reacting physically
to his touch. Her right hand rested against the royal-blue
damask of his wedding coat, a futile effort to keep herself
as far as possible from contact with his broad, hard body.
Those massive arms of his held her easily but tightly, forcing her to use her left arm to lean on his shoulder. Almost
her whole left side was against his chest, and his hands
seemed to burn where they touched her back and thigh.
This was much worse than simply having his hand wrapped
around her arm, and she found it impossible to breathe
freely again until he carried her up the steps past his staff
and into the house, and had put her down in the hall.

"Allow me to present my new wife, Mrs. Rianne Lockwood Machlin," the brute announced to the people who
had followed them inside. "We were married just a short
while ago, and will therefore be celebrating the occasion
here until we leave on our wedding trip. Mrs. Raymond,
have my wife's rooms been prepared?"

"They certainly have, sir," a young woman answered
with a smile. "And those of her gowns and possessions
that were sent over have already been unpacked and put
away. We all wish you a great deal of happiness, Mr.
Machlin, and Cook is preparing a very special dinner just
for the two of you."

"Thank you, my friends," the brute said with his own
smile as the others gathered around him, echoing the congratulations first given by the woman who seemed to be
his housekeeper. "Now let's get the new mistress of the
house settled in. You'll all be introduced to her individu-
ally after she's had time to rest."

Murmurs of understanding agreement came from the staff, and they began to disperse. One man in livery closed the front door before taking himself off, but by then Rianne was back to having the brute drag her around by one arm, this time toward the stairs. They climbed after the woman, Mrs. Raymond, who led the way holding her dark skirts carefully high, then walked a short distance before turning into a wide corridor. Three quarters of the way down the corridor Mrs. Raymond opened a door, and Rianne's loving husband pulled her inside after the two of them.

"This is the sitting room, through there is your bed-chamber, Mrs. Machlin, and that door leads to the maid's quarters," Mrs. Raymond told Rianne with a smile, gesturing toward the appropriate doors. "Please look around, then tell me if there's anything you need that isn't already here. I'll be more than glad to have it fetched at once."

"How about a nice, large rock," Rianne said without looking at the woman or the room. "That's something I would really enjoy having."

Since the brute had freed her arm again she strode across the sitting room to the door that led to her bedchamber, walked inside, then swung the door closed with more strength than was necessary. She hadn't failed to notice the fact that the sitting room, though lovely, had no windows at all, and the same was true in the bedchamber. She was being put in a cage—decorated with silk and lace, but it was still a cage.

The room was cool and lovely in the lamplight, rose and gold blending in an effort toward beauty. The chamber was large enough to have four upholstered chairs and two settles, three tables of varying sizes, a vanity and bench, a fourth table holding a pitcher and basin, a very large wardrobe, and two low chests along one wall. The curtained bed was also larger than the one she'd had at home, the curtains now tied back to the posts.

All the material used was either rose, gold, or a combination of the two, and all the wood and leather was dark-brown. The effect was one of sedate calm, but for Rianne it might as well have been moisture-dripping stone walls and a dirt floor covered with putrid straw. She *hated* being a prisoner, hated the way her life and dreams had suddenly crumbled to sand. If she couldn't escape it would all be gone for good, but how was she supposed to escape from a room with no windows?

Just as she stood in the center of that room asking herself that very important question, a brisk knock came at the door. She didn't answer immediately, but an instant later it was opened anyway. Rianne already knew it was her husband; who else would have the bad manners to simply walk in without waiting for permission?

"Mrs. Raymond will bring you a tray, and then help you get comfortable," he told her, only one step inside the room. "Lady Margaret told me what you did with your breakfast and brunch, and I was there myself to see that you didn't touch a thing at the reception. Dinner is still too many hours away, and will deserve something better than to be swallowed whole. I'll see you then."

Rianne wanted to ask whether that was a promise or a threat, but he left before she had the words put together. A moment later she heard the sound of a key in the lock, and wasn't in the least surprised. Cages did have to be locked, after all, or the dumb, helpless creatures inside might find it possible to blunder out to freedom.

It wasn't more than a few minutes before the door was unlocked again, but this time it didn't open almost immediately after the knock. Rianne was sitting on the floor beside the large wardrobe and leaning back against the wall, her knees drawn up for her arms to rest on. She wanted nothing of what any of them might give her, and that included use of their furniture. She would sit and sleep on the floor of her cage, and continue to think of nothing but escape.

"Mrs. Machlin, is it all right if we come in?" Mrs. Raymond's voice called through the closed door. "Have you fallen asleep?"

Rianne couldn't see that it was her job to be pleasant to those who were loyal to her captor, so she made no effort to answer. Another moment passed in silence, and then the door was finally opened. Mrs. Raymond came in with two girls who were dressed as maids, one of them carrying a tray, and Rianne sighed to herself. It looked like the morning at her own house was about to be repeated.

"Why on earth are you sitting on the floor?" Mrs. Raymond blurted when she saw Rianne, finally locating her after looking around the room. "I mean, with all these lovely chairs, not to mention the bed— Is something wrong?"

"Why, no," Rianne answered in her most reasonable tone, staying right where she was. "Whatever would give you an idea like that?"

"All right, it's clearly obvious that something *is* wrong," the woman said, no longer sounding quite like a servant. "Would you like to tell me what it is? Maybe I can help."

"Your kind offer comes just a little late," Rianne said, not about to give away anything concerning her escape intentions. If they thought she was giving up, someone might forget to lock the door sometime. "At this point, no one can help."

"Ah, I see," the woman said, and now she wore a faint smile. "Your doom is upon you because your husband punishes your bad temper by locking you in your bedroom. Well, the solution to that is simple enough. Mr. Machlin is a fair man, and as soon as you begin behaving yourself properly, I'm sure he'll let you out."

"How good of you to solve my problem, Mrs. Raymond," Rianne said dryly as she stared at the older woman. "Your solution has one small difficulty, though. I don't *want* to behave myself properly with your Mr. Machlin, and have no intentions of doing so."

"He has become *your* Mr. Machlin much more than he's mine," the woman returned with a wider smile, apparently now even more amused. "I doubt if that state of affairs will be quite as bad as you're picturing it, and might even become rather restful. Now, would you rather eat first, or bathe first?"

"Neither, thank you," Rianne answered coldly, finding

a lot less amusement in the situation than the older woman had. What could she possibly have meant by "restful"? Did she know her employer had other women, and therefore would not be bothering his bride? "I'm perfectly fine just as I am. Please don't let me keep you from your other work."

"You seem to be determined to make this as difficult as possible," Mrs. Raymond said with a sigh. Obviously, she was much more perceptive than Lady Margaret had been. "Your husband would like you to eat and bathe and then nap for a while. You find the request too outrageous to agree to? You would prefer that I inform him of your refusal?"

"If you're trying to make it sound as though I've chosen a horrible death over continuing to live, you misunderstand my position," Rianne told the other woman dryly. "Right about now a horrible death would look rather good. And yes, I do refuse."

"You're very young to have learned how to show such cool self-possession," Mrs. Raymond mused, head to one side as she studied Rianne thoughtfully. "If I didn't know better, I would believe you really felt that way. Very well, Mrs. Machlin, the choice was yours."

Mrs. Raymond inclined her head to Rianne, then gestured for the two maids to leave with her. They left the tray behind, but as far as Rianne was concerned they might as well have taken it with them. She was too depressed to have anything like an appetite, no matter how long it had been since she'd last eaten properly. As long as the staff of this house thought she was simply being punished, the door to her cage would not be left unlocked. She was trapped for as long as the brute cared to keep her like that, and the thought was almost enough to make her cry.

But that was one victory she refused to give the overgrown monster. He would *not* make her cry, no matter what he did. She had more than enough experience in refusing to let the tears show, so let him come and do as he pleased. She would never give in and be a good little victim, *never!*

* * *

After seeing his new wife settled into the rooms that had inexplicably but very conveniently been built without windows—it was the main reason he'd bought the place— Bryan went to his own rooms. He took off his coat and vest and tossed them away, then poured himself a stiff drink. He was really tempted to swallow it in one gulp, but as upset as he was it wouldn't have been a very good idea. That girl had a positive talent for ignoring all attempts at explanation, and it had taken quite a lot to keep from telling her everything. But he couldn't betray his brother's memory by jeopardizing the plan, so things would have to continue the way they were for a while.

Even if she *did* think he'd only married her for her inheritance. Bryan sat himself in a chair and took a thoughtful sip of his whisky, remembering how close he'd come in the coach to telling her that her inheritance didn't interest him at all beyond his need to use it against her stepfather. When Robert Harding showed up for dinner the next evening, expecting to leave again with a purse bulging with gold, Bryan would give him the sad news. "B. G. Machlin" was the legal signature he'd established all over the country and the world; "Bryan Machlin" meant nothing. If Harding tried to sue—assuming he had the time for it—he would get exactly nowhere. Nothing less than answering Bryan's questions would get Harding the gold he needed, and then everyone would walk away satisfied.

Except for the girl who was now his wife. She was the one who most wanted to walk away, but just a few minutes earlier, when he'd had her in his arms and was carrying her across the threshold of her new home, Bryan had made an unsettling discovery.

He'd been able to feel the warmth of her flesh even through her clothing, had felt the healthy musculature beneath her rounded softness. Mentally and physically she was different from any woman he had ever met, and the sudden revelation came that she was also his. They'd been married that day in a ceremony that was, for all its haste and informality, completely legal.

"Which means I don't *have* to give her up," Bryan muttered, almost as though in argument against someone who had insisted on the opposite. "That might have been the original plan, but plans are always subject to change. Besides, it's more than time I was married. Settling down will do me a world of good."

That's assuming, of course, that she'll be willing to let you live, a part of him thought, deflating all that justification he'd been building. *She doesn't want to be married to you, and no marriage can be really satisfying unless both partners are willing. Can you see yourself settling for even an armed truce in place of the real thing? Is it just marriage you want, or do you want* her?

The answers to those questions were easy. No, he would not settle for anything short of the real thing, and marriage in and by itself was nothing that attracted him. It was the girl Rianne whom he wanted, a girl who spoke her mind freely even to a man Bryan's size. He admired her for her reckless courage, and wanted to be there always to protect her from the consequences of it. He also wanted to see her smile again, hear her laughter once more from shared enjoyment, feel the touch of her hand in sweet and gentle concern . . .

That's a lovely dream, that other part of him commented, once again ruining his mood. *I can't wait to find out how you intend to arrange all that. Will it be cantharides in her tea, or do you expect to be able to talk her into cooperating? You threatened the girl instead of courting her, and now you expect her to fall panting into your arms?*

Bryan closed his eyes and put the glass against his forehead, unable to argue the truth of that. The girl herself had commented on the lovely way he'd courted her, which made that a large, unwieldy obstacle in the path to marital bliss. Since he'd never gone courting he was at something of a disadvantage, but surely lots of compliments would be a good enough way to start. As soon as he was able to start. First there was a wedding night he didn't want to miss out on, not if there was any way at all to enjoy it.

He smiled faintly as he thought about how she might feel in his arms that night, his hands and lips exploring and caressing her smooth, exciting flesh. He'd meant to tell her over dinner that he would be leaving her untouched, but as it turned out the message would be different. But not in a way that would make things even worse. He'd find a way around her objections, and then they would both enjoy themselves.

He sipped his whiskey while savoring the thought, but after a moment was brought out of it by a tap at his door. When he called out permission to enter, Sarah Raymond came in.

"Well, we brought her the tray, Bryan," she said, walking over to sit in the chair opposite his. "I also offered her the choice of eating first or bathing first, and she was very polite."

"But?" Bryan prompted, knowing well enough there was a but. Sarah Raymond had been a friend for a long time, and he'd learned to tell when she was trying to break something to him gently.

"But she was sitting on the floor with her back against a wall and her knees up," Sarah answered with a sigh. "She's determined not to trust or like anyone, and especially not you. She has also made up her mind not to obey you about anything, and thinks she can hold firm to that decision. She doesn't seem to be the spoiled, arrogant brat we pictured when we discussed this part of the plan, and I have to admit I don't understand what she is instead. I said something to her about being locked up in punishment for throwing a temper tantrum, but I don't believe now that that's why you did it."

"She's an incredibly attractive woman who doesn't like the idea that I bought her, and has made up her mind not to cooperate with the situation," Bryan said with a sigh of his own. "You know I expected to leave her to cry her eyes out alone while I concentrated on her stepfather, but that part of the plan has changed. I *won't* be leaving her to herself, and hopefully after tonight she won't meet the requirements for an annulment."

"I never thought I'd live to see the day," Sarah replied with a slow grin, her eyes suddenly bright. "Bryan Machlin, untamed adventurer, finally married and intending to keep it that way. I'm delighted for you, my dear, but what about that girl? She looks as comfortable in britches as a man, and I'd hate to see her get too close to a weapon. She may turn out to know how to use it."

"No 'may' about it," Bryan said with an answering grin, then told Sarah everything that had happened during the last two days. "So you can see how pleased she was that I forced her to marry me," he concluded, having lost his amusement along the way. "She knows her stepfather sold her, and I'm the cad who did the buying in order to get my hands on her inheritance. If I turn my back at the wrong time, she's very likely to try making herself an immediate widow."

"And all this time I thought you preferred petticoats and shy smiles," Sarah said with a small shake of her head. "That girl must be the only one of her kind in the entire world, and *you* managed to find her. Don't you think it would be safer, not to mention less exhausting, if you told her the truth?"

"I've been tempted to do just that, but I decided against it," Bryan said as he took another sip. "I don't want *anything* to ruin my plan with Harding, and the thought of telling his stepdaughter what I'm up to makes me uneasy. Once I have the answers I need I'll tell her all about it, and in the meantime I can work at smoothing things over between us. I don't intend spending the rest of my life sleeping with one eye open."

"Jamie tells me the two of you did a lot of that when you were forming the first of your guard companies," Sarah said with a soft laugh. "The two of you went about recruiting adventurers like yourselves, then had to fight them into some semblance of a disciplined group so that people needing the protection and services of armed men would be willing to hire them. He told me how hard you worked to make it happen."

"Your husband worked just as hard as I did, which is

why he and I are partners now,'' Bryan told her, meaning every word. "If you hadn't insisted on pretending to be my housekeeper during this game of stalking, you would now be back in your own house, running it the way you always do and waiting for Jamie to get back. Are you sure—''

"I'm positive,'' Sarah interrupted, her tone very determined. "We all loved Ross and grieved when he killed himself, and we all want to get our hands on the man responsible for his death. Since you're the one best suited to taking care of the problem, your family is letting you pursue the matter alone, but you can't do it *all* alone. If Jamie were back I would leave it to *him* to help you, but since he's still away I'm taking his place. And so, *Mr. Machlin*, your loyal housekeeper would like to know what you intend to do next. Do we leave your bride alone to brood in peace, or do we make an attempt to have her see us as something other than monsters?''

"We don't do any of that,'' Bryan answered, then drained his glass and put it aside. "She's *my* wife, so I get to do the honors. Now that I have a better idea of what I want out of this, I may be able to find a way to make her want the same. I hope.''

"I think you ought to tell me which of your estates you like the best before you go in there,'' Sarah mused thoughtfully as he stood. "Just in case we need to know where to send the remains, you understand.''

She peeked up at him after saying that, as though trying to judge whether or not it would be wise to run. Rather than disappoint her Bryan gave her the scowl she'd been expecting, then shook his head at her immediate laughter.

"I can see I'd better keep you away from my little bride,'' he said, the words as dry as a good wine. "If the two of you ever got together, I'd need one of my toughest fighting companies to quiet the resulting riots. When Jamie gets back, I'm going to insist he take you firmly in hand.''

"Isn't that funny,'' Sarah said with a wicked grin, also rising to her feet. "I intend insisting on the same thing myself. Good luck, Bryan, and *do* be careful. I'm sure I would miss you.''

Bryan nodded with a snort of amusement, then headed out of his rooms. His new wife might not be the safest female to associate with, but that just made her better than the others. What he really wanted was to get to know more about her, to find out the little things that made her what she was. And to let her get to know *him*. Maybe he *was* the sort of man most girls would fear rather than love, but wouldn't a very special girl learn to see it the other way around? Storybook romances weren't meant for men, he knew, but did that mean he couldn't hope? Maybe, in spite of everything, she *would* change her mind about him . . . even when she found out he was using her for a purpose that had nothing to do with love . . .

Chapter 5

R ianne continued to sit leaning against the wall, waiting for the wrath of the universe to descend because
of her actions. When it didn't immediately happen she was
surprised, then became more than surprised.

"I don't believe I'm getting bored," she muttered,
looking around at the beautiful room she sat in. "Being
held captive is supposed to be terrifying, especially when
you've been forced to marry the man. How can I possibly
be bored?"

She didn't know how it could be possible, but there was
no doubt about the feeling. She wished fervently there was
something to *do* there, even if the something turned out
to make more trouble.

"But how much trouble can there actually be?" she
asked herself with an exasperated sigh. "He can't kill or
seriously harm me until all the property has been transferred by the trustees, and he isn't even interested in rape.
That leaves him very little in the way of options. Maybe
he'll decide to write nasty letters."

She was laughing softly at the idea when the sound of
unlocking came at her door. A polite knock followed the
sound, but Rianne didn't respond. As much as she was
looking forward to having company for even a little while,
she was continuing to operate on the theory that caged
animals needn't be polite to their keepers. The pause after
the knock wasn't very long, and then it was the brute
himself who entered.

"You *can* acknowledge a knock on the door, you
know," he commented as soon as his searching gaze found

her where she sat. "It won't be a commitment to a life of depravity, and since the rest of us do it you won't be the only one who can be pointed to for indulging in scandalous behavior."

"Ah, I see," Rianne replied, forcing herself not to smile at what he'd said. Why did he have to choose *now* to be funny again . . . ? "I'm supposed to do it the way the rest of you do. All right, I'll go along with that. Is it my turn yet to lock up one of *you?*"

"I'm afraid it doesn't work like that," he answered, and Rianne thought she saw amusement in those gray eyes. "As soon as that rule changes I'll be sure to let you know, but until then you'll just have to put up with it. It won't be for too long, so don't let it bother you too much. Now, you've had a very tiring and unpleasant day. Why haven't you eaten and bathed yet, and lain down for a nap?"

"Possibly because I didn't care to do any of those things?" Rianne said, grimly satisfied to have her guess confirmed. She'd be locked up only for a short while, because he intended to murder her! "Yes, that sounds about right, so that must be it. I didn't want to do any of them, so I abstained. If you need a more simplified explanation, please don't hesitate to ask."

"I enjoy conversing with a woman who has the good manners to say 'please,' " he told her with a grin, infuriating Rianne with the way he refused to get angry. "My main problem now, though, is that I can't be mannerly in return. The circumstances are what they are, and for the moment can't be changed."

Rianne was about to demand to know what he was talking about, when a quick knock came at the still-open door. She looked around to see three of the housemen entering with two large buckets of water each, which they carried to the wooden bathtub standing in the far corner of the room. Once they had emptied the buckets into the tub they headed out again, and this time the brute closed the door behind them.

"You'll enjoy that bath more if you take it now, while it's still hot," he said as he turned back to her, his voice still mild. "When you sleep in clothes they grow rank enough to make you sick, and I don't want you getting sick. You have the choice of taking the bath yourself or having me do it, and I don't know which way I'd *rather* have you choose. Doing it yourself will be better for *you*, but the other way . . ."

"You can't possibly expect me to take this seriously," Rianne scoffed when his words trailed off. "You're too old to be trained as a lady's maid, not to mention probably too clumsy. And if you're trying again to suggest in a subtle way that you're interested in something other than my inheritance, don't waste my time. Your previous wives might have believed that, but I don't."

"Previous wives?" he asked with brows high, looking honestly bewildered. "What previous wives? I've never been married before."

"Of course you haven't been," Rianne said with a small smile, shifting just a little where she sat. "You earned whatever gold you have through honest toil, and never ever married for it. Well, just keep one thing firmly in mind. When you decide it's time for me to have the same sort of accident I'm sure your previous victims had, don't think I'll be as easy to kill as they were. If you're silly enough to forget that, *I* might not be the one having the accident."

"Now you're giving me fair warning along with the threat," the brute observed, the amusement in his eyes having increased. "That's a very honorable thing to do, in light of the fact that you've discovered my sinister plans concerning you. I'm truly impressed, but not so much so that I've forgotten the question I put. Are you taking that bath yourself, or do I get to give it to you?"

"You try putting your hands on me, and you'll be in for a fight like you've never had," Rianne growled in answer, feeling warmth in her cheeks from the faint grin the beast wore. He was *laughing* at her, and after he'd as much as admitted that he did intend to kill her! "I'm not afraid of a lowlife like you, and I never will be!"

"I really do admire your courage," he said mildly as he began to walk toward her, the grin still in place. "I don't *want* you to be afraid of me, so I'm delighted that you aren't. But none of that changes the fact that you still need a bath.''

Rianne tried to get to her feet to keep from being trapped sitting down, but she needn't have bothered. The brute came close and reached down to grab her arms, then hauled her erect with no trouble at all. It continued to startle her that he was able to move her with so little effort, but that didn't stop her from immediately kicking him in the knee. His grip loosened as he hissed with pain, and she lost no time pulling free and running for the door. If she could only get through it and lock it behind her—

''No!'' she screamed as two arms closed around her before she'd gone more than a few steps, arms that pulled her back against a large, hard body. The next instant she was being lifted in those arms, and even kicking and struggling with all her strength wasn't helping to free her.

''Yes,'' the brute disagreed in the same mild way, his words clipped, but not in the least labored. ''It pains me to contradict a lady, but sooner than watch you get sick. Your not having eaten adds to the danger, but that I can't do anything about. This I can.''

Rianne had gotten nowhere pushing at his chest, so she raised her fists to beat at his face. But the brute had crossed the room in a very few strides, and just as she raised her hands he dropped her on the bed. Her breath drew in with automatic fear as she fell, but hitting something soft didn't help. Two big hands immediately turned her onto her belly, and then the brute was using his weight to hold her legs down.

''First we'll get rid of these boots,'' he told her conversationally as she struggled uselessly to squirm loose. ''After that we'll see to your clothes, and then you'll be all ready to be given your bath.''

''Damn you, let me go!'' she screamed as he pulled her boots off, then shifted around to grab her arms again. ''Let me go and fight like a man!''

''You've fought that many men that you know how one does it?'' he asked as he returned her to her back, then quickly knelt across her. "If you're that much of an expert, please, do go into detail."

"I'm not surprised you need to be told how real men do things," she said through her teeth, panting with the effort to keep her wrists out of his oversized hands. "But telling about it won't help, not with someone like *you*."

"It saddens me that I'm so far beyond helping," he returned with a heavy sigh, then snatched at her wrists. "I guess I'll just have to keep on acting as I always do."

His movement was so fast that Rianne found it impossible to avoid. Before she could even react, his hands were wrapped tightly around her wrists. Granted her wrists were small for a woman her size, but she didn't know *how* small until the brute put them together and held them with a single hand. It was outrageous that he would be able to do that, and she was furious that pulling with all her strength still didn't free her.

And then Rianne was more than furious. The brute's free hand was unbuttoning her trousers while his body held her relatively still, and with her wrists pinned it wasn't possible to make even a token effort to stop him. It was then Rianne realized that she felt something other than just anger at the thought of this man undressing her. There was a feeling almost of trembling anticipation, a tingling when his fingers brushed her. She thought of the way she'd felt when she'd first seen him—there was nothing left of that now, of course, not when she now knew the truth— but some shadow of it still touched her. He was a cruel beast for making her experience that, heartless even though he couldn't know it was happening. A decent man would have kept his hands to himself . . .

"You just wait," she whispered hoarsely, totally incapable of speaking in a normal voice. "My life may not continue on for much longer, but before I die I'll pay you back, so help me God, I will."

"That's very kind of you," he answered with a glance and a smile before starting on the buttons of her shirt. "I've always wanted to be undressed by a woman, and now you're volunteering to do it. We'll have to make the time soon, or I'll be too distracted with looking forward to it to pay attention to my everyday duties.''

Rianne blew her breath out in exasperation, hating the way nothing she said bothered the man. He apparently loved to twist both her words and their meaning, or simply ignore them altogether. But there must be *some* way of reaching him, *some* way to make him sorry he ever came anywhere near her . . .

''Would you like to tell me what you think you're accomplishing?'' she forced out as evenly as possible, trying to ignore the continuing flame in her cheeks. ''If you believe stealing my clothes will intimidate me, you're in for a surprise.''

''More than one thing about you is turning out to be a surprise,'' he answered, and suddenly those gray eyes were looking straight down at her. ''But that doesn't include your opinion of me. I know just how you feel about me and I wish you didn't, but we *are* still married. Do you think you might . . . *pretend* to be a proper wife, just to see how it feels? You don't have to mean it if you don't want to, and you certainly don't have to do it all the time. Once or twice would probably be enough to start with.''

''But I never said I'd be a proper wife,'' Rianne pointed out, trying hard not to notice that her shirt was completely unbuttoned. ''You forced me to agree to marry you, but that was all I agreed to. And since you plan to kill me like the others as soon as you have my inheritance, what difference can it make to you *how* I act?''

''Although I'm willing to admit I might have been tempted once or twice, my killing you was *your* idea, not mine,'' he said, faint annoyance now mixing with the wistfulness on his broad, masculine face. ''And I repeat, I have never before been married, so there aren't any 'others.' What kind of trash have they been letting you read? Young girls with vivid imaginations should be kept strictly to the classics.''

''Is it my *imagination* that you'll soon have control of my inheritance?'' she countered fiercely, beginning to feel the outrage again. How *dare* he suggest that the beautiful books she read were trash? "Or possibly I'm dreaming that you walked in and forced me to marry you without even the slightest attempt at courting? Most of the words we exchanged were the sort that often come before duels, but you were so enchanted you refused to be satisfied with anything less than marriage to me? Really, Mr. Machlin, I'm not as innocent as you obviously believe."

"Your biggest problem is that you're a lot more innocent than *you* believe," he returned, and suddenly his big hand was at her face, gently brushing back strands of loose hair. "Every one of those men chasing after you knew exactly what your nature was like, but they still continued to flock around. If you believe it was nothing more than your inheritance they were after, you don't know men as well as you think you do. What kept them coming back was picturing their wedding night with you, just as I've been doing. The only difference is, I'm in a position to *have* that wedding night."

"I—don't believe you," Rianne managed to get out, suddenly so far off balance that she felt as though she were facing him with swords again. "You can't possibly be interested in anything but—"

"*Please* don't tell me what I can and can't be interested in," he interrupted, those gray eyes now pinning her as thoroughly as the rest of him. "Circumstances have made you my wife, but that doesn't have to be anything like the tragedy you're picturing. If we make the effort to get to know each other, it might not be bad at all. And right now I'd like to claim the first kiss from my bride."

His face came down and his lips touched hers, but not with the sort of brutal demand she'd been expecting. His kiss was gentle but much more unavoidable than it had been the night before, and trying to squirm free didn't get Rianne very far. He kissed her slowly and gently but in a way that refused to allow *her* refusal, just as though he intended to taste her thoroughly before he stopped. She had never been treated that way before, and it didn't take her long to know she didn't want it to continue.

"Well, at least this time you moved a little," the brute

said with a sigh when he finally let the kiss end. "You didn't kiss me back, but you did move. I suppose I'll just have to be patient with you."

"You can be anything you like," Rianne growled, hating the way his words brought a hot flush to her cheeks. "If you're waiting for me to respond to you with enjoyment, you have a long wait ahead. I don't like you, Mr. Machlin, and all the patience in the world won't change that."

"Ah, I see," he said, nodding in a suspiciously neutral way. "You don't like me, so you won't respond to me. Since you're so certain of that, I'm sure you won't mind if I amuse myself for a moment or two. Will you?"

Rianne had no idea what he was talking about, but she trusted him just about as far as she would have been able to throw him. It came as no real surprise when his free hand reached to her shirt, but when he brushed it open to expose her breasts she became more than simply uncomfortable. His entire attitude—interest was too simple and inadequate a word—made Rianne feel as though more than her freedom was at risk.

"Now this is part of what those popinjays were after," he said, briefly sending her a glance filled with amusement. "That green gown you wore teased about what it covered, and every man in the room pictured himself looking down at you without that covering. If they'd been able to manage it, this is what they would have done."

His face lowered so that his lips might touch the tip of her right breast, and as they did his tongue flicked out to taste what he'd kissed. If Rianne hadn't been holding her breath she would have gasped when he blew lightly on the flesh he'd dampened, causing her nipple to immediately harden into a point. He shifted to her left breast and did the same, the touch of his tongue almost burning her, and then he raised his head again with a grin.

"That wasn't so bad," he had the nerve to tell her, devilment now dancing in those normally cold gray eyes. "In case you aren't aware of it, little one, what you just did was respond to me. It looks like you've changed your mind about not liking me.''

"You *do* think I'm completely innocent," she answered, what *had* to be anger making it impossible to keep her voice steady. "That was my body responding to you, not my mind. Aren't you experienced enough to know the difference?"

"My, don't we sound worldly," he said with brows raised, once again refusing to be insulted. "Yes, I know the difference, but I didn't think *you* did. How did you come by this vast store of knowledge? More trashy books?"

"What I do or don't read is none of your business," she stated, stopping herself just short of mentioning Angus and Cam. "I might have learned that from all the lovers I've had. My stepfather never mentioned the possibility, now did he?"

"No, you've got me there," he allowed with a sober nod. "Your stepfather never did mention you might have taken lovers. How many were there?"

"That question just proves again how little you know about being a gentleman," Rianne replied, trying not to hope too hard that he would believe her. If he did and felt humiliated enough to throw her out . . . "I wouldn't think of going into details."

"A gentleman never discusses his conquests," he commented with another nod, those gray eyes very thoughtful. "I'm familiar with the concept, but once again I'm surprised that you are. Most gently reared young ladies aren't even told that gentlemen have conquests, let alone that they're not supposed to discuss them. Did you find that out from one of your lovers?"

"I might have," Rianne answered with the blandest look she could manage, the hope growing. "I told you—I don't intend to discuss it."

"That's really odd," he observed with a small shake of his head, his stare unmoving from her face. "The men I know refrain from discussing their love affairs in an effort to keep other men away from so accommodating a lady,

but women don't usually behave the same. Among the
ones I've met who have had multiple lovers, not one will
hesitate an instant in discussing everything about the men.
As a matter of fact, you're lucky if she doesn't start comparing your performance while you're still in the middle
of it. You can see why that leads me to wonder about your
behaving like a man rather than a woman.''

Rianne felt that he was waiting for her to add something
of her own, but in all truth she was too shocked to do it.
Women who had lovers *talked* about them? As though they
were discussing the intricate stitch they'd used on a new
dress? And to *men?* Cam had never told her that, and
Angus hadn't even *hinted* . . .

''That expression you're wearing now makes your eyes
look three times wider than normal,'' she heard, and then
she noticed his grin. ''Those two you do your highway
work with must be very close to you, close enough to tell
you things that most girls don't hear. Haven't they told
you that men with experience *know* when the woman in
their bed is a virgin? Or are they too young themselves to
have gotten that kind of experience?''

The heat of embarrassment filled Rianne, but then it
drained away again when she realized the brute had been
lying just to make her look like a fool. He hadn't believed
her at all, hadn't had the least intention of throwing her
out. He was interested in nothing beyond using her—in
one way or another.

''I do hope you've been enjoying this little amusement,'' she said, the words as flat and cold as any she'd
ever used on a man. ''I'd hate to think I've been put
through this for nothing.''

''I'm not the one who tried suggesting you had lovers,''
he reminded her in a halfhearted way, suddenly touched
with what looked to be guilt. ''But you're right, and I
shouldn't have done it. I just seem to get carried away
when I talk to you . . . Let's go back to what we were
originally doing.''

With that he stood up from the bed, taking her hand
and drawing her up after him. Two tugs and her shirt was

gone, one push and her breeches were down around her feet. An instant later she was lifted out of them, and then was being pulled by the hand toward the tub.

"If the water is too cold for enjoyment, you have no one but yourself to blame," he said, lifting her and setting her into the tub with a small splash. "If you weren't so adorable, I would have had no trouble rushing that undressing. As soon as you finish washing, you can—What in hell is this?"

Rianne didn't need the touch of his fingers to the scar on her lower back to know he'd found it. Any time a new maid had found it, the girl would gasp and pale. It was an ugly, lumpy thing, horrible despite its being relatively small. She folded her arms across her breasts, and tried not to think about what had brought it into being.

"How did you get this scar?" the brute asked, his voice having turned very hard as he moved her hair even farther out of the way. "I could almost swear it was made by a knife. And it looks old. How long have you had it?"

"Probably as long as it will take you to learn to mind your own business," she answered, pretending she wasn't hugging herself to keep the chills from starting. The water she sat in was still warm enough to be fairly comfortable, but that had nothing to do with it.

"Look, you really don't have to make this harder than it is naturally," he said, and then he had moved to stand beside the tub on her left. Rianne wasn't looking up, but she could feel those hard gray eyes on her. "As of today *you* are my business, and I'm afraid your not liking the idea doesn't change that. A scar like that isn't come by accidentally, and I want to know who gave it to you. Was it your stepfather?"

She couldn't help the sound of ridicule that escaped her, but that was all the commenting she did. She *wasn't* this big brute's business, which she intended to prove when she got away from him.

"Doesn't it matter that I'm concerned about you?" he asked after a moment, and then he was crouching down and using one hand to turn her face up to him. "I'm asking you to trust me only enough to give me an answer."

"And if I don't?" Rianne countered, raising one brow. "What will you do about it, add a scar of your own? That would be an unexpected surprise."

"I've got half a mind to haul you out of there and put you across my knee for that," he growled, furious anger suddenly blazing from him. "I've never hurt a woman in my life, but that's the second time you've accused me. I want an apology, and you'd better be damned quick getting it said."

"I'm terribly sorry if my knowing nothing about you offends you," Rianne couldn't help coming back, distantly confused about that anger. Why would he be mad . . . ? "I based my estimation of your character on the beautifully romantic way you proposed, but obviously that was a mistake on my part. I do hope you'll forgive me."

Once again his expression shifted dramatically, and Rianne had the ridiculous feeling she'd hurt him with her response. He seemed to know she'd spoken the truth, and therefore couldn't bring himself to contradict her. But that was stupid. He'd forced her into marriage, and now was holding her prisoner. If he really did feel guilty about what he had done, he'd let her go.

"I stand corrected," he said at last, the words almost painfully neutral. "Your apology was completely in order, and is therefore accepted."

He straightened then and walked back to the middle of the room, leaving Rianne to wonder who he thought he was fooling this time. He'd been trying to pretend he was decent, but when she'd proven otherwise he'd simply dropped the subject. It was just like it had been all those years ago, the way she was supposed to pretend nothing had happened . . .

Suddenly Rianne knew she had to get out of that tub. It was all that brute's fault, making her think about things that were better left buried in the past. She stood abruptly and stepped out, ignoring the way the bottom half of her hair was dripping, then looked up to see the beast turning away from a chest with what looked like a cloth in his hands.

"I'm finished," she announced curtly, ready to fight if he tried to make her go back in. "Now I want my clothes returned."

"You'll have to do without them for a while," he answered after the briefest hesitation, shaking out the cloth in his hands as he moved toward her. "Even just barely rinsed you're cleaner than those clothes, and you still have a nap to take. You can cover and dry yourself with this."

"This" was the cloth he'd gotten from the chest, a very large, double thick length of soft yellow cotton. Rianne barely had time to wonder if it was that big because it was what *he* used after a bath, and then he was swirling it around her. It covered her from head to toes, and as soon as she had it pulled closed in front he surprised her by picking her up again.

"Don't you get bored showing off how strong you are?" she asked as he carried her toward the bed. "I can tell you I'm getting bored seeing it."

"You'll be able to stand it better if you grit your teeth," he commented, apparently paying very little attention to what he was saying. Most of his attention seemed to be focused on moving the covers down, and then putting her into the bed under them. Once he pulled them back into place, he leaned down with his hands on the pillow to either side of her head.

"You're in this bed to take a nap," he said slowly and patiently, as though he were speaking to a child. "The rest won't do you any harm, and might even do some good. I'm asking this as a favor, you understand, but if you can't see your way clear to granting it, I'll just have to stay to keep you company. Would you prefer *that* instead?"

"No," she answered at once, in no way uncertain. "I'd rather take the nap." The quicker he left her alone, the better. She intended to use the time to make plans.

Her decision seemed to satisfy him to a certain extent, enough so that he straightened again, gave her one last glance, then turned to leave. After the door closed she heard the sound of a key, telling her she was back to where she'd been. Or almost back there. She'd learned something from the brute's visit, and that despite his effort not to show her anything but a facade of supposed concern.

It had suddenly come to her that what he called her was "little one." Not Rianne, not Mrs. Machlin, but little one. The books made it perfectly clear that a man who was truly interested in a woman spoke her *name,* softly and lovingly, savoring it like the taste of ambrosia. As a matter of fact, even her pack of suitors had usually done that, even though they obviously hadn't meant it. If a woman's name was too long the man in love with her might shorten it, but then he spoke *that* name softly and lovingly. Calling her something else entirely meant he had no real interest in her at all.

So her new husband had let slip something he didn't realize, but nothing very surprising. And he'd had the nerve to ask her to trust him. Of course she would, almost as far as she would trust a *complete* stranger. After all, didn't one always put one's trust in a man who did *everything* wrong?

Including asking her ridiculous favors. Rianne wasn't tired enough to nap so she wouldn't, but this bed was a good deal more comfortable than she'd been expecting. The lounge she'd spent the previous night on had been hard, and the floor she'd been sitting on even harder. Still, she wasn't tired enough to sleep no matter how comfortable that giant cotton wrap made her feel. Comfortable, and warm, and held, and safe . . .

Bryan waited until he reached his sitting room before he stopped to close and rub his eyes, and then he went for another whisky. He didn't realize that Sarah was in the room until he turned away from the decanter with glass in hand. His partner's wife sat staring at him with brows raised, but he didn't care. He sipped at his drink with the fond hope that it would raise his spirits from the depths they'd fallen to.

"I was going to ask you how it went," Sarah offered, her voice filled with compassion. "Now I don't think I have the heart."

"I was right in all my estimations of her but two," Bryan said with a sigh, walking to the chair opposite Sarah's and dropping into it. "She does have more guts than any man in her house, and she *does* hate me with everything in her. I miscalculated in thinking I could smooth things over with mere Herculean effort, but it wasn't a total loss. I did get her *into* a bath, and I left her in bed to take a nap."

"Two out of three isn't bad at all," Sarah ventured, refraining from commenting on the wetness of his shirt and the rumpled look of the rest of him. No *man* had ever been able to do that to Bryan Machlin . . . "What was the second thing about her where you guessed wrong?"

"At some point in her life, that girl was very badly hurt," Bryan said, leaning his head back against the chair and resting his glass on its arm. "Rather than weakening her the episode made her stronger, possibly too strong. She isn't in the least afraid of me, and intends fighting me with everything she has. I'm her enemy, and that's what one does with enemies."

"Once she knows the truth, that should change," Sarah said, aching for the deep weariness she could see in her husband's best friend, needing to try to ease it. "She'll know then that you're on *her* side, and she'll stop fighting you."

"Sarah, I married her for no reason other than to reach her stepfather," Bryan reminded her with strained patience. "She wanted nothing to do with marriage, but I involved her in my plans and forced her to go along with me. Haven't you exchanged enough words with her to guess how she'll undoubtedly take *that* truth? To give you a hint, my favorite estate is Gray Willows."

Sarah Raymond blinked as she contemplated Bryan's words, trying to make sure of them. A *girl* was getting the best of Bryan? He was bigger even than her Jamie, both taller and broader in the shoulders, and his gray eyes were never easily met. She had seen men step aside for Jamie with tremulous smiles on their faces, praying they'd done nothing he would take offense at. And Jamie had once told her he hoped he would never have to face Bryan as anything but a friend, but a *girl* . . . !

"Oh, Bryan, what are you going to do?" she asked anxiously, then noticed that he watched her through half-closed lids above a faint smile. "And stop laughing at me! If she's crazy enough to threaten you, she might be crazy enough to try carrying through. Since you admitted you don't want to spend the rest of your life sleeping with one eye open—Why don't you reconsider that idea about an annulment—"

"No, sweet Sarah, no annulment," Bryan interrupted without losing his smile. "I never knew I was looking for a girl like her, but now that I've found her I have no intention of giving her up. She'll take a lot of convincing, but I happen to believe I can do it. Do you think I can't, or are you just afraid she'll overpower me?"

"Now *that's* why so many men lose out to so many women," Sarah returned in annoyance, pointing a finger at Bryan. "They know they're bigger and stronger than the woman, so they discount her entirely and laughingly turn their backs at the wrong time. At least Jamie was smart enough not to turn his back on *me* . . . ! Why do you have to keep her? If you really want her, set her free and then go courting."

"Sarah, dear, that worked with you because you're a reasonable woman," Bryan pointed out with even more amusement. "My gentle little bride is a too-strong, willful girl who was raised by a man who couldn't stand up to her, and courted by dandies who gave in to her every whim in an effort to reach her bed. If I turned her loose now, I doubt if I'd ever see her again."

"And you've decided not to accept that," Sarah said, leaning back as she studied him closely. "You're seeing her as the ultimate challenge, and you've never turned away from a challenge in your life."

"Something like that," Bryan murmured, sipping again

at his drink. In memory he saw the girl lying under him as he opened her clothing, completely unaware in her struggling how extremely desirable she was. And how tempted he'd been to have her then and there. Her body was silk to the eye and hand, curved and soft and demanding to be explored. If he hadn't sworn to himself that after the wedding itself, at least the wedding *night* would be properly done . . . And when she'd escaped from the tub and he'd seen the look on her face, he'd been damned glad he'd kept his vow . . .

"She has a small scar on the left side of her back, low down where most people would never see it," Bryan said, all amusement gone from him now. "It has to be a knife scar, but it's more than that. Do you know how you make a permanent, easily visible scar like that one? The natives did it on that island Jamie and I saw on our voyage to Spain a couple of years ago. The natives we came across used scars on their chests and arms to indicate social status."

"No, Jamie never mentioned it," Sarah said, suddenly fighting to keep her voice calm. Bryan was very distracted, otherwise she was sure he would not be saying these things to her. Jamie was always careful to keep his discussions of their travels light, emphasizing the exotic landscape they'd come across but ignoring strange customs such as this.

"They did it by not letting the original wound heal before using the knife on it again," Bryan said, his gaze still turned inward. "After that kind of treatment the wound healed ridged and very visible, and honor demanded that they make no sound while the scar was being put on. Any of the times. I think my wife would have gained very high social status among those natives."

Sarah knew that her face had gone pale, but she didn't care. As long as she wasn't being violently ill, she knew she was ahead and winning. And then she really looked at *Bryan*'s face, and the blood chilled and froze inside her. His handsome face was set without any expression at all, but there was slow, painful death in his eyes for whoever had done that to Rianne. *My wife*, he'd said, as though that were all she was to him. Sarah could see the girl had already become a good deal more, even in so very short a time. And the way he'd smiled when Sarah had called the girl a challenge . . .

"You think she didn't—cry or scream—when *that* was being done to her?" Sarah managed to say, one hand to her throat. "But Bryan, who would do such a thing, and why? Could it have been Robert Harding?"

"That's what I asked," he said with a sigh before raising his glass again. "Her reaction told me I was right in believing it would be beyond someone like Harding, but when I pressed her for details she told me to mind my own business. I'm sure it was done to her when she was very young. I—Sarah, are you all right?"

She could see by the way he came out of his chair that he'd just noticed her pallor, and she smiled just a little as he knelt in concern beside her.

"Jamie will have my heart, and I'll deserve it," Bryan growled, urging a sip of whisky on her. "Of all the mindless, sickening things to tell you! Go ahead, take a second swallow. If you pass out, I'm sending you straight home."

"Byran, I don't want a second sip, and I'm not going to faint," Sarah told him more forcefully as she pushed the glass away. "And I'm glad you told me what you did. That poor child! Obviously you're going to have to be very gentle with her, and be certain you don't lose your temper. After all—"

"Sarah," Bryan interrupted again, frustration now heavy inside him. "I've been *trying* to be gentle with her, and *she's* been trying to knock me down and walk across my face. I can't see myself terrorizing her into cooperating, not after everything she's gone through, and that leaves me with nothing to choose from. I don't know what the hell I *can* do with her, and that's what's driving me crazy. Can I count on you and Jamie to keep me chained here in the cellar rather than sending me to a bedlam?"

"Oh, Bryan, of course you can," Sarah answered with a laugh. "What else are friends for?"

"Certainly not sympathy," Bryan returned, now eyeing

her closely. "Or am I wrong in believing you're now on my wife's side?"

"I'm on the side of both of you," Sarah assured him— without the grin he could hear in her voice. "If you're afraid I'll try getting between the two of you, you already qualify for a bedlam. No one in their right mind would willingly step into a situation like this, not if they could possibly avoid it. I want you to know I'm firmly behind you in all this—*way* behind."

"Out of the line of fire," he acknowledged with a nod and a grin. "Smart lady. I wonder what that feels like."

"With your nature, you'll never find out," she countered with a laugh, then got to her feet. "Since you have a rather special night ahead of you, you might want to think about taking a nap of your own. I'll keep a discreet eye on your bride, and if you're needed I'll have you called."

He straightened up as she patted his arm, then watched as she left, closing the door behind her. He felt too keyed up to sleep, but maybe lying down wasn't such a bad idea. His body was still remembering what touching the girl had done to him, and if he didn't find *something* to relax him his wedding night would be about five minutes in duration. Which, at the moment, his bride would certainly appreciate . . . and never let him forget . . . even if he somehow found a way to reach her . . .

His bride, his little one. There was no question about her being fully grown, but sometimes when he looked in her eyes he saw a frightened little girl peering out. He wanted to hold that little girl close and comfort her, make her know he would never let anything hurt her again, but she insisted on pushing him away. That was what really hurt, that she couldn't yet see him as being on *her* side. His mind knew it was much too soon to expect that, but his heart wasn't able to be so practical. *It* wanted to banish that frightened little girl from her eyes, and see instead a woman's love for a man.

Bryan finished his whisky before going to his bedroom, in the process admiring his self-control in leaving the glass

behind him rather than refilling it. If he began to make a
habit of taking a stiff drink every time he had to deal with
his wife . . . his wife, Rianne Lockwood Machlin . . .
Rianne . . .

Chapter 6

A voice was saying, "Mrs. Machlin, it's time to get up."

Rianne raised her lids partway to see Mrs. Raymond standing over her, a tender smile on the older woman's face. Tender it might be, but to Rianne it looked like the same expression worn by her old nurse all those years ago, an expression that meant Rianne was about to be forced into doing things she hated. Ladylike things; proper things.

"If you don't mind, I'd rather not be called that," Rianne said as she stretched hard before sitting up. She'd spent more time thinking than sleeping, or at least that was the way it felt. "Feel free to choose almost anything else, but stay away from *that.*"

Once she was sitting, Rianne discovered that her hair was almost dry. It was also horribly tangled, which wasn't much of a shock. She hadn't been paying much attention to grooming lately.

"What do you mean by 'that'?" Mrs. Raymond asked with a frown of confusion. "The only thing I called you was—Oh." The woman sighed, and a sad smile replaced the frown. "You don't want to be called Mrs. Machlin. But that's what your name is now, and you do have a tall, handsome husband. Don't girls dream about marrying men like that any longer?"

"Some do, I suppose," Rianne answered with a yawn. "The ones who think only about making love." She'd spent a lot of time listening to Cam's enthusiastic tales involving his and Angus's sexual exploits, and had long ago decided that she really wanted to try it for herself one day. She hadn't done so until then because she had never found a man she wanted to do it *with*, with the single exception of Angus. When the possibility had occurred to her she'd asked her adopted brother if he would be willing, and had gotten the response she'd thought she might. He'd thanked her with a smile and a hug for suggesting the honor, but had also gently refused. The right man for her would be a very special man, Angus had said, and when he came along she would know it at once.

Or, as it turned out, he would simply be the man who bought her. Rianne refused to think about that man, especially after all the thinking she'd already done about him. She should have been furiously disappointed that he would be the cause of her missing a magical time with the special man she'd always dreamed of, but part of her was being very obstinate. That one small part of her kept fluttering around, imagining *him* as her special man, eagerly anticipating the coming night. It would be their wedding night, and he'd said he was looking forward to it . . . But he'd certainly ruin it for *her,* she knew, no matter *what* that one small part believed. If only her first impression of him could have been right . . .

Sarah saw Rianne just staring off into space, and wished she could offer real comfort. The girl was pretending to be completely uncaring, but she must be frantic. It wasn't the place of a housekeeper—even a young one—to intrude in the private lives of her employers, and having to keep quiet was killing Sarah. She shouldn't even be there to help the girl get ready for dinner, but that she'd refused to be denied. If she had the chance to make things better she would, but until then . . .

"Well, it still *is* time to get up," Sarah repeated lamely, also wishing she was better at playing a part. "Why don't you get out of bed now, and I'll help you to wash and dress."

"What happened to my clothes?" the girl asked at once, looking to the place on the floor where they'd been left or thrown. "They were there before I fell asleep, but now they're gone. If anyone has done anything to them—!"

"They're downstairs being cleaned, and your boots are being polished," Sarah interrupted quickly, disturbed by the sudden anger the girl showed. "As soon as they're ready, they'll be brought back to you."

"They'd better be," the girl muttered, then she threw the covers aside and stood up. Sarah studied the girl who was only a few years younger than herself, and thought she understood why Bryan had refused to give up his new wife. The new Mrs. Machlin still looked very much annoyed, but that coldly furious anger had faded. Rianne Lockwood Machlin was an astonishingly beautiful woman despite her unusual height, but when she grew angry that beauty flared and intensified, turning her into a living flame that seemed born to draw men to her. If Sarah wasn't mistaken Rianne would also be as dangerous as a flame, and that was what a man like Bryan would find impossible to resist.

Sarah had brought in a pitcher of cool water to be used in the large ceramic washbasin, but the only help the girl accepted was to take the towel Sarah handed her. Sarah could almost see Rianne regretting the bath she'd had no more than a taste of, but apparently an inward shrug let her dismiss the matter. The girl wasn't concerned over the possibility of Bryan's being displeased, and that made Sarah sigh for her friend. Rianne would have to trust him before she was able to care about him, and his new wife wasn't about to trust anyone, much less him.

"Once you're dressed I'll brush your hair," Sarah said, suddenly determined that Bryan would *not* be totally disappointed. He didn't deserve to be treated with casual disregard, and if she had anything to say about it he wouldn't be.

"That's your idea of being dressed?" the girl asked, looking at the blue silk-and-lace nightgown with matching robe that Sarah had laid out. "I'd be better off going down to the dining room just as I am. Less for that brute to rip off later."

"Bryan—Mr. Machlin—is not a brute!" Sarah snapped, thrown into outrage by the horrible, offhand comment that was so completely untrue. "I know him a good deal better than you, my girl, and I refuse to stand here and listen to such disgraceful slander. He's a kind, generous, and *decent* man, and if you only knew—"

Sarah choked off the rest of the words, not about to betray Bryan's wishes as to what this girl was told, but it was a close call. It was also out of character, but all she could do was stand there with fists clenched as she glared at the younger, larger woman. It would have been nice if the outburst could have been missed, but she knew it hadn't been when she got a raised eyebrow sent in her direction.

"My, my, such touching loyalty," the girl drawled. "Does *Mr.* Raymond know how you feel?"

"He certainly does," Sarah returned, inwardly fighting to control her reflaring temper. "He not only knows, he feels just the same way. I think you're deliberately trying to make me angry, but I don't understand why. Are you trying to force me into leaving? What good do you think *that* will do you?"

"How can I know until I've managed it?" the girl countered with a small shrug, apparently unembarrassed that her ploy had been noticed. "If you go right now, I might be able to find out."

"I'm not going anywhere, *Mrs. Machlin,*" Sarah told her, seeing with grim satisfaction the annoyance that ghosted through Rianne's eyes. "I'm here to make you look presentable for your husband, and that's what I intend doing. And if *your* intention was to make an enemy of everyone in this household, allow me to congratulate you on a really fine beginning."

The girl shrugged and turned away in what was supposed to be total unconcern, but Sarah was startled to see a glimpse of something else entirely. Very, very briefly a look of painful weariness had shown in the green eyes that were usually so self-assured, a window opening onto another truth that had been revealed for no more than an instant. Sarah realized that Rianne was neither the cool regal lady nor the conscienceless brat she presented to the world. The pose was her armor, and she would consider any attempt to breech it an attack against her very existence.

"Oh, Bryan, what have you gotten yourself into?" Sarah whispered low to match the sinking feeling inside her. "And how in God's name will you get yourself *and* her out of it again?"

Sarah knew there were no mystical answers to those questions. Of course it was Bryan who would need them, she admitted privately as she moved toward the nightgown the girl was trying to ignore. Thank God she'd promised to stay out of the mess.

"For your information, you and your husband won't be dining downstairs," Sarah said, deciding it would be best if she pretended to still be insulted. "A table has been set in your sitting room, and the two of you will be served there. If *you* have no modesty to consider, you might think about the men and women who will be serving you. Despite your very obvious opinion to the contrary, they're *also* decent people."

"Too decent to look at a naked body, but not too decent to *over*look a forced marriage," the girl muttered, then asked, "Now I'm being accused of trying to corrupt the innocent?" One golden-red brow raised high. "Apparently there's no end to my perfidy, but even that can be boring. Find a different gown, and I'll agree to wear it."

So you do *have normal modesty,* Sarah thought, swallowing the grin she felt. *It's a good thing I managed to stumble across an argument you can't ignore.*

"Someone your age should avoid words like 'perfidy,' " Sarah continued aloud, showing a smile that was mostly teeth. "It gives one the impression of a four-year-old dressed in matronly clothing. I really do hate disappointing you, but there *are* no other nightgowns among your things. Whoever did your packing must have decided you'd have no need of them, so it's either this gown or nothing at all, and I'm glad to know now that even you are too modest for that."

The fact was, there *were* other nightgowns she might wear that had been sent over, but Sarah was determined that Bryan's new wife was going to look as desirable as possible for him, even if Sarah had to lie through her teeth to get it done. The girl's beautiful face was flushed at the thought of being naked in front of so many strangers, and that was all to the good.

"I don't know why you would consider this gown unacceptable," Sarah pressed her advantage, lifting the gorgeous thing to look at it more closely. "This lace is softer than a sigh, and the blue is the color of glorious summer skies. You must look absolutely lovely in it—even though I would swear it's never been worn. Is it new?"

"Yes," the girl answered, obviously too distracted to remember to be insulting. "A gift from a friend—Are you sure there aren't any others?"

"Positive," Sarah told her despite the stab of guilt for the lie. Why wouldn't the girl want to wear such a beautiful gown? "Here, let me help you put it on."

For the second time that painful, vulnerable look flashed in the girl's eyes, and then it was gone as she seemed to gather her strength to face whatever came. She straightened up to full height and let Sarah approach with the gown, then raised her arms to slip into it. She wore a small, grim smile, and Sarah had the crazy thought that Rianne was thinking about her earlier comment and was glad. The "brute" would rip the gown off her, and that would be the end of it . . .

"Sit down at the vanity and I'll see to your hair," Sarah directed with no outward sign of the trembling she felt within. She'd had her own trouble with Jamie in the beginning, but there had been nothing even half as dismal and hopeless as what this girl thought she faced. And Sarah couldn't even imagine what that was! There must be *something* she could say to make things easier, but what if she chose the wrong thing? If she blundered and made it worse, Bryan would never forgive her. Or, worse yet, he *would* forgive her, making it impossible for her to forgive herself. And what would Jamie say . . . ?

"Don't you think that's enough?" Rianne's voice came, drawing Sarah out of the deep, dark twisting thoughts she'd fallen into. She blinked, and was pleased to see that she'd brushed the girl's hair to shining splendor, the golden-red mass spread wide and flowing down Rianne's back to her waist. If Bryan found any fault with *that,* she would check him for a fever.

"You're right, that *is* enough," Sarah agreed, reaching over to put the brush down before going for the gown's robe. If only she could find something a little more meaningful to say . . .

Rianne was silent as Sarah helped her into the robe, spread her hair again, then went around to tie the ribbons in front. The gown itself had a sheer lace bodice that enhanced the girl's full breasts rather than covering them, but the silk robe hid the deeply veed arrangement behind two ribbons long enough to be tied into bows. Sarah formed both bows as carefully as it was possible to do, then stepped back to examine her handiwork. The girl wore nothing on her feet, because there had been no matching slippers to the outfit. The skirts were long enough for someone of her height, showing that both gown and robe had undoubtedly been made for *her,* but without slippers. Strange that someone should give a gift that was incomplete . . .

"Staring at it won't make it look any better," Rianne said, once again bringing Sarah out of a brown study. "If it's as bad as your expression seems to show, I'm glad you talked me into wearing it."

"I've decided that the best wedding gift your husband could give you would be a sound spanking," Sarah pronounced, again fighting to keep the temper the girl so obviously wanted her to lose. "You just suggested I've helped to ruin Bryan's wedding night, and practically all by myself. If you deliberately twist my feelings like that one more time, I'll—"

Her furious words were cut off by the sound of a knock, and she turned away from the sight of the amusement in Rianne's eyes to answer the door. The girl was playing some sort of game, but Sarah would be blessed if she understood why. Maybe she *ought* to make that suggestion to Bryan about the most appropriate wedding gift . . . before she did something very unladylike to his lovely young bride . . .

Bryan stood at the bedroom door, knowing that this time his knock would be answered. Sarah was in there with the girl, and he'd told her he would call for his wife when the food was ready to be served. He wore the dressing gown his sister and her husband had given him some time ago, a fancy affair in blue velvet that he'd never before had the occasion to put on. His life until then hadn't provided many times when his wearing a dressing gown wouldn't have looked ridiculous—or been downright dangerous—but now that he was a married man—

The door flew open so quickly in front of him, he almost reached for a weapon out of sheer reflex. He stood there blinking down at a furious Sarah Raymond, while she glared up at him like a small powder keg with the fuse running short.

"Mr. Machlin, your wife is ready for you," Sarah growled, sending Bryan's eyebrows even higher. "Now please get out of my way!"

Bryan lost no time stepping aside, and Sarah stomped past and slammed out of the sitting room. He'd had the distinct impression she would have gone over anyone foolish enough to hesitate, and those of his people preparing the table seemed to have realized the same thing. None of them had even considered getting in her way, and Bryan couldn't help wondering what had gone on in his new wife's bedchamber . . .

He didn't quite sigh as he turned back toward the bedroom to see his bride staring at him with a look of bland disinterest. She was breathtakingly beautiful dressed in flowing blue silk, her golden-red hair edging out from behind her arms like angels' wings. And was it his imagination and the distance, or had her eyes taken on a bluish sheen to match what she was wearing? She held her long-fingered hands demurely in front of her, the rest of her calm and regally straight, a vision of beauty and desirability that made Bryan wish their dinner was already finished so that he might take her in his arms . . .

So what in hell had the little wildcat done to poor Sarah Raymond?

Rianne watched Mrs. Raymond storm past her employer and out of sight, and sighed only on the inside. The way the older woman had gotten angry rather than indignant had made Rianne feel she might have met the first woman with whom she possibly could have become friends. But a friend was the last thing she could afford to have in this house, not when that friend might show up while Rianne was trying to escape. It would be a lot simpler if no one wanted to have anything to do with her, just the way it was in her own house, and there was no sense in feeling regret. Besides, Mrs. Raymond was so *easy* to drive wild . . .

"Good evening, wife," the brute said as he came closer, looking down at her with those hard gray eyes. "Our dinner is ready to be served, and I'm ready to welcome it. Shall we go?"

"I think I have a headache," Rianne said, ignoring the arm he held out to her as she looked up into that gray gaze. "Perhaps some other time."

"No, *this* time," he corrected with a faint smile, taking her right hand and wrapping it around his left arm. "Some other time we'll do it again."

He turned then and began moving back toward the sitting room, and with her hand still held against his arm Rianne had no choice but to go along. It was incredible how much strength he seemed to have, so much that he was able to be gentle with it. She couldn't pull her hand out of his grip, but he wasn't hurting her at all.

One of the serving men bustling around the sitting room paused to hold a chair for her at the elaborately set table, and her escort made sure to guide her into it before releasing her. His own chair was held as he took his place across from her, and once he was settled he smiled at her again.

"I had tea brought up for you to drink until we've gotten some food in you," he said, leaning back to allow his glass to be filled. "If you'd eaten from the tray earlier the tea wouldn't have been necessary, but you shouldn't be drinking champagne on an empty stomach. I don't want to see you sick or drunk."

"How beautifully considerate of you," Rianne murmured, reaching for her teacup in an effort to hide the newest flash of confusion she felt. What difference could it make to him how she felt? He meant to force himself on her even if she passed out—didn't he?

"Speaking of beautiful, I'd like to say how lovely you look tonight," the man went on, his glass now held between his fingers as his gaze moved over her. "That blue is very becoming, and I do believe your eyes have definitely turned blue to match it."

"Thank you," Rianne acknowledged, trying to make her voice sound unimpressed and uninterested. She sipped from her teacup again, wondering if he knew his dressing gown was almost the same blue. She was beginning to hate that color.

Angus had given the gown and robe to her for her last birthday, specially made and meant to be put away. *For the man you fall in love with,* he'd whispered with a grin, *to be worn on that very special night.* Angus had had to work like a slave to earn enough extra to buy the gift, and Rianne had been very careful not to tell him that slippers usually went with an outfit like that. He couldn't have afforded the slippers without even more slaving, and now the whole thing was to be worse than wasted . . .

"By the way, I was wondering if you knew why Sarah— Mrs. Raymond—was so upset?" the brute said, drawing her attention again. "I hadn't expected her to leave quite that abruptly."

"Actually, I'm sure it was something *I* said," Rianne answered, giving him the ghost of a smile. "She kept going on about how marvelous she thought you were, and

I'm afraid I wondered aloud why her name was Mrs. *Raymond*. I can see now that that was very indiscreet of me.''

The man had been about to taste his champagne again, but instead of lifting the glass he closed his eyes. The two housemen and the serving girl who had been busy with tasks around the room all froze for an instant wherever they were, then movement resumed with a very deliberate air.

"Listen to me very carefully, little girl," the brute said, and he seemed to be struggling to keep his voice at a normal conversational level. "Jamie Raymond is the best friend I have, and his wife is almost as dear to me as she is to him. You can insult *me* in any way you like and that will be your business and mine, but you're not to include Sarah Raymond in your games again. Have I made myself clear?"

"Oh, absolutely," Rianne said with more of a smile, holding her teacup with the fingers of both hands. "The gentlemanly thing to do, and all that. I quite understand."

The man's cold gray eyes began to heat up from the flames of his anger, but before his glass shattered from the pressure of his grip there was an interruption. The serving men were putting bowls of soup in front of them, signalling the beginning of their meal and incidentally drawing their attention. Rianne wondered who they were trying to protect, her or the man they worked for. For someone who was usually so completely in control of himself, the man was unbelievably easy to reach with ordinary drawing-room tactics. At this rate she might not even have to use any special plan to discourage the man. If her new husband stormed back to his own rooms filled with unquenchable fury, she might enjoy her wedding night after all.

The bowl put in front of her was filled with a delicate meat-and-vegetable soup, and after one taste Rianne had to force herself to eat slowly. It was very nearly the best soup she had ever tasted, and that would have been true even if she hadn't been so hungry. She could feel her dinner partner's eyes on her while she ate, and made certain

not to look up. Her ignoring him in favor of a bowl of
soup should add to her husband's displeasure, which hopefully would lead to another outburst and then to a hasty
exit from the room . . .

Bryan gave silent thanks that his champagne glasses were
metal-bound. He'd paid a lot of money for their otherwise
delicate loveliness, and wouldn't have enjoyed breaking one.
Even with the metal it had been a close call . . .

And that little hellion knows it, he thought, watching
his bride enjoy the soup she ate. *She's been trying her best
to start a fight with anyone and everyone near her, and
her best is a little* too *good. What I damned well ought to
do is—*

He cut off *that* thought in a hurry, and applied himself
to his own soup in an effort to regain control of his temper.
A fight wasn't what he intended having that night, but it
would take some effort to keep remembering that. The girl
was *trying* to get him angry, so the best response he could
give her was calm and peace and friendliness.

He'd always believed women were there to be protected
rather than abused, but this one woman kept reaching to
his rage and pulling it out in large fistfuls. If he wasn't
very, very careful . . .

"Damn!" he muttered under his breath, reaching for a
piece of fresh-baked bread to distract himself from the
thundering of his thoughts. If he kept on like this, he'd
have to leave rather than subject the girl to the danger of
his temper out of control. He had to calm himself for his
own sake as well as hers, and find something to distract
him from her deliberate machinations.

"You made a very good point earlier today," he said to
the girl as soon as he'd swallowed the bite of bread. "You
reminded me that you knew nothing about me, which is a
lack that needs remedying. What would you like to
know?"

"Have you contracted any fatal diseases that are likely
to do you in in the very near future?" she asked after the
briefest hesitation, using those devastating blue-green eyes

to silently laugh at him. "If you have, I would love to hear about it."

"If I had, you would become a very wealthy widow," he returned, finding it impossible to hide his grin. "I may be a younger son in my family, but all of us were provided for. That was before I went into business for myself, of course, and turned my start-up capital into a really excellent investment."

"Ah, then you're a merchant," she said with a graceful nod and a small, disparaging smile. "I really should have known."

"But I'm not a merchant," he corrected, hanging onto his temper with both hands and a fervent prayer. "I recruit and train private fighting companies, primarily, which I then hire out to people who need competent, trustworthy protection. If you have something valuable to ship, say jewelry to France or gold to Spain, you may not have enough men in your regular employ to guard the shipment. Or you may have *enough* men, but not ones who would do any good as guards. You don't often find a clerk, valet, or gardener able to use a pistol or sword very effectively, and keeping fighting men on your payroll all the time when you only ship once in a while is very expensive."

The girl nodded vaguely, as though doing nothing more than being polite, but at least she was listening. At this point Bryan was willing to take anything as encouragement, so he smiled and continued.

"If you don't have men of your own, your biggest problem is to find guards you can trust. Hiring twenty fellows off the street probably won't cost you much, but then you'd have to spend your time wondering if they'll keep your shipment safe even from themselves. My company takes care of that worry, since my partner and I stand behind every group of men we supply. You can even trust them to escort your sweet young daughter on a trip to Paris or Madrid. Our men know that if they ever stepped out of line, Jamie and I would come after them personally."

"I don't have a sweet young daughter," the girl commented, reaching for her teacup again. "But do go on, I'm absolutely enthralled."

"I'm delighted to hear that," Bryan returned, deliberately matching her blandness. "We supply however many men are needed, and guarantee both their ability as guards and their honesty. A full company is rarely needed, unless it's for something like guarding a large wagon train in America. Businessmen there usually make do with a quarter company when they have a shipment to protect, or fewer if the shipment is only moderately valuable."

"You've—been to America, then," she said in a way that seemed *too* casual. "Is it as backwardly awful as everyone says?"

"As a matter of fact, I find it very attractive," Bryan said, wondering why she was paying so much attention to her teacup. "It's a very young country and therefore vitally alive, and every time I go over I find myself adding something to my holdings. A house here, a plantation there, a mining company, a freight company, a newspaper—things like that."

"But you came back here to buy a wife," she pointed out, and now she was looking only at him. "Weren't there any primitive women for sale, or did they simply lack an attractive dowry? I wonder what you'll buy first when my inheritance is in your hands. A *real* plantation or mining company, or will you decide on a newspaper with an actual circulation?"

"You don't believe that I'm rich," Bryan stated with surprise, seeing the scorn in her eyes. "You think I'm lying to you."

"That's right, I do," she answered with another smile, then leaned back to allow her soup bowl to be taken. The next course was ready to be served, and she seemed ready to give it all her attention. Bryan thought about pursuing the question of his wealth, then it came to him that he would be much better off letting the matter go—but just for the moment. He would be right there when she finally learned the truth, and if he handled it properly her fluster at being wrong might counterbalance a lot of her anger at being misled.

Yes, Bryan thought, doing his own leaning back. *If I handle it right, I can end up with a proper marriage after all . . . and the flame of fury will be softened to a candle's glow . . . and shine only for me . . .*

Chapter 7

Rianne didn't know what she had said to stop the flow of conversation, but the rest of the meal took place in silence. The big man across from her seemed to be smiling to himself most of the time, and then he transferred the smile to her. By then she had a glass of champagne of her own, and she used it to hide the annoyance she felt. If calling him a liar hadn't caused him to explode, there was little else that would. It looked like she would have to think up a plan to discourage him after all.

"Let's take our glasses into the next room where we can be more comfortable," she heard, and looked up to see that the serving people were no longer in the sitting room. "Yes, we've been left all alone, and they won't be back to clear away the rest until tomorrow. Tonight the world contains just the two of us."

"You have the nerve to complain that what *I* say comes from reading trash?" she responded, shaking her head. "If I weren't so pleasantly filled, I'd probably be very ill."

"The law frowns on women who are nasty to their husbands on their wedding night," he scolded mildly above amusement. "The nastiness won't do what you want it to anyway, so you might as well come along quietly."

He stood then and held out a hand to her, and she gave him her own with confusedly mixed feelings. Now that the time had come to be alone with the man, Rianne was wondering if she would be *able* to think up a plan. That one small part of her mind was still fighting her. What if she couldn't think of a plan, and had to go through with letting him—

"Steady," he said, and his arm was around her back to do the steadying. "It won't be any worse than execution for treason against the Crown. You have my word on that."

Rianne looked up to see the teasing gleam in his eyes, and her cheeks warmed with embarrassment. She was letting what he was about to do intimidate her, and that was no way for a woman intent on revenge to behave. She wanted him sorry for ever having come near her and then she wanted to leave him behind, but right then she most wanted him back in his own rooms.

"No," the brute said before she'd even parted her lips, apparently reading her mind. "There's nothing you can say that will cause me to leave. We're husband and wife, and tonight we share a bed for the first time. But it certainly won't be the last."

He bent his head to touch her lips with his, then began urging her toward the bedchamber. It was ludicrous and Rianne almost didn't believe it, but she really was beginning to be afraid.

"So you *are* going to rape me," she said, speaking softly in an effort to keep her voice even. "After all that blabber about honor, you're going to use the law to justify rape."

"Nonsense," he disagreed with a laugh, looking down at her in a way she could feel. "There won't be any rape involved, with the law's justification or without. You'll want me to make love to you, and so I will."

"But if I don't want you to, you won't?" she asked, now finding it necessary to look up at him. "You're willing to give your word on that?"

"My word is yours, madam," he said with a grin and a silly little bow. "But on second thought, we'll leave the champagne behind. We'll soon be too busy to want to bother with it."

"Busy with what?" she asked distractedly. He couldn't possibly mean what he'd said about leaving her alone if that's what she wanted, but for some unknown reason she believed him. "Busy with what?" Rianne repeated, stopping to watch him close the door. "Or did you say that about giving your word just to get me in here?"

"If all I'd wanted was to get you in here, I could have carried you in," he replied, leaning one arm on the door as he looked down at her. "Since you didn't enter this marriage of your own free will, I thought it only fair that you be allowed a say in its consummation. On the other hand, however, this is *my* wedding night too, and it's only fair if *I* be allowed certain things as well."

"What—sort of things?" Rianne asked. If he really was going to be fair about it, could she do any less?

"I now have a very beautiful wife, little one," he said, the softness of his words reflected in the gray of his eyes. "I can't make love to her until she tells me I can, but I'd still like to look at her and touch her gently. Is that so much to ask? Are you afraid you won't be able to control yourself being that close to me?"

"You think I'm worried about *my* self-control?" she asked with an honestly amused laugh. "I've already been close to you, and you can take my word for the fact that I felt nothing—nothing at all."

"Then you're willing to give me my part of this wedding night?" he pressed, remaining where he was. "I promise I won't hurt you, so you don't have to be afraid of *me*, either."

"I think I've already told you that I'm *not* afraid of you," she answered, then reluctantly made up her mind. "All right, fair is fair. As long as you keep to your end of the bargain, I'll keep to mine."

"You have a deal," he replied, straightening off the door with a grin. "It's always a pleasure to deal with someone who has a sense of honor. There's very little trouble in predicting what they'll do. Come with me."

He took her hand and led her toward the center of the large room. Of course it was possible to predict what someone with a sense of honor would do, she thought, but why had he sounded amused by the fact? Or had he been trying to compliment her? With people like him, it was so hard to tell . . .

"The first thing we're going to do is take off your robe," he said when he released her hand. "Since I've already seen you without any clothing at all, there's nothing to be embarrassed about."

Rianne watched as his big hands went to the ribbons on her robe, opening the bows one at a time. She'd been about to say that she *wasn't* embarrassed, but that wasn't strictly true. For some reason being entirely naked with Angus and Cam was easier than being scantily clad with this man, and that in spite of his having given his word. Maybe it was because he was so different . . .

"How beautiful you are," he breathed as he slid the robe down her arms and let it fall to the floor. "Knowing you're my wife makes me feel like the luckiest man in the world."

She looked up at him to see if he was teasing again, but his eyes moved over her breasts and belly and thighs, the sheer silk and lace of the gown enhancing the soft curves of her body rather than hiding them. His expression suggested he might not know he'd said anything at all, and then his arm was around her waist.

"Let's sit down," he said, drawing her back with him toward a wide, thickly upholstered chair. "This will probably take a while, so we might as well get comfortable."

Rianne started to say, "But that chair won't hold the both of—" when she was startled into cutting the sentence short. The man had put himself in the chair, but at the same time had lifted her into his lap. That way their faces were just about on the same level, which meant she had no trouble seeing his smile.

"You were saying?" he inquired mildly, his left arm still around her waist. "If we were in two separate chairs I could look at you, but touching would be somewhat difficult. And you did say you weren't worried about your self-control when close to me."

"That's exactly what I said," she returned with a smile that hopefully matched his. The words were completely true, of course, since she *wasn't* worried. But as far as other feelings went . . . was there any reason to mention what even she didn't understand?

"Good," he approved with a wider smile. "Now I can start looking at you in the right way."

She expected his gaze to drop to her body, but those gray eyes kept staring at her face. They moved down very slowly to her neck and shoulders, then worked their way up again.

"Would you like to tell me what you're doing?" she asked after a moment, tired of being confused. "If this is a joke, you should be able to see I'm not laughing."

"I'm enjoying the way the angle of your face draws my eyes down to the softness of your throat and the slender grace of your shoulders," he answered with distraction, and then his right hand came to touch her cheek with nothing more than fingertips. "Don't you know how marvelous it all looks, especially framed by that magnificent hair? Or did you think a man gave his attention to nothing but his wife's breasts?"

"You mean I was imagining your interest in my breasts earlier today?" she countered immediately, stung by his very superior explanation. "Maybe I was light-headed from lack of food and dreamed it."

"I never said I wasn't interested in your breasts," he corrected, sounding as though he were instructing a child. "I said I wasn't interested in *nothing but* your breasts, which is an entirely different thing. I saw enough this afternoon to know what I need to about them, including the fact that I won't even have to touch them to harden their nipples. Having learned that, I can wait before trying to discover more."

"That's ridiculous," Rianne said very flatly, ignoring the warmth that had flooded her cheeks. "I know better than to believe you could do something like that without touching me, and I resent the fact that you think I'm too innocent to notice. You can't—"

"Stop right there!" he ordered with a growl, the look in those gray eyes no longer distracted. "What I said happens to be the truth, and I won't have you accusing me of lying. If you doubted me you could have offered to bet on the point, but you have no right—"

"All right, then let's bet on it," she jumped in at once, determined not to let him get away with scolding her for catching him in a lie. "If you're all that sure of yourself, you won't worry about losing."

"I *am* that sure," he agreed with a thoughtful nod. "All right, I accept your bet, but let's get straight exactly what it is we're betting on. I say I can make your nipples harden without touching your breasts, and you say I can't. If I prove you don't know as much as you think you do, you have to pay me."

"How much?" she asked, suddenly remembering she'd brought no money with her. "If I lose I'll have to stop back at my house to get it, but—"

"This is your house now," he corrected with weary patience, then gestured the point aside. "It isn't money I'll be asking for, little one. If I win our bet, you'll pay up by making an effort to kiss me back when I kiss *you*. No drawing away, no purposeful lack of response, just an honest effort."

"And if *I* win?" she asked, suddenly as ready to take advantage of him as he thought he was taking of her. "If I prove you've been indulging in the telling of tall tales, you'll leave this apartment immediately. No arguments, no calling it unfair, you'll simply leave and not come back. Is it still a bet?"

"You're a hard woman," he said with a small shake of his head, and then he grinned faintly. "But you're definitely on. Just remember that any attempt to stop what I'm doing to you will be considered an admission of defeat."

Rianne nodded warily. Though certain that the beast could never win, there was something disquieting in his confidence.

"Here we go," he said with amusement, and then Rianne felt just as amused. He'd taken her right arm and had begun kissing her hand, just the way it had been done countless numbers of times by countless, faceless men.

She was so used to having her hand kissed that she no longer even noticed it, let alone felt anything from it. Of course, the brute's kisses were slower and more lingering than the ones she was used to, but they still—

Rianne almost gasped and pulled her hand back when he turned it over and began slowly kissing her palm, but that was only due to surprise. No one had ever kissed her palm before, and they certainly hadn't tickled it gently with their tongue as they slowly trailed the kisses all around. She realized he was making her very uncomfortable, but it wasn't anything she couldn't stand.

Not even when the slow, teasing kisses began to rise up her arm. The inside of her wrist twitched to the tickling of his tongue, and when he began to move up her forearm she had to exert conscious control. The sensation was unbelievably strange, an overly intimate exploration of the tender skin of a part of her that shouldn't be intimate at all. She'd had her arm touched a thousand times, but it hadn't been kissed and it hadn't been licked. Rianne shifted slightly where she sat on her husband's lap, wondering why his thumb was keeping her hand from closing into a fist. He'd brought his left arm from her waist to support *her* arm at the elbow, and he slowly made his way higher and higher.

By the time his lips reached the inside of her elbow, Rianne had closed her eyes. For some reason it upset her to watch his patient upward progress; feeling it was bad enough, especially when his fingers began caressing the underside of her arm. She wanted desperately to shiver and pull away, ending the sensations that were trying to drown her, but then she would lose the bet. If she hung on she might still win, and then could have privacy in which to pull herself together.

"Your hand can stop crushing my knee now," his voice came in a murmur that was perfectly fitting. "The taste of you is delicious, and you've lost the bet."

She would have preferred to call him a liar again, but it wasn't necessary to look down to know he had told the truth. Her nipples were hard and stiff against the lace of her nightgown, a condition she'd been trying to deny the awareness of. It still seemed incredible to accept, but he'd done it without touching her breasts even once.

"And you won't even have to admit in words that you were wrong," he said, that deep voice faintly husky. "All you have to do is start paying up on what you owe."

His right hand came to her chin and tilted her face up, and then the lips that had investigated her arm were settling in a new location. His kiss was still as gentle as it had been, but there was now a demand behind it that she wasn't permitted to deny. She had to kiss him back, or renege on what she owed.

And, strangely enough, it wasn't all that terrible. For some reason she felt as though she *wanted* to kiss him, a feeling she had never had with any other man in her life. His lips felt odd, both soft and hard at the same time, and his tongue flickered out to taste her as though there were no reason why it shouldn't. Both of her hands were against his dressing gown, one on his chest, the other on his arm. His left arm encircled her and held her close with that giant's strength which brought no pain.

"Oh!" she gasped, pulling her face away from his. Without her noticing, his right hand had moved aside the lace covering her left breast. His fingers had begun toying with the nipple he'd made so hard, and sensation had flashed through her body like a flare of sunlight in darkness.

"What's wrong?" he asked, now stroking the side of her breast. "I'm just touching you the way you said I could. Are you finished already with paying your debt? I know most women will back out after no more than a token payment, but somehow I thought you were different."

His accusation distracted her from what she'd been about to say, and then his lips were on hers again, demanding the rest of what was his. She met his kiss and returned it the way she was supposed to, but couldn't quite remember what she'd wanted to tell him. Something about the way he was touching her, the way he was stroking her nipple

with his thumb. The feel of it was dissolving the glue
holding her bones in place, but she couldn't think of a way
to explain that in words he would understand.

He had made her part her lips and was tasting her tongue
with his own when she nearly choked, trying to cry out at
the touch of his hand in the new place it had found. She
needed to end the kiss to speak, but wasn't able to move
her face away from his. Her head was leaning back against
one thickly muscled arm that held it in place, and he hadn't
seemed to notice her reaction.

But she'd noticed! The skirt of her gown had been lifted
to her knees, and the hand that had been on her breast
was now between her thighs. Her left hand flew down in
an effort to push his away, but it was like pushing at the
walls of a house. His fingers continued to stroke and caress her in the most sensitive place she had, and then he
made a sound of pleasure deep in his throat. He must have
thought she was encouraging him to touch her there, but
she wasn't, she wasn't!

Rianne moaned as she felt the strength drain out of her
body, turning her into a helpless mass of squirming desperation. His lips were devouring her mouth as his tongue
fenced hers down, and the hand between her thighs was
driving her insane. All teasing arousal it was, a demand
for response she couldn't refuse, and the longer it went on
the worse it became. She whimpered as he touched her
everywhere but where she *needed* to be touched, and he
chuckled at what he undoubtedly thought was a sound of
pleasure. Her hands were claws closed convulsively on his
dressing gown, but he hummed to her and idly increased
her insanity.

It was almost too late when she finally freed her face
from his. Her ears were filled with the sound of her racing
pulse and she was just short of being unbearably dizzy,
but she was still able to force out the single word: "Stop!"

"Stop what?" he asked, touching his lips to the side of
her face and her throat. His fingers continued to stroke
her in a way that made her wish she could get up and run.

"Stop . . . touching . . . me," Rianne croaked, nearly closing her eyes. "I can't . . . stand . . . any more."

"You should have told me sooner that I was hurting you, little one," he murmured, his hand finally moving to take a gentle grip on her thigh. *"Was* I hurting you?"

"No," she whispered, needing to speak the truth. What he'd done was worse than pain, but he hadn't hurt her. She waited for the blessed relief she expected now that his hand was gone from her, but for some reason it wasn't coming. The burning itch still raged between her thighs, and her blood still felt as though it were on fire.

"What's wrong?" he asked as she moaned and tossed her head back and forth against his arm. His hand was now stroking her thigh, and even that small a thing was more than she could bear.

"You have to stop touching me altogether," she whispered, not caring how ragged the words were. "I need some time to—pull myself together, so you'll have to stop."

"Anything you say, little one," he answered. "My stopping won't do what you expect it to, but I promised to abide by your wishes and I will."

"What do you mean?" she asked, looking up into his face. She had noticed before how handsome he was, but now there was something more there than just good looks. His face was broad with the planes of masculine beauty, cleanly shaven and smooth to the touch. Her fingers went to that face, touching it lightly, searching for—she didn't know what. The gray of his eyes was the color of dominance, sure with the knowledge that everything about him was his. The strong brows above those eyes were dark with the same red that made up his hair, the black-red mane that suited him so well. Rianne discovered that she wanted to bury her hands in that mane, but didn't understand why.

"What I mean is that my not touching you won't bring an end to your arousal," he said, his voice very soft and sure. "I was hoping you would enjoy the way I touched and kissed you, but now I can see it went far beyond that.

You're completely aroused, little one, and if something isn't done it can only get worse.''

"No, that isn't true!" she whispered, wanting to disbelieve him but finding it impossible. Every nerve in her body was screaming for the relief that hadn't come, and it did seem to be getting worse. And he'd already proven he knew what he was talking about when it came to her body! What was she going to do?

"I think you know it *is* true," he said, his hand now stroking her hair. "There's only one thing to be done, but that's a decision *you'll* have to make. I gave my word not to make it for you."

Rianne closed her eyes again in misery, but that did more harm than good. Even his touch to her hair was driving her wild. She felt a small, odd thrill when she realized she couldn't go on like this.

"All—right," she conceded with difficulty. "The decision is mine, and I've made it. I—want you to do something about what I'm feeling."

"I'm sorry, sweet girl, but I'm afraid that won't do it," he said, and she opened her eyes to see those icy gray eyes staring unblinkingly at her. "If this was some tawdry affair I'd accept being invited like that, but you're my wife and this is our wedding night. I want to be invited with tender passion, and I want to hear the proper words."

Rianne searched the eyes looking down at her for signs of teasing but there weren't any. He was perfectly serious about what he'd demanded, and would not ease her torment without getting it. Her temper flared without reason, or maybe it was the knowledge that she *had* to do things his way that enraged her. He was being ridiculously formal at such a stupid time, and before she knew it she was trying to beat at him with her fists. She was absolutely furious, but he refused to accept that. Those giant arms closed more tightly around her, and then her lips were again in his capture.

And what a capture! His kiss immediately began to devour her but she was already responding, trying to devour him in turn as her tongue lured his into her mouth. Her

hands had risen and turned to fists in his hair, holding him
more tightly than the fist he had in *her* hair. And his other
hand! Rianne moaned as it slid up the outer side of her
thigh, rising under her gown skirt to reach her hip before
sliding around to her buttocks. She shivered at the exquisite gentleness of his touch, burning for more that *wasn't*
gentle. She wanted all of his strength, needed the easing
he could give, and was now beyond worrying about how
much of a fool the asking would make of her.

"I've got to have you," she panted around his kisses,
able to speak only because he allowed it. "I want you to
make love to me, to take me and finish what you started.
If you refuse me now, you aren't human."

"You have no idea just how human I am," he murmured back. "But you'll soon be finding out, and it's about
time. Come to your husband's bed, wife, and learn to know
the man you belong to."

He pulled her head back by the hair and slowly licked
each of her nipples in turn, then finally consented to leave
the chair. Holding her in his arms he moved toward the
bed, dropping light kisses on her face as he went. Rianne
knew she would die if he didn't hurry, but tightening her
arms around his neck didn't increase his speed. It took
forever until they got there, and then he bent to put her
down.

"All freshly made and already turned down," he said
with a smile. "Do you think someone knew we'd be using
it this quickly?"

He chuckled and then his hands went to the belt of his
dressing gown, untying and opening it. Rianne's eyes widened as he shrugged out of the covering and let it fall to
the floor, leaving him even more naked than she was. Seeing him clothed, even in just a shirt and breeches, hadn't
prepared her, and she couldn't imagine what would have.

He really was a giant, with shoulders twice the size of
Angus's and Cam's, and arms thick with corded muscle.
His chest was covered with reddish dark hair over the deep
tan of his skin, and his waist was trim above flat hips that
couldn't possibly be called slender. Below that—below that

was his desire, the hard knot Rianne had felt but not noticed while she writhed in his lap. It was a lance rather than an arrow, a tree limb rather than a branch; even as she realized she'd never seen anything like it, it came to her that *that* was what she'd demanded of him.

"Don't worry, sweet one, I would never hurt you," he murmured, obviously aware of what bothered her. "You have my word that you won't be given more than you're able and willing to accept. If you find acceptance beyond you, you need only say so . . ."

He let the sentence trail off as he climbed over Rianne and onto the bed, but he didn't *have* to finish it. Her body was already flaring again from his nearness. She wanted him no matter *how* big he was, and if he killed her at least she would die after having been satisfied.

She parted her lips to tell him that, but his own lips stopped the words even before they started. His kiss was growing more and more intense and ever more demanding, and she found she couldn't refuse to join him. Vague feelings of worry became wild response to his passion, and in an instant she was lost again.

Just how long his lips held hers she didn't know, but she *was* immediately aware of it when they released her. He had put her down flat on the bed and his big hands lowered the bodice of her nightgown to her waist, and then he was kneeling over her with his mouth to her breast. Rianne groaned and tried to escape what was being done, but those hands came to her shoulders and held her in place. With her nightgown straps keeping her arms from lifting very far, she had no choice but to accept what he was giving.

Until, that is, his hands left her shoulders to grasp her thighs. She was so lost in the swirling fog of burning need that she hadn't known her knees had been spread, and that now the man who was her husband knelt between them. Her nightgown had been raised all the way to her waist, and his face was lowering to the golden-red hair at the base of her belly. Giddily she wondered what he was doing, and an instant later found out.

Rianne mewled and writhed at the touch of his tongue, but she couldn't escape the frenzy-making sensation. The hands holding to her thighs had the strength of steel, red-hot steel that burned through her skin. He was making her kick the air rather than him, and he still wasn't hurting her . . .

But he *was* sending her into insanity! She moaned again as she tried to raise up to force him away, but those hands were tilting her back and not letting her up! She pounded the bed with fists of madness as his tongue slid around her cleft, her eyes squeezed shut as she fought not to cry. She needed him so badly now, but all he wanted to do was torture her.

And then his tongue was gone, magically replaced by a shaft as hard as rock. The shaft was beginning to push into her, seeking the place of her greatest frenzy, just what she needed and where she needed it. Without stopping to think Rianne arched violently upward, meeting the down-ward push with a thrust of her hips that refused denial. Somewhere far away there was a brief flash of pain, un-important and instantly buried under the explosion inside her. Rianne spasmed in the thick arms that had come to hold her, and the world tried to melt in an effort to match her mind.

Complete unconsciousness never did come. Very slowly the humming satisfaction of her body eased, and she re-alized she lay panting in her husband's arms. The next thing she became aware of was that his shaft was deep inside her, gently stroking in and out. It felt so thick she had no idea how it had the room to move, not to mention bury itself to the hilt.

"It looks to me as though you enjoyed the first taste of your husband," he murmured, bending his head to kiss her face. "The pain wasn't too much for you, was it?"

"Pain?" she echoed, trying to remember, and then it came back to her. "Oh, yes, when you pushed inside. I guess I just didn't notice at the time."

"Good," he murmured with a chuckle. "That was the way I wanted it. You may have had pain from others, but you'll never have it from me. How are you feeling now, little one?''

Rianne wasn't quite sure about that, not with the way he continued to stroke her; the sensations caused by the movement were very distracting. She tried to move away from him as a means of solving the problem, but a gasp was forced from her as she stopped. Movement had quickly reminded her that his body still had possession of hers.

"Mmm, that was nice," he said, moving his lips to the side of her throat. "Do it again, and if possible, harder."

Rianne realized that she'd accidentally tightened her inner muscles around him, and the sensation hadn't been quite the same for her. He'd obviously enjoyed it, but in her case it had caused her eyes to widen. She didn't *want* to do it again, even if she could figure out how to do it on purpose, and then she made another unsettling discovery. The demanding desire that had so recently been shattered was beginning to build again, just as though nothing at all had been done.

"No, I can't," she gasped, bringing her hands to his giant arms in a useless effort to move them. "I can't go through that again, so you'll just have to let me go."

"What can't you go through again?" he asked, the motion of his hips slowly picking up speed. "You haven't actually experienced a thorough loving, so you still have that ahead of you. And wasn't that what you asked me to do? Make love to you?"

"Yes, of course that's what I asked for," she answered, now desperate enough to squirm. "But you're making me feel that way again, and I can't stand it."

"This time you'll find it easier," he said, reassurance in the eyes that had turned smoky-gray. "I'll work to satisfy your arousal even as it grows stronger, and try not to let it take you over as it did earlier. I hoped from the first instant I saw you that you'd find it impossible to resist the birth of your own passion. This time we'll flame together, and quench each other at the same time."

"You did that to me deliberately?" Rianne whispered, the only sense she could make out of what he'd said. "You gave your word, then made that bet—and all the time you knew exactly what would happen?''

"I was hoping, and my highest hopes came true," he said, as if that made any difference. "Now I'm going to finish making love to my wife on our wedding night, and she's going to respond to me just the way she did earlier.''

You can't do that to me again, she wanted to whisper, feeling betrayed not just by him, but also by herself. But the words refused to come, for despite everything she *wanted* him to continue. And then his hands were behind her head, holding her still for his kiss. Rianne fought her own feelings with all the strength she had left, but it wasn't nearly enough. His mouth enticed hers to respond, while his shaft stroked her in a way she couldn't resist or deny. Her mind might have felt betrayed, but her body wanted his thrusts, knowing them as the thing it craved. It didn't matter that he'd lied to her when she'd trusted him; she wouldn't have been able to walk away even if he'd released her.

It took longer the second time, but the incredible frenzy eventually built to the point it couldn't go beyond. It exploded into shards instead, but the shards weren't only hers. The brute exploded at the same time to end his own frenzy, and when Rianne became aware of him again he was lying stretched out on the bed beside her. His arm was draped heavily across her waist, as though holding to what belonged to him completely, and Rianne hadn't the strength to move it. Absolute exhaustion was closing her eyes, but not before she remembered what he'd done. Right then she had to sleep, but once she woke up she would not forget again . . .

Bryan waited until the girl was obviously and deeply asleep, then stroked the softness of her skin a bit before getting up to see to the lamps. Her magnificent hair was soaked in sweat and her body was only just beginning to cool, two ways in which he matched her perfectly. She'd given him the sort of wedding night he'd always dreamed about: without disappointment, and filled with a genuine eagerness for more of the same. She'd been so responsive it had felt like a fantasy come true, having beneath him a woman who could match him stride for stride. In the past the women he'd used had responded cautiously, those who hadn't been out-and-out frightened. For some men full satisfaction didn't depend on full response and abandon from their partners, but for him it did. Too often he'd ended up disappointed and frustrated, wishing the woman he'd shared his bed with hadn't been so timid. Now he'd found a woman who demanded everything he had to give, and magically, unbelievably, she was his wife.

But she was also upset with him. Bryan slipped quietly back into the bed beside her, knowing he would have his hands full once she woke up. He'd used her own innocence against her to get what he wanted, and no matter how much pleasure she'd had she would not be quick to forgive him. Possibly he'd been unwise to tell her the truth just then, but that was the way she affected him. He wanted to tell her about everything he was doing and make her a part of it, which meant it was a good thing that his business with Harding would soon be over. Once it was, he would tell her all about it.

And then she would blame him for that, too. He sighed as he rearranged the quilts to cover them both, then lay down and put his arm around her again. He'd save himself some trouble if he left both points to be covered at the same time, so that's what he would do. Just how he would handle it all he didn't yet know in detail, but he still had his general plan. If it didn't work out, he would think of something else.

It's too bad I had to put you through that, little one, he thought as he spread his hand against her middle and moved close. *I could be ready for you again in no time, but you're too drained to wake up very soon. Well, that will change once you get used to being a man's wife, and tomorrow night will be better. And so will tomorrow in the morning, and in the afternoon, and . . .*

Bryan smiled as he fitted her against him, wishing that her nightgown wasn't still around her middle. But the thing belonged to her, so it wasn't his place to take it. When he finally won her over, *she* would be the one who got rid of it. The first step in that would be gaining her trust, which wasn't likely to be easy. But he would do it, somehow, and then . . . and then . . .

Chapter 8

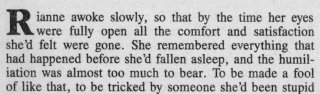

Rianne awoke slowly, so that by the time her eyes were fully open all the comfort and satisfaction she'd felt were gone. She remembered everything that had happened before she'd fallen asleep, and the humiliation was almost too much to bear. To be made a fool of like that, to be tricked by someone she'd been stupid enough to trust . . .

Someone. Rianne looked around the room. A single lamp burned low to keep full darkness at bay, showing her that she was alone. So, he'd left without waking her, probably as soon as she'd fallen asleep. Well, why not? He'd already gotten what he'd wanted . . .

Rianne sat up and put her face in her hands, trying to push away the idiot satisfaction her body felt. It shouldn't have been possible to feel that way, not with the kind of turmoil that was twisting her mind. It was impossible to understand how she could have wanted him that badly, how she could have responded to and desired a man without character or honor. He must have bewitched her in some way, but that didn't mean it wasn't still mostly *her* fault. She'd let herself forget that no one but Angus and Cam could be trusted, and now paid for that lapse with all the humiliation that was possible.

But also with anger, the slow, seething kind that burned hotter than high-jumping flames. Her first objective still had to be escape, but if she ever found the chance to get even with that brute . . . It was more than time he learned what humiliation felt like, especially the sort you were helpless against . . .

Thoughts of helplessness drove her from the bed, along with another point that added to her annoyance: she had no idea what time of day it was. Her cage had no windows, the lack of which was beginning to grate harder.

But first things first. Her hands moved fast to rid her of the blue silk nightgown, and she left it puddled on the floor as she hurried to the wash basin. She could almost feel *his* hands and lips still on her, and that was the last thing she wanted just then. The memory of last night almost made her forget how much she hated the man, and she wasn't *about* to forget.

Rianne managed a fairly thorough job of scrubbing herself from the basin before drying herself. After that she went to the wardrobe that held her clothes, and pulled out the first morning gown her hand touched. She would have preferred dressing in her breeches and shirt, but they and the boots hadn't been returned yet. As soon as they were, though . . .

It was impossible to dress without help, a fact she had to admit by ringing for a maid. She had never had to do without a maid, which made her wonder how she would manage once she and Angus and Cam had made good their escape. They didn't have enough gold for her to hire a girl, but maybe—

"You're an idiot," she muttered to herself once the maid was gone again, staring at her reflection in the vanity. "You can worry about who you will and won't hire once you're out of this room. Until that happens you're simply wasting your time. Stop dreaming and get to work."

Which was easy enough to say, but not quite as easy to do. She sat at the vanity and brushed her hair, fully aware that the door had been locked again after the maid had left. Her thoughts had begun swinging from rage to depression and back again, making it a virtual certainty that the wrong emotion would emerge at exactly the wrong time. If she could only regain control of herself—

A soft knock came at her door, intentionally unintrusive. She put down the hairbrush she'd been using, but otherwise didn't make a sound. She *hated* the false cour-

tesy being given her, and wasn't yet able to force herself
to pretend acceptance.

No more than three heartbeats went by before the door
opened again, and Mrs. Raymond came in. She carried
Rianne's shirt and breeches and boots, and when she saw
Rianne she smiled. The smile, however, didn't last long in
the face of Rianne's own expression. Rianne was remembering what she'd seen in the wardrobe: other nightgowns
all neatly arranged, nightgowns Mrs. Raymond had told
her weren't there. Her gift from Angus had been fouled
for no reason at all, and Rianne would never forget that—
or forgive the lie.

"Good morning, Mrs. Machlin," the woman tried, her
tone going for friendliness. "It's a lovely morning, and
Mr. Machlin is in your sitting room, waiting to share
breakfast with you. I've brought back your things just as I
said I would . . ."

The woman let her words trail off as her forced smile
died, finally admitting the weight of Rianne's stare. Her
cheeks went red as though she'd been accused aloud of
the lie she'd been caught in, and her dark gaze dropped
away as she bit her lip. *She knows exactly what I'm thinking,* Rianne realized, but before the smaller woman could
say anything else, *he* appeared behind her. His broad face
was creased into a smile, and his big hands gently moved
Mrs. Raymond aside. The small woman used that to her
own advantage. As soon as she was no longer being stared
at, she put down Rianne's clothing and boots and immediately left the room.

"Good morning, wife," Machlin said as soon as Mrs.
Raymond was gone, warmth softening his tone as he
neared her. "I'm not surprised to see you looking as beautiful in pale-gold as you do in blue or green. I've been
waiting to thank you for the wonderful wedding night you
gave me. I doubt if any other woman could have done as
well."

He bent to pull her off the vanity bench and into his
arms, acting as though she had laughed and run to him as
soon as he'd appeared. He was dressed in shirt and

breeches and boots, but when his lips touched hers it was almost as if he were naked again, as if they both were. Rianne felt a shudder inside as part of her fought to return the kiss, while the rest tried to struggle wildly to escape. She'd never felt such insane confusion and didn't know how to deal with it, but the conflict had one blessed side effect. It held her motionlessly in place, so that after a moment the brute released her with a sigh.

"I was afraid of that," he said, an odd sadness in the cold gray of his eyes. "We'll have to talk about this over breakfast. And I have something for you I think you'll like."

His big hand touched fingertips to her face, and then he was urging her toward the sitting room with an arm about her shoulders. Rianne thought briefly about refusing to go, then abandoned the idea. The brute wasn't above carrying her out, and if that happened she'd probably fall into a foaming fit. It was a miracle it hadn't already happened . . .

"Just sit right here and your breakfast will be brought to you," he said, guiding her into the same chair she'd used the night before. "Do you prefer tea in the morning, or coffee?"

Rianne, who had never been in a coffeehouse or near a cup of the brew in her life, suddenly found herself distracted. It was said that those in America drank nothing *but* coffee, another point usually used to show how barbaric they were. She really ought to find out what the drink was like, since she would certainly have to get used to it . . .

"Tea," she forced herself to say, at the same time raving silently, *Stop daydreaming, or you won't* need *to know what coffee tastes like, you idiot! Pull yourself together right now, and don't even try to understand why being close to him scatters every thought in your head. Just remember that he's doing it to you on purpose, exactly the way he did last night!*

Embarrassed memories of the night before burned through Rianne, enough so that she was able to get something of a grip on herself. By then the brute was seated in his place across from her, and a serving man was putting a plate of food and a cup of tea in front of her. Eggs, and a wedge of fresh bread with honey, and a chunk of ham.

"For some reason, I'm starving," the brute said, a similar plate having been put in front of him. "After this you'll have to tell Cook what you prefer for breakfast, as well as what you want served at other times. As lady of the house, you can arrange things to suit yourself."

Rianne watched him take a huge bite of bread before starting on his eggs, his loudly announced appetite keeping his full attention on his plate. It was amazing that he'd been able to keep away from the food long enough to make his casual comment about how much control she would have over his house . . .

He really does consider me a fool, Rianne growled to herself, giving her own plate full attention. *Buy the girl and do whatever you please to her, but don't worry about her temper. As soon as you tell her* she's *in charge of everything, she'll be simpering and smirking and eating out of your hand.*

The brute thought he could get away with playing games with her, but he didn't yet know the *meaning* of game-playing. It would be interesting to see how long it took to make him really regret his bargain with her stepfather . . .

Bryan kept most of his attention on his plate, especially once Rianne began to eat from her own. He wanted some food in her before he tried to calm her down, before he tried to melt those eyes of green ice. Sarah had gone even before he'd brought Rianne into the sitting room, staying out of the line of fire just as she'd promised to do. For a brief moment Bryan envied her . . .

But only for a very brief moment. Life had taught him that what was worth having was worth fighting for, even if it meant getting up early and sneaking around his own house like a thief. He'd had a stage to set before his new wife awoke, and a stage required carefully rehearsed players. He'd spent a lot of time with his people that morning, telling them exactly what he wanted, and now he was as ready as he could be.

He drained his cup of the strong black coffee he'd gotten into the habit of drinking in the morning, wondering how much of his planning would succeed. His first ploy, reminding the girl she was lady of the house, hadn't worked as well as he'd hoped. She hadn't refused the food put in front of her, but she also hadn't said anything. Silence wasn't a good sign, not with a woman like her, but maybe she was just waiting for him to apologize. Since that was next on his list, he'd try it and see.

"As I said a little while ago, we have to talk," he began, at the same time gesturing for more coffee. "Since you're not finished eating and I am, I'll start."

He waited until his cup was refilled and the serving man had left, hoping she would at least comment once they were alone, but she didn't even glance at him. All her attention was on her plate, and the unexpectedly large amount of food it still held. For someone who had spent a good number of minutes eating, she hadn't managed to swallow much.

"I've been thinking about last night, and it's come to me that I owe you an apology," he said, trying hard to sound ashamed and regretful. "You accused me of taking advantage of your innocence, and you were perfectly right. I did do exactly that, but it wasn't entirely my fault. If you weren't so desirable, so much a woman who makes a man forget his honor—What in *hell* are you doing?"

Bryan hadn't meant to add that last, but the words had simply popped out. He'd been distracted by Rianne's distraction, following her gaze to where she was simply moving things on her plate. Every time her fork went to her mouth it was empty, and that was why her plate looked so full.

"I'm rearranging things to suit myself," she murmured in answer to his blurted question, still not looking up. "You were saying . . .?"

"I wasn't saying, I was apologizing," he pointed out,

now fighting to hold down a growl. "Don't you even care?"

"Of course I care," she responded, still not looking up. "Please go on."

"How can I—" Bryan began, then broke off the protest. He'd been about to say something about not being able to talk to the top of her head. Right. With an opening like that, she'd— Better to just get on with it, and remember he'd known it wouldn't be easy.

"All right, back to the apology," he said after taking a deep breath and a sip of coffee. "You really are due one, a sincere one, and that's what I'm trying to give you. But if I didn't feel that way, I'd have to point out how much pleasure we shared only because I took advantage of you. If I hadn't, we both would have missed out."

"Then you think it's all right to take advantage of someone if the act brings eventual pleasure?" she asked when he paused, moving egg scraps carefully into some obscure pattern. "That means *whatever* you do is all right, as long as it leads sometime to pleasure."

"No!" Bryan almost shouted, then reestablished some vestige of control. "No, it means nothing of the sort," he went on more softly. "Looking at things only in terms of your own pleasure is shallow and stupid, not to mention dishonorable. I was simply trying to point out— God, I don't know *what* I was trying to point out. All I'm saying is that I know I did wrong and I'm sorry."

Bryan had expected this second ploy to succeed a lot better. Women loved it when a man asked for their forgiveness, revelling in the power it gave them. They also usually gave that forgiveness, just to prove they were better people. He'd hoped his sweet little wife would do the same, getting some of the satisfaction that really was due her, but now . . . He wouldn't have bet a copper penny on the possibility, not any longer.

"That was very nicely said," she granted, moving her ham a bit more toward the center of her plate. "Was there anything else you wanted to talk about?"

Bryan felt the urge to close his eyes. Nothing he'd said

had reached her, and all he wanted to do was grab up that plate she toyed with and send it smashing into a wall. Couldn't she see he really *was* trying to patch things up between them . . . ?

"Yes, there *is* something else," he said, then made a major effort to smooth the growl out of his voice. "I still haven't given you my wedding gift, but that's easily remedied. This is for you, wife."

He opened the case before standing it on the table between them. He expected her to look directly at it, and then be caught by the beauty of the set. A necklace and earrings in diamonds and emeralds, shaped into a delicately spreading cluster of leaves in the center of the necklace, the earrings smaller clusters that matched. The exquisite workmanship had caught Bryan's eye some years earlier, and he'd bought the set with the express purpose of giving it to the woman he would someday marry . . .

"That's very pretty," the woman he'd married said after no more than the shortest of glances before ignoring the set entirely. "Thank you."

This time Bryan did close his eyes, the better to struggle with the rage that wanted to erupt out of him. Not since the age of three had he had so much trouble with a woman, or felt so helpless to stop it. Any other woman would have melted at the sight of that gift, or at least given a *little*. If he'd had any doubts about how determined the girl would be to fight him, they were now gone. She'd formed her own plan of attack, and so far it had been a damn sight more successful than his own. He finished his coffee in a single swallow, then got to his feet.

"Let's go," he said, a good deal more curtly than he'd originally intended. "I planned to show you the house this morning, and there's no reason to change that. You also have to have the rest of the staff introduced to you."

She hesitated a moment, as though debating whether or not to argue, then rose smoothly to her feet without a word. Bryan realized he would have been a lot happier if she *had* argued. No argument meant the attack would come from another quarter, almost certainly when he least expected it. A sane man would have marched her back to her bedchamber and locked her in, saving his resources for the conversation he would have that night with Robert Harding . . .

But Bryan was feeling too stubborn to be sane. After he had what he wanted from Harding he'd be able to tell the girl everything, and that would probably bring problems of its own. But there was also a chance she would understand what he'd done and why, and even beyond that would approve. That was the reason he was working so hard *now*, trying to reach her *before* she knew the truth. He wanted her to trust him without knowing the reasons for his plan. He wanted her to care for *him*, who he was, alone.

Right. As he followed her silent figure out of the sitting room, he knew beyond doubt that he was living in a fantasy world. His new wife was determined not to trust him again no matter what he said or did, but he refused to give up. He *had* to try, and keep trying, until he'd won or was dead . . .

Rianne winced as the door was slammed shut behind her, the sound of the key turning in the lock coming immediately afterward. She was still angry herself from the heated words she and the brute had just exchanged, but she was also grimly satisfied. Treat *her* like a backward child, would he . . . ?

She went to a chair and sat, glad to be able to do it after all the time they'd spent walking around. He'd insisted on showing her every inch of that very large house, and had introduced every person they'd come across. Rianne continued to be distant and gratingly agreeable, and he had kept on with his clenched-teeth patience. Waiting for her to be a fool again and start believing him, surely . . .

But it hadn't worked out like that. The women in the house had gushed at her, the men had shown the most grotesque smiles imaginable, but she hadn't let any of it fool her. They didn't want her there any more than she wanted to *be* there, but for some reason they'd felt it necessary to pretend. They all acted as though they were very happy about the marriage. *His* doing, probably, in an effort to make life more pleasant for himself. Too bad he didn't know she would scarcely be there that long . . .

No, *not* too bad, she amended to herself, remembering how he'd been when he'd finally stopped pretending patience. He had taken her outside to show her one of the outbuildings, a large carriage house and stables that had been converted into a barracks and training area. The men inside had been hard at work, practicing with weapons in small groups. Most of them hadn't been very good, and the brute must have read that opinion in her expression.

"These men are new recruits, only just getting started," he said, obviously trying not to sound defensive. "I have a dozen experienced men here instructing them, and by the time they're through *these* will be almost as good."

"I'm sure," Rianne commented, idly examining each of the groups. "How much do you pay these recruits?"

"Ten coppers the fortnight and keep," he answered with a frown. "Why do you ask?"

"I was just curious about how much I'd be earning," she replied with a shrug. "You *do* remember offering me a position, two days ago on the road? Since I have to be here, I might as well consider accepting."

"I made that offer to a likely *boy*," he returned with a snort. "Pretty girls don't fit in well in men's barracks, even if the men themselves would enjoy it. And you seem to forget—you already have a different position."

"Since I'd be starting out better than most of these, I think I should get more than ten coppers," Rianne mused, ignoring the brute's comments as she strolled closer to one group. "Just look at that one. Not only doesn't he know how to stand, I'll be surprised if he doesn't end up dropping his weapon. A child could best him."

Rianne made no effort to keep her voice down, and no one in the area had missed what she said. The recruit had been clumsily fencing with blunted training swords with a man who was clearly an instructor. When the other men watching began to laugh out loud at Rianne's observation, the object of her ridicule disengaged and whirled around with a murderous scowl. Dark-haired and light-eyed and not recently shaven, the young man's sweat had stained his cheap homespun shirt and breeches. His darkened skin added to the low, menacing look of him, but Rianne just smiled in answer to his scowl.

"Ignoring insults should be the first lesson you learn around here, fellow," Machlin said quickly to the man. "When you get mad you lose control of yourself, and right after that you lose the fight. Just calm down and take it in stride."

"You didn't call him 'boy,' " Rianne hurried to point out, still smiling in a superior way. "You called my— friend 'boy,' and he's much better than this creature. As a matter of fact, so am I."

"That's enough, woman," Machlin growled as the recruit bristled up again. He also sent her a furious glance as he tried to add, "We'll talk about this later—"

"But what good will it do him not to be told how bad he is?" Rianne immediately interrupted. "He should know even a woman is better. And I *am* better, aren't I."

She stared up at Machlin with that, daring him to lie just to calm the young man. He'd been quick enough to know she was trying to trap him, but searching for where the trap lay made him hesitate just a little too long. The recruit's touchy temper flared when Rianne's latest insult wasn't immediately denied, and he threw the training sword down to draw a fully edged and pointed dagger.

"I'll not have no bitch puttin' on the airs with *me*," he snarled, his thick accent slurring the words. "Treatin' honest folk like dirt, that's all *your* sort be good fer. Took it all me life, I did, but won't be takin' it no more."

He started toward her with the dagger tight in his fist and fury blazing from his eyes. Rianne was briefly sorry she'd had to use the young man in her schemes, but she'd needed *someone* to start a riot. Men who were gentle-natured didn't join a company of fighters, and with that sort a single spark could well ignite the lot of them. One of the instructors would try to stop the young man, a fight would start, and then everyone would be joining in.

Chances were excellent that the brute would become embroiled, and then she would be able to slip away . . .

Only it hadn't happened like that. Remembering, Rianne shifted in annoyance in her chair, still unsure as to why it hadn't. The instructor of the group had stepped forward to keep his other students back, letting the one with the dagger continue on without interference.

"To me," the brute had said quietly to the young man, stepping out in front of Rianne. "You come to me with complaints like that."

He hadn't armed himself for the tour of his house and grounds, just put on his vest and coat, but the young man didn't seem to notice. Or maybe he did, and considered the difference in their size enough to justify his weapon. The recruit, though broader of shoulder, was barely taller than Rianne. His furious gaze and menacing advance shifted immediately to Machlin, and the next instant he attacked.

Or, to be precise, tried to attack. Rianne had watched the brute lean to his right as the dagger flashed to his left, and then he had both oversized hands on the young man's wrist and arm. One quick, complicated twist later the recruit was turned away from the brute and bent over, making soft sounds of pain as he himself held very still. The dagger lay on the floor where he'd dropped it, useless and already forgotten.

"Lose your temper, and you'll always lose the fight," the brute had said then into absolute silence. Not another man in the whole room made a sound, not even so much as a shuffling of feet. "She's right about being better with a sword than you, but that's only because she's had more practice. And when she's fighting, she ignores what's being said and pays attention only to what's being done. You'll learn that yourself, but first you have to learn something even more important. I'm better than everyone in this room, and I'll kill the next man who comes at me in serious attack. Is there someone here who thinks I can't? Or won't?"

He'd looked around deliberately then, giving them all a

chance to answer, but no one took it. Here and there someone who must have been an instructor smiled quietly, but no words were spoken. A long, heavy moment passed, and then the brute released the young man with a small push.

"All of you get back to work," he said, no warmth at all in his voice. "I want you able to join a company before the colonies are all settled."

The silence was immediately broken by men returning to their practice, and then the brute had come over to her.

"Now you and I will have a few words," he growled, wrapping one of those hands around her arm. "Right this way."

He'd pulled her out of the practice room and back to the house, and hadn't stopped until he'd reached the front hall. With no one in sight he'd finally come to a halt, then had looked down at her with furious gray ice.

"What in hell did you think you were playing at back there?" he demanded, one big hand closed into a fist. "I didn't hire those men to see them dead, but if that boy had come at me again I would have had to kill him. What did you think you were trying to accomplish?"

"I was simply trying to find out about that offer you'd made me," Rianne had answered with chin high, fighting to keep her voice steady. She'd never seen *anyone* do what he'd done unarmed against a weapon, hadn't even known it was possible . . . "Are you saying you lied about the offer, that your word really is worthless?"

"I thought I was making that offer to a *man,*" he'd repeated slowly and deliberately, unblinkingly enunciating each word. "When I have the time to coax the names of your two friends out of you, you'll see I wasn't lying. I promised them hire and they'll have it, because they're *men.* You, on the other hand, are my *wife.*"

"Is that supposed to be *my* fault?" Rianne had flared immediately, finding it impossible to keep calm. "I'm not the one who demanded marriage, but maybe you've conveniently forgotten. And you'll never—'coax'—those names out of me, not if you had all the time in eternity.

You can do your worst, or even kill me as you threatened to do with those men. Go ahead, kill me!''

Rianne had regretted those overly dramatic words as soon as they were out; seeing immediate amusement in the gray eyes looking down at her made it that much worse. The brute wasn't about to kill her, at least not until her inheritance was in his hands and he'd tired of using her body. Her temper had pushed her into sounding like a silly child, and it was certain he could see the flush in her cheeks.

"You're mistaken, little one," he said, his voice now very smooth. "I didn't threaten those men, I gave them a solemn promise. They know that, even if you don't." And then, suddenly, all amusement was gone. "And although I've mentioned this point before, you seem to need it repeated: I do *not* kill helpless women, even when provoked."

About to hotly contest the idea of her being helpless, Rianne had found it necessary to pause. Those cold gray eyes were looking at her so strangely . . .

"Then I'd like to know what you *do* do," she demanded, mostly to keep from showing how unsure she was. It was possible to hurt people terribly *without* killing them, something she'd learned all those years ago . . . "Go ahead, tell me what awful thing you'll do instead."

"If you don't start behaving yourself I'll take away every one of your dolls," he'd said as she waited for the worst, then raised one dark-red brow. "Can we stop playing games for now? I really do have some serious business that needs my attention."

"You despicable lowlife," she'd choked, absolutely livid with embarrassment. After everything she'd been picturing, he had the utter gall to say *that?* "You low, mean brute of a man! You fiend, you—!"

"Look, I still don't know why, but you started that trouble in the training hall deliberately," he interrupted her to say. "I really have been trying to be patient, but some things I simply can't allow. If you *start* trouble, you can't expect not to have some of it come back at you."

"Then you have to be given something to expect, too," she'd countered hotly. "Retaliation."

By then she'd raised her skirts a bit, but not to show the soft slippers worn by most women at home. Rianne, with escape in mind, had put on short but sturdy walking boots. Her kick landed on his shin with a greatly satisfying thunk! and he drew his breath in with a hiss as he flinched.

"All right, that does it," he'd said in a growl. "We'll see how much you like retaliation after you've spent the rest of the day in your rooms. I'm sure you'll find it a good deal more pleasant than my company has been."

And then he'd dragged her to her bedchamber, thrust her inside, and locked the door again. She turned her head to glare at that door, but the situation wasn't the complete loss it might have been. It had finally come to her notice that the key to her prison was kept in the very lock it opened. Since more than one person needed to open the door that made sense, but it also gave Rianne a means of escape. Those wonderful books she read that the brute didn't approve of—with their help and the fact that her husband hadn't yet realized she *meant* to escape . . .

Rianne was lost so thoroughly in making plans that when a knock came at her door it startled her. She didn't know how much time had passed, but when the door opened almost immediately she found out. Mrs. Raymond came in leading a girl carrying a tray, but didn't speak until the tray was put down and the girl was gone.

"That's your lunch," she told Rianne then, a weariness in her voice, then she blurted, "I can't understand why you insist on fighting with him! He's the man you'll be spending the rest of your life with. If you think you'd rather have that life filled with struggle instead of love, you're a hopeless child."

"I would say that was my choice rather than yours," Rianne drawled, trying to get rid of the woman. "Why don't you find someone who's *interested* in the wisdom of maturity."

"Because I haven't finished saying what I was told to," the woman replied with a deep sigh of defeat. "Your husband has left word that he'll be spending the day with the men, but will return to the house at six and will see you then. He asked me to remind you that there will be a guest tonight for dinner, which will be at eight. He'll discuss the matter with you when he returns at six."

Mrs. Raymond then gave a small curtsy before going out, leaving Rianne more than a little upset. She *had* forgotten they would have a guest for dinner that evening, and the worst part was who that guest would be. Robert Harding, her stepfather, would walk in with a smug and dirty laugh, already knowing what had been done to her by her new husband, and revelling in her degradation! And what if Machlin came back at six and somehow bewitched her into doing it again? That would be only a short while before her stepfather arrived, and would be even worse yet! She would be completely and totally humiliated, and she couldn't bear the thought.

"But I won't be humiliated if I manage to escape," she muttered after a moment in an effort to calm herself. She had all the rest of the afternoon to accomplish it, and if she didn't get away she'd deserve whatever happened afterward. And she would do justice to her lunch, since there was no knowing when she would be able to eat after she was free.

She went to the tray and began uncovering dishes, firmly refusing to think about last night, and the way she would never be bewitched again.

Rianne was sweating by the time she had the key in her hand. She'd eaten and changed her clothes, but being well fed and in breeches and shirt and boots didn't bring immediate escape. She knew what had to be done, but finding the means to accomplish it became the problem. Something to poke through the keyhole to dislodge the key, and something else to catch the key when it fell and carry it back under the door.

The more urgent need was the something to go under the door. Pushing the key out would be wasted effort if there wasn't some way to reach it, but nothing in the bed-

chamber seemed right. Rianne tore apart everything in her
wardrobe and then searched the storage chests. Those
items stiff enough to position were too thick to fit under
the door, while those that were thin enough were too limp
to be properly positioned. More wasted time went by while
she searched through the wreckage again, but nothing had
been missed. And there certainly wasn't anything that this
all but empty room itself could offer—

Except for one thing. Rianne laughed with relief as she
hurried to the modest painting on one wall, certainly hung
there because of its colors. Its depiction of a woods at
dawn, all rose and gold rather than green and brown,
blended so well with the room's decorations that she'd
looked at it any number of times without really seeing it.
Its canvas would be perfect for her needs—as soon as she
got it loose from its mounting.

Fighting the canvas free took even more time, but finally the medium-sized landscape was hers. A brief test
showed it fit easily under the door, but Rianne didn't leave
it there. She still had to find something to push the key
out with, and didn't care to leave the canvas where someone might see it.

As she looked for something suitable, she began to
worry. What if the brute had set a guard on her, someone
who was waiting only for her to step through the door?
What if someone had seen the canvas, understood what
she was doing, and was right then informing her husband?
What if—

"No more!" she hissed at herself, one hand in her hair
where she stood uselessly still. "If he finds out and stops
you, then you'll be stopped. But if he doesn't—do you
intend to do his stopping *for* him?"

Not likely was the only response possible, one which
sent her back to searching with renewed enthusiasm. She
had no idea what the man would do if he caught her, and
if her luck held she would never find out.

A moment later she came across exactly what she'd been
looking for, hidden away in the bottom of a chest: a silver
candle-snuffer with a long, tapering handle that ended in

a slender point. What the thing was doing in there Rianne had no idea, nor did she care. Being perfect for her purposes she immediately set to work with it, first sliding the canvas into position.

Nudge the key out gently, she told herself. *Be careful not to make it snag somewhere on the lock. Also, don't push too hard, or it will bounce off the canvas and out of reach.* Rianne had to shake her head twice to rid her eyes of sweat-soaked hair, and by the time the key was out her knees were aching. She heard the soft "plop" of its fall, slid back quickly along the polished floor, began to ease the canvas back under the door . . .

And there it was, the shiny brass road to her freedom. Once she had it in hand, she paused only long enough to hide the canvas and its frame under the mattress on the bed, and returned the candle-snuffer to its place in the chest. No sense in letting everyone know what she'd done; if worse came to worst, she might need to do it again . . .

Unlocking the door and peeking into the sitting room was a time of heart-thundering nervousness. Rianne kept expecting to get caught, an attitude she found new and utterly frustrating. She snarled at herself in annoyance while relocking the door, leaving the key protruding as it had been before, then hurried through the sitting room to the hall. Putting the key back where it belonged would mean more time before her absence was discovered— assuming she could get out of the house without meeting anyone.

But luck was really with her. Not only was there not a single soul to be seen anywhere in the house, slipping through the front door showed the grounds to be equally deserted. Granted she still had to cross the drive and lawn before reaching the cover of trees, but excitement flared too strongly in her for doubt to have a chance. With the stables and training barracks around at the back of the house, no one would see her go.

Rianne started out walking toward the trees to keep from attracting attention, but when she reached the halfway mark she just *had* to run. She'd realized that anyone seeing

her would know her by her hair color, so not running
would be helping *them* rather than herself. She hadn't been
able to bring herself to look back at the house . . . hadn't
wanted to see a giant, dark-red–haired figure chasing after
her . . . God, what would she do if she did see him . . . ?
Run, you stupid girl, run!

Panting and gasping turned running into a stumble, but
not immediately. By the time Rianne just *had* to slow, she
was among the first of the trees and moving deeper into
safety. A forced glance back showed no one at all, no
alarm being spread, no one giving chase. She brought herself to a stop by throwing her arms around a tree, but
didn't collapse to the ground as she might have at another
time. As soon as she had her breath back—

"Ssst, Ree!" came from so close that she nearly took
off again. If she'd had the breath she would have, which
made it a lucky thing she didn't. It came to her through
the fog of panic that the voice was Cam's, and then he
stepped out from behind a tree to gesture her to him. Only
ten feet away to her left. If she'd kept running, she would
have gone right by him.

When she reached his tree he pulled her behind it, and
then they took a moment to hug. It was incredible that he
would be there, when she'd expected to have to go all
the way to the cave before she saw him or Angus again.
She closed her eyes as she clung to this tall brother of
hers, and his right hand came up to stroke her hair.

"Are you all right?" he whispered, the words choked
with anger. "Angus and I didn't find out what happened
yesterday until this morning, when I went back to see to
our chores. If only we'd known sooner . . ."

"You still wouldn't have been able to do anything," she
finished when he didn't, raising her head to look at him.
"It's true, Cam, so don't beat yourself for not being there.
We couldn't have gotten away with everyone within twenty
miles chasing after us, which would have happened if we'd
tried it. But what are you doing here? You couldn't possibly have known—"

"That you would escape as soon as you could?" he

interrupted with a snort. "Come on, Ree, remember who
you're talking to. And besides . . . if you hadn't made it
by tonight, I would have gone in after you. Angus and I
talked it over and agreed I had to try. He's healing well,
but he still has to rest. You should have heard him cursing
over not being able to go with me."

"I can imagine," she said with a soft laugh, deliriously
relieved to be with her own again. "But let's save this for
when we're back at the cave. The clock I passed in the
hall said it was after four, and by six o'clock at the latest
they'll know I'm gone. When that happens, I don't want
to be anywhere near here."

"Ree, wait," Cam said, catching her before she took
off through the woods. "We don't have to go back to the
cave. Angus had me load everything onto the coach and
that's where he's waiting, less than a mile from here. All
we needed was *you,* and now that we have you we can get
going. Toward London and freedom."

"Freedom," Rianne whispered, taking the hand he held
out and squeezing it. "Oh, Cam, I can't believe we're
finally doing it. But what about Angus? Are you sure he's
strong enough to travel?"

"He said that if we won't go with him, he's going
alone." Cam's grin was wide in the late-afternoon sunshine, sharing reassurance along with the joke. "He really
is a lot stronger than I thought he would be at first, and I
haven't been letting him do any of the work. He's riding
in the coach like a great lord, but he'd better not get *too*
used to it. Once we reach the colonies, I won't be doing
anyone's share but my own."

"Just as we all will," she agreed with another laugh.
"So what are you waiting for? Let's get on with it."

He joined her soft laughter and began to lead the way,
through the woods toward the waiting coach. Rianne
thought briefly about six o'clock, but didn't let herself turn
back for a final look at the house she'd escaped from.
There would be anger when her absence was discovered,
but no real sense of loss. Only her brothers missed her

when she wasn't there; everyone else felt relieved, which was certainly what a giant with dark-red hair would feel. After all, her inheritance would be his whether she was there or not . . .

Chapter 9

Bryan stood barefoot in breeches, staring into his wardrobe and trying to decide what to wear. He was clean again after working up a good sweat with the men, but just being clean wasn't enough. He felt the need for something special, something that would be just the right touch. What did other men wear when they went to attack their wives? He really wanted to make love to Rianne again, but after the way they'd argued earlier, attack was probably the only way he'd get her. If he could just think of a way to get *her* to attack *him* . . . or learn to keep his big mouth shut and his temper firmly in hand . . .

"Bryan, are you there? Bryan?"

The voice was Sarah Raymond's, and he realized he'd been hearing her knock for the last minute or two without really being aware of it. Great. Now he was going deaf as well as stupid.

"Yes, I'm in here, Sarah," he called back. "Come on in."

The door opened and the small woman walked in, but no more than a step or two. When she saw Bryan's bare chest she stopped short, upset rather than embarrassed.

"Oh, I'm sorry, I hadn't realized you weren't dressed yet," she said, beginning to step out again. "I'll come back in a few—"

"No, it's all right," Bryan interrupted as he reached for a shirt. "Did you need me for something?"

"I've—come to make a confession of sorts," she answered with a sigh, her dark eyes troubled. "I couldn't keep from opening my big mouth when I brought your wife her lunch and your message, and she looked really disturbed. If I made things worse between you two I'll never forgive myself, even though I only told her she was foolish for fighting with you. She pretended to be uninterested in my opinion, but she still looked disturbed.''

''I'm probably more responsible for that than you are,'' Bryan said, and not just to reassure his partner's wife. ''You told me to be gentle with her and I agreed I would be, then I turned around and let her force me into an argument. I'm beginning to feel like a hopeless case, but I know I can count on *you*. You'll tell me the best thing to try next.''

''Me?'' she countered with brows raised, watching him stamp into his boots. ''I'm not even sure what day this is. And I'm busy getting ready for your dinner guest, yes, very busy. Most of the staff will be out of sight, but close enough to call in case they're needed. That will depend on what size escort he brings. If there's only a coach driver, the man will be kept occupied in the kitchen. We—''

''Sarah,'' Bryan interrupted again, getting to his feet. ''I know the plan. Since I'm the one who developed it, I should know. After tonight I'll have what I need—except for a way to deal with my wife. Which I need before tonight, but I'm not about to get *that*, am I.''

Sarah shook her head with a commiserating smile.

''So there's no sense in putting off the confrontation,'' he said with a sigh, then cocked his head at her. ''Is this the way the beginning of Jamie's marriage went with *you?*''

''Oh, absolutely,'' she said with a small laugh. ''All marriages start like this. Didn't you know that?''

''People were kind enough to leave me in ignorance,'' he responded with a shake of his head. ''I thought there would be nothing worse than hysterics, which right now I'd happily settle for. Even if they came from me.''

''Now there's an idea,'' Sarah said, backing through the doorway to give him access to it. ''If *you* have hysterics, she'll have to do something to calm you down. Then, while she's feeling tender, you can go on to the fun part of marriage.''

"Tender, *my* sweet wife?" Bryan asked with brows high. "Sarah, you must be feverish. She'd probably stop the hysterics by hitting me with something hard. And with that in mind, you'd better come along and collect her lunch tray. Putting extra ammunition into her hands would be stupid.''

Sarah nodded ruefully, then led the way to the girl's rooms. Bryan spent the short trip thinking about the woman who was waiting for him, the woman who was now his wife. He wanted her so badly it was a physical pain, but even more he wanted *her* to want *him*. He could make it happen. He could, if only he found the right path through the swamp . . .

"I've stopped waiting after knocking," Sarah said, turning the key in the lock. "And it *is* silly, asking for permission to enter a room you'll be entering anyway. Here we go.''

She knocked once before opening the door, then started into the room. Bryan, still distracted, followed—and almost ran her down when she stopped short.

"What happened in here?" Sarah asked, looking around in bewilderment at the clothing strewn every which way. It wasn't clothing alone, Bryan saw after a moment. Everything that hadn't been nailed down was part of the debris on the floor.

"And where's your wife?" Sarah pursued, this time making him blink. "She couldn't have gotten out, but I don't see her anywhere.''

"She has to be hiding," Bryan responded, refusing to acknowledge the clutch of fear around his heart. "She couldn't have run away before I found a way to—Go get some of the staff. I want every inch of this room searched.''

Bryan watched her hurry out, but refused to let himself think while he began the search himself. Rianne would *not* be gone, not when he'd had less than two days with her. *No* one could have reached her in so short a time, so it wasn't his fault that things had gotten worse instead of better. She *hadn't* run away with his first real chance for happiness, it just wasn't possible . . .

He stopped in the middle of the room when Sarah came back with two housemaids, finally admitting he was wasting his time. The girl couldn't possibly be hiding in there, so it was time to head for the barracks. Some of his men were top-notch trackers, and he'd forced himself to admit that that was what he needed now. It was starting to get dark, so he'd better hurry.

Once he'd set them to it, it didn't take his men long to find the story left in the ground. She'd gone out of the house and headed straight across the lawn, walking at first and then running. She may have been a big girl, but her boots were smaller than any other pair on the estate. She'd made it to the trees, stopped briefly, then joined someone in a man-sized pair of boots. The two had gone off together through the woods . . .

"Damn me for the fool I am!" Bryan fumed when he heard that. "Those two she rode with! She must have known at least one would be waiting, and was only waiting herself for me to turn my back. I should have gotten their names out of her first thing, and made sure they were too well occupied to interfere in what was none of their business. When I catch up to them . . ."

"Terry's followin' 'em through the woods right now," Jake supplied, phlegmatic as always. Jake was in charge of the barracks, and was due for promotion to leader of a company as soon as an opening became available. "When he finds where they come t'roost, he'll get back here on th' gallop."

Bryan had no time to nod in acknowledgment. As soon as the words were out of Jake's mouth, Terry's horse burst from the woods and headed straight for them. Terry had followed the trail on foot, but there was no sense in doing the same coming back.

"Bryan, it's haste ye'll be needin'," Terry said as he slid out of the saddle almost before his mount had stopped. "Them two I was followin'—'tis a coach they were headin'

for, an' it not far from th' road. The way they turned—
sure an' it's to London they be goin'."

"London?" Bryan demanded in shock. "But how can
she— Of course, *that's* why they needed the gold! They
may even be planning to leave the country. Jake! Get the
rest of the experienced men mounted, and have someone
saddle my horse. We're going on a rabbit hunt. Terry: how
much of a lead do our rabbits have?"

"Couple of hours at least, maybe more," Terry answered before shrugging. "Won't be matterin', though,
not with them in a coach an' us in saddles. We'll be ridin'
'em down before they're anywhere near to London."

"Which is exactly the way I want it," Bryan growled,
anger a burning weight inside him. "And when I get her
back here . . ."

By the time the horses were brought out, Bryan was
already armed and in his vest and coat. He mounted up
and led his force toward the road at a canter, all memory
of the purpose he'd spent years and a fortune on gone from
his thoughts.

". . . and that's how I got out of the room," Rianne
said to Angus. "When I reached the woods Cam was there,
and now we're halfway to London. Are you sure you're
all right?"

That must have been the twentieth time she'd asked the
question, but not without cause. The coach her brothers
had bought and repaired was a good one, but no coach
gave an easy ride. The four horses pulling it were as
matched as the boys had been able to manage, but they'd
also had to be trained to the saddle in case the three fu-
gitives needed to ride. Saddle horses did badly pulling a
coach in tandem, even when they knew how to do it. The
trip was not proving an easy one at all, and the sweat on
Angus's pale face from the very beginning confirmed that.

"Ree, I'll be fine," Angus replied, also for the twentieth time. "I'm not wounded seriously at all, but even a
small wound can hurt. Cam's looking for an inn or a post-
ing house for us to stop at, and after a meal I'll be even

better. Right now we have to make all the time we can, so don't mention slowing down again. Cam has to keep to this pace for as long as the horses can manage it.''

"I don't see why," Rianne countered with exasperation. "If anyone had come after us, they would have caught us by now. And if no one's chasing you two, we're completely in the clear. I *know* no one's after *me*."

"I thought you said your husband might not know you were gone until six," Angus reminded her, sounding annoyed. "From what I saw of him two days ago on the road, he didn't strike me as a man who easily gives up what's his. You—"

"I am *not* his," Rianne snapped, beginning to get angry. "The brute wanted my inheritance, and now he'll get it. Our wedding was witnessed by enough people that there's no question about his right to it, so why would he need *me*? He can find a woman who *enjoys* being lied to and tricked."

"You told us he didn't hurt you," Angus said after a brief pause, his tone harder. "Were you lying to keep us from going after him? You sound as if he—"

"Angus, I *wasn't* lying," Rianne hurried to assure him, one hand going to his shadow arm. "The man's a brute, but he seemed to be trying not to hurt me. But trickery hurts as much as a slap, and that he did do."

"Maybe—maybe you just aren't looking at it right," Angus groped, his previous anger gone. "If the man really wanted you and couldn't get you any other way—Sometimes you have to do things you don't like in order to get what you *have* to have. Like us playing highwayman to get the gold for our new life."

"That was different," Rianne protested, wishing she could see him more clearly in the dark. "We didn't just do that because we had to, but also because the people we robbed deserved it. You *know* they did, Angus!"

"I doubt if *they* thought they deserved it," he maintained with typical male stubbornness. "All they were guilty of was being close friends with your stepfather. Sometimes, if we decide we don't like someone, everything they do—including accidents—becomes more evidence against them. We see what we want to see.''

''Are you suggesting I imagined the way he forced me to marry him?'' Rianne asked with even stronger anger. ''Or the way he threatened hanging for you and Cam? I know you like to think the best of people, Angus, but there's such a thing as taking that attitude too far.''

''Were you willing to marry him without being forced?'' Angus countered in a voice that seemed to be weakening. ''Strong men have a habit of taking what they want . . . even if what they want doesn't want them . . . The books all say so . . . and a man would have to be dead not to want *you* . . .''

''You know, I think I'm tired of arguing for now,'' Rianne said hastily, wishing she could check him for fever, but knowing he would draw back in protest. ''Let's save the rest of this for after we eat and are back on the road.''

He might have nodded there in the dark, but there were no more words. Rianne shifted where she sat to his left, trying to get comfortable despite the jouncing of the coach. And despite the sword she wore, which also interfered with the proper closing of her cloak. The night air rushing by felt cold, and she would have enjoyed bundling up against it.

But they were on their way, and that was what counted— even though their original plans had had to be changed. Angus was dressed in some of his new finery, already playing the fine gentleman. She should have been richly dressed was well, with only Cam in his original clothes playing their coachman. Once into London they were to have sold the coach and horses, and then three rich young people would have booked passage to the colonies . . .

But Angus was wounded, and couldn't be expected to use a sword if someone tried to rob them. Cam, as their driver, could retain his bow, but a sword would have looked suspicious. That meant their face-to-face protection until they reached London would have to be Rianne, and she couldn't be expected to fight in skirts. It wasn't that she minded not wearing a beautiful gown on her first visit to London . . . but she'd dreamed of the time so often, seeing herself sweep grandly along a street . . .

I suppose I'll have to save the sweeping for when we come back with our fortunes made, she thought with a wry smile. *And maybe it's better this way. I can't afford to meet anyone I know, after all. Angus says that if we take lodging near the docks that won't happen, and we'll save money on top of it. Money. I wish we had more . . .*

It had occurred to Rianne that she could have taken one or two things from the brute's house, things he would have been able to replace once her inheritance was given over to him. But even if she'd thought of it at the time, she probably wouldn't have done it. She didn't want *anything* of that man's, even if it was due her. Like that wedding gift he'd offered, that magnificent necklace with the matching earrings. It had been put into her bedchamber with her clothing, as though it really did belong to her now . . . the way *she* belonged to *him* . . .

You do not belong to him, she told herself with an inner growl. *Angus was wrong in thinking he might come after you, so you have nothing to worry about. No matter what he tried to make you believe, he doesn't want you and you certainly don't want him . . . Look at those dark trees rushing by as this road takes you farther and farther away . . . No, not away, but to . . .*

Rianne bit her lip as she forced away the foolishness of her thoughts, and then she noticed that they were slowing. A quick look out of the window showed her a gentle river of light in the darkness, on their left a small distance ahead. Lanterns, of course, to show travelers where it was possible to stop.

"I think we've found a roadhouse," she told Angus, suddenly aware of how hungry she was. "I hope their food is decent."

"As long as it's served at a table that doesn't move," Angus muttered in answer. "And they haven't run out of ale . . ."

Rianne smiled at that, telling herself he now sounded

stronger. He was going to be all right after all, just as they would all be. In just a little while . . .

Cam pulled into the drive of the roadhouse and up to its front door, but no one came running from the stables to see to their horses. Rianne moved past Angus to use the door on his side of the coach, and once she was on the ground Cam came down to join her.

"It looks like I'll have to take care of the horses myself," he said, frowning at the dimness of the stables. "I suppose most travelers don't arrive this late, so there aren't any night boys. First I want to get Angus inside, though. How is he doing?"

"He's hoping they haven't run out of ale," Rianne answered with a smile that didn't last long. "If there's a physician anywhere around here, I think we ought to—"

"No physician." Angus's voice came from above them, drawing their attention. "Even if we had the time to stop, we wouldn't want to leave a trail *that* clear. We'll be in London in just a few hours, and then we can stop somewhere and sleep. Tomorrow—"

"All right," Cam interrupted with some small annoyance. "You don't have to go through our whole schedule for the next month. Do you need help getting out of there?"

"Yes, thank you, boy," Angus answered with a grin that was faint, but definitely a grin. "Your lord would appreciate the aid of your strong right arm."

"I'd be happier giving my 'lord' my strong right fist," Cam muttered, then grudged a grin when Rianne chuckled. If Angus was feeling well enough to tease him, then everything really would be all right.

Once Angus was out of the coach, he insisted on walking alone. Rianne followed a step behind, ready to help him if he should need it. His gait was the least bit unsteady, but it got him in the door of the roadhouse and within sight of the tables. The common room was ahead and to the left, spread out around the small entrance area just around the door. To the right was a stairway with a counter in front of it, two closed doors, and one archway beyond the counter.

A small man in an apron stood in front of the counter rather than behind, and one look at Angus's clothing brought him quickly forward. The glance he gave Rianne was almost as outraged as the stares of his patrons, but apparently he was more interested in pleasing a gentleman than in being offended by what the gentleman's companion had the nerve to wear.

"Gud evenin', m'lord," the man slurred. "Ye be wantin' a room?"

"I'm wanting a decent meal in privacy," Angus answered in the sneering tones of a haughty young gentleman. "Is it possible to get that here, or must I continue on to the next house?"

"No, no, a meal ye'll get," the man quickly assured him, glancing again at Rianne. "Fer two, y'r lordship?"

"For three," Angus corrected. "My man is currently seeing to the horses, but he'll join us as soon as he's through. I won't have him sickened by kitchen leavings while I still need him."

"No, o'course not," the man agreed, bobbing as he bowed while moving backwards. "This way, y'r lordship."

The small man finally turned, and then was more easily able to lead them to the arched opening that wasn't quite in line with the front door. Angus followed him without glancing around even once, but Rianne hadn't been able to do the same. The lamplight had shown her more than a dozen men seated at the tables in the common room, all of them with drinks and many of them taking that previously noticed interest in the new arrivals. None of them seemed to have swords or pistols, but Rianne knew she would feel better once Cam came in.

Beyond the arch was a dining area for those who were gentry, and the small man hurried around lighting lamps. What came to view was a fairly large room with three tables, a good deal more distance between the tables than there was in the common room. The walls were a light-yellow that had darkened from dirt and the passage of time, and the skimpy yellow velvet hangings reminded Rianne of a dowager too old to look good even in the most expensive of gowns. The chairs around the tables were darker yellow and upholstered, but seemed to be covered by a layer of dust.

Despite the apparent evidence that members of the gentry usually passed this house by, Angus went directly to the center table and sat. He deliberately positioned himself facing the archway, then threw open his cloak with his right hand. Although he wasn't able to use his sword he still wore it, a pretense that should help to discourage would-be robbers. They'd have no way of knowing he was wounded, and so would see nothing but another opponent.

Or so Rianne hoped as she took the chair to Angus's right, first removing her own cloak and putting it over the back of a chair at the next table. She was good enough to face any single opponent without worrying, but one of the tables in the common room had held five or six men. What if a group like that came at them? Would a single sword be enough to make a difference?

"Bring me ale while the food is being prepared," Angus directed, barely glancing at the small man. "A pity it can't be wine, but in a place like this I don't dare. And something to nibble on as well, and do try not to drag your feet so."

The man bobbed his way out of the room, obviously impressed with his newest guest, and Angus flashed Rianne a quick smile.

"How'd I do?" he asked in a very soft voice. "Working those hours at Riniman's Inn brought me more than the extra money I wanted. Was I offensive enough?"

"*I* probably would have thrown something at you," Rianne answered with her own smile, ignoring the sweat on his forehead. "You sounded like every suitor I ever had . . . Angus, the housekeep noticed that you didn't seat me first. Maybe you didn't remember—"

"I remembered," he interrupted, putting his hand over hers. "As often as we went over those lessons, I'll remember to my dying day. But Ree—I think *you've* forgotten. You're wearing breeches and a sword, not slippers and a gown. Would a lordling like me play the gentleman with the sort of girl *you* probably are? I really don't think so.''

"I hadn't thought of that," she admitted with raised brows, then looked at him with what had to be very visible curiosity. "Ah—just what sort of girl *am* I?"

"I refuse to answer that," he said with a wider grin. "At least not while you can use a weapon and I can't. And I think you'll have to change clothes before we look for temporary rooms in London. There won't be many questions asked out here, but once we get there we don't want *any*."

She nodded her agreement, glad Angus was there to think of things like that. He'd picked up things from reading and talking to people that no one would ever have told *her*, and all of it had gone into their planning.

The housekeep was back rather quickly with a tray, which held a flagon of ale and a pewter cup as well as bread and cheese. Angus let the man fill his cup before gesturing him out, then took a good swallow before turning to Rianne again.

"You can use my belt knife on the bread and cheese," he said, handing over the weapon. "If they looked a little fresher I'd do it myself, but at this point wasting my strength would be stupid. And about that question you asked earlier, concerning what kind of girl you are? I don't think the housekeep knows either, at least not precisely. He didn't bring a cup for the ale for you, but he also didn't bring tea. He just may have seen a girl in breeches before, but certainly not with a sword."

"Is that good or bad?" Rianne asked, slicing off two small pieces of cheese for herself and Angus before trying the bread. It might have been fresh earlier in the day, or possibly the day before . . .

"We'll find out if it's good or bad by what happens afterward because of it," he answered in a cheese-induced mumble. "Hmm. Not as bad as I'd thought it would be.

Better than the dried beef Cam and I had for lunch, and a lot easier to chew. Ah, thank you.''

He took the second, larger slice of cheese she handed him and began to devour it, leading Rianne to believe he hadn't had much—if any—of that dried beef he'd mentioned. She took another slice herself, but not because she found it as good as Angus did. There had been cheese on her lunch tray at the brute's, cut into small, neat squares, fine cheese with a delicate flavor . . . But she'd been a captive, and now she was free . . . Shouldn't she be forgetting what had gone before . . . ?

Forgetting is easier when you have something else to think about, so Rianne went back to dreaming about what they would do when they reached the colonies. There were so many choices that they might decide to do two or three things at the same time, depending, of course, on how much of a stake they had to work with and how much things cost. If necessary they could add to their stake by all getting jobs, even her. She hadn't been serious when she'd told the brute she expected to work for him, but there would certainly be other opportunities he had no part of . . .

"At last," Angus said, bringing her back to the present. "Set it down there, my girl, and go back for the pot of tea your master seems to have forgotten."

A kitchen girl had brought a tray containing three large bowls, and she'd lost no time smiling at Angus and wiggling her body at him. When Angus dismissed her, the girl glared at Rianne before turning and flouncing out. Rianne wondered if the girl knew how ridiculous she looked, and then wondered if *Angus* thought she looked ridiculous. If he'd been alone and unhurt, would he have enjoyed the girl's obvious advances? How *did* men look at these things?

"I'd love to know what that expression on your face means," Angus said after sniffing one of the bowls. "If I didn't know better, I'd wonder if you had already tasted this—stew."

"I was just trying to figure something out," Rianne said with a brief smile and a shake of her head. "It wasn't important, but a good meal is. Are you saying the food is inedible?''

''I'm saying we had better even at the hostlers' table,'' he answered with his own headshake. ''But Cam and I should be able to get it down, and even keep it there. You, though . . .''

''Whatever it tastes like, I'll manage,'' she assured him, then looked around. ''But speaking of Cam, where is he? Should it be taking this long to see to the horses?''

''He had to cool them down before he could water them,'' Angus said, obviously trying to calm her worry. ''He'll show up in another minute or two and accuse me of getting wounded on purpose, just so that he would have to do all the work. Ree . . . I didn't know whether to mention this or not, but I think I'd better. That kitchen girl noticed, so I'm afraid others will, too.''

''Noticed what?'' Rianne asked, completely confused. ''Angus, what are you talking about?''

''Your wedding ring,'' he answered heavily, a compassionate look in his dark eyes. ''You're still wearing it. I don't know if you've kept it on on purpose, but it could cause trouble for us. You know we decided a long time ago not to have *me* pretend to be your husband. You wanted it to be *you* who accomplished things, not some man's wife. I understand how you feel, but giving yourself an absent husband could be a lot worse.''

Rianne nodded as she looked down at her hand, having completely forgotten about the ring. She hadn't wanted to be shadowed by even a pretend husband in her new life in the colonies, and now here she was, wearing the ring of a man she didn't even like. It was stupidly mindless, but the slip could be taken care of easily enough. She reached toward the ring with the intention of removing it—

''Well, hain't it nice'n cozy in 'ere,'' a gruff voice said, immediately drawing Rianne's attention. ''Better'n what *we* was gi'en.''

A chorus of agreement came from the men behind the first, the sort that encourages and eggs someone on. The speaker was a dirty lout in old and well-worn homespun, with worn-out boots and a strip of leather for a belt. He had a full beard that looked like it had strained his food for decades, an unappetizing substitute for what his receding hairline had lost. Two of the men behind him also had full beards, while the other two were obviously trying to grow them. The four followers were a good deal younger than their leader—who also wore a sword.

"Get out of here," Angus ordered in a flat-voiced way, nothing but arrogant confidence showing. "If we feel the need to have riffraff around us, we'll be sure to send for you."

"Hain't no need," the spokesman said, even while some of his followers looked ready to obey Angus. "We's a'ready 'ere. Gold's whut we want, an' it's whut we'll 'ave. An' sum visitin' wiv yon chicky. Give it 'ere, else we'll take yer life 'long wiv it. An' keep th' chicky."

He showed heavy yellow teeth in a grin that let them know how much fun he was having. This was a man who enjoyed terrorizing people and hurting them, a man who attracted weaklings as followers so they might share in cruelty by proxy. Rianne's pulse had begun to thud when the men first appeared, but now a coldness rose inside to still all fear. What she felt was disgust and fury—a fury that was quickly growing beyond her control.

" 'Keep the chicky,' " she mimicked as she rose, pushing her chair back with one booted foot. "You couldn't keep quiet if you were mute. Go find a rabbit to frighten, you slime. No one here is impressed."

"Ree, wait for Cam!" Angus hissed low, trying to put a hand on her arm. "You can't face five of them by yourself!"

"They're probably the reason Cam isn't in here yet," she countered, pulling her arm free as the fury rose even higher. "If they've harmed him I'll kill them all, so help me God, I'll—"

"Slut!" the balding man spat, his eyes narrowed to slits as he foamed over what Rianne had said to him. "Ye thinks wearin' a blade's good enow t' send men a-scurryin'. Well, *this* 'ere man don' scurry fer *no* slut. Better get t' beggin', y'quean . . .''

After calling her a whore he stepped forward and began to haul out his sword, which was all Rianne needed to see. No one who really knew how to use a blade drew that sloppily. He'd accused her of wearing a sword just for show, but that's what *he'd* been doing. So few members of the lower classes had blade skill that he'd probably never before been challenged.

But that was about to change. Rianne drew smoothly as she moved away from the table, and then she went *en garde*. The peasant continued to glare as he came closer, too ignorant to recognize her stance. He faced her fully, as broad a target as it was possible to be, and then he yelled and charged. The way he held his weapon, raised well above his right shoulder, said he meant to beat her to death with it.

Rianne flicked her weapon hard before slipping out of the way, and when the man turned to face her again his glare was filled with pain. Her point had slashed a diagonal cut left to right across his body, and blood flowed out through the ruined homespun. She felt suddenly odd seeing that, the first blood she'd ever intentionally spilled. Visions of Angus's wound rose before her, but she pushed the picture angrily away.

"Luck, 'at's all, luck," her opponent muttered, licking dry lips behind an obvious throb of pain. He was lying to himself to bolster flagging courage, and the other men who now stood to Rianne's left seemed to know it.

"Don't stare, ye fool, *get* 'er!" one of them shouted, more than brave with the other three around him. "Are ye man 'r rabbit?"

Rianne's opponent growled wordlessly at that, the shame he felt darkening his skin. But he also obviously felt fear, which surprised her. Did everyone who terrorized others have their own hidden cache of fear?

"If you come at me again, I'll kill you," she told the man abruptly, trying to sound as serious as the brute had in the training barracks. No threats, just promises, she remembered, but somehow it seemed easier when *he* did it. And more believable. Her opponent tightened his fist on his hilt even as he got a desperate grip on his courage. His sneer said he doubted she could kill *anything,* and then he was screaming as he raced at her again.

Rianne knew that the purpose of screaming when you attack is to freeze your opponent with fear, to make him unable to defend himself against you, and for that reason she usually ignored all noise. But this time it wasn't one of her brothers, coming at her with a practice weapon. The man screaming like a *ban-sidhe* really meant her harm, and her response was more trained reflex than thought. Her swordarm leaped out and stiffened even as she shifted her weight hard forward . . .

And the next instant he had impaled himself on her blade, right through the center of his chest. His forward rush, combined with her lunge . . . The man began to cough blood, horror in his glazing eyes. As he staggered back, Rianne let go of her sword without trying to pull it free. She hadn't really meant to *kill* him . . . !

One hand to her mouth to keep the illness inside, Rianne watched her former opponent fall bonelessly to the floor. He still gripped his sword in his fist, tightly as though he couldn't bear to lose it. *Her* sword dangled from his chest, the length of it showing the very end must be poking out his back. There was absolute silence from everyone—until the dead man's followers looked at her almost as one and began to snarl. Knives appeared then, long, wicked-looking knives, and the fury in their eyes said they meant to take their vengeance.

"Leave her alone!" Angus shouted, forcing himself to his feet. "If you try to hurt her, I'll—"

He'd started to draw his own sword, but he moved too fast and too carelessly. His words broke off as his face went white, and he groped for the table edge to keep himself erect. Rianne could see he was close to passing out, which meant he'd been lying about how well he was doing. The last thing she wanted right then was more to do with weapons, but if those animals killed her they'd certainly

kill Angus as well. She couldn't let that happen, no matter
how sick she felt.

It was only two steps to the table, and then Rianne had
Angus's belt knife in her hand. She turned to the four men
in the doorway, silently ordering her hand not to tremble,
and she was almost successful. But she also had very little
idea how one fought with a knife, aside from holding the
knife out and away from one's body. Two of the four hesitated, but the one who had urged her former opponent on
to his death spoke again.

"See how she shakes," he gloated, pointing with the
hand that held no knife. "Ye'll not be touchin' *us* wi' that,
slut, leastways not held *so*. Nor any ways, I be thinkin'."

And then he began to move toward her, first making certain the others joined him. Just to be on the safe side they
would all attack at once, giving Rianne no real opportunity to defend herself. A pack of craven animals who
weren't even her size, but who would still be able to pull
her down. And after her, Angus . . . and Cam, if he wasn't
already dead . . . She couldn't stand the idea of failing
them . . . Bad enough *she* would die without more of—
Do *something, damn it!*

That silent but frantic demand brought her forward two
steps, not very steadily but definitely determined. If she
hurt them badly enough before they killed her, they'd
probably run off and leave Angus alone. At the very least
she had to try. She gathered herself for a rush just as they
seemed to be doing the same.

Suddenly the sound of a pistol shot made them all cry
out in joint protest. But it certainly got everyone's attention, including Rianne's. She watched the four brutal bullies whirl around with widened eyes, and could imagine
their eyes going wider still when they saw the man who
had fired the pistol. A giant with dark-red hair and cold
gray eyes, followed by other men who looked almost as
dangerous . . .

"My next shot won't be aimed at the ceiling," the big
man said, drawing a second pistol. "Who wants it?"

The four seemed to shrink in on themselves, a clear sign

that there would be no more trouble from them. Rianne simply closed her eyes, feeling as though she'd wandered into a nightmare. It shouldn't have been possible for things to get worse after your life had been saved, but that was exactly what was about to happen.

"Get them out of here," that deep voice ordered. "I'll decide what I want done with them as soon as I take care of other business first."

Other *business*, Rianne noticed he said, opening her eyes long enough to get back to her chair at the table. Angus, also seated, was trying to pull himself together, but Rianne just put her elbows to the table and her fingers to her eyes and waited.

"So, wife, you decided to take a short trip," the deep voice said once the sound of footsteps faded away. "And you indulged in some light exercise as well. Aren't you going to introduce me to your traveling companion?"

"I won't let you hurt him," Rianne said, discovering that she was too tired for her voice to tremble. "I don't care what you do with me, but you will *not* hurt *him.*"

"Never mind me," Angus interrupted, clearly fighting to put strength in his voice. *"She's* the one who won't be hurt, or so help me God, I'll—"

His words broke off as they had once before, and Rianne uncovered her eyes to see him struggling against pain again. She started to go to him, but the brute was there first on his other side.

"Now I know which one *you* are," he muttered, beginning to pull Angus's shirt out of the way. "Sit still and let me look at this . . . Oh, *that* was clever. It could have cost you your life, but it certainly was clever."

"What is it?" Rianne asked, needing to know why Angus was so tight-lipped. "What's wrong?"

"He covered the wound three inches thick with bandaging, then put a layer of waxed cloth over the bandages," the brute answered. "That cloth would be enough to protect a loaf of bread from a river. He's been bleeding into the bandages, but you couldn't tell because none of it got through to his clothing."

"Angus, no!" Rianne's protest was filled with horror, but her brother weakly waved it away.

"Rianne, yes," he contradicted. "We couldn't wait around until my wound healed, and you know it. All I wish is that we hadn't stopped *here.*"

"If you hadn't stopped here, you probably would have died," the brute told him bluntly with disgust in his voice. "And all to satisfy the imagined needs of a willful girl. Boys follow along with stars in their eyes; men must learn to be more practical."

"If being practical means abandoning my sister, I'd rather be a boy for the rest of my life." Angus's statement had very little strength behind it, but there was no doubt that he meant every word. "And if her needs are imaginary, then you won't mind giving your solemn word that no harm will come to her. She's headstrong and sometimes foolish, but doesn't deserve to be hurt."

"Sister, eh?" the brute mused with an odd expression, then shook his head. "I'm sorry, boy, but I can't give my word about her and harm. If I'm there I'll do my damnedest to prevent it, but she could make a habit of trying to see I'm *not* there. What I *will* do is give my word to see if the habit can be broken . . ."

By then the gray ice was looking directly at *her,* the way his words trailed off making Rianne feel very uncomfortable. She thought about the possibility of his killing her, then mentally shook her head. No, there was very little chance she would be that lucky.

"What—what about our driver?" Angus asked as the brute straightened away from him. "There's a chance those thieves did something to him before coming in here."

"The third of your number is just fine," the brute answered, pausing on his way out of the room. "He tried to reach a bow when he saw us, but pistols tend to discourage moves like that. Two of my men have him outside, but they'll soon be bringing him in."

And then he stalked out of the room. Rianne exchanged a glance with Angus, but neither of them could feel much relief. Cam was all right, but only for the moment. Angus

had tried to shield him by calling him their driver, but the
brute had known the truth. He had all of them now, and
God alone knew what he would do. Rianne closed her eyes
again, and tried not to think about it. There were so *many*
things not to think about . . .

Bryan passed through the archway into the common
room, ignoring the nervous housekeep who hovered near
his counter. He and his men had had a long, hard ride,
and now they would have the ride back. Or some of them
would.

"Jake," he said, and the lanky man appeared beside
him. "Get Furnan in to take care of that boy. He's the one
I wounded two days ago, and I don't want him dead. Get
rooms for them and two of our men, as well as the boy
we have outside. Tomorrow a litter can be slung in the
coach, to give the wounded boy protection against the
jouncing. That way they can bring him and other one
back."

"An' them four motherless sons?" Jake asked, nodding
toward the four toughs who moved nervously under the
eyes of his men. Everyone else in the common room was
motionless and silent, trying very hard not to be noticed.

"Have three men take them and their late leader to the
local authorities," Bryan answered. "Make sure the authorities are told they tried to rob the wrong people—and
I'll be checking back to see what's done with them. If for
some reason they're simply set free, I'll have to mention
the fact to some of my friends. *They'll* be the ones who
find out why."

"They won't like hearin' *that,* 'specially if they been
turnin' a blind eye," Jake said with a grin. "Like as not
them four'll end up hanged pretty quick, just to make a
end to it. Do we mention it were th' lady who done for
th' dead 'un?"

"Not unless someone else mentions it first," Bryan decided. "If they do, have the men stress that it was my *wife*
who had to be bothered with defending herself and her
possessions. After that let them say how annoyed I am

that the poor little thing had to make the effort, and how much I'd like to make an effort of my own. Make sure they use those exact words: 'poor little thing.' ''

"You tryin' t' make them wet theirselves?" Jake asked with a chuckle. "Or just make sure they don't want nothin' t' do with you? Second's a sure thing, first's a damn good bet. I'll get it all movin'."

He gestured to others of the men, then joined them to pass on Bryan's orders. It was so much easier dealing with men, Bryan thought. *They* didn't take personal offense at the idea of obeying him, and when they were told to do something they just did it. No arguments, no "better" ideas of their own, no picking up and taking off without warning . . .

Furnan was already making his way toward the private dining area, so Bryan followed along to watch. That boy his wife was so concerned about—Bryan had started out the ride on Rianne's trail furious, but after a while the fury had changed to worry. And hearthurt. It had occurred to him that Rianne was running away with the help of two *men;* what if she and one of them were in love? Could that be the real reason she'd resisted him like that, the reason she'd ignored his every attempt to get closer to her?

At that point he'd nearly turned back, and now he felt an inner shudder at what would have happened if he had. What had kept him going was the determination to find out for certain, to hear the words from her own lips. When she and the boy had each offered themselves in payment for the safety of the other, Bryan had been certain his worst fears were justified. He'd been lower than ever before in his life—and then the boy had called her "sister" . . .

It now began to occur to Bryan to wonder at that. Surely if Rianne had a brother, Robert Harding would have mentioned it. Bryan leaned against the side of the arch and watched his man tend to this "brother" of Rianne's. Furnan, though without official recognition, was a better physician than most who had the name. As he leaned over his patient the boy Angus clenched his fist, plainly determined not to cry out. That meant he believed in controlling what he said and did, acting as a particular situation called for rather than simply *re*acting.

With that in mind it wasn't strange he'd been so quick to mention that he considered the girl his sister. He'd wanted Bryan to know the exact relationship between them, understanding that the girl wasn't likely to explain it herself. The boy considered her a sister, and the youngster outside was another brother.

Great, Bryan thought with exasperation. *That puts me right back to where I was before this happened. My wife wants nothing to do with me, and now sits there expecting the worst. Just look at her, so pale and shaken she ought to be passed out in a faint.*

Two more of his men walked past him, heading for the body on the floor to the left. One of them bent to grab a booted leg, but the other paused to pull the girl's sword free. He cleaned the weapon quickly on the dead man's clothing, then turned to offer it back to the woman it belonged to, who now sat with one hand shading her eyes and the other to her middle, trying not to see anything going on in the room.

So that's it, Bryan thought as he moved forward to take the weapon himself. *Part of her problem is reaction to her first kill. I've seen trained men cry like babies or be sick all over themselves after the first, so she's not doing badly at all. But I won't be mentioning that for a while. She needs to know what a really stupid move this was, that two people could have died, if not three. It's time she learned to think rather than—*

Time. The word jolted Bryan, making him think about it after hours of forgetfulness. Her stepfather was to have come to dinner this night, giving him the answer he'd been searching for. After all this time it was supposed to be over—and here he stood in a roadhouse, hours away after haring off on the trail of a runaway girl. He had to get back as quickly as possible . . .

"Jake!" he bellowed after throwing the girl her cloak, taking her by the arm, and pulling her with him out of the room. "See if there are fresh horses available for those of us going back. If there aren't we'll have to make do, but I want us out of here in no more than five minutes. Move, man!"

Jake nodded once before striding off, but even that wasn't enough for Bryan. He followed on the man's heels to shout down anyone who tried to delay them, and the girl hurried along because of his grip on her arm. She hadn't said a word, and that was very wise of her. The savagery filling Bryan would have lashed out at her as well.

If the trip out was hurried, the one going back was frantic. The horses might have been fresh but they weren't top quality, which eventually brought Bryan to cursing at them aloud. Cursing and shouting made men move faster, but those horses proved to be too much like women. It was past midnight before he stormed through the front door of his house.

"Sarah!" he shouted, standing in the middle of the hall. "Sarah, where are you?"

"Here, Bryan," she answered more quietly, appearing from the direction of the kitchen. "It's no use, he's gone."

Bryan cursed then, totally unable to keep the words inside. He'd been so *close,* and now—

"He said to tell you not to bother coming by with an apology tonight," Sarah put in as soon as she could. "Tomorrow after breakfast would be the most civilized time, and certainly your business could wait until then. He sounded as though he were trying to convince *himself,* but apparently he managed it. He left about an hour ago."

"Did he say anything else?" Bryan pressed, wondering why Harding would have to convince *himself.* "Anything at all, no matter how unimportant?"

"He didn't *say* anything, but when he found out you were riding after Mrs. Machlin he turned pale." Sarah's lower lip was between her teeth, her sight inward as she reexamined her impressions. "He seemed very shaken over her having run away, but I don't know why."

"He was probably afraid I'd renege on the deal if I no longer had what I'd wanted." Bryan was guessing, but it seemed to make sense. "He knew it wasn't the money I was most interested in . . . So now I have to wait until tomorrow. I don't know if I can."

Sarah didn't point out that he had no choice, which was very kind of her. It was his fault that it had to be done, his fault for chasing after a woman who wanted nothing to do with him . . . God, he was tired, more tired than he could remember being in years.

"So you *did* find her," Sarah exclaimed, then moved past him toward the door. "Mrs. Machlin, are you all right? Bryan, she looks so—"

"I'm going to bed," he announced abruptly, only glancing at the girl who all but slumped in the doorway. "Put her anywhere for the night, but get her up for an early breakfast. Assuming she's still here."

He went to the stairs and up them without looking back, and when he got to his rooms he poured himself a drink. At some point during the hours past he'd been hungry, but the feeling had long since disappeared. All he was left with was depression, and a serious question regarding his sanity.

He eased his aching body into the most comfortable chair in his sitting room, trying to convince himself that one more night's worth of waiting would hardly kill him. After five years he ought to be used to it . . .

But that wasn't the major problem. His wife was, and he couldn't decide what to do. Every other woman in the world understood about arranged marriages and accepted them. Only *his* wife considered it a personal and mortal insult, something to be fought with every ounce of her strength. He'd wanted her almost from the first moment he'd seen her, but all *she* wanted was to be free of him.

"And what happens if I spend the next five years trying to change her mind, but can't do it?" he asked aloud. The whisky in his glass had burned some going down, but not as much as the words he'd spoken. The way she'd thanked him for saving her life—*Do anything you like to* me, *but don't harm Angus. That* had felt good, like a kick in the privates. What did she think he was?

"That answer I already have," Bryan muttered, then drained his glass. He was an insensitive brute who had bought her, a brute she was desperate to escape from. Well, that wasn't likely to be hard to arrange, and he'd set things in motion tomorrow. After he completed his business with Robert Harding. The girl would undoubtedly be delighted when he told her . . .

He put his glass aside and stood, trying very hard not to mourn the loss of what could have been. You can fall in love with a woman and try to make her do the same with you, but if you fail there isn't much left. Especially if she's a woman like Rianne Lockwood. Was he supposed to keep her locked up for the rest of her life, hoping she never managed to find a way to escape? And if she did, the way she had that very day, would he simply go after her again, drag her back, and start it all over again?

Bryan shook his head slowly, knowing he could never live like that or make anyone else a lifelong prisoner. His own freedom was too precious to him, and in a very short time he would begin to hate himself for what he was doing. Then there would be two people hating him, and what good would *that* do? It was love he wanted, not hatred, but love can't be forced.

So he would have to let the girl go her own way, and pretend he'd eventually forget her. As if he ever would. She was everything he'd ever wanted in a woman, everything he'd never before been able to find, but she didn't want to be his. You can't force love from someone who won't give it, can't change what is to what you'd like it to be. He had instead what *was*, and he'd have to learn to live with it. And maybe, just maybe, he was exhausted enough to sleep.

Chapter 10

Rianne was awake before the maid tapped at her door, even though it had taken quite a while the night before to fall asleep. Her mind refused to stop clamoring at her, refused to give her any peace. She'd been so tired after that horrible ride, so completely drained. The shock of having killed a man, and then nearly dying herself. Of knowing that *she'd* almost been the cause of Angus's death. Of having to give up her dream of escape . . .

And then they'd arrived back at this house, and she'd had the worst shock of all. He hadn't even helped her to dismount, but had rushed inside and left her to her own devices. Hating the idea of looking weak to his men, she'd dismounted and followed as quickly as she'd been able.

Then to reach the door in time to hear him say *that*. Bryan's words came back to her, speaking to Mrs. Raymond about her stepfather: *He knew it wasn't the money I was most interested in.* He hadn't known she was there, so he couldn't possibly have said it just to fool her. He hadn't married her for her inheritance after all, but because he wanted *her*. Even her stepfather knew . . .

So what are you going to do about it? her thoughts kept demanding. The question had begun pounding at her last night, but still hadn't been answered. What *was* the brilliant and courageous Rianne Lockwood going to do? Start out, possibly, by admitting she'd been wrong?

"But I wasn't *entirely* wrong," she argued in a mutter, still not having moved out of the bed. "When a man forces you to marry him, what are you *supposed* to think?"

Maybe you should have thought to look at more than

that one act, her mind immediately countered. *He never hurt you, not even accidentally, not even when you provoked him. And you may have missed it, but he saved your life last night. In what way did you thank him, or even acknowledge that you noticed?*

Rianne was too ashamed about that to think of even a token reply. It may have been true that at first she was too shaken, and then too confused. She hadn't expected to hear what she had, nor had she thought he would bring her all the way back here just to dismiss her. Her door hadn't been locked last night, as though he no longer cared whether or not she stayed . . .

"Here's yer breakfast, Mrs. Machlin," a voice said, and Rianne looked up to see one of the housegirls with a tray. "If ye'll ring fer me when yer done, I'll help get ye dressed."

Rianne nodded distractedly, finally beginning to get up. They were supposed to be going to see her stepfather that morning, so that he and her husband could conclude their "business." Yesterday she would have been certain only her inheritance was involved, but this morning she wasn't so sure. Why would a man like Bryan Machlin be so anxious to talk to her stepfather? And why did she have the feeling there was a lot going on she didn't know about?

Those were two more questions she couldn't answer, so she put them aside while she worked at swallowing everything on her tray. She felt like she hadn't eaten in a week, especially after yesterday's rides. A coach seat was supposed to be more comfortable than a saddle, but not for a rider as experienced as she. If only her horse had been good enough to have a decent gait, it might have been a bit easier.

Rianne spent as little time as possible over her meal, and had already chosen what she would wear by the time the housegirl responded to her ring. With the girl's help she was quickly into a demure white morning gown with small embroidered flowers scattered across the skirt and bodice. Her hair was just as quickly put up and a hat added, and then she was able to leave her rooms carrying a white parasol in her gloved hands. Slippers felt strange on her feet after all the hours she'd worn boots, but they were undeniably more comfortable.

This time she found the front hall occupied, and in a way that surprised her. Mrs. Raymond was there, in a morning gown of pale blue, also ready to go out.

"Well, good morning, Mrs. Machlin," the woman said in a very—neutral—way, watching as Rianne descended the steps. "We knew you were almost ready, so Bryan has gone to have the carriage brought around. Did you sleep well last night?"

"Perfectly well, thank you," Rianne answered, finding it necessary to fight against clenching her hands. She was now forced to admit that she hated the way the woman spoke about Bryan Machlin, so familiarly and almost intimately. *We* knew, she'd said, and *Bryan* has gone. Them together with her excluded.

"I've been asked to accompany you and Mr. Machlin to Mr. Harding's house," the woman went on as Rianne stopped beside her. "Our visit shouldn't take long, and then there's something Mr. Machlin wants to tell you."

Something you already know all about, Rianne thought. *Just the way you know how long "our" visit will take. And it's suddenly become "Mr. Machlin," as though you've just remembered that's the way you were supposed to talk about him. I'm really beginning to dislike you, Mrs. Raymond, and I think I'd enjoy asking you a few pointed questions in private . . .*

"And what is it Mr. Machlin wants to tell me?" she asked instead, still keeping the conversation cool.

"It has to do with your freedom, and how soon it will be available," the answer came, just as cool. "Mr. Machlin will tell you all about it, as soon as he has a moment. His business here is almost over."

"Ladies, the carriage is ready," a man in livery announced as he came in, holding the door open for them. "Mr. Machlin asks that you hurry."

Mrs. Raymond started immediately for the door, but

Rianne, although upset, was right behind her. That comment about her freedom bothered her, and she wanted to know why there was that much of a need to hurry. She really burned to know what was going on, but couldn't bring herself to ask. But it wasn't as though she would never find out . . . She would be right there to see for herself . . .

Outside, the carriage waited, all right, but not all by itself. Half a dozen men sat mounted behind it, the same men who had returned with them the night before. They looked ready to start a small war or end one, and Rianne couldn't help wondering which it would be.

Bryan Machlin himself stood beside the carriage steps, already helping Mrs. Raymond up them into the open vehicle. Those cold gray eyes touched her in turn, and the pleasant wish for a good morning she'd decided to greet him with died in her throat. He was looking at her but apparently not seeing her, and was obviously not interested in conversation. Rianne took a seat opposite Mrs. Raymond, leaving more than enough room beside her, but when her husband joined them he didn't seem to notice. Without hesitation he sat beside Mrs. Raymond, and then they were off.

The ride to her stepfather's house didn't take long, not at the pace their driver kept to. The trip was a silent one, but not deliberately so. Everyone seemed lost in their own thoughts, Rianne being no exception. When they reached their destination they all got out again, and Harms, the house steward, opened the door to them.

"Please come in, ladies, sir," he invited, surprising Rianne. She'd never before seen Harms looking flustered. "Mr. Harding will certainly be with you as quickly as possible. We were told he expected guests this morning, but somehow he seems to have overslept himself. His valet is rousing him now . . ."

They followed the man to a small sitting room, where refreshments were offered and refused. Rianne took a chair without saying anything, but her mind jumped around in agitation. Her stepfather had *never* slept late, not in all the years she'd known him. What is heaven's name was going on?

The answer to that question, at least, came rather quickly. There was a disturbance out in the hall, and then a muffled scream. When they hurried out to see what was going on, they found one of the maids being led away in tears. Her stepfather's valet stood white-faced beside Harms, who was himself visibly shaken.

"Sir, ladies, I regret to inform you—" Harms's voice, none too steady, broke then. He cleared his throat, did it a second time, then looked directly at Rianne. "Mrs. Machlin, the staff and I offer our most sincere condolences. It's my unpleasant duty to inform you that Mr. Harding has—passed on to his final reward. If you feel faint, I'll send for a girl at once . . ."

Rianne felt more astounded and disbelieving than faint, and her reaction was the mildest of the three. Mrs. Raymond gasped with eyes wide and one hand to her mouth, and Bryan Machlin took her stepfather's valet by the scruff of the neck.

"Show me to his rooms!" he ordered in a voice like doom with an expression to match. "Move!"

He thrust the valet ahead of him toward the stairs, and the smaller man was no fool. He all but ran to keep ahead of his giant pursuer, and Mrs. Raymond quickly followed. Rianne, not about to be left behind, ignored Harms's solicitude and hurried after the others.

Rianne hadn't been to her stepfather's sitting room in many years, but it hadn't changed much. More brocade than leather, many shades of blue and green alternating with gold, few books, no weapons, and spotlessly clean. They all passed through it quickly and continued into his bedchamber, where the entire party stopped to stare.

Mrs. Raymond turned away from what the room's bed held, but Rianne forced herself to look. If she hadn't known it was her stepfather, she never would have recognized him. His body lay grotesquely twisted amid disarranged covers, and his face was bloated and almost

black, with staring eyes bulging hard from their sockets.
Rianne swallowed a couple of times, almost wishing she'd
gone hungry that morning.

"Musta had a fit, like," offered the valet, Arthur. "Him
in bed, an' none near enough t' call to. Thrashed around
t' reach th' bell cord, but din't make it nohow."

"Why wasn't there anyone near enough to hear him
having—the fit?" Machlin asked in a hard but steady voice.
"Don't you sleep in the servant's chamber near this
room?"

"No, sor, not fer some time," Arthur replied, beginning to look really pale. "Din't want the botherin' uv
others about him, Mr. Harding din't. Made me take a
room in th' next corridor . . . Beggin' yer pardon, sor,
but it's there I'd like t' be goin' right now."

The big man waved a hand in dismissal, and Arthur lost
no time making good his escape. Mrs. Raymond was still
turned away, holding a small square of lace-edged linen
to her mouth.

Bryan Machlin had been staring from a few steps past
the doorway, but after a moment he walked closer to the
bed. Bending over, he reached to the top of the nightshirt
covering the body and moved it aside. Rianne shuddered
when he actually touched the body, but his sudden savage
words distracted her from illness.

"Damned if it isn't exactly as I thought," he growled,
straightening again. "The 'fit' that killed him was brought
on by the tightening of something around his neck, like
rope or braided leather. He was strangled, hanged by hand,
and it was no accident."

"But Bryan, who would do such a thing?" Mrs. Raymond protested without really turning. "Certainly not the
one we're after. What good would Harding be to him
dead?"

"Probably as much good as he'd gotten to be alive,"
the big man answered in disgust. "We knew Harding was
desperate for money and had been for quite a while. Remember what you said about him last night, that when he
said our business could surely wait until morning he

seemed to be trying to convince *himself?* Last night had to be his last chance to pay up, the last of whatever number of extensions he'd gotten."

"So why wouldn't they have waited again?" Mrs. Raymond asked. "Could one night have made such a difference?"

"There was no guarantee it *would* be only one night," he pointed out. "Don't forget how frightened he was at hearing that the girl had run off. If I hadn't found her and brought her back, he thought I'd probably refuse to honor our agreement. And I have the feeling he knew by then that I hadn't used my legal signature on the agreement. It would have been his—associate—who told him, along with the fact that he had no legal recourse. I could have refused for any reason at all, and that would have been the end of it. They must have decided he would be most useful as a horrible example to whoever else they have their claws into. It would be ridiculous to think their only victims were Harding and Ross."

"Do you think they realize you are Ross's brother?" Mrs. Raymond asked, turning at last but only to look at the man she addressed. "That you were going to demand answers from Harding in exchange for the money? He could have been killed to keep him quiet."

"It's possible but not very likely," the big man answered with a shake of his head. "Ross was using Mother's family name, remember, trying to do as the rest of us and make good without trading on Father's name. Since I chose a name to use almost at random, no one would have connected us until Ross was successful and his family ties became known. Ross could have gotten clear of any trouble by asking the rest of us for help, but he was too ashamed to do it. He killed himself instead, and now I'll never find the man who drove him to it!"

The big man turned away in a palpable effort to control his pain, and Mrs. Raymond hurried over to put a commiserating hand on his arm. Both of them had apparently forgotten Rianne was there, so she turned and went to a chair in the sitting room. She had a lot to think about, but couldn't quite decide where to start.

From what she'd heard, her stepfather had been even worse than she'd thought. He'd associated with people who killed and drove innocent men to suicide, and all the while he'd pretended to be upright and moral. He'd always tried to set such a fine example—

But no, that wasn't right. The time so long ago . . . he'd known about it . . . had even been made to watch . . .

She shook her head hard, chasing away those nightmare memories. She always tried not to think about that, but she'd been badly disturbed by the sight of the second dead body in as many days. She drew her gloves off and pulled a square of linen from her reticule, using it to dry the moisture on her forehead. Other things to think about . . .

Yes, other things. Like the fact that her husband hadn't been a friend of her stepfather's after all. He'd been following a plan to trap Robert Harding into giving him information, and marrying her had only been a part of that plan. That had to be what Mrs. Raymond had been talking about, the freedom that would soon come with the end of Machlin's plan. Rianne was tempted to feel hurt to know that she didn't mean anything to him after all, but she was used to being disregarded in favor of other things . . .

Disregarded . . . Her mother had been so desperate to rejoin her dead husband, she'd disregarded the presence of a living daughter. Robert Harding, when he hadn't been after her to marry, had forgotten about her for days and weeks on end. The servants, beyond tending to her basic needs, usually pretended she wasn't there even when she walked into a room where some of them happened to be. The years had taught them that Mr. Harding, their actual employer, had no objections to such behavior on their part. Even her suitors, those men who had been so eager for her attention . . . how many times had the whole group of them gotten into a polite argument about something they considered important, and forgotten all about her? Then one or another of them would remember why they were supposedly there, come charging after her, and the others would follow. All of them had their reasons for disregarding her at one time or another, undoubtedly real and solid reasons that could easily be explained.

But Bryan Machlin's reason was a good deal more important than most of the others had been. Someone had caused his brother's death, and he was searching for that someone. In his place she would have done the same, to take the life of anyone who brought harm to Angus or Cam . . .

As had been done to that man so many years ago. Suddenly, memories Rianne fought a constant battle to suppress rose to the surface once again. She sat motionless in the chair, fear tingling along her arms and legs, her inner sight forced back to view that horrible incident once again. She'd witnessed it accidentally, and had been too young to hide her presence . . .

"Stop it, just stop it!" she whispered to herself, fighting the rising illness. "You don't want to remember that, so stop doing it!"

A thing which had always been easier said than done. And those memories had never been so strongly persistent, refusing to be chased away. But why now, after all this time? Rianne didn't know, any more than she knew how to stop it. But she knew she *must* stop it, or she would be very sick. That was a certainty, and an imminent one.

The chair was her only solid anchor to normality in a sea of storming madness. Rianne clung to it with both hands, eyes closed as she searched for the reason behind the hell she was being put through. And there *was* a reason, she knew that, but when the first hint of it came to her she very nearly passed out. *No, not that, please, there has to be another way . . . !*

"It's all right, just get a grip on yourself, you don't have to look at that again." The deep voice came from somewhere far off, sounding as though it had repeated the same words over and over. Rianne became aware of the arm around her shoulders, and opened her eyes to see Bryan Machlin crouched beside her.

"You really shouldn't have looked in the first place,"

he said, those cold gray eyes more concerned than accusing. "Are you still trying to prove how tough you are?"

"If I were, it would be clear I didn't succeed," she answered with as much of a smile as she could manage. "You're sure he was killed by the same man responsible for your brother's death?"

"So you heard that," he said, taking his arm back as the expression in his eyes changed. "Yes, I'm absolutely sure it was the same man and I'll question the staff, but I don't expect to learn anything. The man I'm after is too careful to let himself be seen accidentally."

"But hasn't always been," Rianne muttered, feeling the sweat start again. Bryan Machlin frowned at that, but before he could question her Mrs. Raymond rejoined them.

"I'm certain you were right, Bryan," she said, coming out of the servant's room. "The valet said this servant's room hasn't been occupied in years, but the last thing it looks is unused. The bed sheet *isn't* clean and unused, the washbasin isn't quite spotless, and the pitcher still had a few drops of water in it. Someone slept in that room for at least one night, and I'll wager it wasn't the first time."

"But it was definitely the last," he said, then turned those eyes on Rianne again. "What did you mean a moment ago? That the man hasn't *always* been too careful to let himself be seen? You don't mean—"

"That *I* saw him?" Rianne finished when he didn't. "Yes, I'm afraid that's exactly what I mean. I don't know his name, but I'll never forget his face. Not if I live to be a thousand."

The last of her words weren't strong enough even to be a whisper, but Bryan Machlin still heard them. His arms circled her and he held her to him, one hand patting her back while he made nonsense sounds of comfort. It would have been nice if he'd done that for a reason other than casual concern, but Rianne wasn't about to lie to herself. He was a decent man and therefore concerned, but that's all there was to it.

"It—isn't easy for me to talk about it, but it's more than

time I did,'' Rianne said after another moment. "I've always tried to forget . . .''

"No, wait,'' the big man said, leaning back to touch her hair. "Why are you doing this? Why are you suddenly willing to tell me what you know?''

"You saved my life yesterday,'' Rianne answered simply, giving him the reason that had come to her. "Mine and Angus's and probably even Cam's, and I said not a single word in thanks. That wasn't fair *or* decent, and I like to think I'm both. The best way to prove that is to give you what help I can.''

"I see,'' he answered, that strange expression in his eyes again. Almost as if he were disappointed . . . "Well, I appreciate the effort, and I gratefully accept. Truthfully, I'm too desperate to do anything else. Let's go back to my house, and we can—''

"Bryan, wait a minute,'' Mrs. Raymond interrupted again. "Let's find someplace in *this* house to sit and talk. I agree we need to hear Mrs. Machlin's story, but there's something else we should do before leaving. You said Harding has a study with a strongbox?''

"Of course!'' the big man said, straightening out of his crouch. "There could be something in it to give us a clue. I wonder where Harding's keys are.''

"You don't need them,'' Rianne said, rising from the chair. That woman was *really* beginning to annoy her. "Mrs. Raymond was quite clever to remember about the strongbox, but I happen to know where my stepfather keeps his spare key. It's right there in the study.''

"Then let's go,'' Machlin said, not quite rubbing his hands. "And we'll need a private place to talk, where there's very little chance of our being overheard. There's always the possibility that one of the staff has another employer as well.''

"I know just the place,'' Rianne said, ready to lead the way out of the room. "And I could use a cup of tea . . .''

Bryan took a last look around the study he'd visited only once before, but there was nothing new to be seen.

And then it was Rianne he looked at, the woman who was supposed to be his wife. He couldn't get over how much she'd changed, and literally overnight. When she spoke to him, it was as though she spoke to another human being . . .

But there was a reason for that, and in fact two reasons. The first reason she'd mentioned in Harding's sitting room, when Sarah had excused herself for a moment and they were waiting for her to come back. She'd looked at him with those beautiful green eyes, and then she'd gently touched his arm.

"I was so sorry to hear you'd lost a brother," she'd said, her entire manner one of compassion. "I know how I would feel if— Were the two of you close?"

"Yes, it so happens we were," Bryan told her, encouraged to talk about his loss to someone who *would* understand. "My oldest brother Richard is ten years my senior, and my next brother, Andrew, is only two years younger than Richard. Ross was two years *my* junior, and we were inseparable as children. He once even took the blame for something *I* did, because I'd already gotten into trouble the week before. He said I could help *him* out someday, when we were both grown up and the trouble—and punishments—were worse. I promised him I would do exactly that—but he never gave me the chance. I think he was still trying to keep me out of trouble."

Bryan had had to turn away from her then, memories of Ross rising up to bring tears to his eyes. His brothers had been more than willing to join him on his hunt for the man who had caused Ross's death, but their father had asked them to leave it to Bryan. The grand and wonderful old man had known all about what had been between Ross and Bryan, and knew as well that his two older sons would be more of a burden to Bryan than help. They hadn't lived the hard and dangerous life *he* had, nor were they as ruthlessly dedicated.

"Please try to remember that there's still hope of catching the man," Rianne had said gently, her hand now on his arm from behind. "What you've been doing is quite marvelous, Mr. Machlin, and I admire you for acting just as I would have. When you told me that honorable acts could appear *dis*honorable before all the facts were known, you were absolutely right."

Bryan had turned to her with the intention of pointing out that that wasn't *all* he'd said, but Sarah had chosen that minute to return from refreshing herself. As soon as she appeared, Rianne began to lead them to Harding's study, and the moment for intimate discussions was gone. The second point, he'd realized after thinking about it, was that she *was* grateful for his having saved her life after all. She'd said as much, in so many words, trying to be as fair as she wanted others to be. She was an exceptional, fantastically wonderful woman—but was no closer to being his than she'd been before. She'd joined him in his quest rather than in his life, and the difference was downright painful.

"There's definitely something wrong here," she mused, staring at a sideboard without being aware of his own stare. "These carvings, and that arrangement of prettily polished stones—they weren't here when this study was my father's, or even for years afterward. There was silver and crystal on display, not cheap little knickknacks. I wonder that I didn't notice when it was changed."

"It was probably done so slowly that *no* one noticed," Bryan said. "With the estate income Harding had to spend, no one would expect him to have to sell off valuables to add to it. Did you find anything in the desk, Sarah?"

"Nothing more than casual correspondence," she answered, looking up from a drawer. "There's one from a woman begging him to answer her, but it's dated almost a year ago. I think it's here as a cruel keepsake."

"I'm not surprised," Bryan said. "At the ball I noticed he tended to strut and preen in front of the women, obviously considering himself irresistible to them. It was probably one of his major weaknesses as far as spending money went."

"Did you find anything of interest in the strongbox?"

she asked, closing the drawer she'd been examining. "This desk doesn't even have his accounts ledger."

"The most interesting thing about his strongbox is what *wasn't* in it," Bryan said, glancing at the small pile of papers he'd gone through. "His copy of the marriage agreement is there, but not our private agreement. The only other things were two rather lengthy property lists, and his will."

"His will?" Rianne echoed while Sarah exclaimed in surprise. "Let me see it."

Since Harding's property had nothing to do with the Lockwood estate, Bryan had no idea why she would want to. But he separated the will from the other papers, then handed it to her. She unfolded the document and began to read through it, and after a long moment made a sound of satisfaction.

"Yes, I thought there might be something like this in here," she said. "This is only a copy of his will, the original undoubtedly being on file with his London bankers. I know you wanted *a* name, but I suppose four are better than none."

He frowned as he quickly took the document back, and she was absolutely right. Three men were listed in the will as heirs, all of them to share equally in the estate, and the executor was named as well.

"My stepfather had no family of his own, as he kept reminding me over the years," the girl said. "Most of the funds he got were for maintaining this house for me, but he had a small private income of his own. He left that income to—'friends,' the will said, but I've never heard of any of them. And the income may not come to much, but that agreement you made with him—am I wrong in believing the amount was substantial? If *that* was added in, his estate would certainly be worth inheriting."

"Which means there's an excellent chance we now know where the agreement is," Bryan said with a slow nod. "On its way to the man in charge of settling the estate. It looks like someone is determined to make sure Harding *is* worth more dead than alive. Do you at least recognize the name of the executor?''

Rianne shrugged and shook her head, which didn't tell Bryan anything of value. Her being unfamiliar with all four men could mean all of them were involved with his quarry, or that none of them were. Direct investigation would be necessary to find out which it was.

"Does the fact that the agreement is gone mean they'll actually try taking you to court?" Sarah asked. "But that's wonderful! As soon as we see which of the three heirs is pressing the hardest, we'll know who the guilty one is."

"It might not be any of the heirs, just someone behind one of them," Bryan pointed out. "Whoever this executor is, *he's* the one who'll be doing the pressing, and even *he* might not know what's going on. Our quarry loves to stand in the shadows while puppets do his work for him . . . Let's go somewhere else. This room is beginning to depress me."

Bryan copied down the names and addresses of the three heirs and the executor, and then they returned everything to where it belonged. As soon as that was done Rianne took up the lead again, guiding them to a side hall where she yanked on a bell pull. Almost instantly a houseman appeared, and it seemed very much as though he'd run.

"Set up a table for three on the second veranda, right near the fountain," the girl told the houseman without actually looking at him. "Tea and small cakes, and as quickly as possible, please."

"Ma'am," the man acknowledged with a stiff bow, and then he disappeared. He was back almost immediately with two others like himself, and all three of them went into a room just off the hall.

"We might as well wait outside for them to bring the table and chairs," the girl said casually as she walked to the door and opened it. "It's *such* a lovely day."

Bryan let the two women precede him, and when he stepped outside he had to pause for a moment. He hadn't seen this part of the house before, and it was unexpectedly lovely. Three wide terraces, one beyond the other, stretched down and away from the house toward a broad lawn of very green grass. The terraces seemed to be of baked and brightly colored tile, and the center one held a large fountain in its middle. The sides of the terraces were guarded by tall shade trees, leaving only the center of each in bright sunlight.

"Put the table in the shade," Rianne directed, and Bryan stepped aside to let two of the housemen by with their round burden. The third carried a small silk-seated chair, and followed those with the table. That third one stayed to position the table exactly where Rianne wanted it, while the other two rushed inside and returned with two more chairs. By then two housegirls appeared with trays, and it wasn't long before all three of them were seated with refreshments at hand. Rianne had to dismiss the five servants, or they would have stayed and hovered.

"I'm impressed," Bryan said as soon as the five had gone back inside. "I thought *my* staff was efficient and eager, but these people have them beat."

"Not really," the girl answered, giving most of her attention to pouring tea for them. "They're all terrified, and this is probably the only thing they can think of to do."

"I don't understand," Sarah said with a frown. "What are they terrified of? They can't think *they'll* be accused of Harding's murder?"

"They probably don't even know yet that he *was* murdered," the girl responded, handing a cup to Sarah. "What they're upset about is the very fact of my stepfather's death. He was to have life tenancy of this house after my marriage, with sufficient funds to keep it running smoothly. Now that he's gone it reverts immediately to being part of my inheritance, so they're trying to show what good workers they are. They're too comfortable here to want to go looking for other positions."

"But that still doesn't make any sense," Sarah protested as Bryan was given a cup. "If you grew up in this house you *already* know all about them, so why

would they put on a show? Certainly not for *our* benefit.''

"I think that's exactly what that was," Bryan said when
all the girl did was smile faintly in response to the objec-
tion. "A show put on for *our* benefit. Or mine. If the staff
of this house knew Harding would be its master for the
rest of his life, they'd make no effort to go out of their way
for a girl their master didn't get along with, and who would
never have any say over them. This eager service and all
that heartfelt sympathy earlier—it was probably meant to
show me that anything my new wife said against them was
pure vindictiveness and lies.''

"That would cover more than just not going out of their
way, I think," Sarah said with a different sort of frown.
"Were they actually cruel to you, Mrs. Machlin? All of
them?''

"I believe we came out here to discuss something other
than the staff," Rianne said, those green eyes showing her
determination to change the subject. "No one can approach without us seeing them coming, and if they sneak
up behind a tree the fountain will drown out our words.
Shall we get started?''

Bryan noticed that her gaze was now on the fountain,
but he doubted that she saw its three-tiered loveliness. She
was seeing something else entirely, something that had no
loveliness at all.

"I was about eight at the time it happened, eight or
nine," she began in a lifeless voice. "My mother was
dead only a few months, and I'd taken to wandering all
over the house. It had come to me that she might be hiding
rather than dead, you understand, and if so I wanted to
find her. I'd keep her secret from *that man,* her husband,
and she and I would have lots of happy visits.

"I wasn't supposed to go into the cellars, but it had also
come to me that *that man* might be holding her prisoner
down there. It was so much like a dungeon that it was
perfectly possible. Stone walls shining with damp, heavy
wooden doors, stable lanterns easing the gloom only a
little—if she was down there, I had to get her out. She'd

always admitted she was weak, but I was strong enough for the both of us. She had relied on my strength ever since Father had died.

"I'd crept down to the cellars that day because I'd noticed others going down. A strange man who had shown up and then seemed to spend all his time in my stepfather's study, his personal manservant, and my stepfather. *He* never went down to the cellars, not even to choose his wine for dinner. If *he* was down there, it had to be something to do with my mother.

"But it wasn't." Her voice had grown very soft, and Bryan had to lean forward to hear her. He glanced at Sarah to see that she sat stiffly, gripping the arms of her chair, looking as though she were braced against an unexpected blow. She felt the terrible pain in the girl's lifeless voice, just as he did. He thought about stopping the nightmare narrative, but he had to know.

"But it wasn't something to do with my mother," she went on in a whisper. "There was a big, empty chamber toward the back of the cellars, and the thick wooden door stood partially open. Inside was—that man and my stepfather, along with the manservant and a fourth man. The fourth man was tied to a sturdy wooden chair, and he was trying to scream around the gag in his mouth. They'd taken off all his clothes, and I could see the blood and burn marks all over his body.

" 'He's a stubborn one, all right,' the stranger said to my stepfather. 'If I'd known he would be so difficult to persuade into speech, I would have had you extend the invitation to one of his peers. We'll have to choose more carefully next time.'

" 'You're going to do this again?' my stepfather demanded weakly with horror. He acted as though he wanted to look away from the man in the chair, but didn't dare. 'If someone else disappears from my house, people will begin to get suspicious! Please don't give up on this one, I'm sure he's ready to break. Another taste of the iron, perhaps, or—'

" 'Nonsense,' the other man snapped. 'If the threat to

his manhood didn't move him, what do you imagine
would? He's already given up his life as a man to preserve
the secret entrusted to his honor, so what else would it be
possible to do? Even a spineless wonder like you should
be able to see the obvious. Amuse yourself one more time,
O, and then end it.'

"O must have been the manservant's name, because he
smiled with pleasure. There was a leather case lying open
on a high table beside him, and he took out this small
hooked thing of metal, and then . . . The gagged man
couldn't scream out loud, but I could . . .''

By then Bryan was out of his chair, crouching next to
her and holding her tight in his arms, trying to quiet the
shuddering horror pushing her breath out in gasps. She
was paler than the marble of the fountain, trembling harder
than the water drops at the central tier's lip.

"All right, that's enough for now," he decided out loud,
one hand to her neatly coiled hair. "Since I can guess
what happened next, you can save the details for another
time."

"No, no, I can't," she denied, moving protestingly in
the prison of his arms. "A lot of the memory is blurred,
so I have to try to get it straight. If I push it away again,
I may never remember it all.''

"And wouldn't that be a shame," Bryan muttered, reluctantly letting her go and returning to his chair. He'd
needed to hear the story, needed to know how much more
pain and suffering to charge against his quarry's account,
but telling it was tearing the girl apart. Even though she
was trying to pretend otherwise.

"So, I screamed," she continued after taking a gulp
of tea. "That brought me to their attention, and my stepfather was livid. He was also terrified, but the other man
calmed him down. They spoke in whispers for a couple
of minutes, and then I was escorted back to my rooms
where I spent my time until all the guests left. My stepfather was there every time a tray was brought to me, but
all the rest of the time I was completely alone.''

"To make sure you didn't tell anyone about what you'd

seen, " Bryan said with a nod. "They couldn't afford to silence you permanently, not when that would have taken your inheritance out of Harding's reach. They needed an alternate method of ensuring their safety."

"Which they found rather quickly," the girl said, clearly fighting to keep control of herself. "The day after the last of the guests were gone, my stepfather's—friend—walked in when I was taking my bath. The first thing he did was something no one had ever done before—he spoke to me as if I were an adult.

" 'Even if you tell someone, they won't believe you,' he said. 'None of the servants in this house like you, so they won't *want* to believe you. You've been haunting this place like a ghost ever since your mother died, and they think you've been spying on their private affairs. You may believe I'm lying, but I'm ready to prove the point. I'm going to do something to you, but no one will believe you when you tell them how it happened.'

"That was when he did the second thing—scraping my back with his knife." She faltered, needing to swallow hard. "It was painful, of course, but worse was the—deliberately casual way in which it was done. It seemed to annoy him that I wouldn't scream or cry, but he let it go and left. And he turned out to be correct. When a maid came to help me dress after my bath, she was horrified to find me bleeding. She demanded to know what had happened, so I told her my stepfather's friend had cut me with a knife."

The girl smiled without humor, and shook her head. "You should have seen the storm *that* caused. I was shaken hard, and then lectured about telling awful lies about a grand gentleman like my stepfather. First, the woman said, all his friends had left the day before. He *had* no more guests in the house. Second was the fact that a fine gentleman like Robert Harding would *never* associate with anyone who was capable of hurting little girls. She covered the wound, got me dressed, then marched off to tell someone about the way I'd lied."

"How long did you keep trying to tell the truth?" Bryan

asked, wishing he could smooth the fists out of her hands. Fury was clearly what she was feeling, at those who had hurt her, and those who had refused to hear her.

"He came back and did the same thing again for five days in a row," she answered obliquely, green eyes filled with a coldness Bryan had seen before only in the eyes of men. "That second day he laughed at me, because I'd been confined to my rooms for 'lying.' He took the covering off the wound and did the same thing again, but even though it hurt more than the first time I still refused to cry. He didn't like that at all, and I repeated my story when I was asked about what had happened *this* time. I repeated it every time I was asked, but after the third day they stopped asking."

"That was probably when they decided they didn't *want* to know the truth," Bryan said in a growl, wishing more than ever that he'd already caught up to that filth. "They were afraid that the same thing could happen to *them,* or maybe even worse. That slime knew they would think first of themselves, leaving you to manage as best you could. Did he ever speak to you or come near you again?"

"The last time was the last day he came," she responded, the fury now clearly tinged with illness. "He was in a rage that he hadn't made me scream or stop telling the truth, and his narrow eyes glittered with it. Before he added to the hurt on my back, he told me that was the last time he'd do it. He was leaving, and I'd never see him again.

" 'Unless you decide to be really stupid,' he said, staring down at me with those eyes. 'There will be guests in the house beginning tomorrow, and you *could* try telling them what happened. If you do they won't believe you, but I'll certainly find out. At that point I *will* return, then take you away with me. You won't enjoy living with me, but I'll find it most diverting.' "

"And you were too young to know they couldn't afford to do that to you," Bryan said, this time reaching over to pat Sarah's arm. The poor woman had gone deathly pale and looked about one step short of physical illness. When her husband got back, he'd be lucky if Jamie didn't have his ears for putting Sarah through all this.

"I'm still not sure it was an empty threat," the girl told him with a headshake. "They wouldn't have wanted to lose control of my inheritance, but sooner *that* than lose their lives. If someone had believed me and made an effort to investigate . . . Well, I had no idea who would do either thing, so I just kept quiet. That last time with the knife hurt so *much* . . . knowing it was the last time made his threat to come take me away all the more frightening . . . the thought of having it started again, and forever without stop . . ."

Once again her words broke off, her eyes closed as she fought for control. It came to Bryan that she might have told the story here, beside the house where it had happened, to keep from fouling any other place with the memory of it. But whatever the reason, it had gone more than far enough.

"All right, now you've told me everything," he said in what he hoped was a soothing way. "Now we'll just sit here for a few minutes, drinking tea and enjoying the day. Come on, lean back and relax."

He was speaking primarily to the girl, but Sarah also needed the advice. Her problem was that she shared too easily what others went through, that she felt their pain almost as strongly as they did. Compassion like that was more of a curse than a blessing, a truth she was right then proving. Bryan refilled all their cups with tea, then set an example by leaning back himself.

It was Rianne who first threw off the cloud that hovered over them. Bryan had wanted to hold her close and help her do it, but he'd felt the same thing from her that he had the other day after her bath: with those memories stirring so strongly, she couldn't bear to be touched. Someday she might be able to accept the strength of someone else's support, but now she had to do it alone the way she had as a child. She raised her cup and sipped from it, then lifted her green eyes to him.

"So what happens next?" she asked, looking and

sounding as though nothing at all had occurred. "Does he get away with it again, or is there a chance of catching up with him?"

"Those three heirs and the executor of Harding's will all live in London," Bryan answered, toying with his cup. "That means tomorrow *I* leave for London to pay them each a visit. If there's anything at all to be found, I'll find it."

"I can be ready by tomorrow," she agreed, startling Bryan out of his relaxation. "It would be easier if you could get me the clothes boxes from the coach Angus and Cam and I used, but if not I'll have them pack the rest of my things here."

"You expect me to drag you to London after what you've been through?" Bryan demanded in outrage, straightening in his chair. "What do you think I am, a complete savage?"

"Really, Mr. Machlin, *no* one is a complete anything," she murmured in answer, that same devilish look in her eyes that he'd seen the night of the ball. "And what I went through happened years ago, when I was still a child. Or were you referring to what I went through because of you and your plot against my stepfather? Now *there's* something to think about."

"I'll admit you're due an apology for that," he allowed, trying not to show the discomfort he suddenly felt. "I had no choice about forcing you into marriage, but I never meant to hurt you. And I won't add to it by putting you in danger. The man I'm after won't hesitate to kill if he finds himself cornered, and I won't expose you to that."

"Since the choice is mine, you'll have nothing to feel guilty about," she maintained, stubbornness kindling the glint in her eyes. "And how do you expect to recognize the man you're after? Without me he could tip his hat to you on the street, and all you'd do is nod in return. You *need* me, Mr. Machlin, almost as much as I need to face that cur again. Or don't you *want* to catch him?"

Bryan's jaw tightened as he gritted his teeth, the better to keep the growl he felt on the inside. The little vixen was trying to trap him, and so far had done a damned good job. He *did* owe her something for enmeshing her in his plot, and he *did* need someone who had actually seen his quarry. What he didn't want was to expose her to the danger she refused to admit would be waiting. His feelings for her hadn't changed—nor, apparently, had hers for him. Mr. Machlin, she called him, even now when they were supposed to be on the same side . . .

"We'll have to continue this argument later," he said, seeing the house steward coming down the terraces toward them. "Don't think it's settled, little one, not by a long shot. At least one of those four men ought to know what my quarry looks like, and their lives I don't *mind* risking . . . Yes, what is it?"

"I'm Harms, sir," the man who had first opened the door to them said with a bow. "I thought you should be consulted, Mr. Machlin, about when the authorities are to be informed concerning Mr. Harding's death. The body needs to be removed and prepared, after all . . ."

"Yes, of course," Bryan temporized, rubbing at his face with one hand. He hadn't thought about that at all, not with everything else demanding his attention. "Send one of your people now to tell whoever has to know. I'll wait here and speak to them, but the ladies will be returning to my house. Make sure my carriage is at the front door of the house."

"Yes, sir," the man Harms said with another bow, then turned and retraced his steps toward the house. The show of brisk and loyal efficiency was still being put on, but Bryan didn't mind. He'd take advantage of it as long as it suited him to do so, which meant at least until Harding's remains were seen to. And he'd returned from London . . .

His gaze went to Rianne, where she'd begun gathering herself to leave. There was an air of smug satisfaction about her, as though she considered their argument already won. He'd never in his life seen a woman able to recover control of herself that quickly, especially not after reliving a time of absolute horror. He'd have to come up with something good if *he* intended winning, and he was beginning to get the glimmering of an idea. *Don't count me taken yet, little one*, he thought with an inner smile. *Not quite yet . . .*

Chapter 11

Rianne strolled around the grounds near Bryan Machlin's house, knowing she'd already done everything possible to be ready for the next day. Before leaving her stepfather's house, she'd been able to order the rest of her clothing packed and sent to her. Machlin had been busy speaking to Harms at the time, so she'd been able to specify that she wanted her things by that night.

The ride back had been as silent as the ride going, with Mrs. Raymond staring into space and looking very pale. Rianne noticed that the woman seemed to have had a hard time with her story, and had obviously been trying to keep from being sick. As soon as they'd reached the house she'd hurried inside, and one of the housegirls had later told Rianne that Mrs. Raymond was lying down and had asked not to be disturbed.

"But I'm sure she won't mind if *'Bryan'* disturbs her," Rianne muttered, hating the very sound of the name. She'd *never* be able to speak it herself, not after hearing it so often on the lips of that woman. It made her so mad she wanted to kick Mrs. Raymond, and to emphasize the point she kicked at a leaf in the grass. The leaf disappeared out of sight under the hem of her day gown, leaving her with no idea about whether or not she'd missed. What she hadn't missed was how cozy those two were, each of whom was supposedly married to someone else. What she really ought to do was tell them off right to their faces . . .

But why bother? Rianne sighed as she forced herself to face the truth instead, a disappointing truth but one that couldn't be avoided. Her marriage to Bryan Machlin had

merely been part of his plan against her stepfather, nothing
to do with her personally. He'd also tricked her into his
bed, an act low enough to make her angry, but it also
wasn't unexpected. As Angus had pointed out, strong men
had a habit of taking what they wanted, something all the
books agreed with. Conventions were always disregarded
by men like that, men whose passions were so strong.
They were born to rule everything and everyone around
them, especially their women.

Which meant that that sort of man wasn't likely to want
someone like her as a wife. She wasn't the kind of woman
to let any man rule her completely, which Bryan Machlin
had already learned—and obviously hated. He'd put up
with her until then only because he had to, and now didn't
even want her around to identify their common enemy.

That identification was something she owed *him* as well
as herself, but he must be afraid he'd never be rid of her
if he took her to London. She couldn't blame him for the
belief, but that wasn't how it would be. According to Mrs.
Raymond, he was already prepared to return her freedom.
Once the one who paced her nightmares was found, she
would be gone before she became an embarrassment to
Machlin.

A small breeze touched her face, possibly the same
breeze that had joined her for lunch. She'd had the meal
brought to her outdoors, in a pretty little bower to one
side of the house. She'd shared the meal with the trees and
sky as she often did, usually because there was no one
else to share it with. Being alone was nothing new, she'd
spent most of her life alone. When the time came that was
the way she would leave . . . and never look back . . . to
save herself the sight of no one waving good-bye . . .

"So there you are," a voice said suddenly, startling her.
"For a moment I thought you'd run away again."

"When there's a trip I'm looking forward to taking tomorrow?" she asked Machlin with a faint smile after turning to face him. "Not likely. What did the authorities have
to say about my stepfather's—fit?"

"That's exactly what they decided to call it," he answered with a snort of disgust. "They must have considered the sort of people who usually guested at his house, imagined a murder investigation with *them* as suspects, and quickly gave it up. They glanced in my direction for a moment or two, but dropping a few names put an end to that. Lots of money and friends in high places are a combination they don't care to go up against."

"You can't blame them for being practical," Rianne said with a shrug. "If they tried they'd lose, and not only in the matter of proving guilt. The law seems to believe that money can buy anyone free of any crime."

"The point was more honest when it was a matter of blood money being paid," Machlin grumbled, reluctantly agreeing. "If you killed someone you became responsible for his family, and also had to pay that family a set sum of gold. Now the gold goes to those who declare you innocent, and our modern world considers that progress." He paused and looked at her more closely. "So you still think you want to go to London with me?"

"There's no 'think' about it," she answered, joining him in dropping an unpleasant subject. "I *am* going to London, so you might as well accept it. It's as much my right as it is yours."

"I don't see where risking your life can be considered a right," he countered, folding his arms as he looked down at her. "Since you admire practicality so much, you should be pleased to know I'm thinking seriously about leaving you here under guard. You won't find running away as easy as you did before, not when there are two men at your door day and night."

"That's not *fair!*" Rianne hissed, beginning to be furious with the big fool. "And it's also stupid! What if none of those four men can or will identify your quarry? By then he'll know how close you are, and will probably just move elsewhere. Do you want to lose him, maybe for good?"

"No, I don't, and that's the only reason we're discussing this right now," he replied in a very flat tone. "To be frank, I'd rather gamble that I *won't* lose him, but I'm willing to consider taking you on two conditions: that you understand that *I'm* in charge, and listen to me when I tell you to do something. If you expect to run around doing as you please, you can stay here.''

''Why do men always have to be 'in charge'?'' she demanded, more than aware of the determination in those cold gray eyes. ''What's wrong with a working agreement, a partnership of sorts—''

''I already have a partner, and you're my wife,'' he interrupted in the same tone. ''If you think obeying me for a change will be the death of you, then by all means let's preserve your life. I'll see to it that you're allowed outside your apartment once a day, but the privilege will be revoked if you make any attempt to escape. Meals will be taken in your sitting room, and—''

''All right!'' she snapped in annoyance, ending that hateful list of restrictions. ''You have to be the leader, or you won't play. Go ahead and take advantage of a helpless woman; no one will know, or even care if they do find out.''

'' 'Helpless woman,' '' he echoed with a grin, enjoying his victory. ''If all women were as helpless as you, I shudder to think what would become of men. You agree to obey me, then? And won't constantly insist that things be done *your* way?''

''Yes, I'll obey you and no, I won't insist on doing things my way,'' she confirmed with a heavy, put-upon sigh. He thought he was being clever, but there was something he'd missed. Rianne was hoping he would continue to miss it.

''I really hope you mean that,'' he said, with what almost sounded like relief. ''We'll have enough problems *without* playing games with each other. If we cooperate, we'll make progress instead of difficulties. You agree?''

''Certainly,'' Rianne said, doing nothing to avoid that steady gray gaze. She would do whatever was necessary, just as she always had, in the face of danger or not. Besides, they'd be too busy in London for him to have time to indulge in hysterics. "If that's all, I'd better see about having the rest of my things packed . . ."

"But that's not all," he said, his hand coming to her arm as she began to turn away. "You still haven't agreed to my second condition. Obeying me was only the first."

"What else can there be?" she asked in exasperation, an emotion she wasn't really feeling. Nervous was what she felt, possibly due to the new expression in his eyes. Whatever he had in mind, it was something he would refuse to be denied . . .

"If we travel together to London, we'll be traveling as man and wife," he said, his big hand still on her arm. "I've found it necessary to lie too many times in my life. Adding to those occasions when it's unnecessary is something I simply won't do. If we travel as man and wife we'll have to *be* man and wife, in all ways and not just in name. Do you want to go to London badly enough to share my bed?"

Rianne parted her lips to answer, but the usual spate of words refused to come. She could feel the faint flush in her cheeks at the bald way he'd put his demand, but not so much that she was distracted. He hadn't simply added that as an afterthought; if she didn't agree, he would leave her behind.

Which meant he was back to wanting her body. For a man who didn't intend to stay married to her, he certainly had a nerve. Once their common enemy was found, their marriage would be over even faster than it had come to be. Mrs. Raymond had been very clear on the point, but Rianne didn't need anyone else telling her that, not when it was so obvious. No man wanted a wife who gave him nothing but trouble . . .

And he was also trying to force her to stay behind. He knew how much she'd hated being in his bed on their wedding night, so he'd given her a choice that would suit him whichever way it went. If she refused he could leave her behind, and if she agreed there would be nothing to stop him from pleasuring himself. Come to that, he would probably *prefer* that she stay behind . . .

"I've already said I intend going to London," she announced as casually as possible, silently cursing the blush that refused to stop. "If I also agree to share your bed, will the next thing you ask for be an embroidered nightshirt for the occasion?"

"No, the agreement alone will do it," he answered, his grin back and widened. "You may have forgotten I don't wear a nightshirt, but don't worry about it. I doubt you'll forget again."

"If I do, I'm sure you'll remind me," Rianne murmured, wishing she could change the subject to one that would end her ridiculous blushing. And then she remembered a question she really did want to ask, one a good distance removed from blushing.

"What's wrong?" Machlin asked, apparently picking up on her feelings at once. "Is something bothering you?"

"I'd—like to ask an intrusive question," Rianne replied, forcing the words out past a great deal of reluctance. She'd seen Machlin's reaction the first time they'd discussed the subject, and she didn't want to add to his pain. "If you'd rather not answer, I'll understand, and all you have to do is say so . . ."

"Go ahead and ask," he encouraged her, curiosity shading the gray of his eyes. "If it's something I'd rather not talk about, I *will* say so."

"All right," she agreed, then plunged in before she lost her nerve. "Your brother Ross. Would it be too terrible if I asked what was done to him? I mean, to make him take his own life."

A shadow of grief brushed the big man again, but he shook it off with a small movement of his head.

"I'd say if anyone was entitled to ask that, you would have to be the one." His smile was faint as he touched her hair, but it was still encouraging. "I think I should start by explaining how my brothers and I decided on the best way to go out in the world. We all wanted to make our *own* mark, you understand, as individuals rather than as sons of our father. That way we'd know it was our own ability that got us what we had, not the name and influence of our family.''

Rianne nodded, understanding only too well the need to be one's own person. She'd thought the yearning was reserved to women alone, but apparently there were men who felt the same.

"My next older brother Andrew and I chose family names to use simply because we happened to like those names,'' Machlin continued. "It worked well for both of us, but when it became Ross's turn he decided he would do something different. He fully expected to be as much of a success as Andrew and I were, so he took our mother's family name as his own. Her family has very little money or influence, but it's an old and distinguished name and Ross expected to make it shine.

"Which he would have, if not for the man who wanted to own him.'' Machlin's face was expressionless, but Rianne felt a chill from the look in his eyes. "Ross took his first position as a clerk with a shipping company, a position that would let him support himself modestly while he looked around and decided what to invest his start-up money in. It wasn't a very demanding job, but he did have access to payroll shipping schedules that were supposed to be kept secret. He was given that access after being with the company for only three or four months, which proved his employer knew he could be trusted.

"Fortunately or unfortunately, his employer wasn't the only one who knew Ross couldn't be bribed or bought. He went out one night for a few drinks with some of his coworkers, and the quarry—or one of his cronies—managed to drug Ross. He woke up in a sleazy inn, in bed with his employer's wife, a woman who had been after him since he first began working for her husband. He'd ignored all her hints and not-very-subtle invitations, but suddenly he was there in bed with her.''

"But that's not all there was to it,'' Rianne pounced, knowing the statement as fact. "The books all say a trap like that has to have more, like someone sending a note to the woman's husband. Is that what happened?''

"Not quite," Machlin said, giving her an odd glance. "The quarry wanted to blackmail Ross into disclosing his company's payroll schedules, so he and his cronies could rob the shipments. That's why a disturbance was reported in the room where Ross and the woman were, so a constable would be sent to investigate. He walked in only a moment or so after Ross came around, and he got a good look at him and the woman. If it came down to it, the constable would have made an impeccable witness."

"What about the woman?" Rianne asked. "Was she in on the whole thing, and only just pretending to be having an affair?"

"From what I was able to learn, she'd gotten a note she believed was from Ross, arranging the rendezvous," he answered. "She expected him to be awake when she got there, thought he was drunk when she found him unconscious, but decided to wait until he came out of it."

"Exactly as she was supposed to do," Rianne said in disgust. "She might as *well* have been in on it. So why didn't Ross just make the whole thing public, letting people know he had been put in a trap because he was too honest? Some people might not have believed him, but at least it would have taken care of the blackmail problem."

"But that was the whole point, that some people would not have believed him," Machlin told her wearily. "Ross had trapped himself by choosing to use our mother's family name. Many of the old lines are very rigid in their beliefs about what is and isn't proper, and any breath of scandal at all, even if it isn't true, is completely unacceptable. The quarry knew that and thought Ross was more directly related to the family, which would have been bad enough. That he *chose* the name and then brought dishonor on it would have been absolutely intolerable, truth or not, trap or not.

"It was done and couldn't be undone, but Ross still outsmarted them. He couldn't tell the truth, but that didn't mean he had to let himself be blackmailed. He chose the oldest honorable way out, and killed himself. The problem was solved, and could be forgotten about."

The big man finished his story, and the following silence intensified the pain that had been clear in his words. He missed his brother very much, and Rianne was able to understand that.

"Your brother was obviously a very brave man," she said, putting a gentle hand to Machlin's arm. "I'm sure he knew he could go to his family for help, but chose instead to reaffirm his honor. It isn't possible to be anything but proud of someone like that, even if you happen to think he was hasty. He did what he thought was best for the people he loved, and I'm sure he did it without regret. I know you can't help being sad, but every now and then you ought to try to smile for *his* sake. That's what *I'd* want if I'd done as he had."

"You know, you just may be right," Machlin said, his eyes looking fractionally less haunted as he did smile. "Ross was the sort of man who would have been embarrassed at being mourned, but not at being avenged. And we're going to avenge him together, aren't we?"

"As long as you don't have any more requirements on your list," Rianne agreed wryly. "Like having me walk to London barefoot, for instance, or demanding that I first answer the riddle of the meaning of life. I'd better warn you that if you do come up with anything else, I'm going to start suspecting *you* of being in league with our enemy."

"How can I ask you to answer a riddle I've never even heard of?" he returned with a grin that was trying hard to look innocent. "But as far as walking barefoot to London goes, that might not be a bad idea. It would certainly keep you occupied and out of trouble, especially if I sent some of my men along to keep an eye on you. That was a very good suggestion, and I'll have to give it some thought."

"Then you've given up on demanding that I share your bed?" Rianne came back at once. She knew he was teasing her, and wasn't above doing some teasing herself. "That would only make sense, after all. I mean, you aren't going to *have* a bed on the road to London, and even if you did it wouldn't help. After a full day of walking barefoot I'll be interested in nothing but soaking my feet, and—"

"All right, all right, I surrender," he interrupted with a laugh, holding both hands up, palms toward her. "Making you walk is a terrible idea, and I'm sorry I even considered it. Do you forgive me the mistake?"

"I don't believe in forgiving men quite that quickly," Rianne informed him, trying to keep her amusement out of the haughty statement. "I'm told that hasty forgiving usually ruins a man, and women should avoid doing it whenever possible."

"I'd like to know who could possibly have told you *that*," Machlin said with a mock frown. "It's a dirty lie and probably libelous, and I just may speak to my solicitor about instituting a suit. It wasn't those two adopted brothers of yours, was it?"

"Don't be silly," Rianne said, now showing a superior smile. "It was Lady Margaret who told me that, the lady who told you on our wedding day just how terrible a person I was. You do remember her, don't you? Well, she's the one you'll have to sue, and not just for *that* bit of advice. You'd never believe how much more there is."

"Oh, yes, I would," Machlin shot back, now pretending to be appalled. "It so happens I remember the lady very well, so the suit is off. But only if you promise not to mention any of the other points. If you don't promise, I'll just have to sue the two of you."

"Oh, very well," Rianne conceded, fighting not to laugh aloud. "If you're going to let it get you *that* upset, I have no choice but to promise. After all, how would it look: the two of us just about to catch our quarry, and you suddenly bursting into tears . . ."

"Now that you already know, I can admit I have that problem regularly," he said, putting out one hand to stroke her arm. "Bursting suddenly into tears, I mean. I think it happens because of that terrible disease called the emptyarms plague, and I'm told there's only one cure for it. Let's try it and see."

The hand on her arm pulled her closer to him, and then those arms were around her as his lips lowered to hers. His kiss was gentle and undemanding, but only in the same way drawing a sword from its scabbard wasn't part of an attack. The gesture indicated more to come—of an entirely different nature. Rianne felt an odd, unexpected, but immediate tingling when his lips coaxed hers into joining in . . . and then, much too soon, it was over.

"That was *much* better than the first time, and I may even be cured," he murmured, one hand against her hair. "We'll get some more of that in tonight just to be sure, but right now we both have things to do. Earlier I thought this day would be too short, but now I know I'll find it endless. I can't wait until tonight, when I'll be able to hold you in my arms again, wife."

He released her then, but only to take her hand. Rianne felt that tingle come back when he raised her hand to his lips and kissed it while those gray eyes clung to her face. And then he was gone, striding away toward the barracks at the back of the house. Rianne just stood there staring after him, wondering why she felt so odd, wondering why he had *acted* so odd . . .

"Of course," she muttered with exasperated amusement, watching his broad back recede. "He's starting to play those games again, just the way he did on our wedding night. He knows I don't have much experience with men, and he expects to take advantage again. I wonder . . ."

The thought that came to her was a wicked one, and it made her grin. Belatedly she'd thought of a plan for their wedding night, one she hadn't, of course, had a chance to try. If he enjoyed games so much, couldn't he be expected to enjoy one of hers? It would be interesting to see how well *he* did against something he had no experience with . . . And that she was almost completely certain of . . . No woman would ever have treated *him* like that . . .

Still wearing a small smile, Rianne made her way back to the house. That brief conversation had been amusing and she was really looking forward to that night, but only because of her plan. Without the plan there would be nothing to look forward to, of course, nothing at all . . .

After getting the men taken care of and his wife's two "brothers" settled in after their arrival from the roadhouse, Bryan went back to the house. The wounded boy would be fine, the other was cautiously impressed, and he liked the looks of them both. All the new men's training would continue while he was gone, since he planned to take only four of their instructors with him. Any more than four would make his trained force overly obvious, which residents of London certainly would not appreciate.

Still, to be on the safe side, he'd sent a messenger to arrange for more of his trained men to meet them later. They would wait at a small farm about an hour's ride from London, out of obvious sight but available if he should need them . . .

Need. With everything going on he had a lot of needs, but the one that was taking most of his attention had nothing to do with the man he was after. A couple of hours earlier he'd spent ten or fifteen minutes talking to his wife, and it had been far and away the best time he'd ever had. She'd been so touchingly sweet about the loss of his brother, and then she'd joked with him the way she had when they'd first met at the ball. No threats, no arguments, just mutual teasing that had almost had them both laughing aloud.

And that was what he needed most, more of that sort of attention from the woman of his dreams. She'd even touched him gently on the arm again, a gesture more arousing than another woman's stripping naked would have been. If it had been possible he would have made love to her right there, in the grass with the sky and sun watching and laughing . . . or watching in envy of his incredible good luck. If things kept on improving, he might have the marriage he wanted even sooner than he'd hoped.

Bryan was just short of whistling when he entered the house, but when one of the servants informed him Sarah Raymond was still in her rooms, he sobered quickly and

hurried up there. It had been more than half a day since
their visit to Harding's house, but Sarah still wasn't herself. She might even be lying there needing a physician,
while he'd gone blithely about his own affairs, thinking
she was just sleeping. If anything serious resulted from
his negligence, he'd save Jamie the trouble of having to
kill him . . .

Sarah's sitting room was empty, so he knocked softly
on her bedchamber door. He didn't want to wake her if
she really was asleep, but a moment after the knock she
herself opened the door. She wore a lounging robe in yellow, which pointed up how pale she still looked.

"Bryan, what's wrong?" she asked at once, stepping
out to put a hand to his arm. "You look so disturbed—has
something happened?"

"Sarah, what I'm disturbed about is *you,*" he answered
in exasperation. "You still look so pale—do you want me
to send for a physician?"

"Don't be silly, I don't need a physician," she returned
with a small but very amused smile. "What I do need is
a cup of tea, which I've already sent for. Why don't we
sit down while we're waiting for it."

She moved past him into the sitting room proper, leaving him no choice but to follow. When he sat in the chair
opposite the one she took, she smiled at him again.

"Will you please stop looking so grim?" she said,
shaking her head in mock annoyance. "I didn't expect to
react so strongly to your wife's story, and I'm only now
beginning to get over it. But I *will* get over it, so stop
picturing me at death's door."

"Actually, I was picturing *myself* there once Jamie got
back," he countered, relief turning his tone dry. "I knew
what we would hear would be ugly and evil, and if I'd
stopped to think I would have sent you back here first. Her
willingness to talk about it surprised me, but—"

"Bryan, I am *not* a child or a fragile doll," she interrupted, her annoyance now real. "If you'd tried to send
me back here, you would have had a war on your hands.
Jamie knows that even if you don't, so stop expecting him

to come charging after you with blood in his eye. Whatever happened was no one's fault but mine—and, in another definite way, his.''

"Sarah, you're not making any sense," Bryan said, wondering if it would be smart to attempt to soothe her. "Hearing that story affected you badly, but that can't be considered *your* fault. And it certainly isn't Jamie's fault that you're a sweet, sensitive, feeling woman—"

"Bryan, what I am is a woman in the family way!" she all but snapped, her patience totally at an end. "I didn't want to tell you that, not until I told Jamie, but you're making this absolutely impossible. I'm not sick or sweet or sensitive, just enceinte. I had no idea that your wife's tale of horror would hit me so hard, and I've been taking it extra easy just to be on the safe side. Is that perfectly all right with you?"

"I think you've been spending too much time in my wife's company," he muttered, shocked at her peevishness, and, at the same time, delighted and elated at her news. Jamie was finally going to be a father! Now he'd have a reason to spend more time at home, the sort of reason Bryan was certain Jamie had been looking for ever since he and Sarah had married. But contrary to Sarah's belief, Jamie would *not* be easy and understanding about what his wife had gone through, especially not *now*. That was one point Bryan understood better than Sarah ever would.

"It's strange you should mention spending time in your wife's company," Sarah said, leaning back at ease while she studied him. "She's definitely changed her attitude toward *you,* but for some reason she seems to dislike *me* now even more than she did. Do you have any idea why that would be?"

"Not the slightest," Bryan answered, only just stopping himself from suggesting it was Sarah's imagination. Expectant women were supposed to be pampered, not argued with. "If she has a specific reason, I may find it out in the next few days. I've decided to let her come to London with me, even though it's mostly against my better judgment. If I could be certain that leaving her here would mean she would stay here . . .''

''But you can't be certain, even if you have her guarded,'' Sarah said with too much amusement for his taste. ''We still haven't figured out how she escaped from a locked room, so having guards outside her door might do no good at all. How early tomorrow are we leaving?''

''We aren't,'' Bryan stated, standing just as a housegirl entered with tea service on a tray. ''She and I are, but you're staying here. After being sick most of today, you're not spending most of tomorrow in a bouncing coach. Besides, Jamie is due back at almost any time. Are you going to make him trek from your house to here then all the way to London before he can see you? Do I have to tell you what his mood would be like by then?''

''No,'' she answered with a sigh, the old, reasonable Sarah back again. ''He'd be really angry with me, and I couldn't blame him. And you're right about my not looking forward to spending all those hours in a coach, not so soon. I'll wait for Jamie, then he and I will come together—as long as you're sure you won't need me sooner.''

''I'm positive I won't need you sooner,'' Bryan said, making the statement absolutely firm. ''What I need is to see you back in good health, and then we can celebrate. Especially if Rianne and I happen to catch up to our quarry by then.''

''So you two will finally be working together,'' Sarah said with a smile. ''I'm sorry to be missing that, especially if you intend to be intelligent about the arrangement. If she finally feels she might be able to trust you, it would be the perfect time to do some courting.''

''I'll have you know I've already made a start on that,'' Bryan told her, letting a smug smile show how virtuous he supposedly felt. ''The first of my plans may not have worked as well as I would have liked, but I've only just begun. From now on I expect to do a good deal better.''

''I'm really delighted, my dear,'' Sarah said with a warm, true smile. ''You'll see, everything will go much better that way. There are untold benefits in civilized courting, which you're now certain to learn about.''

"You'll never find me refusing benefits," Bryan said with a grin, ready to leave. "Especially untold benefits. I hear they're much tastier than told benefits.''

Sarah laughed at that, momentarily looking a good deal better, and then she sobered again.

"Bryan, I know it's against your nature, but this time I want you to be careful," she said. "That girl—neither of us will ever *really* know what she went through, and I thank God for that. But quite a lot of what she does is *caused* by what she went through, and I believe there are times she has no control over it at all. If you aren't careful enough for both of you, something—horrible could happen.''

"There's already been too much of the horrible in this," he said with a heavy nod. "I intend to be careful enough for an entire company, so will you please stop worrying?''

When she smiled and also nodded he walked over to kiss her cheek, then left her to the maid who was waiting to serve tea. Poor Sarah was suddenly worrying about everything, but Bryan knew that was only to be expected in her condition. *Her condition.* He drew a deep breath as he reached his rooms, then poured himself a drink and sat down to do some thinking.

He was delighted that Sarah and Jamie were finally going to have a child, but he also felt suddenly abandoned. He had confided in Sarah and relied on her opinion for the last two months, ever since his plan against Robert Harding had begun drawing to an end. She was as easy to talk to as her husband, and Bryan's planning always went better when he talked it out to someone first.

But at the moment Jamie was still away, and Sarah was in no condition to be burdened with any more of his problems. He'd meant to ask a lot of questions about this courting business, specifically the best way to go about it and whether or not you mentioned to the woman what you were doing. It seemed silly to think a woman might *not* know she was being courted, so he'd decided on his own that you *didn't* make any sort of fatuous announcements that would make you feel like a fool. After all, the woman was already his wife . . . That had sounded like the most reasonable answer so he'd stick with it, but he would have felt a good deal better if he'd been able to ask.

But now that was impossible. Bryan sighed, unsurprised that his earlier elation had faded to nothing. Despite the optimism brought on by his short exchange with Rianne, he really wasn't anywhere near to being out of the woods with her. He was certain the girl insisted on going to London with him only because they now had a common enemy. Instead of finding a man to love she'd found one to hate, and now everything was taking second place to a newborn passion for revenge. She was eager and alive, but only at the thought of hunting their quarry. Strange how the same thought completely ruined *his* mood.

And that was one of the reasons why he'd made sharing his bed a condition of her going along. If her days were spent looking elsewhere than at him, at least her nights would be filled with the knowledge of his presence. Maybe then she would begin to really see him, not as a vehicle for vengeance or a brute who had forced his way into her life, but as a man who very much wanted her love. His own love was useless without hers, empty and one-sided and doomed to die for lack of its mate . . .

He finished his drink in a single swallow, then got up to ring for a bath. It was getting on toward dinnertime, and he didn't want to be late. His blood surged at the thought of what after-dinner would bring, and that was the second reason he'd insisted on the terms he had. He'd never wanted a woman as much as he wanted his wife, a wife he'd touched all of once. And unless God took pity on him and granted him a miracle, he could still end up having to let her go once their search was successful. It was beyond him to force her to stay, so against that time he would store all the memories he could, to warm him during the following, possibly empty years of his life.

"But maybe I will get that miracle," he muttered, rubbing his face with one hand. "What I'd like to do is carry

her off to a mountaintop or a cave and make her *know* she
belongs to me. But Sarah wants me to learn to do things
in a civilized way, and she's probably right. Be civilized,
and *win* the girl.''

Right. He smiled faintly as he began again to think about
his belated courtship, which had at least one good side to
it. He already knew he would end up getting the girl into
his bed . . .

Rianne sat at her vanity table, slowly brushing her hair.
Dinner had been served very early, and it had been delicious. She'd worn a relatively plain gown of gold brocade,
and amusingly her table companion had worn a coat and
breeches of the same material. His dark-red hair had been
tied back with a golden ribbon, his dark-red vest had covered a shirt dripping ruffles, and his cravat had been a
snowy-white edged in lace. With gleaming gold buckles
at shoe tops and knees, he'd been a resplendent sight.

And attentive. He'd seated her to his right in the small,
private dining room just off the main hall, and hadn't left
it to servants when her glass of champagne needed refilling. His conversation had been light and charming, filled
with compliments he seemed to be completely sincere
about, and once dinner was over he'd escorted her to her
rooms. She would want privacy to prepare for bed, he'd
told her, and then had left her with a maid to do his own
preparing.

"So what is he up to?" she asked her reflection in a
mutter, free to do so with the housegirl gone. "No threats,
no dragging me around or locking me up, no forcing me
out of clothes or into tubs . . . He *must* be up to *something.*''

Which was undoubtedly true, and she knew he was
playing some game even though she hadn't been able to
figure out what it was. And she'd been so distracted, she'd
unthinkingly chosen a night ensemble from her things sent
over that might not be quite appropriate. Made of sheer
lawn in a lustrous silver, both gown and robe were so
delicate that they seemed as thin as spiders' webs. This

time she also wore matching slippers, but the ensemble created an impression she hadn't intended . . .

"He'll think you *want* to sleep in his bed," she murmured to her reflection, knowing that was utter nonsense. The man was interested in nothing more than her body, which wasn't the same as wanting *her*. She couldn't possibly find herself truly attracted to someone like that, but maybe there was just the least bit of that bodily desire Angus and Cam had told her about. After all, the man *was* impressive in a backward and overbearing way. And, at least for the moment, he *was* her husband . . .

"But he's also up to something," she reminded herself firmly. "If you can't find out what it is, you'll try that game of your own . . ."

Just then a knock came at the door, and not the timid knock of a housegirl. Rianne put the brush down and rose, then went to the door and opened it. Just as she'd suspected *he* was there, wearing his blue velvet dressing gown with his white cravat tucked into the front. This time the ribbon tying back his hair was silver, which couldn't possibly be a coincidence . . .

"And to think I believed you looked good earlier," he said, those gray eyes moving over her slowly. "May I come in?"

"What if I said no?" she asked, looking at him with her head to one side. "Would you simply go back to your own rooms in a huff?"

"I'm too big to fit into a huff," he responded, his answer as mild as her question had been. "*Are* you saying no?"

"No," she replied, finding it impossible not to grin. "It would take the maids forever to unpack all those trunks they only just packed for the trip. Do come in."

"If you weren't wearing those silver moonbeams, I'd probably resist that invitation until I got some of my men up here," he said, glancing around as she stepped back out of his way. "All my instincts tell me there's got to be a sinister reason for such a gracious welcome. Have you figured out a way to dig a pit in the middle of a wooden floor, or have you just poisoned the champagne?''

"Oh, definitely a pit," she said, closing the door behind him. "Poisoning good champagne would be barbaric. But I'm afraid I won't be joining you in drinking what's here. I've had enough for one night."

She tried to keep her innocent expression in place as he looked at her with one brow raised, but it really wasn't possible. He'd been joking about her poisoning the champagne, of course, but suddenly he wasn't quite sure. Since keeping a straight face was beyond her she changed to a pleasant and friendly smile, and that seemed to bother him even more.

"Now I'm really worried," he said, blinking at her. "Inviting me in without hesitation, smiling at me, no threats or accusations— What *are* you up to?"

"I'm just upholding my end of our agreement," she answered with a shrug. He was probably accusing her in an effort to confuse her. "But what about *you?* All those charming compliments and little attentions at dinner—I've been trying to figure out what else it's possible for you to be after."

"Can't a man be attentive to his wife without wanting anything?" he asked innocently. "I've been too involved in other things to do the job properly until now, so I'm trying to make up for it. You don't mind, do you?"

"I don't know," Rianne answered, one finger to her lips in consideration. "I was beginning to get used to being dragged places and locked up and ignored. Now you're asking me to get used to something else entirely. I'll have to think about it."

"A man can't expect fairer treatment than that," he allowed, a gleam of strong amusement in those eyes. "And while you're thinking about it, I'll just continue with catching up on being attentive."

He put his hands to her shoulders and gently drew her close, then bent his head to touch her lips with his. It was definitely a touch rather than a kiss, followed by another two or three of the same. Then his big hand brushed the hair back from her neck, and the warm feather touches of his lips moved to there.

Rianne found it all she could do not to gasp or moan. The physical attraction she felt for this man was much stronger than she'd thought; her body had begun tingling the moment his hands touched her, and now her blood raced around madly while her heart thumped like an ax chopping a tree. But he hadn't told her what he was up to even after she'd asked straight out. He was still playing games, so she had to do the same.

"Will—will you tell me something?" she managed, although the words were a trifle on the hoarse side. She also fought to make her mind work, so that she'd have what to ask if he agreed. Almost . . . almost she wished he would refuse . . .

"I'll tell you anything you like," he returned in a murmur, his breath warm on her neck. "There have been too many secrets between us, and I'd rather not have any more."

Her hands had somehow slid around him to his back, and the soft velvet felt strange over the hard muscularity it covered. She was also pressed against his body in front, the awareness of which made her close her eyes against waves of dizziness.

"I—saw Angus and Cam arriving late this afternoon," she said, accidentally stumbling across an appropriate topic. "They said they'd been treated well and Angus was feeling much better, but— What will become of them? Are you going to send them back to the stables at my stepfather's house, or . . . maybe . . ."

"Or maybe turn them over to the authorities?" he finished when she didn't, raising his head to look down at her. "Little one, when will you understand I'm really not like all those people who lied to you? When I give my word about something, I keep it. Your two—brothers—will be given the chance to train for one of my companies. If they're good enough to learn what they have to, the jobs are theirs."

"Oh, I *know* they'll be good enough," she gushed as

he began to lower his lips to her throat. She was really delighted to hear he hadn't been lying, but somehow she'd half-expected it. When it came to her, though, he was still holding things back. She'd given him a chance to tell her what he was up to, so it was his own fault that she had to go on with her plan. He needed to be taught a lesson, and the opportunity was right there.

"Oh, I *know* they'll be good enough, because we trained together as children," she said, then reached to the side to take his arm. "Come sit down and I'll tell you a little about that time."

A peculiar combination of expressions flitted across his face, as though he was delightfully surprised that she wanted to talk to him, but he kept silent as he let her lead him to a settle covered with a brown leather bench pad. The brown was one of the calm places in the sea of gold and rose that covered the room, but the settle itself was one of the most uncomfortable pieces of furniture Rianne had ever encountered.

"Isn't this better than just standing there?" she asked brightly as they sat. "I've never been able to tell anyone about what the three of us did as children, so I'm really going to enjoy this. You will too, when you begin to understand just how valuable Cam and Angus will be to you."

His expression seemed to suggest he'd been hoping for a more intimate conversation than that particular topic, but he also seemed determined not to discourage her in any way. What *he* probably wanted to talk about was the way he'd already become aroused, but that wasn't part of her plan. Rianne had been told how—deflating—it was for a man bent on pleasure to need to listen to a lot of pointless chatter. It would be interesting to see how long her husband could stand it before he admitted defeat in the game.

She launched into the story of her childhood adventures with her brothers, carefully choosing the most boring instances she could think of. She would know she had him when he began to yawn, but he didn't seem quite to that point yet. If anything he seemed to be thinking, which might be the best reaction possible. The sooner he decided to tell her what he was up to with all that attention he'd been paying her, the sooner they could get on to topics he liked better. Like how soon they would get to bed. Not that *she* had any strong interest in *that* . . .

"Excuse me," he said after a number of minutes, during which Rianne had gone on and on. "I don't mean to interrupt, but I have a question. Did you just say that you and the others swore a blood oath to always keep your word? That you would be careful about *giving* your word, but once given it would always be kept?"

"Why—yes," she answered hesitantly, honestly not quite sure. That *was* something she and the others had done, but she hadn't meant to make such a point of it. Rianne wasn't paying attention *herself* to what she babbled; that would have put *her* to sleep sooner than her intended victim.

"Then I'm afraid it's my painful duty to inform you that there's an instance where you didn't keep your word to *me.*" He now looked at her with commiseration, and quickly held up a hand when she tried to speak. "No, there's no need to apologize, I'm sure you've simply forgotten. Not to mention the fact that you've hardly had the opportunity. A woman like you—I can't imagine you refusing to do the right thing as soon as humanly possible. Am I wrong?"

"Of course not!" Rianne told the earnest gray eyes looking down at her, suddenly very confused. "But what are you talking about? What did I give my word to do that I haven't?"

"I feel—very awkward—talking about it," he said as though it were a shameful admission, turning his face away. "It was probably a mistake bringing it up in the first place, but— Well, never mind. I've waited this long, so waiting a little longer won't kill me. Go on with what you were saying."

"I will not!" Rianne protested, more than a little scandalized. "If I've failed to keep my word about something, I want to hear about it. You can't just bring the subject up and then drop it, pretending it's unimportant. You *know* it's not unimportant.''

''I hope you'll forgive me, but I know something else even better,'' he said, turning his face back to look at her. ''If we start going into this now, you'll just end up being angry with me again. I *know* you will, and I didn't come here tonight to argue. If you'll do me the favor of forgetting about it until tomorrow, we'll both be a lot happier.''

''How am I supposed to forget about it *now?*'' she asked, trying not to show how exasperated she felt. ''I can't forget, so you'll just have to tell me.''

''And cut my own throat?'' he countered with a snort. ''Do I look *that* stupid to you?''

''All right, I promise not to get angry,'' she said, seizing the idea as soon as it came to her. ''I'll give you my word not to get angry, but only if you tell me right now. Is it a deal?''

''Little one, you almost make me ashamed of myself,'' he answered with a sigh that looked real. And was that a flicker of pain in his eyes? Why on earth would he feel *hurt* . . . ? ''I'm accepting your deal, but only to teach you not to play games with me. I've been doing this longer than you have, so there's experience to back up strong natural talent. I really don't want to be your enemy.''

''Would you like to tell me what all *that* was supposed to mean?'' she asked with a sinking feeling. He *couldn't* have fooled her again, he *couldn't* have . . .

''When I first brought you here, I took your clothes off to put you in a bath,'' he said, those gray eyes directly on her. ''While I was doing it you swore to get even with me, and I thanked you for promising to take *my* clothes off. Since you didn't say that wasn't what you meant, I was entitled to believe it was. You promised to take my clothes off, and haven't done it yet. I'm guessing, of course, but I expect I'd enjoy *that* a good deal more than listening to stories even *you* have no interest in. And remember—you gave your word not to get angry.''

In spite of having given her word, Rianne simmered on the inside. Most of her anger was directed at herself, for having fallen to him so easily again, but the rest was all his. He *enjoyed* making her feel like a fool, treating her in a way no other man had ever dared. What she wanted right then was to get him as furiously angry as he'd gotten her, and then *she* could sit back and laugh . . .

"I remember the time you're talking about," she told him at last, only a step away from a growl. "You're right about my having given my word, but you left something out. I said I'd get even *before I died*, not at the very first opportunity. There *is* a difference, you know."

"Yes, I suppose there is," he granted, the expression in his eyes flickering. "I hadn't thought of that, but I can see where you would. And since your word isn't in immediate jeopardy of being broken, I can also see that we'll be putting off keeping the promise."

"Not at all," Rianne disagreed at once, and had the pleasure of seeing him actually startled. "There's no sense in putting off what has to be done at *some* time, especially when we're in the midst of the perfect opportunity. We'll take care of the matter right now."

His confused and disbelieving stare followed her as she rose, wariness lowering his brows. Good, he had no idea what she was up to. If it worked out just right, he'd find out at the same time he lost that infuriating temper . . .

Rianne stood close to the settle beside his legs, and reached forward. The silver ribbon tying back his long, dark-red hair was the first thing to go. She hadn't intended running her fingers through his hair in order to loosen it, but it was so thick and magnificent she found she couldn't resist. It spread to the shoulders of his dressing gown, framing him in a mane of sullen fire.

Next came his cravat, its lacy white looking even whiter against the blue of his dressing gown. It was tucked into the front of his gown rather than secured inside, and so slid free with no effort at all. Her hands loosened it at his throat, then drew it off slowly from around his broad, tanned neck. And still he hadn't made a sound. Those cold gray eyes, no longer quite so cold, hadn't left her face, but there weren't any words to go with the stare. When she

reached down to the belt of his gown he made a very small
sound in the back of his throat, but that was all. She knew
he was aware of the way her breasts pushed against her
gown when she bent, but his gaze stayed locked to her
face. Because of that she was carefully controlling her expression, but controlling what she felt was beyond her.
She had no idea why it was happening, but slowly undressing this man was sending her up in flames. In another
moment her blood would probably begin to boil, but stopping was unthinkable—for more reasons than one.

Finally she was able to push open his dressing gown.
Beneath the blue velvet was tanned flesh over corded muscle, dark-red hair on a chest as broad as a stallion's, thick
arms that strained against the material covering them.
Lower down was his desire, a raging lance that quivered
with barely controlled impatience, and a quick glance was
all Rianne had the courage for. She was in the midst of
playing with deadly fire, and had no need to thrust her
hand in to know how badly she could be burned.

The dressing gown was somewhat difficult to remove
without the active help of the man wearing it, but Rianne
finally managed to do it. It was still behind and under him,
but it was definitely and completely off. She'd had to touch
his warm, hard body more than once, and her struggle to
keep from thinking about that wasn't entirely successful.
But she had to keep at it, since there was still the finishing
touch to add . . .

"And that, I think, fulfills all promises made or assumed," she said when it was finally done, shaking her
hair back from her shoulders and arms and pretending she
hadn't begun to sweat. Out of the corner of her eye she
saw those big hands beginning to rise toward her waist,
and therefore moved fast to regain her former seat. "Now,
of course, we have to test the rest of your guess."

"Guess?" he echoed, his voice a thick rumble of utter
confusion. "What in hell are you talking about?"

"You said you were only guessing that you would prefer
having me take your clothes off to listening to uninteresting stories," she reminded him with a faint smile. "You've

just experienced having your clothes taken off, and now you need to experience being talked to. You interrupted me when I'd barely begun.''

Stunned understanding flashed in two pools of molten gray ice, followed immediately by an eruption of fury. He'd obviously expected to go from being undressed to making love to her, and now he'd have to wait while he sat and listened. After all, *he* was the one who had started *that* game, and if he didn't follow through he would lose . . .

''To the devil with that,'' he growled suddenly, the fury increasing. ''I don't know what *you're* made of, woman, but I'm not made the same. All stories and games are *over.*''

And then his arms were under her and lifting her as he stood, once again making it seem that she weighed nothing. Rianne gasped in surprise and clutched at him, but dropping her wasn't part of his intention. Or at least not dropping her on the floor. He strode to the bed, tossed her in, then followed immediately. She squeaked when she hit the quilt, but she really should have moaned. No matter how much of a hurry he was in, her own desire suddenly insisted he was going too slowly.

Before she could move, his hands were at her robe, ripping it open, just before they did the same to her gown. Dark-red hair fell about his shoulders where he knelt above her, and then his lips touched her breast and his hands caressed her hips. Rianne's breath caught in her throat when his tongue touched her nipple, when his stroking fingers slid across her flesh, when his manhood brushed her thigh. He'd literally ripped the clothes from off her, but it had been nothing like what she'd once imagined. Right now it was intensely stimulating, especially since it was also what she'd been ready to demand.

Against her will her eyes closed, and her clutching hands found the thickness of his mane. Oh, God, what his mouth and hands were doing to her! Lips and tongue that turned her boneless and melting, fingers that stroked with a knowledge of absolute possession. He was trying to arouse her, thinking he would force her to feel what he already did, having no idea she was way ahead of him. Her blood *was* boiling, and he was the only one who could make it stop.

And then his fist was in her hair, holding her still for his kiss. Those lips tried to swallow her even as they demanded a response, but again she was ahead of him. Her own kiss was even more demanding as he crushed her to him, stealing the very air from her lungs. When his other hand touched her intimately, probing for her heat, she nearly choked. Why was he delaying? Why didn't he hurry up and get to it?

And then, blessedly, he did. His knee forced its way between hers, the rest of him followed, and then his spear was sheathing itself inside her. She tried to cry out, in triumph over having been given what she wanted so badly, but his lips refused to allow it. He held her to him and began to stroke deep and hard, possessing her completely and making her mind spin away to a land of blinding frenzy. He brought her satisfaction more than once, and the last of it was shared.

Afterward, while he lay on his back beside her, panting as though he'd run miles, she drew in air more quietly to ease her weary lungs. Although he'd done most of the work, her body hadn't found the time effortless. On the contrary, an hour of sword practice was less tiring.

But not more incredible. At first she felt somewhat wide-eyed over having been *impatient* with a man so wildly aroused, especially one who had lost his temper. That wasn't the way a lady was supposed to feel, but it *had* gotten her exactly what she'd needed and wanted—

Lost his temper! That meant he'd also lost the game, which made Rianne even more delighted. She hated the way he always had control of himself, the way he rarely lost patience with her. Keeping your temper with someone you don't care about is easy, and Rianne had no need of additional reminders that that was the case with her. She'd made him lose that temper, and so for a while had been able to forget that it was only her body he wanted. For the time they'd been locked together, she'd been able to pretend . . .

And she'd never forget what they'd shared. It seemed that even though he'd been as mindless with desire as she, he hadn't been *able* to keep from sharing with her, rather than simply taking. Realizing that turned the experience into one that made her stretch lazily with a silent purr.

"I wonder why you look like you're congratulating yourself," his voice came, and then he was leaning over her to her left. Propped up on one elbow he was still wiping off sweat, and that made her smile even more.

"Why shouldn't I congratulate myself?" she asked languidly. "I just behaved like a full wife, and it took almost no effort at all. That *was* our deal, wasn't it?"

"It wasn't part of our deal for you to goad me into all but attacking you," he came back with annoyance. "Don't you have any idea how dangerous it can be for a woman to do that?"

"Then next time I'll have to be more careful," she allowed blandly, enjoying the situation even more. He'd *hated* losing his temper, but she'd made it happen. He might have no true feelings for her at all, but it would take him a while to forget her.

He swallowed down whatever else he might have said, and simply got out of the bed. Rianne thought he intended to gather his things together and leave, but instead he turned down all the lamps but one. That one was left to burn dimly, giving him enough light to make his way back to the bed.

"When we get to London, I'll have to replace that ensemble," he said, glancing at the now-ruined robe and gown she'd worn. Then he got under the quilt and continued, "Until I do, you'll just have to join me under here like any good full wife."

Rianne hesitated only a moment, then did as he'd said. So he was going to buy her another ensemble, was he? She wanted to ask if it would be another to wear or another to rip off, but decided against it. Some triumphs are sweeter when they're left undiscussed. His presence under

the quilts was an unaccustomed awareness; as she began
to make herself comfortable, she wondered if it would be
possible to experience that shared insanity a second time
before they parted forever . . .

Chapter 12

❧

T he coach's speed was brisk enough, but Bryan, looking out the window on his side, wished it could be
two or three times faster. Or maybe he would prefer if it
was two or three times slower. The whirling indecision
inside him was something he was completely unused to.
If it didn't stop soon . . .

But how *could* it stop? The cause of it was sitting right
there on the coach seat beside him, looking out her own
window. Her travel outfit was brown and tan, the long
skirts covering most of her short, soft boots; her hands
were properly gloved, her hair neatly coiled beneath a
charming tan hat. She looked like a very beautiful, very
proper woman, nothing at all like the naked and passionate girl who had shared his bed.

Now *that* had been something beyond all his expecta-
tions! Bryan felt the urge to loosen his cravat at the
memory; he also had to tell himself sternly that this was
neither the time nor the place. They would be in London
soon enough, and his house would be ready by the time
they got there. The messenger he'd sent off yesterday would
have alerted his town staff, and there might even be some
of the answers he was after . . .

I don't believe this, Bryan thought, removing his tricorn
to let some of the breeze from their passage cool his face.
*I've spent years following this trail, and now that I'm al-
most to the end of it it's all I can do to pay attention. My
mind keeps shifting to a beautiful face with green eyes,
surrounded by incredible golden-red hair . . .*

And that magnificent white body. It had been sheathed

in a cloud of silver shadow when she'd shocked him by beginning to take his clothes off. He'd known almost from the first moment she'd begun chattering at him that she was up to something. He'd been pleased at first that she was actually willing to talk to him, as if she now considered him someone to confide in.

Then it had hurt when it became clear she was only playing some unknowable game, and he'd chosen that nonsense about an unkept word to teach her a lesson. It had been certain that she would promise not to be angry in order to find out what he was talking about . . . She'd promised and then had gotten angry anyway . . . But rather than staying angry, she'd . . .

Bryan fanned himself with his hat, teeth clenched in an effort to stay in control. Last night he hadn't been *able* to stay in control, and he'd used the girl with more wild abandon than he'd had any intention of doing. It had been like making love in the midst of a thunderstorm, with lightning striking all around them. Afterward she'd shown nothing of anger or outrage or pain or fear, but when did she ever? Most of her feelings were "none of his business," and she'd shown how much control of herself she had, even in the face of complete horror.

Which might also explain why she'd seemed to respond to him that morning. He'd awakened to find her in his arms, her gloriously naked body pressed to his, and a touch of his finger had found her as ready as he. He was inside her even before she awoke, and her eyes had fluttered open as she voiced a moan. He'd taken the sound as a moan of pleasure before wrapping himself in the ecstasy of stroking hard and deep, but what if it hadn't been? What if she hated what was being done to her, but refused to admit what she would consider a weakness? Was she accepting what he did to her as the price to be paid if she wanted to reach their common enemy?

Being tortured by questions like those was what had kept Bryan from saying the one thing he most wanted to: that he loved her, and wanted her to stay with him forever. The words burned and ravaged inside him, demanding to be let out, but coward that he was, he didn't dare speak them to her. What if she heard them and then let her disgust show on her face? What if she laughed at so ridiculous an idea, a brute trying to overstep himself? The pain would be more than he could live with, and life itself would be empty with all hope irretrievably gone.

And then there was the possibility that she might pretend to consider what he'd said, but would instead take herself off at the first opportunity. That she would then be gone would mean nothing beside the possibility that the enemy might be able to reach her, without first having to go through *him*. He couldn't let that happen no matter how he felt, no matter how much harder it was growing to keep silent. Often a man finds an end to cowardice, but *her* safety and happiness had to come first, even before the vengeance he'd been seeking for five years of his life.

Those dark thoughts brought Bryan down so fast, he plummeted all the way into depression. She'd been distantly pleasant to him that morning at breakfast, but they hadn't exchanged a single word of serious discussion since the day before. If she hated him even more now it was *his* fault, for losing himself with her like that. She may have goaded him into it deliberately, but had probably only been trying to see how far he could be trusted. And he'd shown her, yes, he certainly had.

Bryan was lost so deep in his thoughts that he was startled when the coach began to slow. The image of highwaymen flashed through his mind, then he remembered the four fighters riding behind the coach. They were trained to be alert for the presence of longbowmen and sharpshooters in the forest, and nothing else would have a chance against them. Then he saw the inn, and realized it was time to stop for lunch.

"I'm glad we're not stopping at that roadhouse from the other night," Rianne commented as they pulled up in front of the inn. "Even if my appetite was up to the memory, the food was worse than you could easily believe."

"I hadn't realized you'd eaten anything that night," he said, just to be saying *something*. He was hungrier for her attention than he had ever been for food, and would even have enjoyed being threatened.

"Well, I didn't eat much," she admitted. "Angus was the one who passed judgment on the stew, and from what he said I wouldn't have been happy to try it. But you'll probably be pleased to know that he doesn't think the same about the meals in *your* service. When I said good-bye to him and Cam this morning, they assured me that the next time I saw them they would probably be fat."

"A fighting man can't do his best on scraps and leavings," Bryan said, then opened the coach door and climbed out. A liveried man was there with a step stool for the lady's use, and Bryan offered Rianne his hand as soon as the stool was in place. When she accepted his assistance with a smile, his agitation simply increased. He'd been wrong about wanting to hear anything at all from her. What he *didn't* want to hear about was her feelings for a man who wasn't him. For *two* men who weren't him. Under the circumstances jealousy was ridiculous, but Bryan couldn't help feeling a pang at the thought that Rianne cared for those two more than she cared for him.

They took their time over lunch, enjoying the food as Bryan had known they would. He'd stopped at the inn before, which was a bit farther along the road to London than the roadhouse Rianne had mentioned. Most of the meal passed in a companionable silence that Bryan was beginning to recognize and appreciate. The girl didn't chatter like most women, saving her breath for when she actually had something to say.

With lunch over and the horses taken care of, they resumed their journey. His driver and four fighters had eaten in the common room, and were probably still chuckling over the sincere way in which the innkeeper had urged him to come again. While his men were there taking their meal, no one had dared even to cough too loud. A disturbance in there might have bothered the gentleman and his lady in the next room, which meant the gentleman's escort would stop any disturbance before it had a chance to start.

The inn hadn't been so peaceful since the last time Bryan had stopped there.

The motion of traveling after the excellent meal caused Bryan to nod off for a while, but he didn't realize it until he came awake suddenly at Rianne's gasp. Once again thought of highwaymen came, but for the second time he was wrong. His wife was staring out her window at a sight much more imposing than mere outlaws.

"We'll be crossing that in just another few minutes," he told her with a small smile. "It's even more fascinating from close up."

"But what is it?" she asked without taking her eyes from what they approached. "It looks like a bridge, but how can it be?"

"It's not *a* bridge, it's *the* bridge," Bryan said with a grin. "London Bridge, and people actually live and work in those houses and shops. I've heard it said that if one of those buildings fell, the entire section around it would go down as well. Do you see how some of them are braced with heavy timbers of wood?"

She nodded in distraction, for the moment too busy staring to speak. They were turning onto the wide span of the bridge proper, and that was when the clattering began. Horses' hooves and coach wheels against the worn wood of the bridge sounded loudly and it was scarcely possible to imagine what the noise was like in the houses and shops. They weren't the only ones using the bridge, not at that time of day.

"Those are mostly shops of pin and needle makers," Rianne said, her voice raised over the clatter. "There are people walking on the street over there, but it's so narrow and ugly-looking. And look at those arches of wood. They're attached to the houses on each side of the bridge, like ribs holding a body together. Why would someone have a house or a shop *here?*"

"Why not?" Bryan asked in turn. "If your house is really your home, does it matter *where* it is? And those shops do a thriving business, with all the customers they get from the St. James district. The ladies there don't mind coming here, as long as they can get their pins and needles cheaply.''

''It all looks like it's about to fall down,'' she said, and Bryan could hear sadness in her voice. ''I hope it doesn't, but if it does I'm glad I got to see it first.''

She fell silent again, staring morosely at the rickety one- and two-story buildings. She seemed to be worrying about the survival chances of the magical town-on-a-bridge, and Bryan could understand that. He also had a tendency to be delighted by the unusual, and for that reason said nothing about the latest rumors he'd heard.

People *were* worried about the houses and shops collapsing, and there was talk of pulling them all down. There had been talk like that before with nothing happening, but every time the subject was raised it had more supporters. One day it would have enough to see the thing done, and the day might not be too many years in the future . . .

Eventually the bridge was behind them, and then, too, many of the streets of an ever more crowded London. The St. James district was still bearable, but only just. Bryan far preferred emptiness and room around him, but in a city like London that was just about impossible to find. His house on the north side of the district was small when compared with those on most of his estates, but it was something else he had to put up with. Not that he *needed* an unreasonably large house. London itself and its standards of the proper tended to make him cranky.

''I think what I need is to camp out for a while,'' he muttered to the street they clip-clopped through. ''All alone, with nothing but a bedroll; maybe even in the rain. If *that* doesn't set things in their proper perspective, nothing in this life will.''

''Are you speaking to *me?*'' Rianne asked, this time drawn away from a fascinated study of stone buildings and cobbled streets. ''If you are, I didn't hear what you said.''

''No, I was really talking to myself,'' Bryan answered with a sigh. ''This city has a habit of making me talk to myself. How do you like what you've seen so far?''

''I don't know,'' she replied, looking troubled. ''From

everything I heard about London, I was picturing—I don't know, maybe the thoroughfares of Rome with gilded palaces to each side. The buildings on the other streets were all so close together, and the streets themselves so crowded. If I didn't see thirty people in one place, I didn't see any.''

"That's because it's the middle of the afternoon," he said with a smile for her country point of view—which he happened to share. "Tonight, when people go out to the theater, and to restaurants, and to clubs—and to other entertainment—you won't believe how many you see. But we'll probably stay in tonight. You have to be tired from the trip, and tomorrow you'll want to go shopping."

"Why will I want to go shopping?" she asked, looking at him strangely. "What do you think I'll need that I don't already have?"

"I find it impossible to believe that any woman alive needs to be given a reason to go shopping," he stated, undoubtedly producing a strange look of his own. "Are you *sure* you're real, and not a figment of my imagination?"

"If anyone should know whether or not I'm real, you're the one," she returned sharply with a bit of color to her cheeks. "And I see no reason to go out and spend all your money, Mr. Machlin. You're hardly likely to have enough time to recover the value in trade, so it would certainly not be fair. If I find I need something, I'll pay for it with money of my own."

"Money of your own," he echoed as she turned away from him, still not quite sure what had set her off. He certainly hadn't meant to force her into stating that she would not be with him for much longer. He would have preferred forgetting about that likelihood, at least for a while. And what was all that about money? Did she still think he couldn't afford to take her shopping?

The question kept him occupied long enough for the coach to reach his drive. As they approached the house he could see a horse tied to the ring post on the other side of the steps, one that looked very familiar. By the time they stopped he was certain he knew who his visitor was, and it was no visitor. If Jack Michaels was there, luck was also with him; rather than needing to wait, he could begin intensifying the search immediately.

His staff, as usual, was alert. No sooner had they rolled to a stop than there were four housemen at the coach door, one with a step stool and all of them calling out a greeting. Everything was ready for him and his new wife, and they all wanted to offer their congratulations on his marriage. They were also there to unload the trunks, which would take something of an effort.

Once again he turned to help his wife out of the coach, but although she allowed it, there was no smile given to him along with her hand. He was determined to figure out what he'd said or done, but as soon as she was on the graveled ground he was hailed from the still-open front door.

"Bryan, man, it's so good to see you back," Jack's voice called, and then the man himself was coming quickly down the stairs. His outstretched hand and wide grin was aimed at Bryan, but his grin soon switched to Rianne. "And in the company of such a beautiful lady. No wonder you took the plunge."

"Rianne, I'd like to present John Michaels, a friend and associate of mine," Bryan said, realizing that Jack wasn't simply being gallant; he seemed to be seriously attracted. "And, as you guessed, Jack, this is Rianne Lockwood Machlin, my wife. I'm glad you managed to be here at this particular time. I have a few things for you to do."

"I know," Jack returned, now taking the girl's hand and bending over it. "I was here yesterday when your man arrived. Mrs. Machlin, it's a true honor and pleasure to meet you. I would have preferred meeting you *before* this lucky dog did, but it's still a pleasure."

Bryan saw the smile *he* hadn't gotten being bestowed on Jack Michaels, and for the first time took a really good look at his friend. He wasn't as tall and broad as himself, but he was tall enough and strongly built. Brown hair that tended to curl, brown eyes that sparkled when attractive ladies were present, a handsome face, whose charm was usually enhanced by a smile or a grin— It suddenly seemed like a good idea to get right down to business.

"We'll talk in my study, Jack," he said, trying to recapture the man's attention. "We've had a long trip, and my wife will certainly want to freshen up. We—"

"As a matter of fact, your wife would prefer joining you two gentlemen," the girl interrupted immediately."If Mr. Michaels was here yesterday when your messenger arrived and is here again today, he may well have something to tell you already."

"I don't believe it," Jack exclaimed with another grin. "Intelligent as well as beautiful. She's absolutely right, Bryan, I *do* have something to tell you already. It was pure luck finding it out, of course, but we don't need to mention that. In addition to the luck I was also brilliant, and that we *can* mention."

"Why don't we mention it sitting down with drinks in our hands," Bryan said, taking Rianne's arm. "After that trip I can appreciate a seat that doesn't jounce."

Bryan led the way inside, and just as he'd expected, Jack followed quickly where Rianne was taken. Jack was obviously infatuated with the girl, probably his seventh or eighth infatuation that month.

His friend Jack Michaels was a younger son of a very well-known and wealthy family, who was given a generous income to stay away from that family and do nothing that would bring their name to common tongues. That was the reason he'd adopted the name of Michaels, and lived in what he considered a modest style. His generous income usually didn't stretch to cover that modest style, so he was also usually in need of money. His acceptance in all the "right" circles had made him valuable to Bryan during the years of his search, so Bryan supplemented Jack's income on a monthly basis whether there was anything for Jack to do or not. He'd also found the man discreet and trustworthy—in his own strange and unusual way.

Bryan's study was the first room to the left off the large circular entrance hall. Harris was there to open the door and light a lamp, and then the elderly servant poured drinks for the men. Rianne had asked for tea, and had been told with a smile that it was already on the way. Harris had ordered it brought just in case the new lady of the house should want it, and received an answering smile of thanks in return. The tea was there by the time the men had glasses of whisky in front of them, and as soon as the housegirl had poured for her mistress, the two servants left quickly and quietly.

"I have to admit I don't understand where you find such perfect servants," Jack said to him as soon as the door was closed. "Even my father has his share of clunkers, but no matter where you are you're surrounded by perfection. In what part of the world did you find the secret to accomplish *that?*"

"As a matter of fact, I found that secret right here in London," Bryan answered with a smile. "When I first went out on my own, no one knew me. I was able to take service with one of the bigger Houses so as not to drain my starting initial capital, and there's nothing like seeing the situation from the other side of the silver. I pay only slightly better wages than everyone else, but that small difference lets me have my pick of the best people available. And not only is Harris scrupulously fair with the staff he manages, if one of them has an unexpected problem he lets me know about it. That way I can supply the help they need before the problem gets out of hand. My taking care of them means they do the same for me."

"Looking at your people as people," Jack said with a laugh. "The idea is positively revolutionary, but I don't expect it will catch on. Most of us don't *want* to know what it's like on the other side of the silver. But that's our loss. Let's get on to a subject that's gain."

"Yes, that stroke of luck you mentioned," Bryan said, leaning back in his desk chair with glass in hand. Jack and Rianne sat in the deep leather chairs on the other side of the desk, and she'd removed her gloves and hat.

"Yesterday was the day of the month I usually stop by your house to see if there is anything I can help with,"

Jack said without going into detail about the monthly financial help Bryan gave him. "I hadn't been here long when your man came galloping up, then burst in to say you and your new wife would be arriving the next day. Your staff went into an immediate flurry, everyone running in all directions as though the place was under two feet of dust with apple cores in the corner of every room. As far as I could see the place was already spotless, but—"

"Jack, please," Bryan interrupted, in no mood to humor his friend's tendency for tangents. "I'm glad you admire my staff, but can we please get on with it?"

"Of course, of course," Jack agreed in his usual pleasant way. "Well, I saved your man a trip, because he also had that letter for me. You listed the names and addresses of four men you wanted to know more about, but believe it or not, one of the names was already familiar. Reginald Tremar. You'll never guess where I know him from."

"Either your favorite club, coffeehouse, or brothel," Bryan supplied with a sigh. This was going to be a long story no matter what he said or did.

"None of them," Jack gleefully informed him. "I said you'd never guess. The man is some sort of official at the Bank of England, where my allowance is deposited every quarter. I've never spoken to him, but I pass his door going to and coming from my own man. Once I saw him coming out of his office with the most attractive young lady, which made me wonder. He's not what one would describe as a handsome, outgoing man."

"He also sounds an unlikely associate for my stepfather," Rianne mused, sounding completely perplexed. "My stepfather would never have associated with anyone who *worked* for a living, which is probably why I don't remember this Tremar ever having been invited out. I wonder what the real connection between them was."

"He may have loaned Harding money," Bryan suggested. "I think I'll have to meet this important man from the Bank of England. You'll need a detailed description of him, and I want to know who his closest associates are."

"Why not make a stab at getting all that tonight?" Jack

asked, looking back and forth between them curiously. "I went by the Bank just past lunchtime today, thinking I'd toddle in and see what there was to see, but the man wasn't in. He'd taken the rest of the day off, his clerk told me, probably to rest up for tonight, he added. The young man isn't very fond of our Mr. Tremar, and didn't mind talking about him."

"Whatever you paid for that conversation, it was worth it," Bryan said in approval. "Where is it that he's supposed to be tonight?"

"Alicia de Verre is just back, and she's throwing a bash," Jack told him. "The comptesse swears Paris is causing everyone to die of boredom, so she's come back here for some fun. She's having the usual crowd in, and somehow Tremar got himself an invitation. He's been after one forever, his clerk said, and was ecstatic that he's finally managed it. He thinks he's finally on the way to being accepted."

"By *that* crowd?" Bryan asked with a snort. "Not unless he can also manage to change his parentage. And why he would want to bother is beyond me. Too many of them spend most of their time sitting around comparing the value of the last things they bought—and making assignations with each others' wives."

"According to his clerk, he should have no trouble joining in on the first part of that," Jack said with a grin. "Tremar's filthy rich, and has been for years. He spent a while working for the Bank as a clerk himself, handling scheduling and some books and the like, and then one day he'd apparently had enough. He had a word with a member or two of the Board, and they suddenly discovered he was eligible for promotion. You know how these things work."

"Yes, give the job to the one who can pay the most for it," Bryan said, nodding. "That way you keep it out of the hands of the common—even if they happen to be twice as competent. If they took those people's clerks away, their business would come to a grinding halt. You'd think they would have learned by now— Well, never mind. One must first be capable of learning. So, if Tremar had all that much money, why didn't he buy a post to begin with?''

"Possibly he wanted to see the business from the other side of the Sterling," Jack ventured with a grin. "Whatever it was, his new post must have repaid his investment many times over. And he enjoys the petty power he wields. He's an absolute tyrant when it comes to dealing with clients—unless they happen to have money and position. Then he bows and scrapes and all but licks their—'' He broke off as he glanced at Rianne, then he finished smoothly, ''—boots.''

"And he'll be at Alicia's tonight," Bryan said with a swallowed smile, tapping his glass with one finger. "Jack, I want you to get me an invitation, but don't get one for yourself. There are still three other names on that list, and you've already gotten too close to Tremar. If someone should notice you're also looking into the others—well, it could be dangerous.''

"Nonsense, man, no one takes *me* seriously," Jack countered with satisfaction. "Which is why they lose so much to me when we game. I'll be fine, so don't you worry about it for a moment, but do consider yourself. All the ladies will be crushed when they find out you've married, and will certainly weep all over you. When you return here soggy to the shoes, you'll have a good deal of explaining to do.''

"He won't if I'm there to see it all for myself," Rianne interrupted Jack's foolishness with a smile. "Which I will be. Seeing someone face-to-face is much better than getting a description of them, much more certain. And we do want to be certain, don't we.''

Her comment wasn't a question, and those green eyes never left Bryan's face even when she sipped at her tea. He knew she was right about needing to be there, but hated the idea of exposing her to such danger. And to a crowd like Alicia's. Rianne Lockwood was a country girl, with no idea about what went on in a city like London. Whatever else happened, the experience would change her . . .

"We'll discuss that a little later," he finally temporized, not about to get into a battle of wills with her in front of Jack. "Right now I need that invitation and, if possible, a start on at least one of the other three names. We won't have a lot of time to settle this, Jack, especially if they find out it's me you're acting for."

"How could they possibly find *that* out?" Jack asked with a snort after finishing his whisky. "As far as anyone knows, we're simply passing acquaintances. Well, I'd better get cracking. If this turns out to finish it, whatever will I do with myself afterward? Die of boredom, I imagine. Mrs. Machlin, I look forward to our next meeting with great anticipation."

After glancing at Bryan he bent over Rianne's hand with one of those full-attention smiles, then bowed himself out like a devoted servant. Jack always had to be joking, or he wasn't being himself. But he did have a definite knack for finding things out, and also seemed to enjoy it. A pity there would be scandal if he ever went so far as to take an actual job . . .

"You really seemed to be worried about him," the girl said, drawing Bryan out of distraction. "Haven't we just about agreed that the men he's checking on are only being used?"

"Yes, we decided on that, but it *is* still only a guess," Bryan answered, enjoying her presence in this room that was so entirely his. "Jack is discreet and clever, but he finds it impossible to imagine personal danger. In a place where others would stop for at least one look around, he breezes in and starts talking. That tactic disarms most people, but I'm afraid it won't work on the man *we're* after."

"No," the girl agreed, her expression distant, her tea forgotten. "I suppose you're right. I have the feeling that he's a man who listens closely to people. I remember him saying . . ." Rianne faltered at the memory, then took a deep breath and continued. "He said people like to believe they're keeping their secrets from everyone else, but if you listen properly at the right time you learn exactly what you want to know. With me he had learned I was almost too stubborn to survive."

"We'll have to show the arrogant bastard that he was wrong," Bryan said at once, getting up quickly to circle the desk to her side. Again her face was pale and her hands trembled, and her voice had lowered to that terrible thready whisper. "You're not alone any longer, little one, and the next time you meet him I'll be right there beside you."

"And I'm also not a child anymore," she said, obviously fighting to pull out of it despite the way she clung to his hand. "He'll never have me at that much of a disadvantage again, not ever. The next time *I'll* win."

"The next time hell," Bryan said, crouching down while still holding her hand. "You won the last time, and don't think he doesn't know it. He tried to break you the way he did with everyone else, but he couldn't even get you to bend. He must have been frantic for days, wondering if you really would keep quiet. You were stronger than him then, and you're stronger than him now. With both of us together, he doesn't stand a chance."

"We'll have to make sure of that," she said, some of her old spark coming back. "He won't be stupid enough to let me live a second time. And since we'll be doing all these things together, I take it you've decided to let me accompany you tonight. Or will you insist that I stay here, all alone and well within his reach if he's as close as we think?"

By then she had slipped her hand out of his, and those green eyes were looking at him with their usual steadiness. He was in charge, so she'd left the decision to him—right after guaranteeing that he had no choice at all. Bryan momentarily considered strangling her, then gave up with a growl.

"Yes, I've decided to let you come with me tonight," he said as he straightened. "I did consider leaving you here, but I *can't* take the chance of you facing our enemy alone. I expect to get *some* part of him, which won't happen if you get to him first. You might want to bathe and rest until dinnertime—or until I have a few moments free. Since I'm your husband and in charge, I may decide to let you help me relax."

"Even though I'm that dangerous?" she asked, trying for innocence despite the amusement in her eyes. "Aren't you afraid I might take horrible advantage of you? You've forced yourself to your—duty—until now, but why take unnecessary risks?"

"Obviously I'm addicted to danger," he answered, pulling her out of the chair and into his arms. "I expect it to be the death of me, but until then I won't show a moment of fear. Two moments, possibly, but not one."

And then he kissed her. Remembering how annoyed she'd been with him in the coach he expected her to resist, but instead she responded instantly. The breath of a murmur reached him as the softness of her lips met his, nothing like the passion of the night before, but in some ways better. There was no abandon to blame for the way she added her own sweetness to the kiss, the way her body all but flowed against his. She was probably doing no more than living up to her agreement to be a full wife to him, but for the moment he could pretend her response was real. He held the wife he loved in his arms and kissed her, and she, returning his love, also returned his kiss. It was only a dream, but *what* a dream!

As with most good things in life, the kiss finally had to end. When he released her she seemed confused, but he didn't understand why she would be. She'd behaved just the way she'd agreed to, the way a woman of honor who had given her word would want to.

"I'll have Harris show you to your part of our suite," he said, walking to the bellpull. "It should please you that these rooms have windows. But if you decide you miss the country and want to go back to it, don't bother using them. I'll be more than happy to have a coach brought to the front door."

"Thank you anyway, but I'll have no need of a coach," she responded, her pretty face flushed. "We made a deal, and since I've been upholding my end, I expect you to do the same. Any other action on your part would be dishonorable, and we've already established that that isn't what you are."

Bryan hadn't needed—or wanted—confirmation that she'd only been upholding her end of the bargain, and hearing it anyway just brought the pain he'd known it would. Mentally he groped around, trying to think of some lucid response, but was saved the effort. A knock came at the study door, and then Harris entered in his usual noiseless way.

"Harris, Mrs. Machlin is ready to see her rooms now," Bryan said as he watched the girl gather up her possessions. "And please tell Cook that we'll be going out tonight, so we'll appreciate an early dinner."

"Certainly, Mr. Machlin," the precise old man responded, and then he turned to the girl with a bow. "If you'll follow me, Mrs. Machlin."

The girl nodded regally and then left the room, giving Bryan nothing in the way of further attention. Honorable or not, he interested her less than the dirt beneath her feet. Once the door was closed behind her, Bryan shook his head.

"I wonder what it would be like to have her be that eager to find *me*," he muttered. "I'd do anything in the world to see it, but that's the whole problem. I can't figure out what would make something like that happen. You can't do what you can't think of to do."

Those statements did too good a job of showing how confused and muddy his thoughts were, so he went back to his desk chair to check what correspondence had come in while he was gone. Later he would spend some more thought on his wife; later, when he might have more luck handling the thoughts . . .

Rianne followed Harris to the rooms that were hers, then let him show her around. She had a very large and formal sitting room, all ivory and gold and green brocade, obviously arranged for intimate receptions. Elegant was much too mild a word, and the chairs even looked comfortable. Beyond the windows was a large balcony, a perfect companion to the sitting room for those times it became too crowded. Two separate withdrawing rooms stood beyond the room to the right of the windows, and to the left there was a small alcove where a footman could be posted. Beyond the alcove were the double doors that led to her bedchamber.

"All of the girls worked together to get your trunks unpacked, Mrs. Machlin," Harris said with a gesture toward one of the huge wardrobes. "If you find you'd rather have things arranged differently, simply ring for one of the girls. If you require anything else, two rings will fetch me, one ring one of the girls. Would you care for anything at the moment?"

"At the moment, no," she answered with a smile. "I'd like to rest for a short while, and then I'll want a bath. When I'm ready for it I'll ring. Harris, please convey my thanks to the—girls—for a truly excellent job. I was picturing the unpacking taking longer than the packing, and frankly I was dreading the time. You and your staff have rescued me from being in the middle of a nightmare of rushing around."

"It was our pleasure, madam," the old retainer replied with a bow that was deliberately more than perfunctory. "On behalf of the entire staff, allow me to formally welcome you to your new home."

She thanked him again, hopefully with all the warmth she should have been feeling, then watched him leave. Once the doors were closed she put her gloves, hat, and reticule on a side table, removed her jacket, then threw herself down in a chair.

"My new home," she muttered, looking around at the bedchamber. This one was blue and white, many shades of blue offset by pure white. All of the furniture was carved of some beautifully-grained wood that had been painted white, the drapes were blue brocade, the curtains white lawn. The bed linen was white, the quilts were blue, and the flounced curtains contained both colors. On the four-poster itself was the only contrasting color in the room—silken throw pillows in a rich wine-red. Here, too, the windows led to a balcony, and one of them had been opened to let in the late-afternoon air.

"All right, enough," Rianne growled at herself. "You can inspect all the pretty furnishings later. Right now you have more important things to concentrate on. Just what did you think you were doing?"

Even being asked the question by her own mind bothered Rianne, sending her back into the sea of confusion she hadn't yet climbed out of. Bryan Machlin had kissed her, and she'd responded so quickly it had literally made her dizzy. Rather than continuing to be angry with him for what he'd said in the coach, she'd forgotten all about anger as soon as his arms were around her. She'd never acted like that before, and had no idea why it had happened *this* time. Maybe she was just tired from the long coach ride, or maybe it had something to do with not being treated like a large porcelain doll . . .

"Yes, maybe that's it." She grasped at the straw hopefully. "Until now only Angus and Cam treated me like another human being, including fights when we were younger, and then sword practice. Now *he* comes along and brings me something other than genteel enjoyment, so my mind is confusing him with Angus and Cam. The only problem is—he doesn't care about me as much as they do."

Not that she really wished he would. He'd been insufferable in the coach that afternoon, telling her she would want to go shopping tomorrow without telling her what he thought she needed. How was *she* supposed to know what she was missing? She'd never been to London before, and he had a house there! It wasn't as though she had female friends, who would have told her what she needed to know . . .

"He's a fool, and I shouldn't even be talking to him," she muttered, looking down at the twisting fingers in her lap. "But instead of ignoring him, I can't wait until he's ready to 'relax.' Please, God, don't let him start meaning something to me. I'll still have to leave as soon as it's all over, and I'm so tired of being the only one who cares. My mother and father . . ."

She'd been very young when her father had died, and it had devastated her that he'd "gone away" without even saying good-bye. It hadn't mattered that it was heaven he'd gone to; he still hadn't said good-bye, and she'd loved him so very much. And then her mother . . . They'd been closer for a while, before she slowly began withdrawing from all contact with life. Rianne would have given her own life for her mother or even gone happily with her, but instead she and her love had been left behind.

And now Angus and Cam were delighted with the new life *they'd* found. She'd seen that morning how happy they were, to know they'd be going to the colonies with ready-made jobs. Men who were smart and good workers got ahead fast in Machlin's companies, earning enough money to stake them to anything they cared to do afterward. In five years or less they could have the beginnings of their own estate, running prime stock rather than sub-adequate scrubs. They'd laughed as everything they'd been told came bubbling out . . .

And she'd smiled and told them how happy she was for them, and then had turned away to find the coach that was waiting. Their lives had moved beyond hers, and she hadn't had the heart to tell them her marriage would soon be over. They thought she had a man who cared for her, when what she really had was a business partner. Once their mutual business was done . . .

She would have to walk away. A thin stream of tears trickled down her cheeks, but she didn't bother brushing them away. Whether she wanted to or not she would still have to go, so what was the sense in wishing she could stay? She'd *never* gotten anything she'd wished for, and prayers had been equally as useless. When the time came for her to leave, there would be no one to wave good-bye . . . or miss her . . . or wish she could have stayed . . .

Rianne leaned back in the chair and closed her eyes again, so tired it was almost beyond bearing. Most of the time when she was about to fall asleep, she prayed she would not wake up again. It still seemed like an excellent idea, but wasn't likely to happen. Even God didn't love her enough to want her in His House . . .

Chapter 13

B ryan helped his wife into the carriage, then climbed
in after her. It had been a silent meal they'd taken
together, and that silence was now continuing. He'd expected anger from her, but it wasn't anger he felt behind
that heavy withdrawal. It was more like a deliberate pulling away, a determined reserve meant to be an unbreach-
able wall. He had no need to ask who the wall had been
built against.

He sighed as the carriage began to move, taking them
to Alicia de Verre's party. The girl had fallen asleep in her
rooms, something he'd discovered when Harris came to
tell him she hadn't rung for the bath she'd wanted. He'd
entered quietly to find her asleep in a chair, and although
he couldn't understand how anyone could sleep in clothes
and corsets and hoops and things, he ordered her left
alone. If she got a good rest, things might go better between them.

But things didn't seem destined to go better, only more
quietly. She'd been awakened in time to bathe before dinner, and then they'd both had to dress. He was conserva-
tively resplendent in royal-blue brocade, white ruffles and
hose, and silver buckles and buttons. She, however, was
breathtaking in a turquoise-green sacque that fell from her
shoulders like a windswept cloak. In front the thing showed
off her breasts to an incredible degree, and the diamonds
at her half-belt were echoed at throat and ears. Whoever
her dressmakers in the country had been, they'd been well
in touch with London style.

But she herself was out of touch, with the world and

256

certainly with him. He was sure he'd really put his foot in
it by being rough the night before, and then failing to
apologize properly. Her habit of not showing fear made
him believe she felt none, and that had goaded him on to
excess. It was true he was beginning to want to tear her
clothes off all the time, but he'd damned well better be
sure never to do it again.

In his limping campaign to court her, he hadn't gotten
much beyond paying her compliments and attentions.
Since he didn't know what else serious courting involved
that wasn't surprising, and having her in his bed wasn't
helping as much as he'd hoped it would. That was due to
his lack of control, and he was growing truly disgusted
with himself. Because of that lack of control, he seemed
to be losing whatever tiny amount of ground he'd gained;
if he lost any more, she would be gone even before they
found their quarry.

Jack had been prompt about getting an invitation to him,
knowing that Alicia's parties were so infamous no one got
in without one. She had a place not far from Ranelagh
Pleasure Gardens, where all those masquerades were held.
She was so wild about the appearance of the Gardens—
even though she'd never *ever* be found at a masquerade—
that she'd had her own gardens designed to match them.
If it had been possible, she would even have had a rotunda. Bryan had been to Ranelagh twice, and each time
had enjoyed himself thoroughly. There was something
about a woman masked and costumed . . . sometimes almost *un*costumed . . .

"How are we going to approach this Reginald Tremar?" the girl asked suddenly, surprising him. "I mean,
we can't just walk up to him and ask whose creature he
is. I've been thinking about this, and I'll be very surprised
if he turns out to be our quarry."

"Why do you say that?" he asked. If she thought there
would be no one at the party for her to identify, why had
she bothered to come . . . ? "Don't you think our luck
could run that good and his that bad?"

"It isn't a matter of luck," she replied with a headshake, her gaze on the darkened streets they rode through. "Don't you remember what Mr. Michaels told us his clerk said? He'd been trying to get an invitation to this thing forever, and now that he had one he was ecstatic. That's not a description of the man we want."

"You're absolutely right," Bryan agreed slowly, looking at it from that new angle. "Our man would have no interest in silly parties with silly people. If *he* tried for something, it would more likely be a knighthood."

Bryan considered that, trying to imagine what their quarry would *really* be after. At least one of his pawns, Harding, had had the sort of social position most of the common-born would happily kill for, but what did that do for *him*? *He* couldn't take Harding's position, even if the man had been willing to give it up. What you got at birth could be lost, but not transferred.

"I think we may have to let Tremar approach us," Bryan said after temporarily shelving an impossible question. "If he's that eager to be at the party, he must be certain he can impress people with what he has and who he knows. We'll let him find out that most of those there won't even listen, and then *we'll* listen. If we play it right, he'll end up mentioning everyone he's ever met. And we'll pretend not to know about his relationship to Harding until and unless *he* mentions it."

"And then we can be totally uninterested," she agreed with a nod. "Or at least I can be. Why is there a big hole in the ground in your neighborhood, when no place else seems to have the same? Wasn't there enough money to finish laying the street properly?"

"That's not a hole in the ground, it's a basin," Bryan explained. It was strange, but he'd gotten to the point of not noticing the thing, even though it was 120 feet in diameter and almost smack in the middle of the district in St. James Square. "They're supposed to be putting in a pond, but the basin was constructed in 1726 and they still haven't filled it in. They swear we *will* one day have a pond, but refuse to commit themselves to what century the day will be in."

"Well, they only have forty-nine years left in this century, so they'd better get moving," she said with a faint smile he could hear in her voice. "If they take a lesson from us, they'll have it finished in no time. We won't be taking half a century to do what *we* have to."

"No, we won't," he agreed quietly, wishing she'd turned even once to look at him. It would have warmed him to see her face even in the dark, a desperately needed addition to the very few memories he would have when she was gone. And she *would* be gone, so terribly soon, as she'd just reminded him . . .

Alicia's place was lit so brightly, it was visible from almost a block away. The street was full of carriages of all sorts, taking turns going up the curving drive to the front of what had been built to look like a miniature palace. Liveried servants were everywhere, handing guests glasses of champagne as soon as they were out of their carriages. By then it had already been determined that the people *were* guests; large footmen met each carriage as it pulled up, and politely requested sight of an invitation. If none was immediately available, the carriage was sent on its way.

After showing their invitation, Bryan helped Rianne out of the carriage, then guided her up the steps to the front door. She moved with such regal grace that most of the men they passed stopped to stare.

They moved out of the pleasantly warm night into the large entrance hall, and from there to the left into the ballroom. The terrace doors on the far side of the room were all thrown open in anticipation of many more people than currently filled the ballroom, and the orchestra played the latest popular tune. Bryan had no idea what it was, nor did he care. He looked around casually, as though he were bored, then began leading Rianne deeper into the room.

"Which one of these women is our hostess?" the girl asked in a murmur, still playing regal and unimpressed. "And wherever did she find enough crystal for all those chandeliers? If they all fell at once, no one in this room would escape.''

"Alicia has a passion for crystal chandeliers," Bryan answered with a swallowed smile. He'd often thought the same thing himself. "She feels that just one or two in a ballroom is positively scandalous, and shows nothing but that a person hasn't the price of more candles. And she won't be down for a while yet, not until almost everyone is here. She also has a passion for entrances."

"But our designated victim for tonight won't be doing the same," she said with a radiant smile that Bryan knew was just for show. "I'd wager on his being already here, quivering and anxious to begin mingling. Which we should begin doing ourselves."

"We'll let everyone else mingle with us," he disagreed, gesturing to a servant with a tray of glasses. "I've been to enough of these things to know it won't be long now. Would you like some champagne?"

"Yes. Thank you." Her reply was somewhat distracted, possibly because of the entrance of a rather large group of newcomers. They greeted some of those who were already there, but paused no more than a moment with anyone. Their ultimate destination drew them, and where they were headed was abundantly clear.

"Machlin, you cur, how could you do that to us?" Sir John Merriman, leader of the pack, demanded as soon as he was near enough. "You arrive with a vision from heaven itself, then walk her past us without so much as a nod. I'd always thought you were raised in a stables, and now I'm certain."

"It's good to see you again, too, John," Bryan responded mildly with a bland smile. "How have you been?"

"None of us is doing as well as *you* obviously are," Pinky Sedgwick came back with a laugh while Merriman growled wordlessly. "Not to mention the fact that we've sworn to return quickly to our ladies in the hall, who believe we're taking a moment to arrange a very private matter of honor. Happily, they won't enter the room without escort to find out the truth, so we've got a few moments to make thorough fools of ourselves.''

"Which we're guaranteed to do as soon as you introduce us to this angel," Peter Albright said with a wide smile. "And please do get my title right for once, there's a good chap. Ladies do so love titles."

Two or three other voices spoke together then, all apparently demanding the same. Bryan wished he could be amused, then said to hell with it. Just then the woman *was* his, so he had a right to be amused.

"Peter can't wait for the day when he becomes earl in his father's place," Bryan explained to Rianne as though they stood alone. "It isn't the estate he's interested in, just the title. Pinky over there will be Baron Holwell after his father, John already has his knighthood, Ian—I forget exactly what it is that he's heir to— Gentlemen, allow me to introduce Rianne Lockwood Machlin—my wife."

There was a moment of stunned silence during which time every eye went to the girl's ring finger. Her wedding band was plainly visible to anyone making the effort. After that the moaning began, right along with the complaints.

"Machlin, you're enough to make a man wish he were a younger son like you rather than an heir," Peter Albright said in disgust. "I don't understand how you do it, not only finding what the rest of us dream about, but actually getting it for your own. Are you *certain* your father's no more than a baronet?"

"Unless he's been hiding things from us," Bryan answered with a grin. "If he has, my eldest brother Richard will be delighted when he inherits. He likes titles as much as you do."

"Mrs. Machlin, I'm Sir John Merriman," the pack leader announced, coming forward to take the girl's hand. "That lout you're married to will never introduce us properly, so I've decided to see to the matter myself. Are you by any chance one of the Southwick Lockwoods? The eldest brother was supposed to have married a distant Hanover cousin."

"My father and mother," Rianne acknowledged with a

faint smile. "They've been gone for years, so I know only a little about the family."

"Her father's title went to a nephew," Bryan supplied from what Robert Harding had told him. "That and the small estate it included, though, were all that went. The family fortune came from a different branch, and so was part of his private estate."

"What beastly rotten luck!" Pinky exclaimed, having taken his turn at Rianne's hand. "Imagine inheriting a title, and then finding it comes with nothing but a piddling small estate. If that ever happened to me, I should sit in a corner and cry."

"But you'll notice the cur Machlin isn't crying," Merriman pointed out with amusement. "Even if this delightful lady had a brother, her dowry would be more than impressive. Do you have any sisters, my dear?"

"Not a one," Bryan answered for her, back to looking bland. "The inheritance is all hers which was, of course, the only reason I married her."

Catcalls and jeers came from every man within hearing, one and all branding Bryan a bald-faced liar. The spontaneous reaction brought a real, full smile to the girl's face, which was the end result Bryan had been hoping for.

"You know, I feel as though it's been more than a few months since the last time I was at one of these things," he said once the noise had died down. "There seem to be more faces I don't recognize than ones I do."

"We've decided someone has turned merchant," Pinky Sedgwick said in agreement. "They— Oh, dear, I believe the ladies have found other escorts into the ballroom."

The rest of the men turned to see the crowd of new arrivals, bowed their regrets, then hurried off intent on reclaiming the ladies they'd brought. Only Pinky stayed, and Bryan was curious.

"What about *your* lady, old chum?" he asked. "Don't you want her back, or did you come alone?"

"It was my honor to escort Miss Elizabeth Bowdler," Pinky answered with a very bland smile. "The idea wasn't mine but Mum's, and now the lady has latched onto poor

Sellars. He'll be fine when she learns he won't inherit, but for the moment his bad luck is my good. Where were we in what I was saying?''

"That someone has turned merchant," Bryan reminded him, exchanging an amused glance with Rianne. She apparently found Pinky as amusing as he did.

"Ah, yes." Pinky nodded. "The rest of us noticed the strange faces as well, and we've decided someone has pinched a handful of invitations. At a sovereign apiece, they'd make the man a tidy night's income. When Alicia comes down, she'll be livid."

"But some of them must be legitimate new guests," the girl protested, using her silk fan in a way that somehow made her look lost and helpless. "However is one supposed to tell the difference?''

"My dear lady, I'm at your disposal," Pinky replied immediately with a smile and a bow. "And do call me Arthur, unlike that husband of yours. He's not only a scoundrel for keeping alive embarrassing nicknames, he has the gall to stay away from our fascinating circle in order to make money. I know three times the number of people he does, and I'll consider it an honor if you'll allow me to help you sort them out.''

"How wonderfully gallant you are, Arthur," she said with a smile that nearly knocked Pinky over. "I would be *so* grateful for whatever help you were able to give.''

When she batted her eyelashes at him, Pinky was done. He bent over her hand again to show that his help and he himself were both hers; that was when she looked at Bryan and closed one eye. Bryan had been keeping his face expressionless despite the churnings of his insides, and that wink was like the balm of the gods. She wasn't encouraging Pinky—she was using him! Bryan couldn't believe the relief that knowledge brought. He still didn't care for the idea of her playing up to *any* other man, but at least she was doing it for the two of *them*.

And you'd better get a handle on that jealousy, you fool, he told himself sternly. *If she finds out now that you don't want to let her go, she could well take off at the first opportunity. You've made a deal with her, so for the moment you'd better stick to it. You need every advantage you can get.*

Bryan let the amusement show in his eyes as he nodded to her, which in turn brought her her own satisfied amusement. Her ploy with Pinky had given her the opportunity to take over the lead in the night's investigations, and she dove into it without hesitation. Taking Pinky's arm she let him begin to lead her around the ballroom, both of them apparently forgetting about Bryan.

Which, for the moment, was fine with Bryan. He ambled along behind, occasionally nodding to acquaintances, carefully listening to everything his wife was being told . . .

". . . and he's rather strange but completely harmless," Arthur said, the third useless description he'd given Rianne. She was beginning to feel a bit impatient, but firmly pushed the emotion away. She wasn't likely to hear anything worthwhile for quite some time, and it wasn't as if she were unused to boring male chatter. If she'd been able to stand it before, now she certainly could.

Remembering that Arthur should have been escorting another woman would have made Rianne feel guilty, if the other woman had been anyone but Elizabeth Bowdler. She and Rianne had more or less grown up together, but only because Elizabeth's father had been a close acquaintance of Robert Harding. It had been hate at first sight between the two girls the first time her father had brought her to Rianne's house to visit, and the snide little piece had never outgrown her nastiness. Dismissing concern for Elizabeth Bowdler was something Rianne had no trouble doing.

But what she couldn't do was keep her mind from darting off on its own trail every time she realized she needn't listen closely to what was being said. Arthur Sedgwick was a fairly handsome young man with a pleasant, friendly disposition, but Rianne couldn't help feeling she'd rather be on a different man's arm. That different man had managed to surprise her again, first by knowing personally all these people of position, and then with the unexpected mention of his family. He'd never even hinted that his father was a baronet . . .

Which was what her own father had been. Rianne smiled and nodded when Arthur pointed out his cousin, who wasn't there under his own name. His cousin's family, much stuffier about appearances than his own, would have been outraged if they'd found their son associating with the notorious Alicia de Verre, so the young man socialized under a pseudonym. Just as so many of the people there seemed to be doing, including her own husband. Everyone apparently knew the truth about everyone else, but proprieties were observed as long as no one spoke proper names aloud . . .

And Arthur was Pinky because of his tendency to color, not because of his hair, which was plain brown. Every time he paid her a compliment and she smiled, his complexion shifted more toward the florid. She could read him as easily as a book, not like someone else she could think of. *He* never let anyone read him, not unless he wanted them to . . .

"And *that* is Miss Lydia Worden," Arthur said, nodding toward a slender blonde beauty who fanned herself vigorously. Her face wore a smile that seemed to be covering the agony of torture, and she shook her head firmly to whatever was being said to her. The man talking to her was tall and thin and nearly old enough to be her father—although hardly likely to be. Miss Worden's gown and jewelry showed excellent taste, whereas her companion's finery screamed expense with no taste at all.

"The poor thing," Rianne murmured, using her own fan more gently. "Imagine needing to accompany *that* sort of relative to a place like this. He must be the oldest man in the room."

"I daresay we do have rather a young crowd," Arthur agreed with a thoughtful look. "When one reaches a certain point in life, one takes one's socializing elsewhere. Alicia quite prefers it that way, as men of her own age hold no interest for her. She's fond of saying the Compte de Verre, her late husband, selfishly used all the years of her girlhood before having the grace to die. Since he left her disgustingly wealthy, she now uses his money to buy back those years. She won't enjoy seeing who Lydia brought—a man, by the way, who is *not* any relative of hers.''

''Then who in the world is he?'' Rianne asked with brows raised in carefully drawn shock, inwardly holding her breath.

''His name, as I understand it, is something like Tremont, Tremar, or something like that,'' Arthur replied, making the chance a certainty. ''He's supposed to be something or other in business, with no family to speak of but a well-bulging purse. Lydia has—too great an interest in gaming, and her allowance is usually gone even before it comes to her. She was into almost everyone in the crowd, if not due to losses, then due to loans. One or two of them were seriously considering going to her father, who believes she's carefully looking around for the best marriage and knows nothing of her gaming excesses. Then, two days ago, she paid everyone off.''

''Let me guess,'' Rianne said with a sigh. ''That was the day the comptesse returned from Paris and decided to hold a party. But what can he possibly think his money has bought him? He looks like a stable man dressed in his very young master's castoffs.''

''I'd wager he's trying to appear young and dashing like the rest of us,'' Arthur said with a self-deprecating chuckle. ''And from the way Lydia looks, he must be demanding that she introduce him around. She knows well enough that the word about him has spread, and probably never dreamed that he would want to do more than stand and stare. She's as competent at judging people as she is at gaming.''

''I wonder what it would be like to meet him,'' Rianne mused, working very hard to make it sound as though she contemplated daring mischief. ''It would have to be under nothing but my married name, of course. If he ever found out I was *someone,* I'd probably never be rid of him. Even people who are supposedly well-bred tend to gush when they learn about my mother's family. Thank God no one's done it here.''

"Those of us prone to gushing have learned to do so inwardly with this group,'' Arthur replied with a laugh. "With so much of the cream showing up under pseudonyms, it's hardly polite to do anything else. I say, I just had a splendid idea. With so many intruders here tonight, why don't we introduce them all to each other? We'd first point them out to each other as dukes and princes and such in disguise, then make sure they understand one never mentions anyone's true identity. Then they could gush at each other, and leave the rest of us free to enjoy the party.''

"That, Arthur, would be terribly wicked,'' Rianne said with mock reproach before suddenly laughing. "Clever and rather fitting, but terribly wicked. Sometimes I feel desperately sorry for all those poor souls who spend their lives wishing they were someone else, instead of enjoying who they are. *You* enjoy who you are, don't you?''

"Yes, indeed, but I'm someone who it's certainly worth being,'' he responded, looking off into the distance. "If I were someone else entirely, someone who had to make his own way . . . The thought is unsettling, possibly even frightening. Your husband is envied more than respected by the rest of us, you know. The mark he made is his own, without his father's name and position. He may have been advanced his start-up capital, but even with it the rest of us aren't certain we could have done as well. Not nearly as well . . .''

His voice trailed off as the ghost of self-doubt came haunting, making Rianne sorry she'd asked the question. Doubting yourself occasionally is natural, but living with the belief that you would probably be a failure on your own . . . She couldn't help shivering, then quickly and deliberately changed the subject.

"I don't know about anyone else, but I think I'd like to be introduced to Miss Worden,'' she stated with an air of decision. "The poor thing looks miserable standing all alone, and will surely be grateful for the company. If you introduce yourself simply as Pinky Sedgwick rather than as Arthur Sedgwick who will be a baron, there shouldn't be any difficulty.''

''Dear lady, your wish is my command,'' he replied, taking a deep breath to banish the heavy mood. ''And poor Lydia does look like she could use a hand. Allow me to escort you over there.''

His short bow was wryly amused, and it gave Rianne the chance to glance over her shoulder. She'd thought Machlin was still as close to them as he'd been at first, but her glance showed he'd been stopped by a group of people at least ten feet away. One of the men in the group was talking to him, and the way he made no effort to escape the conversation said it was probably important.

Which meant he had no idea Rianne was about to be introduced to the person they'd come there looking for. As Arthur led her forward, she felt the urge to bite her lip. Machlin would certainly be annoyed with her for not calling him, but what choice did she have?

Since the answer was none, she was able to relax and smile. The music was lovely, and after their business was taken care of they should even have the time to dance. She would explain it all to him then, while he held her in his arms, and he would have to agree she'd had no choice . . .

''Machlin,'' Bryan heard as he followed a short distance behind his wife and Pinky. ''Just the man I really need to see.''

Bryan glanced around to find Robert Creighton calling to him, a smile on the young Lord Redstone's face. Robert and Bryan's brother Richard were good friends, just as their fathers had been before Robert's father's recent death. Bryan didn't care to be distracted from his reason for being there, but he had no real choice about responding. He had his family to consider, and the conversation shouldn't take very long at all.

''Robert, it's good to see you again,'' Bryan said with a smile as he approached and offered his hand. ''How is your mother doing?''

''She's doing quite well, actually,'' Robert responded

with his own smile as he took Bryan's hand. Being two
years the elder had never shown in Robert before his father's death, but now Bryan could see a certain maturity
in the plain but pleasant features. "Mother believes that
she and Father will be together again one day, so she's
perfectly content to wait until then for him to come for
her. She still has tea with her friends every day, and discusses what to wear when the time comes."

"That's a belief I think we'd all like to share," Bryan
said, nodding to the others around Robert. "I'd love to
stand and chat, but I'm afraid this isn't the best time. Can
we sit down together a bit later, possibly in the smoking
room? I have some news you're certain to enjoy hearing—"

"Won't be possible, old chum," Robert interrupted, his
smile turning wry. "I'll only be here long enough to bid
adieu to the crowd, and give my respects to Alicia. The
time has come to settle down to responsibility, which
means I shan't be by again. And that, by the bye, is the
reason I need to talk to you. I may soon require the services of some trustworthy men who are also capable. Who
else would I turn to but you to supply them?"

"I would, of course, be honored, my friend," Bryan
answered with true warmth. "The only thing is—"

"Come and walk with me for a moment," Robert
urged, putting an arm around his shoulders—or trying to.
"This won't take long, I promise you, and then you can
return to the pursuit of whichever lady has caught your
eye. I promise you, a moment only."

Bryan glanced over his shoulder to see that Pinky was
leading Rianne toward Lydia Worden, and decided he
could spare that moment. He caught a glimpse of a dull-
eyed man standing next to Lydia, but he was more concerned about what Rianne might hear from the Worden
bit. Ah, well, there wasn't anything Lydia could tell the
girl about gaming that she didn't already know, so it ought
to be perfectly safe. Ought to be. Bryan sighed, wishing
he could believe that.

"The problem is rather a delicate one, old son," Robert
murmured as they strolled toward a part of the room that

was less crowded than the rest. "I'll tell you straight out
that I had your enterprise thoroughly investigated, you as
well as your partner James Raymond. That should tell you
how serious this is."

Bryan let his eyebrows rise, and not simply for effect.
In their circle gentlemen trusted one another without question, especially when each knew personally the other's
family.

"You've managed to gain my attention for your moment," Bryan admitted, putting his empty champagne
glass on the tray of a passing servant. "But if it's the
Crown Jewels you're thinking of moving, I'm afraid I'll
have to decline. Even I can't be trusted with *that* sort of
temptation."

"Stuff and nonsense, old son, stuff and nonsense."
Robert chuckled. "Your coffers are full enough to *buy* a
portion of the Crown Jewels, not that that's what we're
discussing. And I'm told you and Raymond have each
turned down lucrative offers for hire that didn't meet your
personal criteria. Your partner may be a commoner, but
there's nothing common about his sense of honor. Or
yours."

"Your saying that means a good deal to me," Bryan
assured him, as serious as Robert had grown. "I'll also
tender thanks on Jamie's behalf, but now I'm even more
curious. If it isn't the Crown Jewels, it must be the contents of the vaults of the Bank of England."

"It's the wrong time of the year for *that*, old son, but
you aren't so very wrong," Robert replied, glancing
around to be certain they weren't being overheard. "The
B. of E. isn't the only one who ships gold and silver on a
regular basis to even out their books with banks in other
countries. Father did rather well abroad with enterprises
of his own, just like a number of his friends. When it came
time for them to send out jewelry or fine furniture or silver
trinkets and decorations and such, and in turn to collect
gold, they got together for the efforts. My father and four
of his friends shipped together four times a year, valuables
out, money in, and never had the least bit of trouble."

"When did that change?" Bryan asked, already knowing it had. If they weren't running into trouble, they wouldn't have needed him.

"Two years ago," Robert told him with a sigh. "Father and the others thought having their gold and silver stolen twice was simply a little bad luck to make up for all the good, but the same thing happened last year as well and once already this year, about two months ago. Now that I'm into it instead of Father, I want to be certain it doesn't ever happen again. If you and yours can't be trusted to handle it properly, no one in this world can."

"I think you might want to do more than simply hire one of my companies," Bryan said, already considering the problem. "Painful as the idea will be, you'll first need to check on your four associates. Are *all* of their businesses thriving, and none of them too deeply into gaming and fast living? If so, you'll then have to check their intimates. Which ones are allowed to know when the shipments are due to go out or come in? Are there mistresses involved, or even wives who can't keep from telling their maids *everything?* The list will seem endless, Robert, but it all has to be checked or you might as well simply hand over your gold or whatever and be done with it. And that's another question: are your shipments being taken right after leaving their place of origin, or just before they reach here?"

"Bryan, old son, you've managed to stagger me," Robert said, nearly wide-eyed as he stared. "I see I've done better coming to you than I thought would be the case, but we certainly can't go into details here. May I call on you at home tomorrow? About eleven?"

"It would look better if I came to you, but I know *my* staff is completely trustworthy," Bryan answered, weighing ideas. "All right, you come to me, but don't let *any* of your people know about it. Take your carriage to a club where you can get a change of clothes, then sneak out the back and hire a carriage to take you to a place two streets from my house. Wait until the hired carriage is gone, and then see if you can get to my house without anyone spotting you."

"By God, but that sounds like a lark," he laughed, the old Robert momentarily back. "Sneaking about like an agent of the Crown in those ghastly books—serious or not, old son, I believe I'll love it. I may even put on false whiskers."

"Just make sure you aren't followed, and we may even have a chance to catch the ones responsible," Bryan told him with a grin. "If we do, my partner and I get a percentage of any monies recovered. We can discuss what the percentage is tomorrow . . ."

"Lydia, my dear, you're looking lovely as always," Arthur said after leading Rianne over, pausing in front of the woman to bend over her hand. "I've brought a newcomer to introduce you to, but a newcomer in the most amusing way. Machlin has actually gone and done it. Allow me to present Mrs. Rianne Machlin. My dear, this is Miss Lydia Worden."

"Miss Worden, a pleasure," Rianne said with a smile and a nod. "Pinky has been telling me about the members of the crowd, but there are so many I'm afraid I'll never remember them all. Please call me Rianne."

"No wonder Bryan has finally done it," the woman replied, looking Rianne over with a faint smile. "Men do so love the obvious. Which is not a count against you, my dear, only against them. Do call me Lydia."

"I see I'm not the only one in the company of a newcomer," Arthur said while Rianne tried to decide whether she shared Lydia's amusement. "Pinky Sedgwick here, sir. And you are . . . ?"

"Reginald Tremar, at your service, old man," the other answered at once as he offered his hand. He'd been all but squirming as he hovered on the fringes of the introductions, and now jumped in with both feet. His attempt at instant friendship made Rianne and the others flinch, but Arthur was up to handling it.

"And what do you think of our little gathering, Mr. Tremar?" he asked while letting his hand be shaken. "Am

I wrong in believing this is your first time at one of Alicia's parties?''

"No, no indeed, this *is* my first," Tremar agreed with a heartiness that seemed forced. "It certainly won't be my last, though, you can be certain of that. Most of my friends felt I'd be out of place, but nothing like it. Feels more as though I've come home, you see. Yes, definitely home.''

He looked around in an oddly possessive way, as though now that he'd made his first conversational breakthrough there was nothing left but clear sailing. The man was narrow-faced with a sallow complexion, and his thinning, light-brown hair hung lifelessly against his scalp. His brown eyes looked washed-out and dull and, in his distraction with the glitter that surrounded him, sullen and vindictive. Rianne felt she would want to be armed if she ever had to be alone with him, and then those eyes were suddenly on *her*.

"Reginald Tremar, at your service, my dear," he said without waiting for a proper introduction. He also took her hand, which made Rianne's skin crawl. "We newcomers should stick together, eh? Those baubles of yours must have cost your husband a pretty penny. Next time have him come to me before he buys. I know where the best baubles can be gotten at the best price.''

Lydia Worden closed her eyes as she began fanning herself furiously again, probably in an effort to keep from fainting. Rianne had met a lot of boors in her life, but Tremar came close to winning the prize. Even a lowly house servant would have known better than to intrude with an offer like that to a stranger, not to mention a lady. A gentleman discussed price with other men, never with their wives.

"How lovely of you to be so thoughtful, Mr. Tremar," Rianne murmured while Arthur turned three shades redder. "And we newcomers certainly *should* stick together. I wonder though—whyever would your friends believe you would be out of place here? Don't *they* like going to parties?''

"Only with the dull and unimportant," he responded

with a grimace. "Fat little men with their big fat fortunes—not a bit of style to any of 'em. The only time they
let down is at Ranelagh, during a masked bash. They think
no one knows 'em, see, and then they can pretend to be
grand. Well, I *want* to be known, and after tonight I will
be. Just needed the chance."

He didn't seem to notice that his accent had slipped
rather badly, and seemed to be worsening as he drained
his champagne glass. Rianne wondered how many glasses
he'd had, to nerve himself to the chore of becoming
"known." It was all but tragic that the man had no idea
how useless his efforts were destined to be. No one *wanted*
to know him, most especially since the story of how he'd
gotten in had already made the rounds. Even if he'd been
acceptable in other ways, his manner would have put people off . . .

"I say, we'd better get back to circulating," Arthur put
in after clearing his throat. "Machlin's counting on me,
after all. Always a pleasure to see you, Lydia . . ."

He was obviously trying very hard not to notice how
pale the woman had grown; escape was uppermost in his
mind, even if it looked like a hasty withdrawal. The tactic
would probably have worked with almost anyone else in
the room. Reginald Tremar, however, proved once again
that he had no idea what "intrusion" meant.

"I'll just walk along with you, old chap," he announced, back to trying to be hearty. "And I don't mind
saying I'll put in a good word for you with the others.
Shouldn't let this Machlin make you do his chores for him,
not unless he's paying you. If he is, I'll let them all know
you deserve double."

A man with less poise than Pinky Sedgwick would
surely have groaned aloud, but the man who would one
day be Baron Holwell was made of sterner stuff. Despite
the reddening of his face he didn't utter a sound—until he
turned to see the two people just in the process of joining
them.

"Well, so there you are," the small, black-haired, pretty
young lady announced in frigid tones after his choked

gasp. "And you do remember me after all. Your mother, the baroness, will be delighted to hear that, after assuring me her son was the most attentive man in London. I did think, though, that she meant attentive to the lady he'd escorted. *Not* to a clumsy horse of an overgrown country bumpkin!"

"Are you still having the same trouble with your eyes, Elizabeth?" Rianne asked with sweet, smiling concern for the dainty girl who glared at her. "I should have thought the problem would have been taken care of long ago. Other than that, how have you been?"

Miss Elizabeth Bowdler began stuttering with fury, too far out of control to think of an adequate comeback. She'd been like that ever since Rianne had learned to pretend to ignore her nastiness, losing more and more control the longer Rianne remained calm. Before that time she had told Rianne that she was too large to attract any men at all, and in retaliation Rianne had stepped on her foot.

"I think you should know that dear Arthur here can't be blamed for not returning to you immediately," Rianne went on when it became clear the other girl was still having trouble speaking. "My husband asked him to introduce me around, to spare me the need of having to listen to tiresome business discussions. I think that was really sweet of him. Did your husband ask the same?"

Rianne held warmly to Arthur's arm as she asked her innocent question, the tiny smile she showed making her escort cough into his hand. Elizabeth's escort, presumably the "poor Sellars" Arthur had earlier referred to, turned away to rub at his face with two fingers. The girl herself was absolutely livid, knowing as she did that she was being laughed at. She'd tormented any number of others with her own laughter over the years, but repayment was something she refused to accept.

"So Robert Harding finally bought you a husband, did he?" the girl taunted with all the viciousness at her command. "It must have cost him every penny he had, but would have been a bargain at twice the price. And now you're married to a merchant! I can't wait to see the silly little man. Do you kiss him on his bald spot?''

Her laughter rang out at Rianne's stricken look, thinking she had finally scored against her old enemy. Rianne, however, was suddenly worried about another game, the one with the man Tremar. The tall, thin Tremar had been staring openmouthed at Arthur ever since he'd heard the words ''your mother, the baroness,'' but that had just changed. Elizabeth had named Rianne's stepfather, and that had taken his attention immediately.

''What's this?'' he interrupted with a scowl as his hand went to Rianne's arm. ''What have you got to do with Robert Harding?''

''He's my stepfather,'' Rianne answered without hesitation, knowing she had to brazen it out. ''I don't understand why you're so upset, Mr. Tremar, but I'd appreciate being released. You're hurting my arm.''

''Don't understand, do you?'' he growled, tightening his grip instead and shaking her. ''Let's take a walk and I'll explain.''

The champagne glass dropped from Rianne's fingers as she was pulled away from the others, trailing gasps of shocked surprise and halfhearted objections of ''I say . . .'' Tremar's fingers were like a band of metal around her arm, and he was clearly heading them toward the terrace doors leading to the side gardens.

''What do you think you're doing?'' Rianne demanded, trying to sound outraged rather than frightened. ''Let go of me this instant, or I'll—''

''You'll do nothing and then some,'' the man interrupted flatly with that cold, lifeless scowl. ''You said Harding *is* your stepfather, but we both know there's no more 'is' about him. The stupid, stuck-up fool is dead, and here *you* are, asking me all kinds of questions. Like I'm supposed to think *his* girl would ever treat me human. I'll know what you're up to, just as soon as we get outside.''

And then they were passing through the doors and out onto the terrace. Rianne suddenly realized she'd missed her chance to shout for help. It was still too early for the gardens to be peopled with those needing fresh air after dancing, which meant she was on her own. If Arthur or that man Sellars had been prepared to stop Tremar, they would have done so immediately. There was obviously a great deal of difference between a man who was wellborn and a man of action.

"This is absolutely ridiculous," she tried next, adding exasperation as she was all but pulled down the terrace stairs to the garden path. "Of course I didn't tell anyone my stepfather is dead. I don't know these people, so why would they care? I don't even know why *you* care. Or, for that matter, how you found out. And what in the world *could* I be up to?"

"That's the question that needs answering," he responded grimly, manhandling her up a side path to the right. It led around to the back of the house, an area that would be all but deserted. Torches had been set in sconces around the garden to flicker in the night breeze, and Rianne quickly decided on the one they were approaching as the place to make her stand. If she waited any longer, there was no telling what might happen.

"All right, I've had *quite* enough!" she announced, using every ounce of her body weight to force them both to a stop. "I want to know what's going on *this* minute. And I also want to know how *you* knew my stepfather was dead. It hasn't even been two days."

Her demanding words and imperious stare put a shadow of uncertainty in the dull brown eyes watching her. Tremar had been startled into stopping, but not to the point of releasing her arm. Rianne could almost see him wondering if he'd made a mistake, but then suspicion reasserted itself.

"You're the one who'll be answering questions," he said in the flat way of someone used to exercising authority. "I'll know what you're doing here, suddenly out of the blue, trying to get me to talk. What did you think I would say?"

"Nothing more than what you did say," she retorted just as flatly, ignoring the pain of his fingers digging into her arm. "I'm here because my husband brought me, and it certainly wasn't *you* we came over to talk to. Pinky insisted on introducing me to Miss Worden, and if I recall correctly you barged in and introduced yourself. I may have asked you a question I don't even remember now just to be polite, but that doesn't make me guilty of a crime. I know you didn't notice, but Pinky and I were trying to free ourselves from you just before all this nonsense began. *You* were the one who boorishly insisted on clinging to people who had had more than enough of your—singular—company."

The man's sallow face darkened with embarrassment, light from the torch just behind Rianne mixing his expression with shadow. She knew she was taking a long chance saying those things to him, but there was nothing else to do. She'd felt the fear under his heavy suspicion, and knew that goading him into rage would be safer. If only she could make him believe it was *all* his imagination . . .

"The bastard was right as usual," Tremar muttered to himself, his grip on her arm finally loosening. " 'They won't want to know you any more than they do me,' he said. 'All they'll do is laugh and turn their backs,' he said. 'I can buy and sell every one of them, even own some, but they'll never consider me an equal. You they'll just spit out and throw away. Stay away from them and be satisfied with what you have, or—' "

The muttered words broke off, and the fear returned, strengthened. Rianne was shocked to also see tears in those dull eyes, something that sent her back a pace.

"And now he'll know I didn't obey him, but went ahead and tried it anyway." Once again his words were spoken to himself and the night, but brought Rianne a sudden chill. "He'll know I called attention to myself, and that's the one thing none of us must do. But it wasn't my fault. It was her fault. What else could I think? He won't care, and now I've got to get away. But first I'll teach *her!* Singular, am I?" He turned to Rianne, his rage plain on his face along with his tears.

Rianne glanced wildly around the empty grounds, and

saw only the four-foot torch set in its decorative metal
sconce. She pulled it free with both hands and swung it
back with all her strength, the hammering of her heart
aiding the effort. She held to it with a double grip of desperation, turning trembling into frantic motion.

She struck Tremar just as he was trying to seize her.
His shout of pain and fear came as he stumbled back,
brushing at himself to be certain he wasn't afire. Rianne
swung the torch again, grimly determined to connect, and
that sent him back even farther. His intended victim was
now after *him,* and the look on his face said that had never
happened before. He'd bullied and bought many people
over the years, and none of them had *ever* fought *back.*

But this crazy woman was doing just that, and Reginald
Tremar was completely out of his depth. He didn't know
how to deal with anyone who wasn't helpless, and didn't
even care to try. Rianne saw the appalled expression on
his face just before he turned to run, but he didn't get very
far. Four paces back toward the main garden path he shuffled to an abrupt stop, every line in his body screaming
true terror. A dark shadow stood beside a bush on the
right, a shadow who was a man.

"No!" Tremar shrilled in a voice like a woman's, obviously having recognized the shadow man. "It wasn't my
fault, it wasn't! He shouldn't have told me not to try, not
when he knew I had to! And it would have worked, it
would! All I needed was the chance!"

The shadow made no answer, his silence that of the
empty night. But he did move two steps forward, casually
deliberate steps that set Tremar trembling and moaning.
He shivered like a small child as he watched the shadow
reach to its coat, and when the hand reappeared elongated
he began whimpering. *It's a pistol,* Rianne thought with
shock as she, too, stood frozen in place. The torch was
still in her hand, but now forgotten.

And then she jumped at the sharp crack of the pistol firing,
but Tremar didn't do the same. His whimpering cut off into
a choked gurgle, and then he began to slide bonelessly to the
ground. *He can't be dead,* Rianne thought in whirling con-

fusion, *but of course he is. That man just shot him, and now he's looking at* me. *If he has another pistol . . .*

But apparently the man didn't. His shadow hand returned the pistol to his coat, then reappeared filled with a different shape. A knife, it was a knife, and as he began to move toward her Rianne wanted to be violently sick. A flicker of torchlight had let her glimpse his face without shadow, bringing immediate recognition. The man she'd known only as O . . .

She knew he would be glad he had no other pistol . . . glad it was a blade he would use on her . . . And he *would* use it on her . . . enjoying the pain and death it brought . . . *Her* pain and death . . .

Chapter 14

❦❦❦

"Machlin!" An excited voice interrupted what Bryan was saying to Robert Creighton, and Pinky was suddenly there beside them. "I say, I've been looking all over for you! He's taken her out to the gardens, and we were all so startled we just stood there like loons. I considered giving chase, then realized *you* would be much—"

"Pinky, slow down!" Bryan ordered, the chill of dread twisting his insides. "Who are you talking about? Who took who out to the gardens?"

"Why, that Tremar lout," Pinky answered unsteadily, his face pale for once at the way Bryan held a fistful of his coat. "The one Lydia was foolish enough to bring. He spouted some nonsense at your lady, then pulled her out of the room with him into the gardens. They—"

But that was all Bryan stayed to hear. He took off at a run through the thickening crowds in the ballroom, knocking people out of his way without even noticing. He should have *known* that girl would do something to get herself into trouble, known it and refused to let her leave his side. Now she was out in the dark somewhere, with a man who would be almost as dangerous as their quarry . . .

"Machlin, over here!" George Sellars called from the left of the terrace. Bryan had just burst through the doors, but hadn't the faintest idea of which way to go. "I came out here while Pinky went chasing off after you. They've taken the first path to the right."

"God bless you, Sellars, for having a mind and using it," Bryan called back, but he was already running again

in the proper direction. If he managed to be in time, he
would owe Sellars more than he could ever repay . . .

Bryan was just short of turning off the path to the right
when he heard the shot. His blood went cold as he caught
himself almost in mid-stride, knowing it would be suicide
to charge someone armed with pistols. His own life didn't
matter, not at a time like that, but if his Rianne was still
alive . . . as she *had* to be . . .

He went to one knee and peered carefully around the
short hedge lining the walk that went to the right. It was
too damned dark to see everything he needed to, but the
most important thing was clearly visible in the light of the
torch she held: Rianne, and definitely still alive. He whispered a prayer of thanks, fervent but very short. The girl
wasn't alone on the path.

A crumpled shadow on the ground showed where the
pistol shot had gone, the one who must have done the deed
just beyond the body. The man was turned away from him,
facing Rianne, and even as Bryan watched the man started
toward her. His right hand held something Bryan couldn't
make out, but there was no doubt that it was a weapon.
Bryan stood and eased onto the path through the shadows,
needing to get closer before he was seen. If the man carried two pistols the way *he* usually did . . .

And then everything began to happen at once. Rianne
had stood like a carven statue as the man approached her,
but suddenly she came to life. Any other woman would
have screamed or tried to run, but *his* wife uttered a strangled, wordless shout and went straight for her would-be
attacker. She held the torch like a broadsword, cocked
over her right shoulder with both hands at its base. That
she was going to use it on the man in front of her was in
no doubt whatsoever.

Bryan cursed as he launched himself again into a run.
The torchlight had glinted off the knife the man carried,
but that wasn't the relief it should have been. Rather than
backing from the woman who came at him in attack, her
pursuer had braced himself and was clearly waiting for her
swing. Once the torch swept past him he would lunge with

the knife before the backswing came, and then there would *be* no backswing . . .

Bryan Machlin moved faster than he ever had in his life. Just as Rianne started her swing, the man she aimed for heard him coming. He jumped back and whirled around, bringing his knife up, and that's when Bryan's shoulder took him in the middle. They went down together and rolled, but the impact hadn't been enough to put the husky man out of the fight. He snarled as the two of them came to a stop, and brought his knife up in an arc that would have ended as it plunged into Bryan's chest.

But that was easier thought of than done. Bryan caught the man's right wrist in his left hand, then swung his right fist at the viciously snarling face. The son of a dog had been going to kill his love, and Bryan wanted nothing more than to beat him to bloody pulp. Even if he'd had a weapon, he wouldn't have used it; only bare hands could have satisfied his rage.

The fist connected with a thud, but Bryan hadn't been able to put too much into the blow. From his back and partially on his right side getting sufficient leverage was almost impossible. His opponent grunted with pain even so, then threw all of his weight behind his knife hand. No man's arm, even one the size of Bryan's, could withstand that sort of strain for long.

But that wasn't something Bryan had to be told. He'd fought big men with knives before, and had already begun shifting his weight to his right under the reach of his opponent. As soon as that was done he suddenly stopped pushing up against the other man, and at the same time began to roll. The other, taken off guard and abruptly off balance, went down to Bryan's left with the knife held between them.

Now Bryan had the upper hand, but the other man used his knee with the intention of doing serious damage. Bryan cursed and protected himself as best he could, and the two began rolling again. And then, with shocking suddenness, it was over. The man tried to twist his knife hand free, but just at the wrong time. Bryan's weight had come down hard just as the wrist slid out of his grip—and the knife was buried hilt-deep in his opponent's chest.

"Blast the scrofulous, blasted luck," he muttered once it was clear the motionless body was not about to move again. He'd been willing to bet everything he owned that the man under him could have told him exactly what he needed to know, but now the dog was dead. Much as he'd wanted to, Bryan hadn't intended killing him—only coming close—but now . . .

And there were also the sounds of a large number of people approaching. Pinky might not have come out after him on his own, but if Robert Creighton led the way more than one would have followed. And that wasn't by any means the most important thing on his mind. He pushed himself quickly back to his feet, then moved over to Rianne. The girl stood staring down at the dead man with no expression on her face.

"Are you all right?" he asked gently, taking the torch as he put his other arm around her. "Did either of them hurt you?"

"I really should be asking you that question," she returned, then deliberately pulled her attention away from the body. "I'm fairly certain this one was here for no other reason than to kill Tremar, and he almost did the same to you. As soon as I saw his face I remembered—he's the one who . . . did all those . . . *horrible* things for . . . *him* . . ."

As the words ended her arms were already around him, clutching tight as though for warmth or stability. Bryan held her to him as she fought with the memory of the nightmare, wishing he could do more, wishing she were holding to him because she needed *him*. Right then she probably just needed *someone,* and he happened to be handy . . .

"I say!" came with the sound of many feet on the path, and then two other torches were brought to join his. George Sellars was there to the front with Pinky, John Merriman, Peter Albright, and others behind. In the lead was Robert Creighton.

"Machlin, old son, are you or the lady hurt?" he demanded as soon as he was near enough. "For the love of God, what's been going on here?"

"It's that Tremar chap, and he's been shot," Pinky announced from near the first body. "Did you have a pistol, Machlin? I don't recall seeing one."

"Nonsense, Pinky, *he* didn't do it," Sellars answered with a snort. "Heard the shot myself while Machlin was still in sight. Must have been that other bloke."

"That's right, it was," Rianne confirmed, loosening her hold on Bryan. "That man came out of the dark and shot Mr. Tremar, then turned on me with a knife. My husband reached him before he could do me harm."

"But what in the world were you doing out here with that Tremar person?" Robert asked. "Pinky said something about him dragging you away— And did you say 'husband'?"

"Yes, she said husband," Bryan confirmed, hating the way she'd moved away from him even that very small distance. "But introductions can wait until later." Then he turned to Rianne and said, "Right now I'd also like to know how you ended up out here."

"Frankly, I have no idea *what* happened," the girl replied, looking perplexed. "One minute Arthur and I were talking to the man, and the next he'd suddenly decided I was 'up to something.' He dragged me out of the room while muttering to himself, and then all the way down the path to here. As soon as he released me that other man appeared, and Mr. Tremar went toward him. I imagine Mr. Tremar expected to have a conversation, but the other simply pulled out a pistol and shot him."

She gave a delicate shudder at that, one Bryan suspected was mostly acting. There was a good deal she *wasn't* saying, of course, but that would have to wait until they were alone. There was one point that didn't have to wait, though . . .

"Do you mean to say he dragged you all the way across the ballroom, and you made no effort to scream or cry out?" he demanded. "Did it slip your mind that I was in the same room, or were you simply trying to keep from disturbing me?''

"Do you mean you would actually have expected me to make a *scene?*" she countered immediately with what had to be shock tinged with mortification. "My dear sir, wherever do you think I was raised? In a barn?''

"Quite right, my dear girl, quite right," John Merriman soothed her, sending a scowl of disapproval toward Bryan. "Really, Machlin, the lady isn't one of your wild colonial frontier females. There *is* such a thing as propriety, you know.''

"Of course, John, I must have lost my head for a moment,'' Bryan muttered, looking down at the serene smile the girl wore. The little wildcat had done that deliberately, just to make him drop the point. Well, that was another item for later . . .

"We shall first thing return this lady to the house,'' Robert announced, gesturing someone into taking the torch Bryan held. "Once that's done, we'll send a houseman to fetch a constable or one of Magistrate Fielding's people. Can't imagine where that ruffian came from, but he's definitely not one of ours. They'll need to know that.''

"But he did have an invitation," someone at the back of the crowd contributed. "He arrived just when I did, and I couldn't help wondering what sort of new collection Alicia was beginning. He entered the house without a word to anyone, and then disappeared.''

"I really detest those with no manners," another voice complained. "If one *must* be murdered or do murder, surely good breeding would dictate that it be done away from gentlefolk. And they wonder why we dislike having them among us.''

"Yes, how ill-mannered of them to die and ruin our party,'' Bryan murmured, but no one heard. They were all too busy helping his lady back to the house, leaving only Robert to suggest he brush himself off. Not five minutes earlier he'd fought for his life, but it would never do to return to Alicia's house *looking* it. The comptesse would surely be highly offended . . .

* * *

Even once she was seated in a high-backed chair to the side of the ballroom, Rianne didn't let herself relax. She accepted a glass of champagne from Arthur with a smile, then sipped it as she looked casually around. Too many people were paying much too close attention for anyone who might be watching for their quarry to stand out among them, and then Lydia Worden was taking the chair beside hers.

"Mrs. Machlin—Rianne—are you all right?" she asked, looking seriously worried. "That horrible man—if I'd had any idea he would behave so—*insanely*—! Oh, it's all my fault!"

"Lydia, please," Rianne soothed her, patting her twisting hands. "You couldn't have known that would happen, so you mustn't blame yourself. We all do things in this life that under other circumstances we would choose not to. Necessity dictates, and we bow and pay the price."

"You're not just saying that, are you?" The other girl's blue eyes were wide in a still-pale face. "You really do understand. I don't deserve understanding, but what a blessing to have it. And from someone with enough good taste to despise our Miss Bowdler. Things were at least partially in hand before *she* flounced over."

"Yes, Elizabeth does tend to show up at the most inconvenient times," Rianne answered dryly. "And I can never refrain from responding to that waspish manner of hers. That makes me at least partially responsible for what happened, by not keeping quiet. *She,* at least, must have been delighted by the nonsense."

"Oh, no, she was much too busy being affronted," Lydia said with a full, real smile. "Not only did Pinky run off in one direction, George Sellars took off in another. In an instant she was completely unescorted, abandoned by one and all. The girl doesn't know what to do with herself if she hasn't a man's arm to cling to, so she stalked back out to the entrance hall. Hopefully she won't find another, and will therefore need to leave in a huff."

"No such luck," Rianne murmured, seeing the object

of their discussion approaching with yet another man. Her pixie-like beauty had always attracted admirers, but her complete lack of personality usually drove them away again in boredom. Rianne knew Elizabeth's father doted on his lovely little angel, and that had to be the reason she wasn't yet married. He hadn't yet found the man who would truly appreciate his darling.

"Well, so there you are again, Rianne," Elizabeth said as she strolled up, all but waving the man to whose arm she held. "And this time Arthur has deserted *you*. For myself, I'm delighted. Roger is so much more a man in every way, but I'd never have been able to accept his company if I hadn't come with a gadabout."

The man Roger, who didn't seem to mind not being properly introduced, smiled down at Elizabeth and patted her hand. He had blond hair, blue eyes, and a very handsome face, but something about him said he would be as good a conversationalist as Elizabeth herself.

"Oh, but I really must ask you to forgive me," Elizabeth went on, now looking sweet and sincere. "Just before we were interrupted, you'd begun telling me about your dear little husband. A merchant, wasn't he, with something of a bald spot? I know I'll just love meeting him. You're not hiding him, are you?"

"Not at all," Rianne answered. The girl's sleekness was sickening, and there was no real reason to accept it. "That's my husband coming now, but as far as a bald spot goes you'll have to look for yourself. Maybe—Roger—can help you."

Elizabeth's smirk of anticipated enjoyment was clear as she turned, and her gaze swept around everywhere but at the three men approaching their little group. Arthur had gone to bring Machlin to where Rianne sat, and with them was the man who had led the group storming to their assistance earlier. Rianne wondered who he was.

"Shame on you, Rianne," Elizabeth scolded, clearly enjoying herself. "You were fibbing, and you *are* hiding him. Confess now—he's gone for a short nap, hasn't he?"

"Elizabeth, you're amazing," Rianne said with a sigh

while Roger chuckled at his young lady's clever repartee. "You make yourself look more ridiculous every time you open your mouth. That's my husband standing directly behind you."

The small, dark-haired girl was instantly incensed at what Rianne had said. She drew herself up and then deliberately turned to sneer at whoever was behind her—and saw nothing but Machlin's coat, vest, and ruffles. She had to tilt her head back to see his face, and by then she was openmouthed with shock. Machlin's cold gray eyes looked down at her with puzzlement, and Lydia Worden's laughter tinkled out.

"Have you ever been introduced to Bryan Machlin, Miss Bowdler?" she asked, the words literally carved from amusement. "If not, I'm certain you've seen him around. And I'm afraid he can't quite be described as a merchant, although he does sell a certain service. Bryan, this is Miss Elizabeth Bowdler, who insisted on meeting Rianne's husband."

"Miss Bowdler," Machlin acknowledged with a nod, proving they *hadn't* been introduced before. And then those gray eyes were on Rianne. "I hope you'll all excuse us, but my wife and I will be leaving. Tonight's hospitality has been a touch more—brisk than I care for, most especially with her involved."

He'd extended his hand to her, so Rianne put her glass aside and let him help her stand. The champagne had braced her just enough to do so without wobbling, something she hadn't been sure would happen when she'd first sat down. She'd tried not to think about what had happened, but the reaction to it had still hit her hard . . .

"I'll extend your apologies to Alicia, old son," that other man said, clapping Machlin on the shoulder. "But before you go, I'd like that introduction you promised me. I'd just about given up hope—along with Richard and your parents—that you would ever settle down. You're certain to enjoy married life quite as much as I do."

"I'll have to admit that it isn't at all what I'd been picturing," Machlin said dryly with a glance for her, and then he performed the introductions. As soon as Robert Creighton had finished with her hand and gone through the standard compliments, Machlin said good night again and led her out to a carriage. The crest on the door indicated that it belonged to Lord Redstone, and had probably been handier than their own.

Machlin gave the driver directions to his house, then came to sit silently beside her. Rianne knew they couldn't discuss what had happened where the strange driver might overhear them, so she simply paid attention to the night. It was dark and quiet once the house was well behind them, street lamps casting pools of pale yellow about their own feet. There was also something of a breeze now, bringing with it a hint of damp. Tomorrow it could well be raining . . .

Harris was at the door even before they were both out of the carriage. His face and manner showed nothing whatsoever of surprise at their early return, nor did he seem curious. Rianne wondered if he was simply that perfect a servant, or was he used to his master's early return from parties? Then she wondered, if the latter *were* true, had his master come home early *alone* on those occasions . . . ?

"I'm going to get out of these clothes," Machlin said as he guided her toward the stairs. "I suggest you do the same, and then we can talk."

Rianne, having noticed the spots of blood on his vest, could understand that he'd want to be out of his clothes. She had the feeling something was bothering the big man, something beyond the evening's unexpected excitement. She nodded her agreement as they climbed the stairs, certain she would know soon enough what the problem was.

Rianne's maid was brushing her hair when the knock came, and the girl hurried over to admit her employer. She curtsied at his gesture of dismissal and left, but Machlin didn't move from the doorway until he'd made sure she was gone from the sitting room. Then, leaving the door of the bedchamber open, he crossed to a chair and sat.

Once again he wore his blue velvet dressing gown, but this time without a cravat.

"I think you look better in gold than in silver," he remarked, referring to the gold tissue gown and robe she wore. "Now tell me everything from the beginning."

Rianne, on her vanity bench, did so, putting back in what she had left out with the others around. It didn't take long to tell, and when she was through he stared at her thoughtfully for a moment.

"So Tremar caught it immediately when the Bowdler girl mentioned Harding's name," he said at last. "And he already knew about the man's death, and was suspicious over your not having mentioned it. What do you think he meant by all that muttering he did?"

"He had to be talking about *him*," Rianne said, firmly keeping herself from shuddering at the memory. "And *he* must have at least one of that crowd's regulars under his thumb. When the story spread about who Lydia was bringing to the party, he must have arranged to send his pet torturer to kill Tremar."

"I wonder if all that has something to do with the supposed sale of invitations that Pinky mentioned," Bryan mused. "It would be clever of our quarry to arrange the presence of a good number of interlopers, just so his man would be lost among them. When Tremar's body was found the interlopers would be the first suspected, but his man would be long gone."

"Only he isn't gone, at least not in that way," Rianne said, getting up to go to the decanter on a side table. "He was the worst sort of human being there is, someone who *enjoys* hurting and killing, and I'm glad he's dead. Would you like a glass of fruit juice?"

"Thank you, no," he answered gently. "And I appreciate your telling me your opinion of that. I wondered how you felt."

"What I feel is sorry *I'm* not the one who did it," she came back, turning with her glass of juice to face him. "In case you've forgotten I'm a partner in this, not some poor little female who just happened to be there. What do

you make of that comment about masquerades at Ranelagh
Pleasure Gardens? Tremar said that was the only place his
'friends' relaxed and enjoyed themselves because no one
knew who they were.''

"I'm still thinking about it, but I may have the beginnings of an idea," he returned, watching her walk back to
the bench and sit. "If it comes to anything, I'll be sure
to let you know. Now, would you like to tell me what's
bothering you? I can see something is, and maybe I can
help."

Those gray eyes were puzzled again, undoubtedly over
her unexpected outburst, but that was one question she
would *not* answer. Was she supposed to tell him that she'd
realized again how close he'd come to being killed and
how frightened she was at the thought of losing him? It
was that thought which had turned her knees weak at the
party, the realization that Bryan Machlin could well be
dead now.

And she hadn't been able to bear the thought. Even
though they would soon be going their separate ways, even
though she would be gone from his memory not long after that—how could she stand it if he didn't live? It was
stupid and mindless, but she wanted him to be happy—
even if he did it without her.

"What's bothering me is the possibility that our quarry
may now know just how close we are," she answered after
no more than the briefest hesitation. "Tremar mentioned
my stepfather, and demanded to know what I was up to
before he dragged me out. If the wrong someone overheard that or is told about it later . . . even if they find
out you're the one who killed Tremar's murderer—there
isn't a chance he won't be warned, and he may even be
packing to leave at this very moment."

"I seriously doubt that," Machlin replied, leaning forward in his chair. "From everything I've learned about
that man, he isn't the sort to panic and run. If he goes,
he'll do it when he's good and ready. And is that the *only*
thing upsetting you? The possibility that our quarry might
take off?"

"What else is there?" Rianne asked unsteadily, having noticed the sudden anger in his eyes.

"You're asking what else?" he demanded. "How about telling me *now* why you didn't shout for help when Tremar was forcing you outside. And also why you went near him alone to begin with. Those are a good couple of choices to get upset about."

"Why—I didn't shout because I honestly didn't think to," Rianne stammered, trying to find an explanation he would understand. "Even the people we stood among didn't try to stop him. Why would a room full of strangers make the effort?"

"Because that room full of strangers included me," he returned very flatly. "But you didn't think of me then any more than you do at any other time. And you still haven't told my why you went ahead to meet him without me. Tremar wouldn't have left if you'd waited. If he hadn't been killed, he would have been the last guest out the door at the end of the evening."

"I—was certain you would be right along," Rianne temporized, suddenly unwilling to point out the truth. She'd promised to obey him, yes, but he hadn't been there to tell her not to go ahead. Without a specific order to the contrary, going ahead alone hadn't been disobedience.

"If you were all that certain I would be right along, you would have waited," he countered, refusing to accept the lie. "What you really thought was that I would take too long, so you shrugged and went ahead alone. When I first saw you in the gardens, you were already holding that torch. Why did you take it out of the sconce?"

"It—I felt the need to defend myself with something," she stumbled, half-turning to put her glass on the vanity. He was changing subjects so fast it was making her head spin, and that soft, menacing edge to his tone . . . "Tremar was behaving so strangely—was I supposed to just stand there and let him hurt me?"

"So Tremar didn't just release you before his murderer appeared," Machlin pounced, reminding Rianne of the story she'd told and had tried to maintain. "He was going to hurt you, and you used the torch to keep him away. Why didn't you tell me that earlier?''

"You're getting me all confused!" Rianne protested, wishing she hadn't had so much champagne at the party. "All I did was swing the torch at him, and he began to run away. They're all such cowards, that bunch of bullies. They want someone helpless to attack, not someone willing to fight back!"

"There are times when that doesn't hold true," he growled, suddenly rising to his feet. "If you really knew what you were doing instead of just thinking you do, you would have learned the difference. That man with the knife wasn't a simple bully, he was a devil with a real taste for blood! He was just *waiting* for you to swing that torch at him, and when you did he would have sidestepped and put his knife in you! I was *there* and I saw it about to happen!"

By then he was standing over her and shouting, and Rianne could feel all the blood draining from her face at the memory. She'd been terrified at the sight of that horrible man coming toward her with a knife, and then something inside her had snapped like faulty laces. Insanity had taken her over, and she'd gone for the man with the intention of bashing his brains in.

But maybe it hadn't been total insanity. If she'd just stood there doing nothing, he would surely have hurt her terribly before killing her. Attacking instead would have forced him to kill her at once, forced him to forego his usual pleasure. Yes, she'd done the right thing, no matter what Machlin thought. A quick death was preferable even to living a certain kind of life.

"You *think* you saw it about to happen," she countered, making no effort to look up at his anger. "What if he misjudged his sidestep, and I caught him after all? Since I meant to swing in an arc, what if I'd gotten him first with the backswing? You can't just assume—"

"He almost killed you!" Machlin roared, reaching down to pull her to her feet by the arms and shake her. "Can't you get that one simple fact through your stubborn head?

If I'd been even a moment later, you would probably be dead! What did I tell you about risking your life? What did you say about obeying me?''

His furious anger shocked Rianne, coming out as unexpectedly as it had. She'd seen the man angry before, even out of control as he'd been the previous night during their lovemaking, but this—

And then she understood. Machlin was feeling guilty about not having been there from the first when she'd needed him, and so had taken to blaming *her* in order to ease his conscience. Considering what he'd done afterward it was ridiculous for him to feel that way, most especially since it put *her* in such an uncomfortable position. She admired the man for being so concerned about a woman under his protection, but concern wasn't what she wanted from him, nor was pointless scolding.

"Stop it!" Rianne shouted back almost immediately, struggling to pull free. "Just because you're feeling guilty doesn't mean I have to take this! There was no way either of us could have known a simple conversation would turn out so badly, so stop blaming yourself for almost not being there. God knows *I* don't blame you, so why must we have these hysterics?''

He stared down at her for a moment, those gray eyes filled with such fury she thought he would explode. Then, with great effort, he regained his usual, rigid control.

"So to you I'm having hysterics," he said, the words so flat Rianne almost flinched. "It's nothing but guilt moving me, and you see no reason for it. I don't happen to agree, but we won't go into that now. What we *will* go into is the question of why you risked your life. Didn't you promise to do no such thing?''

"Why do you refuse to understand that I didn't deliberately risk my life?" she demanded, wishing he would stop looking at her like that. "And I admit I promised to obey you, but *you* have to admit I didn't *disobey*. You didn't tell me not to talk to Tremar, now did you? In fact, we'd agreed we had to talk to him no matter what. Isn't that the reason we went there in the first place?''

"Stop looking so triumphant," he ordered, obviously completely unimpressed. He wasn't holding onto her arms any longer, but that wasn't the comfort Rianne thought it should have been. "You know very well I didn't want you taking any risks at all, and we were supposed to have approached Tremar *together*. You deliberately went ahead without me, and *that* is my definition of disobedience."

"But you can't send me back to your other house," she said as quickly as possible, suddenly terrified that he would do exactly that. "Tremar never would have identified the quarry for you, he was much too frightened of the man. If the others are the same, and there's no reason to believe they won't be, that leaves me as the only one able to identify him. Without me, you'll never find him."

"Under certain circumstances, I'd be willing to accept that," he said, the meaningless words almost a mutter. "If there was any chance he would go away and never come back . . . But there *is* no chance of that, and very soon he'll come to realize the very thing you just said. There's no question that tonight's events won't get back to him, and he's sure to hear stories about Harding's stepdaughter. You're the only one he really has to worry about now, the only one who not only can, but is *willing* to identify him. If I send you back alone he'll find some way to reach you, so that means I have to keep you here, where I can watch you myself and keep you safe. But that's also a problem. The second most important aim of your life seems to be the risking of that life, and I refuse to allow it. I'll have to do something else to be certain you're protected."

"What sort of something else are you talking about?" Rianne asked, bothered by the determination she could see in those gray eyes. "You know I won't stand for highhanded treatment, so what do you intend to do?"

"You'll find out," he said, then turned away from her to walk to the decanter of fruit juice and began to pour himself a glass. Rianne waited for him to add to what he'd said, but he didn't. Three small, uninformative words, and he refused to add to them!

"You can't just leave it like that," she said, watching him drink the juice he'd poured. "If you're going to threaten me with something, you have to tell me what the something is, or else the threat will be ineffective."

"I wouldn't dream of threatening you," he returned, the most infuriating blandness covering him all over. "You're my wife, after all, and a lady. No gentleman would ever threaten a lady."

"That didn't stop you the night before our wedding day!" Rianne snapped, seeing the same blandness in his gaze when he turned back to look at her. "If you could do it then, you can do it now."

"The night before our wedding day I threatened a female highwayman, not a lady and not yet my wife," he corrected mildly. "Tonight, all I've done is make up my mind about something. That can't possibly be considered a threat, so the question doesn't arise."

"Then tell me what it is that you've made up your mind about," she said through clenched teeth, fighting the urge to shout. "If this whole thing is so innocent, you shouldn't mind discussing it."

"Oh, I *don't* mind discussing it," he answered immediately, full innocence now joining the blandness. "It's just that discussion is so unnecessary, when you *will* find out all about it. Are you ready for bed now? We've both had a very long day."

Rianne couldn't hold back a sound that was a mix of infuriated frustration and a growling desire to commit serious bodily harm. He had no intention of telling her what she wanted to know, and any more words would be more of a waste than the ones she'd already spoken. In high fury she stalked past him to the bed, really wishing he was more the size of the men who had been her suitors. If he was, she was angry enough to have knocked him to the floor, then jumped up and down on his prostrate body.

It didn't take long before Rianne was in bed, and once Machlin drained his glass of juice he went around turning out lamps. Rianne lay on her side, hating him with every ounce of passion she possessed, determined not to acknowledge his existence in any way whatsoever.

Soon the room was completely dark, except for the slightly lighter black of the night coming in through the open terrace doors. Rianne expected to hear him leave, and was startled when she felt him climbing under the quilt instead. Her body flared instantly with desire, turning her mind wide-eyed with shock. She *couldn't* want him after the way he'd behaved, it just wasn't possible! And *he* couldn't be barbaric enough to expect that she would . . .

And he didn't expect it. His hand came first to her arm, stroking gently, probably to see if she would flinch away. When she couldn't make herself do so, the hand slid down her arm to her side, and then to her thigh. Her nightgown skirt was raised slowly and deliberately, giving her more than enough chance to protest, but that, too, was beyond her. The heat of his flesh had set hers afire, and it was all she could do not to move under its caress.

And then the hand was under her skirt, sliding between her clenched thighs to the secret she would rather have kept. Her body flowed with eagerness for him, and when his fingers thrust gently in to discover that, she wailed. She hadn't wanted him to know how weak and idiotic a female she was, how she couldn't even refuse him after he infuriated her. She expected him to laugh, to gloat in his triumph, but all he did was sigh as he turned her toward him.

"Don't cry, wife," he whispered as he held her tight in those arms, misinterpreting the sound he'd heard. "It isn't as bad as all that, and I'll try to make it even better. Don't cry, Bryan will make it all better."

And then his lips came to hers, unaware of the fact that they'd just spoken a lie. Bryan would make it worse rather than better, but he had no way of knowing that. A moment ago she'd wanted to murder him, but one touch of his hand had made her his without question. It was just as she'd feared might happen, she'd fallen in love with him. But he didn't love her, and once they'd caught the man they were after, he would return her freedom as Mrs. Raymond had said he was prepared to do. She would be alone in that freedom, once again facing the loss of someone who meant everything to her, but just then she lay in his arms. That reality forced away the awareness of everything else, thrust all regret behind her as she instantly merged with him.

Much later, after Machlin had fallen into an exhausted sleep beside her, she lay there and wept. This time the loss would be unending agony, but there was nothing she could do to stop it. Nothing . . . nothing . . . nothing . . .

Chapter 15

Bryan was up early the next morning, taking breakfast alone in the small dining room. Rianne had still been sleeping when he left her, snuggled under the quilts against the gloomy damp coming in through the windows. It was raining just then, and would probably continue to do so for the rest of the day.

Bryan filled a plate and sat with it, then ignored it in favor of the coffee he'd poured. He had a busy day ahead of him, but somehow he wasn't ready to start it. His mind was still on the night before, and the fact that he'd just posted two men outside under the girl's windows. A third would check on them every ten minutes to make sure they weren't eliminated without him knowing about it, but he still wasn't satisfied. Only catching the quarry would turn *that* trick, and they were still too far from doing it.

But also too near. Bryan toyed with the food on his plate, scattering rather than eating. After last night he knew it would only be a little while before the man they were after would turn to face them. They'd penetrated too far toward his identity for him to feel safe even if he ran, since he couldn't afford to run far. To be completely safe he'd have to abandon his very lucrative business of theft, and Bryan didn't believe he would do that. Destroying his pursuers would seem like a better idea to him, and for that he would have to turn and fight.

So they would soon catch up to him, and then they would either win or lose. If they lost they would both most likely be dead, but if they won—Bryan would still lose. His wife would no longer *be* his wife, but trying to avoid a final confrontation would solve nothing. The girl's life would be in danger as long as their enemy remained alive, and Bryan would sooner lose his own life than see hers taken.

"And that means I have to get to him as soon as possible," he muttered to the coffee in his cup. "But the sooner I get to him, the sooner I lose *her*. There's no way out, especially not after last night."

He leaned back in his chair and rubbed at his eyes, knowing how furious Rianne would be with him today. The decision he'd made had been to have her closely guarded by his men, but when she'd asked him what he meant to do he'd refused to answer. Some devil had jumped up and poked him, and the more she'd questioned him, the more he'd refused to answer. She'd been close to stuttering with rage when she went to bed, and then he'd compounded the torture by asking her to make love to him. She'd continued to uphold her end of their deal by complying, but that wailing sound she'd made had shown how mortified she felt. She'd *never* forgive him for doing that to her, and he had only himself to blame.

Even though it had probably been hurt rather than a devil that had made him do it. It tore him apart that she hadn't even remembered about him when she was in danger. She thought he felt *guilty* about almost losing her to that torturer's blade, when he'd never been so terrified in his life. How could she pretend she didn't know what he was going through . . . ?

"Pardon me, sir, but Mr. Michaels is here," Harris said, interrupting his rampaging thoughts. "He wonders if it's too early for you to receive visitors."

"He wonders if it's early enough for him to invite himself to breakfast," Bryan corrected with a smile. "You know how he loves Cook's efforts. Show him in, Harris."

The man bowed acknowledgment of the order, and a moment later Jack was striding into the room. His morning coat was rain-spotted here and there, but otherwise he was as impeccably dressed as ever.

"Bryan, how good of you to invite me to breakfast," he said with a grin as he headed straight for the buffet.

"I always miss your congenial company when you leave London."

"If it's my company you miss, why do you always come looking for it at mealtimes?" Bryan countered with a grin of his own. "Someone would think that what you miss is my food."

"Absolutely not, old friend," Jack denied with solemn assurance. "I would still continue to call on you even if you *didn't* have the best cook in the city. Since it's raining out, you should now know I'm not just a fair-weather friend."

"Forgive me for having doubted you, Jack," Bryan returned dryly as the other man brought a hasty plate to the table. "Are you here with news for me?"

"Of a sort," Jack agreed, going back for tea. "How can you drink coffee at such an early hour? It would have me all strung out before mid-afternoon."

"I picked up the habit in the colonies," Bryan answered. "Tea is less available out of the cities, and you're left with the choice of coffee or rotgut. Take my word for the fact that rotgut is very aptly named."

"I'll never understand how people put up with such a life," Jack said, almost serious for once as he returned with his tea. "The idea of having to leave the modern amenities and splendor of London for the squalor and struggle of the colonies—I would never survive, and probably wouldn't want to."

"People do what they have to *when* they have to," Bryan told him with a smile. "I'm sure you'd do just fine, Jack. In fact, you'd probably end up wealthy—if you could also manage to stop gambling. Have you found the second man on my list?"

"Yes and no," Jack replied around a mouthful of food. "After asking around, I discovered that Edmund Lawler is a leftenant in the military. He's known at one or two of the clubs who accept military rank as well as civil, and apparently he's on the brink of being promoted."

"But he still wasn't good enough to be invited out to Harding's place," Bryan commented, having finally started on his own food. "When will this up-and-coming military man be available for some conversation?"

"In about a month, when he returns from being on holiday," Jack responded, looking glum. "He was called away last night by a family emergency, and took advantage of accumulated leave. His squadron leader, a corporal Something-or-other, was quite firm about not mentioning where this emergency occurred. If I'd wanted to leave my card, the corporal would have been delighted to have it forwarded. He was most polite for such a beastly day."

"You saw him this morning?" When Jack nodded, Bryan did, too. "Well, that answers one of the questions about last night. The man *did* have someone at Alicia's, someone who lost no time getting him the word. Either he ordered Lawler away to save him for future use, or because his pet assassin would no longer be available to silence him if it became necessary. Don't bother to check on the third and fourth names, Jack. Crowns to pennies they've also been 'called away.' "

"What was that about Alicia's gathering?" Jack asked, finally paying more attention to the conversation than to his food. "You were supposed to see Tremar there, weren't you? Lydia *did* bring him?"

"He was there, and I did see him," Bryan agreed. "The only problem was, by then he was no longer in any condition to tell me things." He then ran through the official version of what had happened, just to get it straight in his memory. He'd certainly have to repeat it later, probably to one of Magistrate Fielding's people. When he was through, Jack looked at him strangely for a moment before shifting his gaze back to his plate.

"So the man went mad while speaking to your wife, and nearly caused her death," Jack summed up, sounding shaken. "If I'd known there was a possibility of that, I'd never have gotten you that invitation. And you say you're certain the man you killed was a creature of the one you've been after? How can you know that?"

"By the very fact that he killed Tremar," Bryan answered, unwilling to explain Rianne's recognition of the

man. "Could it possibly be a coincidence that so weak a
link was eliminated just as he was about to bring attention
to himself? He was where he didn't belong, a place he'd
been warned to stay away from. When he decided to go
anyway, he signed his own death warrant."

"That man you're after must be quite—ruthless," Jack
said, apparently fighting a shudder. "And you killed one
of his people. What's he likely to do now, do you think?"

"I have no idea," Bryan said, finally giving up on eating. "I don't even know what *I'm* going to do. I suppose
I'm hoping he makes some kind of move. At least that
way I'll be able to reply to it."

"Isn't there anything else *I* can do?" Jack asked, clearly
concerned and anxious. "You know I want to be in on
this with you, right to the very end."

"Yes, I do know, and I'm grateful for your help," Bryan
said with a soothing smile. "If I think of anything, I won't
hesitate to ask. Other than this, how have things been going for you?"

Jack smiled and began telling his usual lies about enor-
mous gambling wins and the large number of women they
attracted. He also finished what was on his plate, but didn't
go back to refill it as he often did. He simply finished his
tea, and then rose.

"Since you don't need me for anything, I'll be toddling
along," he said, offering his hand. "To be absolutely
truthful, I did leave the bed of a lady this morning to see
to my duty. Now that that duty is discharged and I've been
fortified as a reward, I'd like to return before she awakens.
When sleep still clings to her, it's possible to coax her into
doing the most—interesting things. We poor bachelors
must settle for an occasional taste of what you married
men feast on."

Bryan smiled as they shook hands, then saw him to the
door before going back for another cup of coffee. The
smile he'd produced had been a difficult one, the comment
having reminded him how short a time he'd be doing his
"feasting." For him that included pleasant conversation
and honest laughter, but she wasn't likely to consider what

he'd done last night amusing. He'd have to talk to her later, to see if apologizing would do any good. And he'd try to reassure her that she wouldn't be missing out on catching up to her enemy. Maybe *that* would make her less reckless, less ready to throw herself into the thick of things. He'd be happy even if it did no more than make her hesitate long enough for him to catch up. Assuming he was stupid enough to lag behind again . . .

He carried his second cup of coffee into his study, and once settled behind his desk he sent for his secretary, Jeffers Banyon. The man had a small, permanent office at the back of the house, and ran things for Bryan when he was away. Jeff was the perfect secretary—intelligent, efficient, and filled with a passion for order and simplicity.

But he was also one of the most well-trained fighters Bryan had ever seen, even taking lives when it was necessary without batting an eye. He'd joined one of Bryan's companies without needing training, and Bryan had never asked where he'd learned his deadly skills. He'd meant to promote Jeff to the position of company commander, but when they'd spoken during the interview Bryan had found him uninterested. Business matters were what interested Jeff, but no one had been willing to give him a chance with them.

Bryan gave him that chance, but not as just his secretary. Jeff was learning every aspect of the business, and sometime in the next year or so would open a company office in the colonies. He and Jamie had agreed the man was the best one for the job, someone they'd never thought they'd find. Jeff was absolutely trustworthy, and would probably end up becoming a partner.

"Bryan, I'm sorry I wasn't here yesterday to welcome you back," Jeff said as soon as he walked in, offering his hand. "I was entangled in personal business, and didn't get back until very late."

"I won't ask her name," Bryan said with a grin, standing to shake hands. "I stopped trying to keep track of your 'personal business' when I first found out how complicated it was. The question is, do *you* know her name?"

"I always know the names," Jeff answered with a grin that almost reached his pale-blue eyes. "The only problem is, I haven't yet found one I want to remember. I understand you can no longer say the same, and are now due congratulations. I wish you all the happiness possible, and if you think it's best, I'll stay out of her sight."

Bryan felt the urge to frown as Jeff sat in one of the chairs in front of his desk. A stranger would have thought from that comment that there was something wrong with the way Jeff looked. The man was dressed casually for their conference in a plain, off-white cotton shirt and brown breeches, off-white hose and buckleless shoes, his blond hair tied back with brown ribbon. He wasn't quite Bryan's size, but few men were.

In point of fact Bryan knew the man was considered handsome, and tended to attract a large number of ladies. Some, however, felt frightened by him, and actually hurried from a room if he happened to enter. It was almost as though they knew exactly how deadly he was, just from the look in his pale, cool eyes, and imagined they might be in danger from him. Which was completely ridiculous, of course. The tall blond man was a gentleman and honorable; no woman would ever have anything to fear from him.

"I wouldn't worry about staying out of my wife's sight," Bryan said after a moment. "She might be the least bit annoyed with me today, and if she is you'll be better off staying out of her line of fire. Jack brought a lead yesterday which I tried to follow up last night, and there was more than a little trouble."

Jeff asked for the story, so once again Bryan went through it. This time, though, he also went into detail about the man he'd killed, knowing Jeff could handle it all much better than Jack. Jeff nodded when the narrative was over, and then he smiled.

"She attacked an armed man using nothing but a torch?" he asked, apparently really amused. "You may be right about my not needing to keep out of her sight, but this time I might want to. How good a shot is she?"

"It's not funny, Jeff," Bryan growled, back to being more than annoyed. "She's better with a sword than half the recruits we get, but she will *not* be having anything to do with pistols. I'm having a hard enough time keeping her safe now. If she ever had a pistol to rely on— I don't even want to think about it. And speaking about keeping her safe, I don't want both of us out of this house at the same time. There's an excellent chance someone will come after her."

Jeff's brows rose at that, but on this point he didn't ask any questions. Again Bryan hesitated, then he told Jeff everything of the story so far, explaining why the quarry would want the girl dead. Jeff would be much more effective if he knew what was happening.

"Yes, she's definitely the prime target," Jeff agreed when he'd heard it all. "I'll be sure to keep my eyes wide open. The poor thing must be frightened half to death."

" 'The poor thing' doesn't think much of anyone's chances of taking her," Bryan countered flatly. "I could see that opinion on her face while we were having words last night. She's convinced she'll be able to avenge herself when they meet again, so she's actually looking forward to it. One of the things you have to watch out for is the chance she'll take off alone to look for him."

"How did you ever find a woman like that?" Jeff blurted. "The only ones *I* ever meet are too delicate to even breathe the air the rest of us do. They'd faint if someone frowned in their direction, but *this* girl . . ."

He let the rest of it trail off, and Bryan knew he wasn't expecting his question to be answered. He'd voiced what Bryan himself used to feel before meeting Rianne Lockwood, a woman who put all the shrinking violets he usually met to shame. And all too soon she would be out of his life again . . .

"We'd better get to work," Bryan said, finding his coffee cold but drinking it anyway. "I have a couple of errands I need you to do for me this morning, and you have to be back by this afternoon so *I* can go out. My father has a good friend at the Bank of England, and I need to ask him a favor. I've always thought of the Bank as the grand lady of the Empire who knows the secrets of all men who come in contact with her. Right now I need access to some of the lady's secrets, and my father's friend can help. *If* I can talk him into cooperating, which might take some doing. We'll get this work and your errands out of the way, and then I'll try.''

Jeff nodded and leaned forward, and they began to go over business matters. There wasn't that much to be covered, not with the way Jeff ran things, but what was there needed Bryan's touch. When everything was done and Jeff had his instructions, the two parted. Bryan had just enough time to realize how much he would miss having Jeff around when the other man left for the colonies, and then Harris was at the door, announcing the arrival of a visitor.

"There's a—person—here to see you, sir," Harris said from the doorway. "He insists he's expected, but refuses to give me either a card or a name. Shall I ask Mr. Banyon to put him out?"

"Mr. Banyon is on the way out himself, so we won't bother him," Bryan answered without showing the amusement he felt. "I *am* expecting someone, so why don't you show the gentleman in."

"Yes, sir," Harris responded immediately, making no effort to disagree with the word "gentleman." "Shall I have tea brought in, sir?"

"Please," Bryan agreed with a nod, then had to work at not laughing aloud. Robert Creighton, dressed like someone off the streets of West End, shuffled into the room past a silently suffering Harris. He was rumpled and slightly stooped, thoroughly wet from the rain, and altogether an unappetizing sight. He'd obviously taken Bryan's cautions to heart; at the moment, no one but his own mother would have recognized him.

"All right, fellow, come and sit down," Bryan ordered, playing the game. "And do try not to drip on my rugs, they're worth ten of your sort."

Robert waited until Harris had closed the door, and then he straightened up to give Bryan a reproving look.

"Really, old son, they couldn't possibly be worth more than five of me," he said, then grinned like a boy. "Even if nothing comes of this, it will still be the most fun I've had in ages. And I'm able to state positively that no one followed me here. Having the weather conspire with us has helped enormously."

"Then let's not waste that help," Bryan said, watching him sit in the chair Jeff had used. "I've been thinking about what you told me, and I'm afraid it almost has to be one of your associates who's responsible for the trouble you and your father's friends have had with your shipments."

"Why do you say that?" Robert asked, no longer amused. "Have you any idea how long my father and those men were friends? I can't believe one of them would betray the others like that."

"Most men will do anything they have to in order to survive," Bryan answered, trying to be compassionate. "Haven't you asked yourself why only two of the four quarterly shipments were stolen? Why not all four?"

Before Robert could answer, a knock came at the door. It was Harris and one of the housegirls with a tea tray. They waited in silence until each of them had a freshly poured cup and the servants were gone, and then Robert sighed.

"No, I have to admit it hadn't occurred to me to wonder," he said. "I assumed they weren't *able* to take all four shipments, not that they *chose* not to. That's what you're suggesting, isn't it? That they chose not to?"

"Exactly." Bryan nodded. "It probably wasn't the head thief's idea but the insistence of whoever was selling him the information on the shipments. An uncaring employee *would* have sold out all four shipments. Only someone more personally involved would try to keep everyone else from being ruined. He must have become involved because he needed the money, or possibly he was caught in a compromising position and thereafter was forced to cooperate. I'll need a list of the four partners involved in the joint shipping."

Robert wasn't happy, but he supplied the required list. As Bryan wrote down each of the names, he realized that if he didn't know the man personally, he at least knew *of* him. And a disturbing thought came, one that kept his attention until Robert cleared his throat.

"I meant to tell you this sooner, old son, but the memory of it escaped me until now," Robert apologized. "That row last night with those two interlopers—someone will be coming by after lunch for your statement. No one understands why those two chose Alicia's party to stage their production, but they're fairly certain none of *us* is involved. And Alicia, of course, was livid. Her invitations, from now on, will include the name of the guest invited, and that list has been cut quite a bit. She'll no longer be able to throw parties on the spur of the moment, but at least she'll know who'll be *at* them. Much of that is a direct quote."

"I'm not surprised," Bryan said with a faint smile. "When she began to send out invitations without the guests' names, people were impressed with her daring. *No* one did *that,* they said, so of course Alicia had to. She considered it young and reckless, but in point of fact it was foolish. Something like last night was bound to happen sooner or later."

"But at least now she's learned her lesson," Robert agreed. "If anyone wants to bring someone not already of the group, they'll have to clear it with her first. I think I'm relieved that I won't have to go through that. There aren't such stringent restrictions for a ball at the palace."

"The pendulum has swung to the other extreme," Bryan pronounced, just as glad he had no immediate intentions of going back. "Let's talk about the information you'll need to get for me, and how you should go about getting it. We'll also have to find a place to meet regularly and quietly, at least until we identify the guilty party. Afterward, I may have some suggestions on routine precautions for the shipments. If not, I won't bill you for that part of the consultation."

"Damned big of you, old son," Robert returned dryly,

making Bryan grin. "Ah, well, not to worry. When we
find the culprit, we'll let *him* pay all your fees. Probably
stagger the chap so badly, he'll never leave the straight
and narrow again. Let me have another cup of tea, and
then you can tell me what you need."

Bryan poured for the both of them, then went through
his requirements. Robert counted off the covered points to
be sure he had them all, promised to find a private place
for them to meet, then rose to take his leave. Bryan had
the stumbling ne'er-do-well use a side door rather than the
front as he had when he'd come. It had never occurred to
Robert to use the tradesman's entrance . . .

Once Robert was out the door, Bryan noticed that it was
almost lunchtime. That meant it was also time for the talk
he'd decided to have with Rianne. Another, more foolish
man might have hoped she *wouldn't* be angry, but Bryan
knew better. Her temper would never let what had happened the night before pass without *something* in the way
of reaction, and he couldn't wait to see what it would be.
After all, he was the one addicted to danger and cata-
clysm, wasn't he?

Bryan sighed, then started slowly up the stairs. *Of course*
he couldn't wait to see what she had in store for him . . .
not longer, certainly, than the end of the century . . . *next*
century . . .

Rianne stood by an open terrace door, looking out at
the drearily falling rain. It had been doing that ever since
she'd awakened, which was why she'd changed into a velvet and silk day gown. All morning she'd felt chilly in
muslin and lace, at least on the outside . . .

Inside she'd been just as furious as she was right then,
which would have been enough to send her former suitors
scurrying in all directions. When she'd awakened Machlin
was gone, but the memory of his infuriating behavior was
right there and waiting to kindle the blaze. How *dare* he
treat her like someone who could be kept in the dark
whenever he cared to do it? Whatever he meant to do
concerned *her,* and she had a right to know about it!

Her hand closed into a fist on the sheer white cloth of the curtain, an anchor to keep her from starting to pace again. She'd paced out every step of her rooms that morning, not once but over and over. She'd tried to tell herself it was anger making her do that, but far beyond the anger was a memory of how she'd felt last night in Machlin's arms. She loved a man who didn't love her, but some small, stubborn part of her mind discounted that. It gloried in what she felt when her husband touched her and she touched him, ignoring everything but that. That part of her didn't want to acknowledge her husband's lack of love, but it didn't matter. The rest of her had wearily given up on the idea of ever being loved, knowing it for the child's dream it was.

And that left her free to hate Machlin the way she should. The man was as stubborn as he was oversized, as impossible to talk to as he was to reason with. It added to her fury that she had to obey him, even when she didn't want to. If he ever decided to send her somewhere "safe," she would have no way to refuse.

But at least he couldn't chance sending her back to the country. The enemy would find her too easily there, although it wasn't likely he would come after her himself. Or maybe he would, just as he'd done so many years ago. He would still be thinking of her as a helpless child, and that would be her most powerful weapon against him . . .

"Does this open door mean callers are welcome?" a deep voice asked, one she had no trouble recognizing. "And today you're wearing brown and gold. Is there a color you *don't* look good in?"

Rianne had to forcibly keep herself from turning, at the same time silently cursing the distraction that had made her forget to close the door. She hadn't closed any of the doors she'd paced through, hadn't even noticed she'd had to open them. She was really tempted to answer the question Machlin had asked and say he *wasn't* welcome, but that wasn't part of what she'd decided. She would have nothing to say to the man until he told her exactly what she wanted to know.

"The chill in here is sharper than even the weather calls for," he commented, his footsteps bringing him closer. He must have been hoping she would comment in return, and when she didn't, he sighed.

"I want you to believe that we *will* get our common enemy," he said, now directly behind her on the right. "You don't *have* to risk your life to make it happen, or sneak around trying to do it yourself. I'm here to do it with you, and together we'll make him pay what he owes."

Sneak around! Rianne drew herself up at those words, angry all over again. How dare he accuse her of sneaking, when everything she'd done had been completely out in the open! She could see that the explanation she wanted would be some time in coming, but that didn't change anything. She was more than prepared to wait.

"You still aren't saying anything," he observed cleverly, the faintest touch of vexation is his tone. "Is this silence and chill something you intend to continue for a while?"

That was one she could answer by not saying a word. She watched the rain coming down, the world gray and wet behind its transparent curtain, a small amount of satisfaction beginning to rise. He seemed to dislike her lack of response; if he disliked it strongly enough, that explanation might be forthcoming sooner than expected.

"I could always order you to talk to me," he mused, obviously having understood her answer. "Since that's part of our deal you would have to obey me, but I think I'd rather do something else. Lunch will be ready soon, so I hope you'll forgive me if at any time you feel rushed."

Rianne had no idea what he was talking about, but his hand to her arm began to give her a hint. He used that gentle grip to draw her away from the window and into his arms, and then he was kissing her as if she'd run happily into his arms. She tried to keep herself from responding to the kiss, needing nothing more in the way of pain, but it simply wasn't possible. That one small part inside forced her to respond, most especially since the kiss was sweet rather than passionate. It was unlike any other kiss he'd ever given her, almost like something from a friend rather than a lover. But that didn't keep the contact from being painful, and when it ended she was almost as relieved as she was sorry.

"Would you like to tell me what this was all about?" she asked once he had released her and she'd caught her breath. "If you were making a point, I'm afraid I missed it."

"I—didn't want you to be angry with me," he groped, suddenly looking like a guilty little boy. A very large, guilty little boy. "I thought this would—bring us close together again, the way two people working together should be. I wasn't trying to upset you last night, I was just wrapped up in trying to protect your life. I would appreciate it if you could bring yourself to believe that."

"I do believe it—but I *don't* appreciate it," Rianne stated, realizing he still meant to keep his secret. "If that's your usual manner of protecting things, I'd rather be in danger. Did you say lunch was ready?"

He parted his lips to say something else, but the distance Rianne had put in her manner apparently made him change his mind. Rather than speak he nodded, then waited for her to lead the way out of the room. His sigh told her he hadn't accomplished whatever it was he'd really been after, and that brought some small satisfaction.

Lunch was a quiet affair, after Machlin stopped trying to make small talk. Rianne resisted every attempt, more than aware that he was trying to make things better between them. It was such a futile effort, smoothing things over so that they could part on good terms. She didn't *want* to be on good terms with him, she wanted to hate him. Which she would certainly do after they'd finally caught up to the enemy . . .

"I'll be going out this afternoon," he said after a long while. Rianne looked up to see him sitting back in his chair, apparently finished with his meal. "I don't know when I'll be getting back, but it might be late. Don't feel that you have to wait up."

"Do you have another lead?" she asked, something in

his manner suggesting he did. "If so, I want to go with you."

"All I really have is our original lead and a vague idea," he answered, dark-red brows knit with frustration. "I learned this morning that the second heir in Harding's will left the city last night on a 'family emergency.' That tells me the third is probably gone as well, and possibly even the executor has disappeared. I've decided to speak to a man I know, someone who can give me information the public isn't usually permitted to know—if I can talk him into it. That's why I have to go alone."

"And what do you expect this man will be telling you?" Rianne asked, foolishly feeling unwanted and unneeded. Of course she was, at least until it became time to identify the quarry.

"I don't know," he admitted. "It's all part of that vague idea I just mentioned, but that doesn't mean you're now uninvolved. I have the feeling we'll be going out again in the next couple of days, for a social event similar to the one last night."

"Does that scenario include dead bodies too?" Rianne asked innocently, annoyed that he refused to go into more detail about his immediate plans. "If it does, I'm definitely going to be bringing my sword."

"No bodies," he returned flatly, those gray eyes not in the least amused. "And certainly no sword. Aside from the fact that Londoners thrive on scandal, I refuse to tempt fate. Weapons draw their like, and I don't want that sort of thing drawn to *you*."

"My being unarmed last night didn't keep things from being drawn to me," Rianne pointed out. "But if you're that concerned about scandal and public opinion, just forget about the sword. If the need happens to arise again, I'll manage the way I did the first time."

Her concession didn't soothe him any more than she'd intended it to, but the disagreement didn't continue. It was a long moment before he spoke again, and then it was on another subject.

"When I go out, I'll be leaving my secretary in charge

of the house and your safety," he said. "His name is Jeff
Banyon, and you can trust him completely. If something
happens, do as Jeff tells you and don't worry. He's as good
with a sword, pistol, bow, and whip as he is with figures
and appointments."

"Whip?" Rianne echoed, never having met anyone who
could handle the weapon called a bullwhip. She'd heard a
number of people in the colonies could, and so had become interested. She was about to ask another question,
but Harris chose that moment to appear.

"Excuse me, sir, but there's someone from Magistrate
Fielding's office here," he said to Machlin. "He has one
of the magistrate's cards rather than his own, and he asks
if you might spare him some time."

"Tell him I've been expecting him, Harris, and take
him to my study," Machlin said, reaching for his cup of
tea. "I'll be there shortly."

Harris bowed his way out, and Machlin waited for the
door to close before he looked at Rianne.

"That's about last night, of course," he said very softly.
"Fielding is the most respected magistrate this city's seen
in a long while, and he often has his people help the con-
stabulary with investigations. I'll give the man a statement, and that should take care of it."

"At least until the next time," Rianne muttered, but
too low for Machlin to hear. He simply finished his tea,
pushed away from the table, then left the room. Rianne
wondered if they would want to question her as well, then
laughed at herself for being ridiculous. They'd never consider talking to a poor, helpless woman, even if she *was*
the only one who had been there for everything that had
happened. Statements from the men involved would be
much more thorough and useful than anything a *woman*
could have to say.

Rianne stayed in the small dining room for another cup
of tea, trying to figure out how Machlin would test his
idea. She pushed and prodded at everything she knew for
a while, then realized he might have learned things that

morning which he hadn't shared. Unless she found out what those things were, she was wasting her time.

"And if he meant to tell me, he would have already done it," she muttered, pushing her chair back and standing. "If I miss out on the end of this, I won't have any trouble hating him afterward."

She stood there next to the table for a moment, watching the rain through the curtained window, then decided to go back to her rooms. At one time she had enjoyed rainy days, but after her mother was gone there had been nothing to do when it rained, and no one to talk to. After a while she'd gotten into the habit of staying in her bed-chamber and sewing, a pastime she'd never admitted she enjoyed. Since Machlin intended taking off on his own, it would be a good time to return to the habit.

She expected the front hall to be empty, but Machlin was there dressed to go out, talking to another man who seemed to have just come in. His coat and the hat he held were spattered with raindrops, and he gestured toward the large envelope he held as he spoke. Machlin nodded as he listened, clearly paying careful attention to whatever he was giving his approval to. *Business matters,* Rianne thought with annoyance, *and nothing to be discussed with a woman.*

The man Machlin spoke to was almost as large as he, with blond hair that looked unruly even though it was neatly and properly tied back. Even from where she stood Rianne could see how light his eyes were, a pale, pale blue that suggested ruthlessness and soullessness. The man who was probably Jeff Banyon was very handsome, but Rianne couldn't help wondering how many women would be able to meet that death-blue gaze. And then the man's voice rose ever so slightly, just enough to let her hear what he said.

"I recommend that you be especially charming to the guardian of that grand lady you're so intent on getting together with," he said to Machlin with a laugh. "If you don't get past him you'll never get to *her,* and that would be a pity."

"More than just a pity," Machlin replied with a laugh of his own. "I've made up my mind not to take no for an answer, no matter how long and hard I have to talk. I—" That was when he noticed Rianne where she stood, and continued, "Oh, Rianne, you're still down here. Good, I'm glad you are. I'll be leaving as soon as the carriage horses are changed, but right now I'd like you to meet Jeff Banyon. Jeff's been taking care of something for the both of us."

"Mr. Banyon." Rianne acknowledged the introduction with a nod as she approached them, then returned her attention to Machlin. She was still puzzling over the partial conversation she'd heard, but Machlin's comment diverted her. "Something for the both of us, did you say?"

"Collecting your inheritance," Machlin clarified, pointing to the large envelope. "Once I sign and return those papers, the trustees will begin turning over everything. As soon as I have a moment, I'd like you to sit down with me. I'll show you everything involved, and you can tell me if there's anything special you'd like done with any of it."

"Me?" Rianne almost squeaked, taken totally by surprise. "You want to ask *me?*"

"Why not?" Machlin countered, obviously amused behind the mildness of his tone. "It comes from your family. If you want a say in what's done with it, you should be able to have one."

"What if I decide on the wrong thing?" she demanded, certain he had to be joking or lying. "Are you just going to sit there and let me ruin things?"

"Of course not," he returned, still with that mild amusement. "If you choose the wrong thing, I'll tell you why it's wrong and let you choose again. No one is *born* knowing all about business. Even Jeff here had things he needed to learn."

"Mostly things I didn't *know* I needed to learn," Jeff Banyon said with a grin. "It came as a shock, but luckily Bryan—Mr. Machlin—was here to soften the blow."

"And Jeff also brought back something *just* for you,"

Machlin went on, at the same time gesturing to the man who had appeared at the front door. The carriage was ready, and Machlin was eager to go. "I'll see you get it later or tomorrow, depending on when I get back. A substantial stack of sovereigns, so if you want to go shopping tomorrow you can do it with *your* money. Call it an advance against the coming inheritance."

He raised her chin with his hand to give her a brief kiss, then strode out after the man who was obviously his driver. Rianne stood there in confusion, staring at the closed door, and then she looked at Jeff Banyon.

"Is he serious?" she demanded, certain the blond man would know the truth. "He sounded serious, but this has to be some sort of elaborate practical joke. No man alive would do for a woman what he says he intends."

"I'd say he's considering the woman," Banyon returned, his smile amused. "He believes in teaching those capable of being taught, those with an interest in it. *Do* you have an interest in being taught?"

"I don't know," Rianne answered honestly, seriously bothered. "I never thought I'd have a reason to think about it. Now that I do . . . Damn the man. He ought to know by now that I hate surprises."

"You're not alone in that," Banyon agreed with a laugh. "Only people who have never had anything unpleasant happen to them feel differently. Is there anything I can do for you before I get back to my work?"

"Yes, but I doubt if you'd be willing." Rianne looked at him, the beginnings of vexation showing through. "I'd *love* to see that man damaged a little, preferably with something heavy over the head. I'd do it myself, but I hate mussing my gowns."

"Quite understandable," Banyon murmured, trying to swallow a grin. "I'd certainly oblige you, but this is a new coat. I'm sure you understand."

Rianne smiled, understanding even better what he *wasn't* saying. Machlin was right to trust him, but she had other things to think about. She excused herself and headed for the stairs, thoughts of decisions and sovereigns chasing themselves around in her head.

Jeff Banyon watched his employer's wife disappear up the stairs, then turned silently toward his office at the back of the house. He'd liked her immediately, he realized, even though he'd been reserving opinion on the suitability of *any* woman for Bryan Machlin. Bryan was a special man who deserved something special in a mate—and it looked like he'd found it.

Rianne Machlin was just a little too tall for his taste, and would probably be the same for any man who didn't have Bryan's size. And she cared about him, that had been easy to see once he was no longer standing with them. She kept control of her expression when Bryan looked at her, even when she was shocked and disbelieving. Must be that argument Bryan had said they'd had . . . an angry woman doesn't want *anyone* to read her deeper feelings, especially the man she's angry with . . .

Jeff closed the door to his office behind him, hung his hat and coat on the rack to dry, then sat at his desk. The woman had asked him to take something heavy to Bryan's head, but it was a good thing he'd answered in the joking manner he'd been sure *she* was using. He had the distinct impression that girl would go after *anyone* who tried to harm her husband, him included. The idea was warming, in a way only men like himself and Bryan could appreciate. People asked *them* for protection, they never offered it.

But it was now easy to see why Bryan had such a problem. Jeff leaned forward to frown at the envelope he'd carried in, sitting damply on his desk. To have a woman like that risk herself was something that would also have driven *him* crazy, but stopping her couldn't be as easy as he'd thought. Ordering her to obey wouldn't do it, not if she'd made up her mind differently. She'd die in her tracks rather than back down.

Jeff sat thinking for another moment, then got up to retrieve his coat. Bryan had assigned one of his men to check the guard posts, but Jeff would feel better if he checked them himself. And while he did, he could be asking himself what *he* would do with a woman like that . . . short of tying her hand and foot . . .

Chapter 16

The next day passed strangely for Rianne. It started when she awoke that morning to a fresh, sunny day. She'd tried to wait up for Machlin's return the night before, but sleep had come before he had. But he'd been in her bedchamber, the proof being the heavy purse of sovereigns left on her vanity. He'd kept that part of his word, at least, and hadn't even stopped to take payment for the gesture.

"He must be planning on doing that later," she muttered to herself before ringing for a maid. Along with the sovereigns he'd also left a gift, a rose-shaped brooch in rubies and diamonds. The thing was beautiful and obviously expensive as well, but for some reason it disturbed Rianne. She finally decided he had private reasons for being so generous, reasons he would probably share once she was sufficiently grateful. It was a cynical thought that should have made her feel ashamed, but what it actually made her feel was sad.

She took breakfast alone in the small dining room, Harris having told her that Mr. Machlin was still asleep. He hadn't gotten back until the wee hours, and had left word not to be disturbed unless there was an emergency. Rianne shrugged in agreement, then asked Harris to arrange for a carriage and driver. She wanted to see all those wonderful places to shop she kept hearing about.

When she and the carriage were ready, so was Jeff Banyon and a discreet escort. The carriage driver wasn't the one who had taken Machlin the day before, and this new man had a companion who moved like a hunting cat. All

three of them did that, Rianne realized, the two men and
Jeff Banyon. And Machlin, although it was harder to see
because of his size. She asked casually how dangerous
shopping was supposed to be, and Banyon grinned. She
didn't need the words to know that with them there, it
wasn't going to be dangerous in the least.

As it turned out, it was more boring than dangerous.
There seemed to be quite a lot of carriages out, especially
on the streets where the most popular shops were. In places
it was very slow going, and while Rianne looked out at
the people and buildings and cobbled streets, she had
enough time to think about the gold and the brooch Machlin had given her, worrying at the why of his actions.
Much of the gold lay heavy in her reticule, and the first
thing it did was cause a stir.

Rianne spotted a gunsmith's shop not far from the first
dress shop Banyon said they were going to, and a display
in the window caught her eye. When the carriage stopped,
she first led Banyon back to the gunsmith's. What had
caught her attention had been a pair of pistols, a matched
set with silver-inlaid ebony grips and barrels polished to
the same shining silver.

Seeing them up close convinced her they were something any man would love to own, and only then did she
realize she wanted them for Machlin. Why she would think
of buying him a gift she didn't know, but the money was
hers and she could do what she pleased with it.

And so she had bought the pistols, along with the ebony-
and-silver case they came with. The gunsmith's clerk, who
had been startled to see a lady entering, suddenly became
delighted—until *she* was the one who produced the sovereigns. He'd expected to send the bill to her husband, or
at the very least be paid by her male companion. It scandalized him that *she* was the one handing over the gold,
and for a moment looked as though he'd refuse to take it.
That was when Banyon stepped forward, and although the
big blond didn't say anything, the clerk gulped and quickly
completed the transaction.

It was just as they were leaving the shop that the thought

came to her, the sudden understanding of why Machlin's gifts had bothered her. It had been a memory trying to break through, one linked to the short conversation she'd overheard the day before, and the distraction caused by the clerk had apparently been enough to let it all come together.

The memory was of another of the books she'd read, a novel about a wealthy lord who was very hard to please when it came to women. He would invite ladies to stay at his estate for a while, and when he tired of them he would give them gold and send them away. He would do it even if they cried and begged to be allowed to stay, the tears and pleas never moving him. He'd seemed very cruel until it was pointed out that he searched for someone *he* could love, not just someone who loved *him*. He finally found the girl, but not until he'd sent away other women without number.

Of course, he'd never married any of the women he lived with, but that was only because he hadn't had to. When he'd first brought them to his house he was very attentive, but then he'd grown bored and began to look elsewhere. Angus, who had also read the book, had said that was because the man was the sort he, Angus, had heard about. That sort was eager for what he didn't have, but as soon as he got it he began to grow bored. Angus had warned Rianne to be careful about becoming involved with a man like that, since the upper class was supposed to be full of them.

Rianne was rather badly shaken, but was surprised she hadn't seen the answer sooner. Especially after the comments she'd overheard about the grand lady Machlin was determined to get together with. Now, with all the rest, those few words made sense. That man in the book—when he was through with a woman, he usually gave her an expensive trinket as well as some gold. The piece of jewelry was meant as an extra thank-you, and could either be kept as a remembrance or sold. The man considered the gesture only fair, after what the woman had given *him*.

Fair. Yes, the man had been very much concerned with what was fair . . .

After that Rianne visited the dressmaker's shop, but couldn't really concentrate on finding a fabric she wanted another gown in. She finally bought ten yards of short-napped velvet in dark-blue and the same of cotton in off-white, along with matching thread. The purchase, among other things, was to give them a reason to leave, and when it came time to pay she gave the money to Banyon, then had him take her back to Machlin's house. She no longer cared who paid for what, not with the new understanding filling her thoughts.

It was past lunchtime, and Machlin had already eaten and gone. Rianne asked that tea be sent to her rooms, but said no to any food. Despite her outing she wasn't at all hungry, which was hardly surprising. She thanked Banyon for having accompanied her, had a manservant take her purchases upstairs, then followed silently after.

Once she was settled by a window with a cup of tea beside her, Rianne deliberately made herself think about the new circumstances. She *had* wondered why Machlin had given her all that money, and at first, when she'd had trouble in the gunsmith's shop, she'd thought it might be to embarrass her. These London people considered it scandalous for a lady to have anything to do with money, and Machlin might have wanted her to learn that the hard way. It would have been just like him . . .

But then she'd realized that *he* was the one who would be most embarrassed, to have people talking about the outrageous thing his wife had done. They were people *he* knew, ones whose opinions he seemed to care about. That had meant he had to have had another reason, specifically the one she obviously hadn't wanted to see.

Could anyone possibly argue the truth of that? She didn't think so, not when you looked at the facts. All that money, given to a woman who couldn't spend it without making a spectacle of herself . . . given at the same time as a gift of jewelry and an unexpected amount of freedom . . . along with an overheard conversation that made sense no

other way . . . and a sudden lack of interest on the part
of her previously very attentive husband. He was telling
her as politely as possible that he'd found another woman
who interested him more, a woman who was surely a
proper lady, and one he might come to love. When the
hunt was over he expected Rianne to be gone, and had
even given her the means to do it. All the talk about getting her opinion on the disposition of her inheritance had
been just that, nothing but talk.

The tea she sipped at was warm, as warm as the golden
sunshine just beyond her window. Rianne hadn't wanted
to wonder where he'd been all night, and now she didn't
have to. He'd been with a lady, a woman who was that in
truth rather than just in name. He'd finally gotten tired of
all the trouble she caused, more trouble than her beauty
could justify. He'd appreciated her beauty, but had never
been overly concerned with it.

And so she had taken the first step toward leaving forever. The velvet and cotton she'd bought—she'd need
something to wear on the voyage to the colonies, and that
something certainly couldn't be gowns. She still couldn't
afford a maid, and without Angus and Cam she'd never be
able to dress herself. She'd wear her special outfit of
breeches and shirt when she left, and during the voyage
would have plenty of time to make more. Breeches from
the velvet and shirts from the cotton, a wardrobe that
would take little time to sew.

Rianne put the teacup down and closed her eyes, the
pain so deep in her breast that it was a wonder she didn't
cry out. She didn't *want* him to have another woman, she
wanted him to love *her*. It wasn't likely to happen, but she
was still weak enough to pray that it would. Maybe tonight
at dinner . . . if she asked him to stay home and he did . . .
that could mean he really didn't prefer that other . . . please,
God, let it be that way . . .

But he didn't even come home for dinner, which told
all the story Rianne needed to know. She prepared everything she would very soon need, then got numbly into
bed. Her dreams were filled with terror and pain, but that

meant nothing at all. Waking was filled with worse. Sometime during the night she resolved to do exactly as he wanted her to, without embarrassing him with a scene. She was strong enough to do that, surely . . . at least until she was out of his sight . . .

Bryan took breakfast in his rooms the next morning, *the* morning of *the* day. He'd had very little sleep the last two nights, but all his efforts had paid off. He knew where to be tonight, and most of his preparations were made.

"Come in," he called to the knock at his door, and Jeff Banyon did so, raising his brows in surprise at the way Bryan was practically inhaling his breakfast.

"Would you like me to send for more of that?" Jeff asked, one brow still raised. "As far as I know, that isn't the last of the food in the kitchens."

"Don't worry, I'm only eating like it was," Bryan said with a grin. "I don't really believe it, so you can relax. I haven't had a decent meal since lunchtime yesterday."

"And it's almost lunchtime today," Jeff observed, taking a chair not far from him. "I hope all that sacrifice paid off."

"Ask me again tomorrow at this time," Bryan replied, all amusement gone out of him. "I'm fairly sure I've located the right man, but there's very little actual evidence against him. Everything points to him, but only in a circumstantial way."

"That's definitely not good," Jeff mused, studying his expression. "Can you tell me anything about what you learned?"

"Certainly," Bryan agreed with a nod, going back to eating. "I visited that friend of my father's, but not until I had a talk with Magistrate Fielding. The magistrate helped me to get a look at the pertinent Bank records, and we found some things of interest. To begin with, do you remember our friend Tremar, the man who worked for the Bank of England?"

"The one who was killed by the man *you* killed," Jeff said. "What about him?"

"We discovered that he bought his highly placed position about six months after the Bank lost a very large shipment of gold," Bryan answered. "It was gold being sent to France and Spain to balance accounts with banks *there*, and the shipment details were known to no more than a handful of men. Tremar was one of them, but another man disappeared shortly before the shipment was stolen. Everyone assumed that that second man, who was never seen again, sold the secret he had of the shipping details before running off with his ill-gotten gains. This happened about ten years ago."

"What do you know that doesn't agree with that?" Jeff asked, frowning. "There has to be something, or you wouldn't have mentioned it."

"You know it too, if you stop to think for a minute," Bryan reminded him. "Remember what I told you about that scene Rianne witnessed as a child? I'm willing to wager that the man she saw tortured to death was the one who was ultimately blamed for selling the information on the Bank of England gold shipment, even though he died without speaking. The man who had been directing the torture said something about having chosen the wrong one to deal with, and now needed someone else. Tremar was the someone else, and rather than needing to be tortured simply sold the information. The dead man was blamed, and my quarry walked away with most of the gold."

"With no one the wiser," Jeff said, leaning back in his chair. "Tarnish the name of an honorable man, and then go blithely on your way. The whoreson probably laughed when it worked out so well."

"He won't be laughing when people learn the truth," Bryan said, comfortably grim. "The world will know about the man who died with his honor intact, but they'll also have to know about some others who sold their honor for gain or out of shame."

"Who are we talking about now?" Jeff asked. "Besides Tremar, I mean."

"Robert Harding, for one," Bryan answered, watching Jeff's immediate surprise. "I'd thought it was just a matter of unmanageable debts, but Harding was dancing to a blackmailer's tune. That, I discovered, included paying over most of his wealth on a regular basis.''

"And you found that in his bank records?'' Jeff asked, even more surprised now. "How could it possibly have been entered? 'Blackmail, payment thereof'?''

"Not quite, but almost,'' Bryan said with a chuckle, pouring another cup of coffee. "Every quarter for more than ten years, ninety percent of his income has been turned over to an 'investment advisor' named George Haynes. That part is perfectly aboveboard, but not the fact that there's never been so much as a copper deposited as returns. It all went out, and nothing ever came back.''

"You'd think he would have been smart enough to change investment advisors after the first year or two,'' Jeff commented dryly. "But you were right about that being only circumstantial proof of blackmail. There's no law against being bad in business if the people whose money you lose don't complain. Is that all you got?''

"Not quite,'' Bryan said with a headshake. "We had to do a lot of cross-checking, and that's what took so much time. Once a pattern began to emerge I appealed to Magistrate Fielding for help, and then it went a little faster and easier. What we got is as follows:

"The dates of large deposits to the account of this same George Haynes coincide with a number of the reported robberies of gold and silver shipments. Shortly after these deposits, transfers were made to certain accounts which turned out to belong to people who were involved with the particular company which had just been robbed. But these people getting the payments were never suspected of complicity in the crime. In every instance, someone else had already been accused and arrested.''

"Fielding must have loved *that*,'' Jeff put in. "Imagine sending a whole string of people to Newgate—or the gallows—and then finding out you'd been had. But I still can't believe this Haynes would just deposit stolen money like that, or transfer what have to be payoffs. What if someone noticed?''

"There wasn't much chance of that," Bryan told him. "Our friend Reginald Tremar was in charge of his account, and as long as Tremar's figures balanced, the Bank minded its own business. They're very discreet with their larger depositors, and George Haynes qualifies for that sort of treatment. Now that Tremar is dead, however, and not just dead but murdered, there's reason to look into everything he was handling."

"So if Haynes *was* the one who got that stolen gold shipment from the Bank, he used Tremar in two ways," Jeff said with a thoughtful nod. "First as a source of information on the gold shipment, and later, after Tremar bought his higher position, to keep his financial information private. If he was that useful, I wonder why Haynes had him killed."

"At this point we can't be certain, but I do have a theory," Bryan said, finally pushing away his food plate. "From what my friend Pinky Sedgwick said, Tremar had been drinking rather heavily. If he was known to talk too much when he drank too much, he would suddenly become a liability rather than an asset. He meant to impress the people at Alicia's party, and if he became desperate enough—as he probably would have—he might have resorted to mentioning the secret things he knew. And even if he kept quiet this time, what about the next time or the time after that? Haynes decided not to risk it, and so had him killed."

"So much for thieves sticking together," Jeff commented. "Was there anything else?"

"Only one thing," Bryan said. "When we found the copy of Harding's will, I made the mistake of thinking none of the names in it would match the man I'm after. One name does match, and that's the name of the executor."

"Don't tell me," Jeff interrupted with a snort. "If it isn't George Haynes, I'll resign my post with you and take up embroidery. Is that his real name, or a conveniently adopted alias?"

"That we don't know yet," Bryan admitted, taking another swallow of coffee. "The man's account at Bank of England shows he's incredibly wealthy, but it's everyone's opinion at the Bank that he's from the lower classes. Without that wealth it might have been possible to charge him with *something*, but with it it's a waste of time. Sending him to Newgate on anything but a capital conviction will let him buy his way out again, and that will be the end of our effort. We need more, and this is the part I had to be talked into. Fielding wants to catch him attempting murder against someone of standing."

"Who could that possibly be—" Jeff began, and then, looking at Bryan's expression, the answer became clear. "You don't mean your wife," Jeff protested. "I know she's the natural choice and she'll *want* to do it, but— If you're right next to her, he's hardly likely to try."

"That was *my* argument," Bryan growled, forcing the chilling fear back down. "Along with pointing out that I had no intentions of leaving her unguarded to give that scum a chance at her life. Fielding quietly remind me how many people were dead because of the man—shipment guards, people who refused to speak under torture, those like my brother Ross who were forced to suicide, accomplices like Tremar who became liabilities. Then he asked me if I really wanted to have to guard her for the rest of her life, never trusting anyone even if they were friends. After all, since Haynes likes to use blackmail, *anyone* could become his victim. I didn't have to think about it long to know he's right. If we don't get Haynes, Rianne will never be able to stop looking over her shoulder."

"If it were me, I would call him out," Jeff said, his light-blue eyes glittering like winter ice. "With someone like that it would probably be more slaughter than duel, but I can't think of anyone who's done more to earn it."

"If I thought there was any chance of his facing me, it would already be done," Bryan agreed. "The point you're forgetting is that in a matter of honor, both parties have to *have* honor. Haynes would arrange for someone to stand for him, and I'd end up killing a helpless dupe instead of the man I want. And while we're on the subject of violence, tell me about the attack that slime sent against my wife. When I first heard about it, I said to hell with the research and was about to come back here. That was the second time Fielding talked me around, pointing out that I had adventurers on the job good enough to protect the king, and I had to admit he was right. And Harris said you took care of it alone, so I want the details.''

"It wasn't as heroic as you're making it sound,'' Jeff said, thawing just a little. "It was yesterday afternoon, after Mrs. Machlin and I got back from her shopping trip. I was at my desk working, and two men came through the terrace doors. They'd avoided the men on watch, then apparently went looking for someone to lead them to their victim. They had knives and I was alone, so they were feeling very brave. I killed the first one fast with a fist punch to the throat, intending to save the second for questioning, but he refused to cooperate. He came at me so fast with that knife, I'd forced it around and into him before I knew it. Afterward I was really annoyed.''

"I can imagine,'' Bryan said with a grudging grin. Jeff Banyon prided himself on never killing unless it was necessary or desirable, and that second man had ruined his intentions. "But as long as Rianne is safe and doesn't know what happened, I'm just as pleased. Did she spend that money I gave her down to the last penny, or did she actually save some?''

"Well, actually, there was something of a problem there,'' Jeff temporized, his eyes suddenly compassionate. He obviously found it easier to talk about killing and death, which made Bryan just as suddenly worried.

"What sort of problem?'' he asked. "She didn't take it into her head that the money was really mine rather than hers? I could have sworn she believed what I said—''

"Bryan, it wasn't her,'' Jeff interrupted. "It was something we should have both considered, but for myself I don't have enough experience shopping with women. With the very first thing she bought, the clerk nearly threw her out of the shop for not billing the purchase to you. When he saw I wasn't amused he took her money, but still acted

as though she'd committed a crime. After that she lost
interest in looking, and finally had me pay for the only
other thing she bought. When we got back, she went
straight to her rooms without even stopping for something
to eat.''

"Damn," Bryan breathed, then added a few stronger
words under his breath. "I can't believe I didn't think of
that. I wanted her to enjoy herself for once, on her own
terms, and instead I made things worse. Nothing I do with
her seems to go right. I've never in my life felt like such
a gawky, unhandy boy, but with her I can't seem to be
anything else.''

"When a woman doesn't demand things from a man, it
seems to be harder on him," Jeff observed gently. "How
are you supposed to act when you don't know what's expected of you? You try to do your best, then spend your
time wondering if that's good enough. After this is over,
you'll have to ask her to be a little less reasonable.''

"Reasonable," Bryan echoed with a smile that had no
humor in it. "Yes, when this is over I'll be sure to try it.
Right now I'll have to figure out some way to apologize
to her for putting her through that sort of embarrassment.
She doesn't know this city but I do, and I shouldn't have
let that happen. But to get back to our original conversation, I want you along tonight when we go to Ranelagh
Pleasure Gardens. Magistrate Fielding and I have a plan
to make Haynes try for the cheese in our trap, but it's
going to be tricky.''

Jeff leaned forward to listen carefully while Bryan spoke,
agreed he understood what his part would be, then left to
begin preparations. Bryan leaned back in his chair and
sipped the cooling coffee, more than reluctant to go looking for Rianne. He had to tell her what they'd be doing
that night, but it was the need for apology that kept him
from rushing to see her. He didn't believe how much he'd
missed her over the last two days . . .

But how do you apologize for hurting someone who has
already been hurt more than any mortal should be? By
saying it was an accident, that he'd really meant to please

her? Bryan cursed as he pushed the coffee away and got to his feet. It had to be done so he would do it; he just wished he wasn't so certain he would mess it up . . .

Jeff Banyon paused outside Bryan's rooms, trying to decide if he'd done the right thing. He'd told Bryan about Rianne's "first purchase," but not that the purchase was a pair of pistols. He remembered what Bryan had said about not wanting the girl to *have* pistols, but damn it all, he *knew* she hadn't bought them for herself. Hadn't the shopping trip been enough of a disaster? Was he also supposed to ruin the surprise of the gift she'd bought?

Jeff stood and stewed for a minute, then resolutely headed for his own rooms. Right now he had things to do. If he decided later that he'd been wrong, he'd correct the error then . . .

Rianne was feeling almost calm when she walked into the small dining room for lunch. She'd spent the entire morning sewing and thinking, and she'd finally been able to see everything in the proper light. Of course Machlin had found a woman to really care about. Why shouldn't he? He had never made any promises to *her,* and just because *she* had been born to lose the people she loved didn't mean others had to go through life alone. When the time came she would simply get out of his way, the best repayment she could give for the times he'd saved her life.

"Well, good afternoon," Machlin said pleasantly as he rose from the table. "I haven't seen you in so long I almost feel like a stranger again. Have things been going all right while I was away?"

"They couldn't have been more perfect," Rianne answered, actually managing a smile. "Harris and his staff are good enough to tend the king, but I'm glad they're here instead."

"I'll tell them you said so," Machlin acknowledged with a smile of his own as he seated her. "They'll be very pleased."

A moment later he was back in his own chair, but

seemed to have run out of small talk. Rianne, not really
in the mood for conversation, reached for the bell to begin
the serving of the meal. Her fingers had only just touched
the crystal handle when his hand stopped her.

"Before we eat, there's something I have to tell you,"
he said, the look in those gray eyes making her insides
lurch. He'd decided to tell her about that other woman . . .
"Tonight we get a chance at the quarry, but there's a good
deal more to it than that. If you think the plan is too dangerous or that you'd rather not be a part of it, just say so.
I'll tell you frankly that if I'd had any other choice, I never
would have considered it."

"That sounds positively ominous," Rianne said with
brows high, so relieved she felt all but light-headed. "Why
don't you tell me about it, and then I'll decide."

"Our quarry's name is George Haynes," he began, taking his hand from hers in order to pour them both tea. "If
that name sounds familiar, it should. He's the designated
executor of Harding's will, and you were right to consider
him a definite suspect. He's also had someone in his service for years, a man who's been identified as Alfred
Homand. Homand is no longer among the living."

"Is he the one you killed after he killed Tremar?"
Rianne exclaimed, suddenly excited. "That name—
Homand—and what I thought I heard as a child. It wasn't
'O, and,' it was Homand!"

"Exactly," Machlin confirmed. "It was one of the
things that convinced me. But something else you told me
was even more important. Do you remember Tremar's
ramblings about *him* and masquerades and Ranelagh Pleasure Gardens? It seems our Mr. Haynes has a passion for
masquerades, and never misses the really big turnouts.
There's going to be one tonight, and if you agree we'll be
joining him."

"I agree," Rianne said at once, all those feelings from
childhood rising up again to infuriate her. "What are we
going to do?"

"Not so fast," he warned, one hand held up toward
her. "You haven't heard it all yet. We were able to identify

some of Haynes's people, so we arranged for one of them
to 'overhear' talk about my plans for tonight. They think
I'm going to bring you to Ranelagh to identify the man
I've been after for years, and once you do I'll appeal to
Magistrate Fielding for justice. With your testimony the
magistrate should be able to move against Haynes, but
there isn't enough evidence for him to do anything without
it. I haven't bothered Fielding yet, but as soon as I'm
certain about my facts, I will.''

"So you're saying Haynes will be expecting us," Rianne
said with a frown. "Will he really believe we mean to
walk in there alone, take a look at him, and then walk out
again? And how are we supposed to see his face at a masquerade? Pull the masks off everyone one by one?''

"He's been led to believe I'll only have a couple of my
men with me,'' Machlin answered. "More than that would
draw attention to us, most probably unwelcome attention.
As for the mask problem, that takes care of itself. We
locate Haynes and his party during the evening by asking
discreet questions, then make sure we're near him at midnight. That's when everyone unmasks together, and it
won't matter to *us*. Haynes won't know who we are even
if he sees us.''

"Yes, that *does* sound logical,'' Rianne agreed, liking
the idea. "Unless we're very unlucky, it should work perfectly. That means we'll go ahead with it—''

"Wait," Machlin interrupted, holding up one hand.
"The most important part hasn't been mentioned yet. If
we go, at some point I'm going to have to leave you alone,
to give Mr. Haynes the impression that he can get to you.
He'll certainly take the opportunity to silence you, and
when he tries we can catch him at it. But that means you'll
have to risk yourself, and after everything I've said about
that . . .''

"You feel silly making this suggestion," Rianne finished when he didn't. "Well, don't. This is too serious to
worry about feeling silly, so we'll ignore it. Tell me what
these masquerades are like. I've heard about them, but
never in any kind of detail.''

"Actually they can be a lot of fun," Machlin answered, eyeing her as though trying to decide if she meant what she said. "Everyone dresses up in costume and goes masked, and except for rare instances you might not know who the people are around you until everyone unmasks together."

"What about costumes for *us?*" Rianne asked after sipping at her tea. "I don't know about you, but I don't have any. What can I possibly make in one afternoon?"

"You don't have to make anything," he soothed, patting her hand. "As soon as I heard about Haynes's fondness for Ranelagh, I had a feeling we might need to visit there. That's why two days ago I arranged for a costume to be made for you. I have the one I wore the last time I went, and yours will be delivered this afternoon without fail. And the way we'll recognize Haynes is simple: he'll be the one trying to kill you. I want you to keep that fact firmly in mind, so if you have to defend yourself you won't hesitate."

"What will I be defending myself with?" Rianne asked, for some reason certain he had something specific in mind. "Does Ranelagh use torches to provide light?"

"No, they don't," he responded with a grin. "You'll find out what I mean this afternoon. In the meanwhile, why don't you ring for lunch."

Rianne did so, at the same time noticing his grin had faded. He was obviously worried about tonight, but she wasn't. She'd waited almost half her life for the chance to face that man again, and tonight it would finally happen.

The meal was delicious as always, but once again it was a silent one. Machlin picked at his food while she ate, something he'd never done before. He was obviously distracted by very private thoughts, and finally it came to Rianne what it would mean if they were successful tonight. The chase would be over and their marriage as well, and he would return permanently to his new woman. She pushed her plate away, still calm but no longer having an appetite. When Machlin saw that, he sighed and looked straight at her.

"I'm going to do this badly, but it has to be done," he said heavily. "I owe you a deep and sincere apology, but I can't seem to find the words. I swear I never meant to hurt you, and I hope you believe that."

"Of course I believe it," she answered in a voice that was low but quite steady. She was finally hearing what she'd dreaded to, but she'd sworn to be strong. If only he could have been talking about something else—but there wasn't anything else. "Sometimes things turn out in a way we can't help and didn't foresee, and there's nothing we can do," she added. "It wasn't your deliberate fault, so there's no need for apology."

"I know that, but it doesn't make me feel any better," he said, gray eyes filled with the oddest longing. "Happiness is something everyone tries to find, but it usually ends up just beyond us. If, just once, we could close our hand on it, all that effort would be worthwhile. Can you blame me for trying?"

"No, I can't," she whispered, the calm fast disappearing. "Please excuse me, I'm not feeling very well."

She all but ran from the room, needing the solitude of her own bedchamber to pull herself together. If he'd been talking about anything but wanting her to go, he wouldn't have mentioned trying to find happiness. That was the word the lord in that novel had used, the same thing *he'd* been searching for. Now Machlin had said the words and it was finally settled; all *she* had to do was make herself accept it.

Bryan watched the girl disappear, the pain in her eyes making it impossible for him to follow. He'd apologized and she'd forgiven him, and now he felt worse than ever. Did she really believe he hadn't humiliated her on purpose, or did she think he'd used her lack of sophistication to teach her what he considered her proper place? It was a stupid, mindless mistake to have made, but she'd so wanted to exercise a little independence . . .

"And if I had my choice, I'd never refuse her anything," he muttered, putting his hands to his eyes. "But everything I do pushes her closer to seeing how much better off she would be without me. Dear God, why can't I make this work right? I've never failed this miserably before, and nothing's been even half as important. Please tell me what I'm doing wrong!''

Nothing but the muted sound of others in the house came to answer him, which was perfectly fitting. Emptiness seemed to be his lot in life these days, at least where it counted. He pushed away from the table and stood, knowing he needed to get some sleep before tonight. He'd been hoping for something other than sleep, but that was out of the question now. Later, after it was all over, he would have to talk to her . . . But what would he say . . . ? What *could* he say . . . ? There had to be something besides a flat refusal to let her go . . .

Chapter 17

D inner was early that night, of course, but Rianne was ready. If there was one thing she'd learned in life, it was that holding on to people already lost was impossible. All the tears and denial in the world couldn't bring them back, a fact she'd learned by trying. This time she'd taken a shortcut, and had simply accepted the pain without fighting it.

But that didn't mean there wasn't any fighting to do. The cause of her worst nightmares would soon be in reach, and Rianne found it hard to wait. She meant to take out every bit of anguish she'd ever had on his miserable hide, and then she'd be able to walk away with her head held high.

The costume Machlin had mentioned wasn't brought until he and Rianne were on their way into dinner, so Rianne didn't get a chance to see it before the meal. Jeff Banyon joined them at table, which helped quite a lot to keep the conversation on an impersonal level. All they discussed was the preparations for tonight, and where everyone would be. Machlin had plans to have two dozen of his men there, as well as Jeff, to keep watch all over Ranelagh.

Immediately after dinner they separated to dress, and Rianne couldn't believe how eager she was to see what Machlin had chosen for her. Her maid, Meg, was already there to help, but the look on the girl's face stopped Rianne short.

"All right, Meg, what is it?" she asked, almost afraid

of what answer she'd get. "If it's as terrible as your expression says, maybe we can do something to fix it."

"Oh, no, mum, it ain't terrible atall," the girl immediately denied. "I never dreamed nothin' could be so fine,
but— Does th' sir really want you in this—this—"

"You'd better let me see it," Rianne decided when the
girl found it impossible to supply the proper word.
"Maybe a mistake's been made, and they sent the
wrong— Oh, my . . ."

Rianne looked at the costume being held up, for the
moment sharing Meg's loss for words. It was made of
samite, that incredible silver material that glowed like a
polished sword blade, but was still soft and silky and
clinging. It *was* a gown of sorts, but the sort seen on
drawings of ancient Greeks or Romans. Sleeveless and
collarless, it was almost bosomless as well, with a slim
length of braided silver obviously supplied as a girdle. But
the worst thing about it was its length, along with its very
uneven hem. It was so high in front—

"Every one of 'em, mum, they'd *all* see your limbs!"
Meg blurted, shocked into using terms commonly excluded from polite conversation. "An' see there, in th'
bottom of th' box. *Sandals*, no less, and not one but *two*
weapons! What can th' sir be thinkin' of?"

As soon as Rianne saw the small silver bow and arrows,
she was hit by inspiration. "Diana, Goddess of the Hunt,
that's what he's thinking of!" she exclaimed. "What would
be more appropriate? And I think I also understand what
happened to the gown. Meg, hold it up in front of you."

The girl did so, and Rianne immediately saw she was
right. If Meg had put on the gown it would have come
down easily to her ankles, showing little beyond a teasing
amount of foot. Whoever had made the costume couldn't
possibly have been told how tall Rianne was, and Machlin
had been too busy handing out orders and keeping secrets
to bring her in for a fitting. If *she* wore that gown, the
scandal would take a year to die down . . .

And yet, why not? Rianne stared at the costume, having
a fairly good idea how she would look in it. The idea of

scandal didn't bother her; what did bother her was the fact that Machlin had chosen another woman over her. He ought to be given a really solid reason for doing that . . . and maybe a regret or two when he saw her . . . ones that couldn't be forgotten as quickly as she herself . . .

"Meg, help me out of these clothes," she said, the decision already made. "I have a masquerade to attend."

The girl was speechless with shock, but she did as she was told. Rianne took everything off, knowing how clearly every line of her body would show beneath the samite. And she wanted it to *be* body, not corset and lacings. So he would decide she wasn't good enough for him, would he? They'd see how easily "good enough" was defined.

Once the costume was on, Meg seemed struck even more speechless. Rianne studied her reflection in the mirror, seeing how the samite, bound between her breasts and around her waist by the girdle cord, breathed with her like silver flesh. It strained over her breasts and hips, flowing like spring water from the mountains, down to a place in front just below her knees. It fell lower to the sides and back, but in front her high-laced silver sandals could easily be seen. Not to mention her legs.

"That should do it," Rianne murmured, glad she'd decided to also free her hair. It burned above the gown like soft and flowing fire, another point to be added to the eventual talk. To appear in public with her hair unbound and uncovered? Indignity would be piled on affront, and all of it would be *delicious*.

Her feathered silver mask lay in a box of its own, the most gracefully beautiful thing Rianne had ever seen. She was about to put it on when she remembered the silver bow and arrows, and decided to see about them first. Seeing was easier without a mask, and she would have to—

She stopped short with her hand extended into the box, only right then remembering Meg had said *two* weapons. Beside the toy bow with tiny arrows attached lay something that was quite real. Silver scabbarded and silver hilted, the slender blade was of good steel. Rianne assured herself of that when she drew it from its sheath, and that

was when Machlin's earlier comment made sense. If the
need arises defend yourself, he'd said, and now she knew
with what.

Once the sword was resheathed, Rianne discovered that
the scabbard's lockets could be attached to her girdle with
no trouble at all. She'd wondered why the girdle cord had
been long enough to wrap around extra times, and now
she knew: to make it strong enough to support the weight
of a real sword. She let Meg help her into the voluminous
gray cloak she'd chosen; put on the mask and raised the
cloak's hood; picked up the toy bow to complete her costume, and then she was ready.

Machlin and Jeff Banyon waited downstairs in the hall,
and they watched her descend the stairs slowly enough to
keep the cloak from billowing open. She didn't want her
surprise unveiled until they reached the Gardens.

Machlin wore what looked like golden breast armor over
a red-skirted tunic, a heavy sword at his left and a golden
helmet-mask as well as golden boots. The armor wasn't
metal, she saw as soon as she got closer, but a heavy cloth
gilded in some way to make it look real. He was obviously
supposed to be Mars, God of War. Banyon was robed
down to his sandals in white, sporting a long white beard
with hair to match, as well as carrying a trident and net.
He was probably supposed to be Neptune, God of the
Seas. Would the entire pantheon turn out that night?

"Are you sure you're feeling better?" Machlin asked
when she joined them. "Earlier you weren't, and I want
you to tell me if that hasn't changed."

"As a matter of fact, I'm feeling marvelous," she answered with a smile, finding his sudden concern ridiculous. "Isn't it time we left?"

Their driver came to the door then, ending the need for
further conversation. Rianne arranged herself carefully in
the carriage, her cloak well overlapped, then she stared
out the window with the pretense of sight-seeing. In reality she was lost in anticipating the upcoming confrontation, and saw nothing outside the coach. One of the men
said something about it being possible to reach Ranelagh

by boat as well as by coach, but all the rest of their conversation went by her.

And then they were there. The rotunda all but glittered
in the light of torches, and theirs wasn't the only carriage
discharging passengers. More than a few of the new arrivals were cloaked, and once they were inside Rianne saw
why. They each took a great deal of pleasure revealing
themselves to those they'd arrived with and then, with
masks in place and laughter all around, they went to join
those revelers already here.

"You can give your cloak to the servant," Machlin said,
bringing her attention back to him. He and Banyon were
looking around the rotunda, as though checking for familiar faces.

"Madam?" the servant behind her said, echoing Machlin in fewer words. It was time to give up her cloak,
something she'd thought would be easier. Well, easy or
not it had to be done, with or without a deep breath first.
Rianne took a breath, removed her hood and unhooked
the cloak, then let the servant take it.

At first, with her two companions looking elsewhere,
there was no reaction whatsoever. They were the only ones
still near the entrance, and the servants had to be the sort
who could watch a beheading without batting an eye. And
then Banyon turned to her, apparently intending to say
something, but the words were never uttered. He froze
with light eyes wide and staring, what she could see of his
expression filled with such incredulity that Rianne wanted
to giggle.

"Is that a *real* trident, Mr. Banyon?" she asked instead,
forcing her voice lower than normal so that she might
sound sultry. "If it is, you don't by any chance know how
to use it?"

"It—ah—so happens I do," Banyon answered after
clearing his throat. "I've made a study of . . . ancient
weapons . . ."

The way his voice trailed off must have caught Machlin's attention. The big man turned and also began to
speak, but for the second time the words were lost. More

than incredulity flamed from gray eyes behind a mask of gold; for an instant demanding desire burned there, so strong Rianne was about to step back from it. And then it was gone, replaced by anger, and she realized she'd probably imagined the desire.

"What have you done?" Machlin demanded, his gaze inspecting every inch of her. "You look—you're dressed—you're *not* dressed! How could you have come out like that?"

"I wasn't the one who had this costume made," she reminded him coldly, immediately stung by the unfair accusation. "Was I supposed to politely request something else to wear ten minutes before we were due to leave, or simply stay behind? Tell me which option *you* would have chosen, *Mr.* Machlin."

His jaw tightened as he straightened, but once again there were no immediate words. Everything she'd said was true and he knew it, but he didn't seem prepared to be reasonable. Rianne was sure he was about to demand that they leave, but Banyon's hand went to his arm.

"Bryan, we can't call things off now," the other man urged in a low voice. "There are too many people involved, and we may never have this chance again. Are you going to risk the only alternative, the one you said made you change your mind? No one can stay alert forever, not even you."

Machlin's expression changed then, at least what she could see of it. He wasn't pleased, but apparently he'd been given no choice.

"All right, Jeff, we'll go ahead with it," he conceded in a growl. "I can't risk the alternative, and she and I can discuss this later. Allow me to offer my arm, wife."

The unhappiness in his voice was unmistakable, which made Rianne take her turn at straightening with anger and indignation. So he was going to scold her later, was he? Just before he turned his back on her forever? Well, they'd see about *that*, but right then there was something else to see to.

"Mr. Banyon, I would consider it a favor if *you* were

to offer your arm," she said, ignoring Machlin completely. "I have an—aversion—to being escorted by men who feel themselves shamed by my company. I'd rather walk about with no escort at all."

Banyon hesitated and glanced at his employer, waiting for permission or denial. Rianne, who looked only at him, had no idea which it would be until the man sighed and offered his arm.

"Mrs. Machlin, the honor is mine," he said with a bow that looked ridiculous with what he was wearing. "Would you care for champagne, or possibly a fruit drink?"

"Definitely a fruit drink, Mr. Banyon," she answered. She took Banyon's arm, smiling at him as though he were the only one there. As far as she was concerned he was, and it would stay that way for as long as they were there. Afterward she would be free to walk away entirely, and would never need to think about that brute again. She'd wanted to hate him, and for once her wish had come true . . .

Bryan watched his wife walk away with his secretary, and the chaos inside him was difficult to contain. What he wanted most was to kill something with his bare hands, preferably something extremely dangerous. He was already being torn to shreds, and it wasn't fair that he was being kept from fighting back . . .

A servant passed carrying glasses of champagne, pausing to offer one to Bryan. His fingers twitched with the desire to take two or three and empty them quickly, but he shook his head even to the suggestion of one. Drinking and fighting don't mix, not if you intend to survive the fighting. Once their business there was taken care of, he'd be able to drink all he liked . . .

Which is probably the only way I'll be able to stop seeing her, he silently admitted to himself. *My God, there can't possibly be any woman ever who was more beautiful. She looks as though she's been dipped naked in liquid silver, and it hasn't yet dried. I know she isn't wearing anything under that, and she even freed her hair . . . It was all I could do not to take her right here and now . . .*

*How could she do this . . . ? There can't be the slightest
bit of caring for me in her . . .*

And that was what hurt the most, the fact that she didn't
care at all. He was nothing to her, and she'd proved it by
unhesitatingly dressing in a way that would draw men to
her like vultures to a dying carcass. She'd wanted him to
know exactly what he'd soon be losing—as if he didn't
already know. He'd never had a kind word from her except
about Ross, no more than a single touch from a gentle
hand . . .

You're a fool, Machlin, he thought flatly as he stood
close beside a stone bench. *You used to laugh at men who
worshipped at the feet of women who didn't know or care
they were alive. You also swore it would never happen to
you, and now look at you. Almost ready to beg on your
knees, if that would keep her with you.*

*But you've just remembered you don't have to beg. It's
finally come through to you that she's your wife, and if
you refuse to let her go she'll have no choice but to stay.
And you won't have to worry about considering her feelings. She* has *no feelings, at least as far as you're concerned. She'll never love you, and it's time you admitted
it. And gave up trying to make it happen. Just tell her
what to do, and teach her to do it without arguing.*

Bryan searched for the satisfaction his decision should
have brought, and when he didn't find it he decided he
was too distracted by what lay ahead of him. Once the
enemy was met and bested, he'd break the news to her.
She *was* his wife, and that wasn't called capture, it was
called marriage. The law was on *his* side, so where was
the sense in not taking advantage of it? Later was when
the satisfaction would surface, without any possible doubt.
He'd wanted her to want him freely, without coercion, but
this would be just as good . . . almost as good . . . It
would . . .

After what seemed like days, Rianne finally found herself alone for the moment in a quiet corner. It *had* been
much more than an hour, and she wished she had her fan

with her. Not that a fan would have done much good, considering the mask she wore. Under it she was sweating, and that wasn't the only place . . .

She took a deep breath, then forced herself to admit the truth. Her discomfort had very little to do with the mask, and she cursed herself for ever having put on that costume. All those men, most of them faceless strangers . . . Thank God Banyon had been there . . . She must have squeezed every bit of blood out of his arm in her agitation . . .

But hopefully the men coming at her hadn't noticed. They'd been so forward she'd been shocked, but then anger had risen to help her. Strangers had offered every compliment they could think of, before shifting to being slyly suggestive; her own husband, however, had hated what she looked like and had blamed her for it, when all the time the whole thing had been *his* fault. She hated that brute, she really did—most especially for not being there to protect her.

But then she had to admit there was no reason to have expected him to be there. He might not want her life on his conscience, but that was as far as his caring went. He'd found another woman for his bed, but he'd also made sure she had enough money to take care of herself. What more could any gentleman do?

Rianne's throat burned with that question, and she wished Banyon would hurry back with her drink. It was still much too long until midnight, and she wasn't sure she could stand the wait. After that it would be over, completely and finally over, and then she could . . . could . . .

"Well, good evening, Lady Diana," a voice came suddenly from behind her, making her flinch. It was a male voice, and one that sounded faintly familiar. "I do hope you'll forgive my daring, but goddess or no, I felt I had to speak to you. You are a perfect vision of loveliness, and every man here will feel forever grateful for having been allowed this glimpse of your radiance."

By then the man stood in front of her, his costume patterned after the dress of those old-time freebooters who had roamed the waters thereabout, before England was an

integrated island, much less an empire. He wore a leather
mask and boots and dark wrapped-leather leggings, a long
tunic of rose silk, a heavy shirt of imitation ring mail, and
a wide sword at his hip. At the sight of that last Rianne's
hand went to her own hilt, and the man took an uncertain
step backward.

"Mrs. Machlin, I do beg your pardon," he said at once,
his tone uncertain as well. "Have I offended you? It's this
wretched sense of humor of mine, I suppose I'll never
learn— You do know it's me, don't you? Jack Michaels?"

"Oh, Mr. Michaels," Rianne said in relief. "No, I'm
sorry, I didn't know it was you. I thought it was another
of those—people who have been at me since I arrived. I
knew this costume was daring when my husband gave it
to me, but I never dreamed . . ."

"That anonymity erases all sense of good manners in
many people?" he finished when she didn't. "I must admit I understand the point too well personally. What I
don't understand, however, is how Machlin could give you
something like that to wear, and then disappear. Is he
counting on your very realistic gesture of hand to sword
to keep the rogues away? I daresay they'll realize, as I
did, that touching a sword hilt is a far cry from wielding
the weapon. Where has the dog gone?"

"I really don't know," Rianne answered, trying to
sound almost as lost as she felt. According to the plans,
she wasn't *supposed* to know where Machlin was. "I
haven't seen him since we arrived. His secretary, Mr. Banyon, has been escorting me, but *he's* gone off to fetch me
a fruit drink. There are so many people here, and so many
taking advantage of the music to dance . . . It was very
difficult finding a corner in a round hall."

"And even more difficult, I should imagine, finding a
quiet corner," he said with a smile. "Machlin should be
soundly trounced for having abandoned you, even if he's
most likely been detained by those addicted to discussing
business. May I make so bold as to offer *my* company, as
well as a tour of the gardens? They're breathtakingly lovely,

and beyond that they're cooler than this rotunda and a good deal less crowded.''

Rianne didn't quite know how to answer that, but was saved from the need for an immediate reply. They were suddenly joined by a monk in brown robes and rope sandals, who stared at Rianne through a brown sackcloth mask before bending over her hand.

''Mrs. Machlin, is it not?'' he asked, sounding a shade less than sure. ''I hadn't expected to see you tonight. Robert Creighton here—we met at Alicia's do the other night. If it's you, where has Machlin gone?''

''He's abandoned her, Redstone,'' Jack Michaels supplied in a pleasant way. ''I've already taken over, so you might as well be on your way.''

''Jack?'' Robert Creighton said, peering at the free-booter. ''You're someone else I hadn't expected to see. Has the whole crowd shown up tonight? I thought you'd all sworn off this place as being too well attended by the so-called respectable.''

''I've been wondering what all the fuss was about, so I came to see for myself,'' Jack answered with a continuing smile. ''And 'respectable' isn't the way *I* heard this place described, which leads me to wonder what *you're* doing here. I thought you retired from the crowd to take up the straight and narrow.''

Under his mask, Creighton's expression turned odd. He also seemed to be searching for an answer, which suddenly disturbed Rianne. The enemy, Haynes, had people in his power who were forced to help him. If Robert Creighton, the new Lord Redstone, was one of those . . . Maybe it was starting . . .

''Is this area reserved, or can anyone stop by?'' a voice asked, this time a female one. Rianne turned to see a woman dressed as an Oriental empress, her hair dark and shiny and piled very high. Her vibrantly colored silk gown came down to the top of her slippers, but it was almost as straight and form-fitting as Rianne's. Her feather mask echoed the reds and blues and greens of her gown, and once again Rianne thought the voice was familiar.

"Lydia!" Jack Michaels exclaimed. "I think the whole crowd *is* reforming, Redstone. If Alicia ever finds out, she'll cross us all from her list for good."

"I understand she's already done that for *me*," Lydia Worden responded glumly. "Not that I can blame her. I never dreamed a banker could be that irresponsible, which proves how naive I am. I didn't know you and Robert were here, Jack. I came over to spend a moment with Rianne, but not the sort of moment I suspect you two are interested in. I would suggest that you gentlemen go in search of refreshments for us—*before* Machlin breaks loose and finds you here. They haven't been married long enough for him to be in the least tolerant or understanding."

"You may be right," Robert Creighton conceded after exchanging a glance with Jack. "But now that you're here to chaperone, it should be perfectly acceptable. We'll be right back."

The two men moved off, and were quickly lost in the crowd of revellers. Rianne didn't know whether to feel relieved or disappointed, and then realized it didn't matter. They'd be back soon enough, and then the real game could begin . . .

"Am I mistaken in thinking you recognized my costume?" Lydia asked once the men were gone. "What I could see of your expression suggested that, and if you did, you're one of the very few here who have."

"I saw a drawing of that very gown in a book someone brought me as a gift," Rianne replied. "It was an academic work on one of the Oriental cultures, and was really very badly written. If all books on the Orientals are that dry, it's no wonder we know so little about them."

"I'm told all the books on the subject, the few that there are, *are* equally as bad," Lydia agreed with a smile. "But I really must say I was delighted to see you. Until *you* arrived, this gown was considered one step short of scandalous. However did you get Machlin to let you wear that?"

"He didn't have much choice, once we were already here," Rianne answered with a very deliberate smile of

her own. "And I think people are much too easily scandalized. I consider it my duty to inure them to the unexpected and improbable."

"I used to think there should be limits to the unexpected
and improbable," Lydia replied with the same sort of
smile. "I suppose I still do, even though I seem to have
moved beyond so comfortable an outlook. And I really
didn't come over here to insult you. What I came for was
to ask a favor."

"What sort of favor?" Rianne asked in turn, wondering
at the smaller woman's faint sadness.

"I—couldn't help but notice that you were being escorted by Jeff Banyon, Machlin's secretary," Lydia responded, now looking embarrassed and possibly even
flustered. "I've—never had the chance to meet the gentleman, but often felt I would enjoy doing so. Would you—
I mean, is there any reason you would prefer not to—"

"Introduce you to him?" Rianne interrupted, just to
stop her very painful groping for the proper words. It was
odd that Lydia had recognized Banyon under that costume,
but possibly she'd noticed his unusual eyes. A woman interested in a man did notice such things, even though Lydia
hadn't seemed the sort who would find attraction in a man
like Banyon. Ah, well, stranger things had happened . . .
"I can't see any reason why not," Rianne continued, "and
he should be back at any moment. He made me promise
to wait right here for him."

"Probably until he finishes whatever he's doing with
Machlin," Lydia said with a nod, faintly less embarrassed. "I saw the two of them going *that* way just a few
moments ago, and they seemed rather intent. You'd think
they would forget about business while they're supposed
to be having a good time."

"What's through that door that would interest them?"
Rianne asked as casually as she could. Only the chase
could have distracted them, and if they'd started something
without her—! "Most people seem to be passing right by."

"I think there's a small, private apartment back there,"
Lydia replied, something of a frown in her voice. "The

cost of it is rather high, I'm told, but there's usually some-one who takes it for the night. A private party within a party, or a place for secret business partners to meet, or anything you'd care to use it for. I've even heard there are sometimes—assignations—there.''

"Are there really," Rianne murmured, thinking about Machlin's new woman, but then dismissed the thought. Banyon was with him, Lydia had said, and the assignation they were *all* there for would leave little or no time for dallying. But if Haynes had taken the apartment for the night and they'd found out about it, they might also have found a way to reach Haynes without using her as bait.

"Why don't we just stroll over that way," Rianne suggested, again trying to sound casual. "The music may not be quite as loud over there, which will make introductions much easier to perform."

"But—but weren't you told to stay *here?*" Lydia asked in confusion, hurriedly following an already strolling Rianne. "Won't he be furious with you for disobeying?"

"I'm sure he'll get over it," Rianne answered with a smile, feeling more than a little superior. Another woman would have stayed where she'd been put, thereby missing out on everything she'd come there for. Rianne wasn't about to miss *anything,* not when she'd waited so long . . .

Moving around the edges of the masked revelers got them to the door fairly quickly. The music, of course, was just as loud there as it had been in their original position, but happily Lydia never noticed. She eyed the door almost with suspicion, and stopped just short of it.

"I really don't think we should be doing this," she said, looking around nervously. "They're more than likely talk-ing business in there, and won't appreciate the intrusion of two women. Wouldn't it be better if—"

"No, it wouldn't," Rianne said without waiting to hear the suggestion. "Really, Lydia, you *must* get over this be-lief of yours that men have to be obeyed. As you said, this is no place to talk business. Once we remind them of that, they'll certainly be grateful."

She flashed the smaller woman another smile, then

walked directly to the door and opened it. The short hallway beyond was something of a letdown, but not completely. At the end of the empty hallway, no more than ten
feet ahead, was another door, behind which they certainly
had to be.

Without waiting to see if she was being followed, Rianne
moved ahead to the next door. It was always possible the
apartment would contain no one but Machlin and his men,
and then she really *would* be in trouble for going off on her
own. Now that she thought about it, Jack had turned up in
an awfully convenient way. Maybe that suggested walk in the
gardens hadn't been *his* suggestion after all . . .

Rianne reached the far door, opened it, and walked
through, almost automatically. Thinking about Robert
Creighton and Jack Michaels had distracted her, and it
took a moment before she really saw the only man in the
room.

"Good evening, Lady Diana," he said in a low, deep
voice that wasn't in the least familiar. "You've been on
the hunt, but can now consider the hunt ended. Your part
of it, at any rate."

The man was dressed all in black, with a hood-like mask
that covered most of his face. He was certainly supposed
to be a headsman or executioner, and Rianne's insides
chilled at the sight of him. She'd obviously made a bad
mistake, but one step backward was all the retreat she was
allowed. A sound came of the door behind her being closed
and locked, sealing Lydia out and her in there with this—
this—

This executioner, who was slowly drawing a deadly-real
sword . . .

Bryan had watched the men flocking around his wife as
long as he could stand it, then had stalked to the other side
of the rotunda for a few moments of solitude. His temper
was threatening to explode like a keg of the best-quality black
powder, and he needed to reestablish control.

But how was he supposed to do that? he demanded silently. The girl hadn't moved from Jeff's side, but the way

she'd exchanged banter with all those men—she *had* to have been enjoying herself. Well, when that was over he'd teach her a thing or two about proper behavior. Once he was done, she'd never even *glance* at another man . . .

He stopped to lean against a wall, doing his best to rub at his eyes through the mask he wore. Never in his life had he come close to imagining what jealousy could do to a man, not until he'd begun suffering from the disease himself. Every thought in his head was irrational, but more and more he considered them justified and reasonable. He didn't know how it could be considered reasonable to try to force a woman to love you, but that's what too much of him wanted to do.

He took a fruit drink from the tray of a passing servant, once again wishing it could be something a lot stronger. He was heading deeper into hell with every step he took, but there didn't seem to be a way out. Even his decision to refuse to let the girl go didn't help, but he wasn't about to change his mind over that. He *couldn't* let her go, not and still stay sane . . .

Bryan stood and sipped his drink, fighting to clear his mind for the task ahead. He applied himself to the chore with determination, and after a little while actually began to get somewhere. He had just swallowed the last of the fruit drink to celebrate that much success, when Jeff Banyon appeared in front of him.

"Well, at last," Jeff said as he halted. "For a while I was convinced you were deliberately hiding."

"Why would I be hiding?" Bryan asked, putting aside his emptied cup. "That's not what we're here for."

"Exactly what *I* thought when I had trouble finding you," Jeff answered. "Especially when something important has happened. What is it?"

"What are you talking about?" Bryan asked blankly, beginning to bring more attention to the conversation. "If something important has happened, you'll have to tell *me*. And where's my wife? You didn't let her take off alone, did you?''

"My God, Bryan, I'm a fool!" Jeff exclaimed, his face

under the false beard going pale. "I was on my way to get
your wife a drink, when someone dressed like Mercury
the Messenger God stopped me. He said something important had happened, and you needed to speak to me
immediately. I forgot about the drink and came looking
for you, but now I can see it was a trick. They were just
trying to get rid of me."

"And apparently succeeded," Bryan agreed tightly.
"But don't blame yourself," he added quickly, noticing
the stricken look on Banyon's face. "We knew they would
try something like this, but not with either of us watching.
Take me to the place where you left her."

Jeff headed quickly through the crowd, and Bryan had
no trouble keeping up. Right then he was praying hard,
praying that his preparations and planning had done their
job. It had been certain that the two of them would somehow be gotten out of the way, in order to leave a clear run
at the girl. Had he done enough? Would the enemy's tactics prove superior to his? He'd hedged his bet four times
over, but he could still lose everything . . .

"She *is* gone," Jeff growled, peering over and around
the revelers. "And after she promised not to leave that
spot until I got back. Let's ask those two men. They may
have seen which way she went."

Bryan looked at the men Jeff was talking about, and his
heart sank. Even costumed and masked he knew them,
and they shouldn't have been standing there talking to one
another. They made their way closer, and as soon as the
two saw him they began speaking to him together. Then
they stopped abruptly and looked at one another, and
Bryan interrupted rather than wait for the duet to start
again.

"I have the feeling you both had her, then lost her
again," he said. "Which of you got to her first?"

"I did," Jack answered, sounding more surprised than
put out. "Are you telling me I was wasting my time protecting her from Creighton?"

"Me?" Robert huffed indignantly. "You thought you
had to protect her from *me?* I came to rescue her from

your clutches, old son. And I had no idea I wasn't the only one doing this.''

"Neither of you was told about the other," Bryan interrupted again, his fear, he knew, showing plainly on his face. "Where did my wife go, and was she alone when she went?"

"When we left her here, she was perfectly safe," Jack said, speaking for them both. "When the suggestion was made that we go for refreshments, it was almost done in your name. I thought you were briefly calling me off, so I went without hesitation."

"And I," Robert agreed, exchanging glances with Jack. "She said we ought to go for the drinks 'before Machlin finds you here,' or some such, which I certainly thought was a signal. I had no idea—"

"You said 'she,' " Bryan interrupted once again, the sick feeling inside him increasing. "I hope you don't mean you left her with Lydia Worden."

"How did you know?" Robert demanded while Jack put a hand to his masked eyes. "And are you suggesting she's now a pariah, just because she made a mistake letting that banker buy her out of financial trouble? Really, old son, I thought you were more understanding than that."

"Robert, I'm afraid that's not the way it went," Bryan said, wondering if he should have shared his suspicions. "I can't prove it yet, but I don't believe Tremar *bought* his way into Alicia's party. Sir Alastair Worden, Lydia's father, is one of your associates. I think the money she paid back on her gambling debts came from selling Haynes the details of your most recently stolen shipment. Tremar found out she'd been doing that all along, and blackmailed her into bringing him to the party. She in turn let Haynes know, and then spread her own version of the story because she *expected* Tremar to be killed. If she chased you two off, it's because she's still working with Haynes. You have no idea which way they went?"

"I was too wrapped up in my own theories to keep watching," Jack responded with a lot of self-disgust. Rob-

ert simply shook his head, and Jack continued, "Why
don't we separate, Creighton and I to check the gardens,
you and Banyon to circulate in here. Surely *someone* noticed two unescorted women in such unusual gowns."

"I don't think that will do it," Robert disagreed. "If
Lydia deliberately spirited her away, she'd want to be as
sure as possible that no one was watching. In her own odd
way, Lydia is as efficient and capable as her father."

"That's the way I see it," Bryan told them with a nod.
"Lydia would try to be certain no one was watching, so
looking for casual witnesses is a waste of time. There's
only one chance, and I hope to God it works. Jeff, pass
the signal that we're starting to move, and pray it isn't a
lie."

And then Bryan headed for his very last hope without
waiting for a reply. But not without doing the praying he'd
suggested to Jeff. What if it *hadn't* worked? What if he
got there too late? Rianne . . .

"Yes, the door has been locked," the masked executioner said to Rianne. He'd drawn his sword, but he held
it down and away from her. "You can't get out and no
one will be coming to your rescue, so you might as well
resign yourself. Come over here, and I'll make it as quick
and painless as possible."

"That's very kind of you," Rianne replied, fighting to
keep her voice even. The room was the next thing to an
alcove, unfurnished and unembellished. There were two
doors in addition to the one she'd come through, one to
her left and one to the right. "So Lydia is one of you. I
never guessed."

"You weren't supposed to," he answered with a grin.
"We knew you would never allow yourself to be left out
of what was happening, so we told you your husband was
up to something and suggested you keep out of it. With
your sort of rebellious nature, that brought you to us faster
than the best racing pair in the kingdom could have."

"I ought to be insulted that you consider me so pre-
dictable," Rianne said, carefully taking off her mask and

tossing it away along with the small silver bow she still held. "The only thing is, your predictions are somewhat off the mark. If I'd known you were waiting here, I would have come even faster than I did. I know your voice isn't the one I remember so well, but in tonight's game, where a minion is, the master won't be far away." Then she drew her sword. "It's his life I want, not yours. Tell me where he is, and I'll let you walk away."

The man's grin had disappeared, and his hand tightened around the hilt of his sword. Rianne knew she was supposed to be terrified of him and his awful costume, but she *had* been braced for something like this. She would defend herself against the man if necessary, if for no other reason than to get something back for all their victims who hadn't been able to. Besides, what did she have to lose . . . ?

"You don't expect me to take that seriously?" the man demanded, gesturing toward the sword she held. "The suggestion that a woman can use a blade is as ridiculous as the offer you made. You should have stayed home where you belong."

And with that he brought his sword up and attacked, clearly expecting her to be too outraged to be prepared. With a snort of disgust Rianne stood her ground, parried his rush rather than back from it, then flicked her tip in a very short backswing. The pointed steel sliced shallowly down his sword hand, and he retreated fast with a sound of pain.

"Losing your temper during a fight also loses you the fight," Rianne lectured as she slowly pursued her opponent. "My fencing master taught me that, along with a number of other things. Are you going to answer my question, or would you rather see more of your own blood?"

The man in black bared his teeth, but didn't speak as he came *en garde*. His light eyes showed fear, and not just because of the blood running down his fist, she realized; he was held so tight by the man who owned his soul that he would rather face her steel than expose him.

This time the man's attack was in good form, as close

to it as his ability allowed. Rianne parried and countered, and her opponent's parry almost didn't work. He'd had training, all right, but he wasn't as good as she was and they both knew it. He backed from her advance, sweat showing beneath his mask. He had to be in pain from the wound on his hand, but he refused to stop trying, and that disturbed Rianne. She wasn't nearly as experienced with real fights as she'd tried to make him believe, and the thought of killing someone again after the way she'd felt the first time . . .

As it turned out, she needn't have worried. She was trying to convince herself to press her own attacks, when her opponent gave in to desperation. He hadn't been able to get through her guard to reach her, and must have decided he never would. The only thing left to try was strength and berserker rage, before his wounded hand became useless. He *did* have greater strength, and he did have the rage of fear . . .

He snarled and came at her fast and hard, using the strength of his blows as the weapon to drive her back. Once he had her pressed to a wall she would be helpless, and he could kill her at his leisure. Rianne could almost see him thinking like that, and something inside her twisted darkly. He wanted to hurt her, just as *he* had done all those years ago . . . This one worked for him, and had said so . . .

The hard-edged cold that took her over frightened Rianne, but only in a distant, unimportant way. An icy flame took control of her mind and body, so that rather than retreating from the now-desperate man in black, she parried, slipped aside, then lunged. Right through the middle of his chest her blade plunged, his flesh resisting but not enough. Her weapon was swallowed up to the hilt, and even his mask didn't hide the way the man's eyes bulged with knowledge of his coming death.

He choked and lurched to one side, possibly trying to reach her before the end, instead accomplishing a different end. His own forward motion had helped to impale him, and for the second time Rianne was unable to withdraw her weapon. He pulled it from her grip as he went down sideways, and that was when the hands grabbed her from behind.

Thinking it was Lydia, Rianne immediately began to struggle in an effort to free herself. But the hands closed tighter with a grip no woman could have, and she was pulled around to see that it was not the door to the hallway that had opened. It was the door to the left of the one she'd come through, and the masked man who held her wore the toga of a Roman senator, complete with laurel wreath.

"How dare you do that?" he quavered, as though she'd broken a precious porcelain cup or ruined a rug. His accent was that of someone educated to an upper-class position, rather than one born to it. "You'll regret it, girl, you'll certainly regret it!"

With that he thrust her toward the open door, apparently not caring how much his grip hurt. Rianne fought with fright as strongly as with her captor, but with the former she was more successful. Her sword was gone and she couldn't free herself, but *something* in the way of a plan would come. She'd sworn never to be helpless in front of that man again, and no matter what it took she wouldn't be . . .

Where that first room was small and starkly unfinished, the second made up for it. Three or four times the size of the first, it had wall drapes in purple and gold, with many matching brocade-covered couches ranged all around. Most of those couches held men dressed in togas and masks, replicas of the one who pushed her forward. They seemed to be reclaiming their places after having stood, and Rianne was certain many of them had witnessed the end of her sword fight.

Which would be one reason for the way they muttered and cursed and reached unsteadily for golden cups. Her victory must have badly unnerved them, just the way bullies were usually disturbed. They'd thought no one would be able to oppose them, that they could do whatever they were doing in complete, superior safety. They certainly

must have been assured of that by their leader, the biggest
and most cowardly bully of them all . . .

And that one lounged on a dais at the far side of the
room, his couch larger than any of the others and also
decorated with gold. Behind him to either side stood men
who were almost naked, except for the very large feather
fans they held. He himself was dressed as a masked Au-
gustus Caesar, his toga embroidered with silver and gold.
The cup he held gleamed with jewels to rival the ones he
wore on his fingers. As Rianne was forced closer he put
the cup aside, slowly stood up, then stepped down from
the dais.

"I see the years in between have made you forget," he
said, and that very soft voice coupled with those eyes made
Rianne want to shiver violently. Then he looked at the
man who had brought her to him. "What did she do out
there, beguile my executioner into bowing over her hand?
I wouldn't put it past the useless fool, and then he'd wonder how he'd been hit on the head. The so-called nobility!
When he wakes up, tell him—"

"Sir, she killed him!" her captor blurted with a gulp,
obviously hating to break the news. "I saw it all, but I
still have no idea what she did! He'd been taught how to
use a sword, and she—"

"She blinded him with beauty, then took him un-
awares!" Haynes snapped, close to fury. "A woman has
neither the courage nor the ability to make herself a real
threat to a man, and you should know that. All she *can*
do is give him trouble with words, but that's easily stopped.
This one will never speak out of turn again." Then he
turned his head to Rianne. "You've grown into more than
I imagined you would, girl, and that will keep you alive
for a while. I once promised you something if you spoke
out against me, but now that you're no longer a child I've
decided on something else. I'm going to take you with me
when I leave here tonight, so we'll be able to discuss the
matter later."

"You flatter yourself if you think I'd discuss anything
with the likes of *you,*" Rianne said coldly, holding her

voice steady only at great cost. "Go ahead and make all the decisions you care to, continuing the pretense that you're someone important. All I know is, you're a lot shorter than I remembered."

And she smiled with all the amusement she could muster, stabbing as brutally at the man as he had once done with her. He was thin and slight; the top of his head came a good two inches below hers, and she wearing no more than sandals. Realization of the truth of that fact struck Haynes like a slap, and his face went white as madness blazed from his eyes. He tore his mask off and hurled it away, and then fingers like stone were digging into her arms.

"You would dare?" he demanded in a hiss, the words spraying with spittle from his lips. "You would speak so to *me?* Did you learn nothing from the lesson I so carefully taught?"

Those hands shook her hard, adding to the pain of fingers dug deep, but that wasn't the worst of it. The sight of that face pulled Rianne back, back to the nightmare past, to the terror and agony she'd lived through then. Despite everything she could do the trembling began, the need to mewl out her fright a shuddering storm twisting within. Her throat closed against the need to scream, nearly choking her just as it had back then. She would die rather than give him the satisfaction . . . but please, please, not the way the poor man back then had died . . .

And then those eyes of madness filled with triumph, telling her that he knew. He could see the fear she refused to voice, and simply knowing it was there was his victory. He began to laugh, the sound telling her how alone she was in a roomful of people. She'd let herself be lured away from those who would have helped her, and now she was just as alone as she'd been in a house full of people . . . No one would help her, not even herself . . . Once again he would do exactly as he wanted to do, and no one would stop him . . .

The familiar, heavy cold of abandonment began to wrap its cruel tendrils around her again, this time like a shroud.

Rianne stood unmoving in the grip of the man who had tortured her as a child, wishing desperately that she could cry. She hadn't understood back then, and he didn't understand now. It wasn't the pain that brought terror and deepest despair, it was the loneliness. Having no one who cared, no one who would open their arms to her, offering a haven of safety and love . . .

And then the sound of a door crashing open ended Haynes's laughter, and brought most of the men in the room to their feet. Rianne twisted in the grip still holding her, and saw what she'd thought was impossible. The entire Roman pantheon poured into the room, and with them came the Greek and Norse gods. How they'd found her she had no idea, but at their head was a raging Mars . . .

"So it was all a ruse devised by *him*," Haynes growled, ruthlessness and soullessness mingling in those eyes that glared at the newcomers. "There were only supposed to be a few of them . . . It was all a lie and now they think they have me, but the game isn't over yet. I may end up losing, but my next move will make sure *he* isn't around to see it."

The man's voice was so deathly cold, that Rianne shuddered again to hear it. That brought her partially back to his attention, but he'd already dismissed her from consideration. An uncaring push sent her staggering away, and that took care of the rest of the dismissal. She was too unimportant to bother with right then, and could be forgotten about completely.

He then began to stalk the new object of his fury. Most of the men in togas had thrown themselves on the invading gods, some with daggers or heavy sticks, some barehanded, and the resulting melee was chaos. The bedlam had swallowed up almost everyone including Machlin, who had been forcing his way forward toward Haynes. Right then his back was turned as he stood with empty hands against a man with a dagger. He was good at that, Rianne remembered, very good . . .

But Haynes had pulled a long, jeweled knife out of his Roman robes, and began to move deliberately toward the

much larger man. Machlin would never see him coming,
or hear him over the screams and shouts of the others.
And his golden armor—not armor at all, but heavy gilded
cloth made to look like metal. That knife would plunge
right through it, through it into *him* . . .

Rianne didn't have to force herself into motion. As soon
as full understanding came she began to run, nothing left
of the fear for herself. Machlin, the man she'd been forced
to marry, the man who didn't really want her, the man
who had already found another woman to take her place—
if he died so would she, so it might as well be her alone.
What he'd given her even without love—it was worth the
price of her life. She'd never be missed, and she'd never
have to feel loneliness again . . .

The scene came to her jerkily as she ran, as though God
moved the world at an uneven pace. Machlin moved carefully against his opponent, unaware of the knife being
raised behind him in a fist of vengeance. Haynes had also
begun to run, and his mouth opened as though he were
about to voice a battle cry. His right arm was all the way
back above his shoulder, and just as he brought it forward
he began to scream—

But Rianne was there to throw herself in the way, and
her own scream erupted from her throat even before the
point of the blade touched her. For the first time in her
life she screamed freely, screamed for victory of life over
death, for love even if it wasn't returned, for the end of
terror and fear and hate—

And then she screamed at the pain of the knife, plunging into her rather than into the man she loved. She'd never
told him that, never could have told him, now never would.
Sharpened metal tore open her flesh, and the blessed darkness took her as its own.

The screams behind him made Bryan's blood freeze, but
he was too experienced a fighter to simply whirl around.
As he jumped to the right he kicked out hard, and the
fool who'd been threatening him with a dagger went down

crumpled over, leaving Bryan free to pay attention to whatever had gone on behind him . . .

"No! God, no!" he screamed, seeing Rianne on the floor, covered in blood. His beloved, his life—! And the man who had done it still stood there, bloody knife in his fist, a look of fury on his face.

"The stupid little fool!" the man growled with annoyance. "She was *always* getting in the way, but now she never will again. Good riddance to the tart, and now I can get on with finishing *you.*"

And to Bryan's disbelieving shock, the man raised his knife and began to advance toward *him.* Just that calmly and easily he'd struck down the most important thing in life to Bryan, feeling no more than annoyance over having been bothered. Now he was coming after Bryan, considering him just as much of a victim since Bryan stood with empty hands. Insanity touched Bryan then, fueled by inconsolable grief, and it no longer mattered that there were constables among his men who were there to arrest Haynes.

Bryan reached across his body to the broadsword he wore as part of his costume, a sword that was in no way a toy. Unsheathing and bringing it up lightning-fast, he gripped it two-handed, the way a broadsword is meant to be held. The heartless monster of a murderer stopped short, no longer the only one who had a weapon and therefore suddenly cautious. He might even have been thinking about surrendering and taking his chances with the law, but Bryan was not about to let that happen. He swung with all the strength in his arms—

And sent the head of George Haynes flying away from its body. Screams of shock and fear came from all around the room, but Bryan didn't even watch the man's body fall. He dropped his red-streaked weapon and went to his knees, gathered up the crumpled silver form all covered with blood, and cried for a loss that could never be repaired. He knelt like that for an endless time, and then Jeff Banyon's voice insisted on intruding.

"Bryan, listen to me!" the man prodded, as though he'd

said the same thing many times before. "Bryan, let go of
her! We have a physician here, but he can't do his job if
you don't let her go! Do you want her to die?"

Bryan was about to tell Jeff what a fool he was, when
the body in his arms stirred and moaned. And it was warm,
the body was warm! In a haze of shock he let Jeff take
her, then sat on the floor with his eyes closed and his head
in his hands. She was alive, still alive, even though she'd
tried to fight Haynes herself bare-handed when *he* was
only a step away. He meant less than nothing in her life,
but at least she still *had* that life. *Thank you, God,* he
whispered silently, *thank you for her life . . . even if she
wants to live it without me . . .*

Chapter 18

"**B**ryan, you're a fool!" Sarah raged. "Why don't *you* talk to her?"

"Because she wants no part of me," he answered, returning calm for anger. "Are you going to claim it's all my imagination?"

They sat in his study, him behind the desk, she and Jamie in front of it. It had been good to see his partner again, and be able to congratulate him on his upcoming fatherhood. That had been the only bright spot for Bryan in the last fortnight, and it had already passed.

"I can't believe things have deteriorated between you two rather than improved," Sarah fretted, then turned to her dark-haired, dark-eyed husband. "Jamie, *you* talk to him. Tell him it has to take time, and if he sends her away they won't *have* that time."

"Sarah, my love, there are occasions when a man runs out of time," Jamie told her gently with a compassionate glance at Bryan. "I've never known Bryan to give up on a fight that wasn't already more than lost. If he feels there's nothing left to be done, then there probably isn't."

"You two are enough to make a woman want to take up weapons," Sarah huffed, then looked at Bryan again. "Where's Jeff Banyon? He usually shows more good sense than the average man, and I'd like to hear what *he* thinks."

"Jeff has been helping to clean up the rest of that horrible mess," Bryan answered, shaking his head. "They wanted *me* to give them a hand, but I'd had enough of it so I loaned them Jeff. He's also in charge of that half company I brought in, and the experience will do him good.''

"Weren't most of the men Haynes used in his robberies there in the room at Ranelagh?" Jamie asked. When Bryan nodded, he said, "Then what has Jeff been cleaning up? And why would he need a half company to do it?"

"What's left is gathering up the people Haynes bribed or blackmailed over the years," Bryan explained. "He carefully chose people as amoral as himself when he could, and it's hard to believe how many of them he found. If he judged wrong and one of them began to develop a conscience, he simply had them killed. The ones still living were the worst of the lot, and Fielding appreciated having the half company there to support his people and the constables.''

"How did the people Haynes bribed keep from being suspected?" Jamie asked curiously. "I can't believe they all looked and acted like such angels that no one ever considered them.''

"That wasn't the way they did it," Bryan said with a faint smile. "He and his paid informants always had someone to blame right there on the spot, someone they'd previously chosen. If there was a worker with a sick wife, say, and that worker suddenly had enough money for a good physician right after the gold was stolen, wouldn't you investigate him first? And if you questioned the worker and found he'd been *given* the money anonymously . . .''

"I'd stop looking altogether," Jamie agreed sourly. "I hate to think how many different ways it would be possible to do something like that. How did the bunch of you find out about it?"

"From Haynes's journals," Bryan supplied. "He kept careful track of everyone he'd paid and how much—or what he had on them to make them obey him—along with what they'd done to frame someone innocent. He wouldn't have wanted to repeat the method unless he had to, and it was another way to keep the ones he'd paid from trying to blackmail *him*. No one could turn him in without doing the same to themselves.''

"So what will happen to the informants who are members of the nobility?" Jamie asked, unashamedly curious. "There are some *I* wouldn't mind helping to arrest, even if the court just sends them back to their families."

"That's not as easy a fate as it sounds," Bryan said with a smile for the glint in Jamie's dark eyes. "Don't forget every one of them betrayed those families, and that fact won't be forgiven or forgotten. Lydia Worden, Robert Creighton tells me, will spend her time under close chaperonage at home until a suitably restrictive marriage can be arranged for her. She was the one responsible for handing out invitations to Alicia's party to eager outsiders that night, and was probably looking forward to Tremar's being killed."

"And Tremar was killed for being too likely to get drunk and talk too much," Jamie said. He and Sarah had already been told about Tremar and the party. "Did you ever find out for certain why Harding was put out of the way?"

"Haynes's journal section on Harding was thick," Bryan answered with a nod. "I haven't yet had the heart to tell Rianne, but Haynes's involvement with Harding started a long time ago. She thinks her father died in a hunting accident, but the truth is Haynes had him killed for Harding. Harding had found out how large a private estate the man had, and wanted control of it. Married to the man's widow he had a lot of control, but then his wife died. The trustees who had approved him for the marriage then had more to say about the estate than he did, because it then became Rianne's inheritance. Harding, already being blackmailed by Haynes for that first murder, was ordered to get back control of the estate and share it with his major benefactor as he'd promised to do. When Harding failed again and again, Haynes grew disgusted. Signing that useless agreement with me was the last straw, and since Harding had been stupid enough to make out a will at Haynes's direction, Haynes decided he'd be worth more dead than alive."

"I'll bet Haynes had plans for blackmailing *you,*" Sarah said, her voice thoughtful. "I don't know what he would have used, but he probably couldn't bear the thought of letting you walk away with all of your new wife's inheritance. And since we're back to that, I'll ask you again: can't *you* speak to her?''

''No,'' Bryan answered shortly. ''Sarah, I'd decided to force her to stay with me, but even if it wasn't done on purpose she did save my life. I didn't know Haynes was behind me, and her attack on him kept him from putting that knife in my back. That means she has a right to be free of me, but I have to know she'll be safe. Will you tell her for me what I've arranged? She should be able to travel soon so it needs to be said, but it should come from someone she knows rather than from a servant.''

''If at all, it should come from *you,* '' Sarah muttered, not in the least happy. ''If only I'd been able to travel to London with you, I might have been able to do *something* . . . Bryan, are you very sure?''

When he nodded calmly into the intensity of her stare, she surrendered with a sigh and answered with her own nod. She would do as he asked, he knew, saving him from doing what he couldn't. He didn't even plan to be there on the day the girl left. He hadn't seen her for two weeks, and if God was kind he would never have to look at her again. If he did see her, he would probably dishonor himself by refusing to let her go. He was doing the right thing . . . He *knew* that . . . He *knew* that . . .

''. . . and what he did was set the *serving men* to watching you,'' Cam enthused, delighting in telling Rianne all about it. ''He knew they always see everything, but those veddy, veddy important people never see *them.* Everyone else had missed where you'd gone—or had been made to miss it—but *two* of the serving men hadn't. He got all his people together and then broke in, and the rest you know.''

Rianne nodded to show she did indeed, and didn't mention that she'd prefer to forget. Cam had been in London for two days, having gotten himself the job as driver for Machlin's partner and his wife, Jamie and Sarah Raymond. The Raymonds were downstairs with Machlin, while Cam was visiting with her.

"Are you *sure* you shouldn't still be in bed?" Cam asked, a repeat of the first thing he'd said to her. He hadn't known she'd been hurt until that morning, or he would have been banging down the door the instant he arrived. "You look—pale, and not even as healthy as Angus did when I left."

"Cam, I'm fine," she assured him, shifting on the lounge she preferred to the bed. "There may have been a lot of blood, but the wound wasn't all that serious. Haynes hit me in the arm, and I must have fainted from the tension of everything that had happened. It certainly wasn't *painful* enough to make someone faint."

"Oh, of course not," he agreed dryly, sounding exactly like Angus. "People get stabbed every day, and most of the time don't even notice. It's a good thing you have someone to look after you now, Ree. If Mr. Machlin can't keep you out of trouble, no one can."

After two weeks of slowly getting used to the truth, Rianne had no trouble keeping her face expressionless. Cam didn't know that she hadn't even seen Machlin since that night she was stabbed, and she had no intentions of telling him. He and Angus thought her life was as happily settled as theirs; if she told them it wasn't so, they would insist on leaving with her when she went. Since she wasn't about to let them sacrifice their dreams, she'd simply keep quiet.

Or be noncommittal, as she was just about to do, when someone knocked at the door. Her maid, Meg, went to answer it, and when she'd opened the door Rianne was surprised to hear a familiar voice say, "I'd like to speak with Mrs. Machlin. Please tell her it's Sarah Raymond."

When Meg turned to look at her, Rianne gave a reluctant nod. She really didn't want to see the woman, but there was no sense in being rude for no reason. Sarah Raymond came in, and her clothes were of better quality than when she'd been pretending to be Machlin's housekeeper. She smiled at Rianne, a rather strained smile, then glanced around.

"Would you mind if we talked in private?" she asked. "If you need anything I can get it for you, and Cameron can come back to continue his visit later. As if anyone would be able to stop him."

Her smile at Cam was warm with friendliness, and he returned a roguish grin. No one *would* be able to stop him from coming back, and as long as everyone understood that, things were just fine. He patted Rianne's hand before getting up, and a moment later he and Meg were gone with the door closed behind them.

"All right, now we're alone," Rianne pointed out when the other woman remained silent. "What do you have to talk about that's so very important?"

"We never got the chance to really know one another, did we?" Mrs. Raymond responded with a faint smile as she walked to the chair Cam had vacated and sat down. "It's one of the things I regret, probably more than you'll ever know. Bryan—asked me to talk to you."

And there it was, the invitation to leave Rianne had been expecting ever since she woke up back in his house. She'd obviously embarrassed him so badly wearing that costume, he couldn't stand the thought of seeing her again for any reason. He must have been spending most of his time with his new woman, and had come back only to tie up the remaining loose ends.

"You can tell Machlin I'm fine, and that I'll be leaving in the next couple of days," she said, forcing herself to ignore the sick feeling inside her. "Was there anything else?"

"As a matter of fact, I'm here to discuss that very subject," Mrs. Raymond answered, looking even more upset. "Your leaving, I mean. Bryan has a really lovely house that he was going to sell, but now he wants *you* to have it. He'll take care of all the expenses, of course, and you'll be able to live there quite comfortably."

"It sounds charming, but I'm afraid I have other plans," Rianne said, reaching for her teacup to hide the bleakness she felt. He was so eager to be rid of her, he was even willing to support her for life. Life. Existence . . .

"Mrs. Machlin—Rianne, I'm afraid you don't understand," Mrs. Raymond protested, her fingers folding the silk of her day gown. "Bryan doesn't want you to have other plans, and I'm certain he's prepared to insist. He doesn't want to worry about whether or not you're safe, so—"

"So he's decided to lock me up again," Rianne interrupted, beginning to fume. "Can't he learn to ignore his guilt like everyone else in the world? All I want him to do is leave me alone!"

"But that's the one thing he *can't* do," the woman blurted, her eyes pleading. "Don't you understand? He said you even saved his life, and now—"

"And now he wants to thank me," Rianne interrupted again, this time very flatly. "Well, he can keep his thanks, along with everything else he owns. The only thing I need is to be out of here, and that I'll have in two days' time. And now, if you don't mind, I'd like to be alone."

The woman's dark eyes searched Rianne's face, but whatever she sought was apparently not there. She shook her head with a sigh, then got to her feet.

"I can see there's no sense in saying any more," she conceded. "I'm sure Bryan won't agree, but you two will have to work that out between you. Do you want me to send your maid back in?"

"No," Rianne answered. "I'm tired and I'd like to rest for a while. When I want her, I'll ring."

The woman nodded, almost hesitated, then shook her head again and made for the door. When she was gone Rianne sat thinking for a moment, then got up, her decision made. Machlin thought he could salve his conscience by burying her somewhere in the country, but it wasn't going to happen. If she was going to be ignored and forgotten about, it would be because she wasn't anywhere in reach. She'd be off living her own life, just as she always had.

She ignored silent echoes of *alone . . . alone . . . alone*

as she went toward the chest where she'd put her breeches
and shirt and boots. She'd used her wound as an excuse
to keep her rooms, deciding that if Machlin had anything
to say, he would have to come to *her*. But he hadn't come,
not even to find out if she were alive or dead, not even to
tell her it was time to get out. If Sarah Raymond was right
and he decided to argue her decision, he'd find no one
there to argue with. She couldn't bear the thought of seeing him again, when that would be the very last time . . .

As she opened the chest, the small twinge in her left
arm came more from lack of use than the wound itself.
Her possessions were all there inside, untouched by Meg
or anyone else. She kept her private things in there, and
no one had tried to invade that privacy. In a strange way
she'd been happy in this house, almost as happy as during
her early childhood. If only things had continued the way
they'd started, if only he could have loved her back . . .

Rianne closed her eyes for a moment, then quickly began to dress. Wishing for "if onlys" was the biggest waste
of time in the world. They *never* came true, not ever, and
if she hadn't learned that by now, she never would. But
she *had* learned it, and from now on would make her own
wishes come true.

Once into her clothes, she remembered she was already
packed. Everything she meant to take was in a single dark-
blue sack, but when she pulled the sack out she found
something unremembered beneath it. The matched set of
pistols she'd bought, intending to give them to Machlin.
Since she no longer had her sword or any other, should
she take the pistols instead?

She carried everything to a table, thought about it for a
moment, then shook her head as though someone were
there to argue with. If she took the pistols, they would be
a constant reminder of the man who hadn't returned her
love. She'd rather be weaponless than hurt herself so,
rather die than save her life with one of them. It was painful just to look at the box . . .

Abruptly she turned away, chose a dark cloak that would
hopefully be inconspicuous, and then was ready to go. But

before picking up the sack, she did one last thing. She put
the jewelry he'd given her on the table beside the pistols,
and left her wedding band on top of the black-and-silver
box. This time there was no chance of her coming back,
and she didn't even want to. Maybe the first time, wanting
it without knowing she did, but not now . . . not again . . .
not ever . . .

Her sight was blurred as she slipped out of the room,
but that didn't stop her from making sure she wasn't seen.

Sarah Raymond headed back to Bryan's study with determination. The interview with Rianne had gone even
worse than she'd expected, and she felt like kicking herself
for letting Bryan talk her into going. That girl's self-control
was incredible, but this time the feeling of deep pain from
Rianne had been so strong that Sarah had almost become
sick again. Like that day when she'd told them about what
had been done to her as a child . . .

Sarah ground her teeth together to regain some of her
own self-control. There was more wrong than any of them
knew, and this time she would insist that Bryan get to the
bottom of it. If necessary she would throw a carefully
calculated tantrum, which would certainly be blamed on
her pregnancy. Men were so vulnerable to pressure plays
like that . . .

She crossed the front hall, went to the study and threw
open the door—and found it completely deserted. Both
Bryan and Jamie had disappeared, and when she called
Harris she discovered that Cam had gone with them.
They'd been called away briefly on some matter that had
to do with business, and had left word that they would
return soon.

Soon to her meant just a few minutes, but at least two
hours and a full pot of tea went by before she heard voices
in the hall. Sarah went immediately to see if it was them,
and it certainly was—along with Jeff Banyon. Jamie and
Jeff looked absolutely delighted, and even Bryan seemed
distantly pleased.

"Sarah, love, come and hear the good news," Jamie

called, putting out a hand toward her. "Everyone was so impressed with Jeff's efficiency these last two weeks, our services are now being demanded by five of the men who had been Haynes's victims. Of course, it did help that it was Bryan who figured out what Haynes was doing, but I'm sure it was Jeff who convinced them we were best for the job. We spent the last hour or so quoting fees and signing contracts."

"I'm glad to hear we won't be starving for a while," Sarah responded, unable to share his mood. "I'm also glad to hear that Bryan is so clever. Maybe that will help him with his private problem."

"What do you mean?" Bryan asked at once, those gray eyes anxious. "What happened when you went to see her?"

"She rejected your offer almost before I got the words out," Sarah told him bluntly. "She said she had her own plans, and would be out of here within two days. She also said you can keep whatever you have, she doesn't want any of it."

"But she *can't* just take off on her own!" Bryan protested, sounding like a hurt little boy. *"Anything* could happen, and no one would be there to protect her! Sarah, you've got to go back and make her understand—"

"No, Bryan, not me," Sarah interrupted sharply. *"You're* the one who has to talk to her. And while you're doing it, you might try to find out why she's still in so much pain. If everything is as simple and straightforward as you claim, why did I get the feeling she was dreading leaving rather than looking forward to it? You can't—"

"She's gone!" a voice suddenly shouted, and they all looked up to see the boy Cam at the head of the stairs. "Mr. Machlin, Ree's rooms are empty! I looked all through them, but she isn't anywhere around!"

A sudden stampede sent Bryan, Jamie, and Jeff flying up the stairs, leaving Sarah to follow at her own best speed. The boy must have gone back to Rianne as soon as he'd brought his employers home, to explain his delay in returning if nothing else. When Sarah reached the sitting room, the men had already checked the smaller rooms attached to it, which meant she was right behind them when they entered the bed chamber.

"See?" Cam said as he pointed to the floor. "Those are the bed things she was wearing. Do you think she just felt well enough to go out for a walk? She was so pale from being indoors so long . . ."

Cam's voice trailed off when he realized Bryan was no longer hearing him. Sarah saw that the big man stared at a table, and when she followed his gaze she moaned and clutched at Jamie's hand.

"What is it?" Jamie asked quickly in concern. "Sarah, love, what's wrong?"

"That's Rianne's wedding ring sitting on that box," she whispered, tears in her eyes. "Oh, Jamie, she's *gone,* and she won't be coming back."

Somehow, Jamie's arm around her brought less comfort than it usually did. Bryan looked as though he'd been run through with a sword, and simply hadn't gotten around to falling down. Cam had gone pale and silent, and that left only one person to say something.

"What are *they* doing here?" Jeff asked, as though everyone would understand what he meant. "I expected her to give them weeks ago."

"Jeff, what *are* you talking about?" Jamie asked in turn. "Who are 'they,' and what have they got to do with anything?"

" 'They' aren't *who,* they're *what,* " Jeff answered unhelpfully as he moved forward. "In that black case. Those are the pistols Mrs. Machlin bought for Bryan, but I thought she would have already given them to him. I wondered if she'd decided to save them for a special occasion."

"What in hell are you talking about?" Bryan himself demanded, more out of control than Sarah had ever seen him. "She didn't buy anything for *me.* Why would she, when she can't even stand the sight of me? If there were pistols in that box, you can bet she's taken them with her."

Rather than answering in words, Jeff walked to the table and carefully moved the desolately abandoned ring before opening the box. By then they were all there, and able to look down at the beautiful brace of pistols. Once again Bryan looked stunned, but he also shook his head.

"That can't be right," he said, his head going back and forth in slow denial. "She *must* have bought them for herself, and left them only because she doesn't know how to use them."

"Of course she can use a pistol," Cam put in from his place at the fringes of their group. "She gave Angus the silver to buy one, and we'd sneak off regularly to practice shooting. She's a dead shot, Mr. Machlin, better even than with a bow."

"And I happen to know she *did* buy them for you," Jeff said, those pale-blue eyes refusing to back down from the disbelief in gray ones. "I was close enough to hear her speaking to herself as she examined them, and what she said was, 'Machlin would *love* these.' They were the first thing she bought that day, and the only thing that really gave her pleasure."

"But—why would she buy me a gift?" Bryan asked, so bewildered that Sarah's heart hurt for him. "And with money she considered hers? That doesn't make any sense at all. She's never even spoken my first name."

"That's not hard to understand," Sarah felt compelled to counter. "You two have done nothing but circle each other warily ever since your original intentions were revealed. How much effort did you make to get to know one another, and I mean in words?"

"There wasn't really time for conversation," Bryan admitted with a frown. "We were so involved with finding Haynes—and any time we did talk, we ended up arguing instead. She knew I wanted her, but always avoided the subject because *she* didn't want *me*."

"Excuse me, sir, but that's not true," Cam spoke up again, also looking troubled. "At first Ree was sure you *didn't* want her, and even said so the night we three tried to reach London. Angus and I were worried about being followed, but she was sure we wouldn't be. She was sure *you* didn't care enough. And two days later, just before you and she left, she came to say good-bye to us. Afterward Angus was upset, but I thought he was imagining things because of his wound. He said she still didn't believe she was wanted, and she had that look in her eyes again. She used to have that look all the time, before he and I got close to her. You know, the look of a little girl all alone in the world, in the midst of people who only want to use her. But I don't understand why she went alone, without me, at least. She should have known I would have gone with her.''

"I'm sure she did, Cam," Sarah soothed him. "And I'm also sure that's why she didn't ask. You and your brother have found places that please you, places that will let you rise in the world according to your abilities. She loves you too much to have asked you to leave all that for an uncertain future with her.''

"And it's all my fault," Bryan said slowly. "I was being so clever, trying not to scare her away, that not once did I tell her how I felt. She must have thought I only wanted to use her to find Haynes, and let me do it because she wanted to find him, too. But if there's a chance she cares for me, why did she attack Haynes alone, literally behind my back? That may have accidentally saved my life, but why didn't she at least wait for us to do it together?''

"But she didn't *attack* him," Jeff objected in bewilderment. "I saw the whole thing, but couldn't get clear fast enough to do anything about it. That cold-blooded murderer was going for your back with a knife, and you had no idea he was coming. Mrs. Machlin ran to get there in time, and threw herself in the way. Bryan, she took the knife to keep it from reaching *you*—I thought you knew that.''

"Oh, my Lord," Sarah blurted with a hand to her throat. "No wonder she was furious. I said something about your knowing she saved your life, Bryan, which must have sounded as though *that* was the reason you wanted her to have the house. As a thank-you for a useful service, a pat on the head as you sent her away. Sent her away—

Oh, God, I've just remembered something else, and I'll bet you never spoke to her about it."

"Spoke to her about what?" Bryan asked, now as bewildered as Jeff had been. "What did you remember?"

"That day we went to Harding's house and found him dead," Sarah answered, fighting to make the words come out lucid. "You'd asked me to let her know that you were ready to return her freedom, and I did. Did *you* ever tell her that you were setting her free because you believed it was what *she* wanted?" Bryan's bewilderment vanished behind closed eyelids, which made his following head-shake unnecessary. "I thought not," Sarah added, sharing his pain. "Now I *know* why she felt so hurt, and I wish I didn't. What are you going to do?"

"Find her," he answered flatly, that old look suddenly back in his gray eyes. "I knew I should never have let her go, but I was trying to be civilized and gentlemanly about it. Now that it's almost ruined my life, I say to hell with it. From now on I do things *my* way, and God help anyone who gets in that way."

"London's a big city, my friend," Jamie called after him as Bryan started for the door. "You'll be using the men to help look, of course, but where will you start?"

The mild words stopped Bryan the way a shout never would have, and Sarah felt like smacking her husband. Why did he have to say that, just when their friend was starting to come alive again? It *was* harder to find someone in a city than out in the countryside, but that didn't mean he couldn't do it.

Sarah looked at the men, all of them now wearing the same expression of frustration, and suddenly felt chilled. Surely Bryan would be able to find Rianne and bring her back . . . Wouldn't he . . . ?

Rianne stood at the far rail of the ship, looking out to sea as the wind tried to toss her hair around. She'd tied it back with a piece of ribbon the way men usually did and tucked the end into her collar, and from behind with her cloak on she looked like a man. The captain of the vessel

knew she wasn't, but he had his own dour sense of honor.
He believed that she wasn't there to sell herself to his crew
and other passengers during the voyage, and had assured
her of his protection once they were at sea.

Protection. The word almost made her smile, but not
with amusement. It was two days since she left Machlin's
house, and she hadn't had much trouble protecting herself.
The room she'd taken on the waterfront had been awful,
but it had also been cheap. People usually minded their
own business down there; she wasn't the only one who
hadn't been asked intrusive questions, but she still felt
grateful.

But not so grateful that she hadn't broken a pitcher over
the head of someone trying to bother her. That had kept the
rest of them away, all the small, dirty men who lost their
grins when she met their eyes. There was no fear in her,
not over anything *they* might do, and knowing that seemed
to have kept them at a distance.

And then she'd learned about this ship, arrived just the
day before and taking on cargo and passengers for the
colonies. She'd come on board and spoken to the captain,
and had even haggled over the price of her passage. When
they'd come to agreement he'd told her to be back today,
for he meant to sail with the evening tide. Just a few more
hours and England would be left forever behind . . .

Rianne put her hand on the weather-smoothed rail,
searching for the eagerness she'd once felt at the thought
of such a journey. The harbor had a perpetual smell of fish
and salt water, bird droppings and garbage, spoiled pro-
duce and grease-protected metal. She couldn't wait to be
away from it all, but no longer cared about the way she
left. Grand sailing ship or scow, carriage or cart, horse-
back or shank's mare—anything, as long as it took her
away. For two days she hadn't been able to sleep or eat
much, and she was so very tired . . .

But would that really change? She stared out at the un-
dulating gray-green sea, no longer filled with plans and
hopes and dreams. She didn't know what would happen to

her, and didn't even care. All she really wanted was to sleep and sleep and never wake up . . .

"It's got to be those clothes," a voice said suddenly from behind her. "Every time you put them on, I end up hopping around like a madman. It's obvious they have it in for me, so you're just going to have to choose between us."

Rianne stood frozen in shock for a moment, then whirled around to find that she *hadn't* imagined the voice. *He* was there, staring down at her with the most awful look in those gray eyes . . .

"What are you doing here?" she blurted, her shock turning the question into a demand. "How did you find me?"

"Unfairly," he admitted without hesitation, actually sounding pleased. "Sometimes that's the only way I can deal with you if I want to avoid utter failure."

"Well, it's too bad you bothered," Rianne said, refusing to show how suddenly torn up she felt. "I'm sailing in a few hours, so you can just go ahead and forget about me. You'll enjoy not having to worry about failure again."

She began to turn back to the rail, hating the reminder of how much trouble she had made for him. Was he there to rub salt in the wound of memory . . . ?

"You're mistaken," he said, one big hand on her arm stopping her. "You're *not* sailing in a few hours, you're coming back with me right now. There are things we have to say to each other, things that should have been said long ago. *I* should have said them before—that was my mistake and now I'm correcting it."

"Look, Machlin, I'm really too tired to play this game," she told him with a sigh, turning only her head. "I already know that I'm an embarrassment to you, and that you've found a woman who suits you a good deal better. Since I'm not about to argue any of that, you can consider everything said. And you can also go away and leave me alone."

She tried to unhook her arm from his hand, but instead of letting her go he turned her all the way back to him.

He was staring at her as though she were mad, and even seemed to be outraged.

"A *woman?*" he finally demanded. "You think I have a woman? How the devil did you come up with that?"

"It was perfectly obvious," she responded, uncomfortable in the face of his anger. "I overheard you and Jeff Banyon discussing the great lady you'd decided to get together with, and you'd made such a fuss about sharing my bed earlier, but after that you were much too busy. Do you think I'm too ignorant to see the truth when it's right under my nose?"

"God in heaven give me strength," he muttered with eyes closed, and then he was staring down at her again. "It so happens that the great lady we were talking about is the Bank of England, where I hoped to get information on Haynes. If you thought I had another woman, why didn't you say so? Don't you think a wife is entitled to know that for certain about her husband? Or that a husband is entitled to the chance to prove it isn't true?"

"I—didn't see any point in making a fuss," she answered defensively, now even more uncomfortable as well as embarrassed. "We were together for a particular purpose, and that purpose was nearly over. You never *said* you wouldn't find interest in other women, so how could I—"

"Of *course* I said I wouldn't be looking at other women," he interrupted with a growl. "I know you weren't paying very close attention to our marriage ceremony, but I was required to give my oath on that. And even if I hadn't, I still wouldn't have gone roving. Why would I have another woman when I'm in love with my wife?"

Rianne stood blinking in confusion for a moment, wondering why he'd said that. He couldn't mean it, of course, not in a world where wishes never come true. And then she remembered he was grateful to her for having saved his life. He *was* a man of honor, and obviously intended to repay that debt in a proper way. He would spend the life she'd saved at her side, pretending to a love he didn't really feel.

"Thank you for telling me that, but now you'd better go," she said, looking away from him. "You don't want to still be on board when the captain sets sail. He—"

"You don't believe me," Machlin stated, refusing to loosen his grip and let her pull free. "For some reason you think I'm lying, but I refuse to accept that. You'll come home with me, and then we'll talk until—"

"No!" she interrupted in turn, trying harder to get loose. "I'm not going anywhere with you, and certainly not to talk. I'm staying right here on this ship, and you can't do anything about it. I've already paid for my passage, which means I'm under the captain's protection. If you try to force me to go with you, he'll have his men stop you."

"Where do you get these ideas?" Machlin asked with a snort. "Even those books you read can't be filled with such drivel. As your husband I can do anything I please with you, and even a dozen sea captains couldn't stop me. Especially while we're still in port. If you want to stay on board that badly, let's do it. But we're still going to talk."

With that he released her, but only to bend and reach for her legs. An instant later she was over his shoulder, and even squawking in panic and kicking her legs didn't free her. He ignored her pounding fists as he carried her forward and then down a ladder that led to passengers' accommodations. Her shouts for help brought nothing and no one, and then they were through a door and into a cabin. When he turned to close the door Rianne had a glimpse of a place three of four times bigger than her own tiny cabin, and then he turned again and resumed walking.

The kidnapping ended at a large bed, built into the deck but much grander than an ordinary bunk. He dumped her onto the bed like a sack of oats, then stood over her, ignoring her glare.

"I want your word that you won't try to leave here until we have everything straight between us," he said. "I can't tell you what I want to if I have to sit on you while I'm doing it.''

"Do you think bringing me to the captain's cabin will make me believe what you said about him?'' she demanded, immediately sitting up. "He can't possibly know what you've done, but once he finds out—''

"This isn't the captain's cabin,'' he interrupted in annoyance. "It's the owner's cabin, and even the captain won't enter here without my permission. Now—''

"*Your* permission!'' Rianne echoed, suddenly seeing what he'd meant about finding her unfairly. "This ship is *yours,* and you brought it here to lure me out! You couldn't find me, so you set a trap!''

"Exactly,'' he agreed, folding his arms across his chest. "Your friend Cam told me where you three planned to go, so I gambled that you'd decide to continue on alone. Now give me your word about staying.''

"Never!'' she growled, hating him for telling her how easily he'd bought Cam's loyalty. "I'd rather be dead than stay in here with you, or anywhere else for that matter! And you have nothing to say that I care to listen to.''

With that she jumped off the bed, and made a try for the door. By ducking under his quickly reaching arms she actually got past him, but he caught her before she could open the door. She screamed and kicked as he carried her back, finding it just as useless as ever, and this second time he didn't simply put her down. He unhooked her cloak and tossed it away, then pulled off her boots and clothes as he'd done once before. When she was bare he rolled her things in the discarded cloak, put the bundle behind him, then took off his own coat and vest. Rianne watched him warily, but that was as far as he went.

"Now I don't need your word about staying,'' he said, sitting down in a chair and loosening his cravat. "If you still want to leave, go right ahead.''

"You—!'' Rianne couldn't think of anything bad enough to call him, not even with a wealth of stable words. She wished desperately that she could just get up and walk out, but if anyone saw her she really would die. She sat up on the bed again with fists clenched tight, and simply glared her fury.

"That, by the way, leads me to an apology I owe you," he said, just as though they were in the middle of a normal conversation. "When I saw you in that silver costume *I'd* been stupid enough not to have properly fitted, I thought you were deliberately showing yourself off. To let me know what I'd soon be losing, you understand, and to attract every other man there. Jealousy does a great job of turning a man into a fool, and it took Jeff's telling me how you'd hated all that attention to bring me back down to earth. You wore that gown in spite of being terribly embarrassed, because you knew you had to be there that night. I apologize for thinking there was any other reason."

As angry as she was, Rianne still had to pause. What he'd just said wasn't entirely true, but how was she supposed to admit that she *had* wanted him to regret losing her? She couldn't, not without sounding like an idiot, so she didn't say anything at all.

"Now that I've apologized, let's get back to what I *won't* be apologizing for," he continued after a brief pause. "We can start from the beginning on that, all the way back to my plan against Harding. I happily let myself be talked into marrying his stepdaughter, because I had no intention of *staying* married to her. I would bring her to my house, install her in her rooms, then get the marriage annulled once I had the information I wanted. Annulments are possible, you see, if the bride remains in a chastely untouched condition."

"But then why did you—I mean, our wedding night—" Rianne couldn't quite get the specifics out, but it wasn't necessary.

"Do you mean why did I take you in my arms and make love to you?" he asked with a grin. "Because I couldn't help myself. The moment I saw you I knew I had to have you, and not just because you're the most beautiful woman I've ever seen. There *is* more to you than beauty, so much more that I lost the fight in the first exchange. I love you, Rianne, and I know now that you also love me."

"That isn't true," she whispered, quickly looking away. It *couldn't* be real, it couldn't, she must be in the middle of a dream. No one would ever love her enough to come after her, not unless there was something else involved. That had to be it, he wanted something else, but—what else did she have to give?

"What isn't true?" he asked, suddenly sitting beside her. "That I love you, or that you love me? I happen to *know* you love me, and I can prove it. You said yourself you thought I had another woman, but instead of flying into a rage and accusing me of compromising you, you tried to quietly step aside. You do that when you love someone, when you consider their happiness before your own. I should know. I thought you desperately wanted to be free of me, so I forced myself to step out of your way."

Rianne still couldn't look at him, but even more she couldn't make her mind think. There was too much confusion in the way, and the very beginning of an unexpected doubt.

"Which should prove what a fool I am," he went on, much too close for any sort of comfort. "What I should have done was tell you how I felt, but I was afraid the truth would drive you away sooner. I even mostly kept myself from buying every beautiful thing I saw and bringing it home to you. You'd said you didn't want anything from me and never mentioned what I did give you, so I gritted my teeth and just let it pass. Seeing that brace of pistols *you* bought for *me* showed me again what a fool I was. It wasn't gifts you'd refused, just meaningless gifts. If I'd brought something that showed my love for you . . . the way your gift did with me . . ."

His big hand was warm on her arm, making things even worse. Rianne closed her eyes as she shivered, part of her fighting desperately to keep from believing him. That part was horribly afraid to believe in anyone or anything, afraid of being terribly hurt yet again. Another part of her *wanted* a man who loved her, this man in particular, the man *she* loved. The two battled inside her, confusion keeping her from knowing which one she wanted to win.

"You must be cold like that," he said, reaching around her shoulders to draw her to him. "I'll keep you warm while we talk, and there won't be much more. Do you know the strongest proof I have that you love me?"

Rianne shook her head against his shirt, her cheek pressed to it while her eyes stayed closed. His arms were wrapped tightly around her, but he made no attempt to touch her naked body in an intimate way. Nevertheless she lay miserably stiff against him, not trusting herself to move or speak.

"My strongest proof is the way you tried to give your life to save mine," he said, and briefly touched his lips to her hair. "You believed I'd found a woman to displace you, but you were still willing to give up your life to save me. At first I was furious when I learned you'd done that deliberately, that you thought I'd *want* to live if you didn't. Now—now I know it was your love speaking, using the same words I would have used. My life sooner than yours, beloved, now and forever."

Tears formed in Rianne's closed eyes, but she did nothing to try to blink them away. That was exactly the way she'd felt. Maybe . . . maybe he did feel a little something of the same . . .

"And so, with all of that in mind, I can now tell you about my decision," he murmured, his lips touching her brow as well as her hair. "Rather than step out of your way, I'm going to hold you captive for the rest of your life."

It took a moment for his words to sink in, but really hearing them didn't also mean understanding them. Rianne raised her head from his chest, stared at him with all the confusion she felt, then said, "What are you talking about? You can't do that."

"Of course I can," he answered with a grin for whatever her expression was like. "And not only can, but absolutely must. It's come to me that you *can't* believe I love you, that you may never let yourself believe it. That means you might try to run away from me again, and I won't allow that. These last two weeks without seeing or speaking to you—I felt like the living dead, or maybe the merely *existing* dead. Whatever, it certainly didn't feel like living, and I refuse to go through that ever again. That's why you're going to be my captive."

"But I can't let you do that to me," she protested, still horribly confused. Again her desires were divided, and part of her actually thrilled to the idea. The other part stood with feet spread wide and fists on hips, furiously outraged that he would dare say such a thing. "I'm a free, independent woman, and you can't—"

"You're a married woman, married to me, which means I can," he interrupted with full assurance. Like magic, he produced her wedding ring from somewhere, and slipped it back on her finger. Rianne couldn't quite force herself to resist his doing that, not with the wordless ecstasy flooding through her. "Of course, there's a way you might make me change my mind," he drawled then, "but I doubt if you would be interested. Being such an independent woman and all . . ."

He let the words trail off, and suddenly Rianne understood what was happening. For the most part he was teasing her, but he was also perfectly serious about not letting her leave him. She suddenly loved him even more than she had, more deeply than she'd known was possible, and couldn't resist joining him in the teasing.

"You expect me to use my body to persuade you to free me?" she demanded, looking at him with fire and challenge. "Well, you're right, I *am* too independent, and I flatly refuse. You'll never find me touching your lips with mine, like this . . . or stroking your face with my hands, like this . . . or pressing up against you with my naked body, like this . . ."

And then his arms were bands of steel around her, holding her motionless while he took the kiss his eyes demanded. One fist was buried in her disarranged hair, and the other hand caressed her as if they'd been apart for years. At one time the furious strength of his desire would have frightened her, but now she gloried in it. She wanted him so desperately she would have killed to reach him, but killing wasn't necessary. He was right there, under her lips and hands, stretching them both out to lie together on the bed.

"Sir! Whatever do you intend doing to me?" she managed breathlessly when he abruptly ended the kiss. "You may think you have me at your mercy, but I assure you that isn't so."

"I know it isn't," he agreed with a laugh, tearing his shirt off over his head. "Right now I have no mercy, so how could I possibly have you at it? But I do have something else to have you at which you might find of interest. Would you like to see it?"

"Is it a gift of love?" she asked in a whisper, looking up at him. She wanted to continue the banter she'd started, but that was impossible in the midst of a dream come true. His gray eyes, filled with all the desire in the world, softened, and he leaned down to kiss her most tenderly.

"It's not only a gift of love, but one that will never again be given to any woman but you," he vowed. "Once we've gone to visit my parents so I can introduce you to them, we'll leave on our wedding trip. Cam told me how much you want to see America, so that's where we're going. You are my love and my life, Rianne, and by the next century I hope to have proved that to you. Will you give me at least until then? If I haven't done it, *then* you can leave."

"Until the next century—Bryan," she agreed, tears of happiness trickling down her cheeks. He came to her then, bringing the ecstasy of his hard, thick presence, and her body greeted him as eagerly as his thrust was into her. Once again they shared total abandon, two halves of the same coin merged into one . . .

Bryan, lost in the love he had finally been able to free, couldn't think; all but pure feeling was beyond him. She loved him, as much as he loved her, and nothing in his future life would ever match the moment when he was finally certain of that. His wife, his woman, moaned and writhed beneath him, urging him on to greater and greater effort . . .

He crushed her to him and kissed her savagely, and her hands closed tight in his hair, refusing to let him stop. Her hips rose to meet him as his thrust down, the matching movements of two people who had become one. His perfect mate, Rianne, his lifelong dream in the flesh . . . and then, inconceivably, she made it even better.

"Bryan," she moaned, caressing his name as her hands caressed his body. "Bryan . . . Bryan . . . *my* Bryan . . ."

"Yes, yours," he panted in answer, reality slipping away to oblivion. "Forever yours . . ."

He was hers, and the flame of fury burned high only for him.

Avon Romantic Treasures

*Unforgettable, enthralling love stories,
sparkling with passion and adventure
from Romance's bestselling authors*

MY WILD ROSE *by Deborah Camp*
76738-4/$4.50 US/$5.50 Can

MIDNIGHT AND MAGNOLIAS *by Rebecca Paisley*
76566-7/$4.50 US/$5.50 Can

THE MASTER'S BRIDE *by Suzannah Davis*
76821-6/$4.50 US/$5.50 Can

A ROSE AT MIDNIGHT *by Anne Stuart*
76740-6/$4.50 US/$5.50 Can

FORTUNE'S MISTRESS *by Judith E. French*
76864-X/$4.50 US/$5.50 Can

HIS MAGIC TOUCH *by Stella Cameron*
76607-8/$4.50 US/$5.50 Can

COMANCHE WIND *by Genell Dellin*
76717-1/$4.50 US/$5.50 Can

THEN CAME YOU *by Lisa Kleypas*
77013-X/$4.50 US/$5.50 Can

ROCH CARRIER

Roch Carrier est né dans la Beauce en 1937. Tout jeune, il publie deux recueils de poèmes, avant d'écrire, au cours d'un séjour en France, un livre de contes, Jolis deuils, *qui lui vaut un Prix littéraire de la Province de Québec. Par la suite, son oeuvre s'oriente vers le roman, notamment dans son importante trilogie de* La Guerre, yes sir!, Floralie, où es-tu? *et* Il est par là, le soleil, *qui, adaptée pour le théâtre et traduite en anglais, fait de lui l'un des écrivains les plus originaux et les plus lus de sa génération. Aujourd'hui, Roch Carrier vit à Montréal et dans les Cantons de l'Est, où il écrit sans relâche.*

LA GUERRE, YES SIR!

Publié pour la première fois en 1968, réimprimé régulièrement depuis, traduit en anglais, adapté pour le théâtre et pour le cinéma, *La Guerre, yes sir!* est l'un des romans les plus lus de la littérature québécoise contemporaine.

C'est, dans une langue et sur un ton endiablés, le récit d'une longue nuit de veille et de prodiges de toutes sortes, au cours d'un hiver des années quarante, dans un Québec villageois où la religion le dispute à l'ivresse, la tendresse à la violence, et le rire tonitruant aux larmes amères. Autour d'un soldat défunt, c'est tout un monde qui se déploie, qui éclate de vie, qui dit ses joies et ses malheurs, ses hantises, ses espérances, et son invraisemblable pouvoir de rêve et de parole. Corriveau tombé au champ d'honneur, le cortège des Anglais impassibles qui transportent son corps au village, Amélie et ses deux hommes, Bérubé et Molly, Arsène, Joseph-la-main-coupée, Esmalda la petite religieuse, toutes ces figures inoubliables animent une merveilleuse fête de l'imagination, de la mort et de la puissance de vivre.

La Guerre, yes sir! constitue le premier volet d'un triptyque comprenant aussi *Floralie, où es-tu?* (collection "Québec 10/10" n° 34) et *Il est par là, le soleil* (collection "Québec 10/10" n° 35), triptyque auquel Roch Carrier a donné, pour cette édition en format de poche, le titre de *TRILOGIE DE L'ÂGE SOMBRE.*